Kara

Kara

Julie Ellis

Five Star
Unity, Maine

Five Star Romance Series

Published in 2000 in conjunction with Julie Ellis.

The text of this edition is unabridged.

Set in 11 pt. Plantin by Elena Picard.

Printed in the United States on permanent paper.

Library of Congress Cataloging-in-Publication Data

Ellis, Julie, 1933–
Kara / by Julie Ellis.
p. cm.
ISBN 0-7862-2839-3 (hc : alk. paper)
1. Plantation life—Fiction. 2. Married women—Fiction.
3. Louisiana—Fiction. I. Title.
PS3555.L597 K37 2000
813′.54—dc21 00-057308

For Shirl

Chapter One

Kara stood in the bright spring sunlight, the crisp morning air brushing the sweep of delicately auburn hair from her face and wrapping the yellow muslin dress about her fragile slenderness, a carpetbag, holding all her worldly possessions and food for the trip, at her feet. Her eyes blurred with sudden tears as she looked up at the sailing ship. The ship, which began its journey in London, stopped here at Cork to collect additional passengers, and thence would ride the seas to New York.

Papa had been right in leaving her this way, before she went aboard. He'd remember her with a smile on her face. It was frightening to cross an ocean alone at eighteen—even in this year of 1852 with so much happening in the world. An age of miracles, Papa called it.

She pulled the cashmere shawl close about her shoulders. A present from Mrs. O'Casey, still elegant despite its much-handed-down status. And it was a comfort to her now, a warmth against the loneliness of the days ahead.

Papa would travel back home, go to the tavern, drink until his credit was cut off again. But Mrs. O'Casey—almost eighty and determined to be around till she hit a hundred—would always see that he had a bowl of hot oatmeal, or some potatoes fried with cabbage. She closed her eyes tightly for a moment, fighting back the tears.

"Oh, you're the lucky one," Papa had said last night.

Hiding his own sense of loss at her leaving. "Rushing off to America, along with half of Ireland."

Kara looked around at the bustling activity on all sides.

Small boats moving about the harbor, clusters of people gazing with fascination at the steam packet anchored at the wharf, ignoring the more commonplace sailing ship. The American steamship would make the trip across three thousand miles of ocean in, perhaps, fifteen days. But the likes of that, Kara thought wistfully, was not for her purse.

Packing cases, carpetbags, boxes were being passed from one pair of hands to another and hauled aboard the steamship with rapidity. Other hands were busy with ropes and oakum yarns and lowering cartons into the hold. A brawny group were getting the cows on board, "taking in the milk" a man explained to his wife. Others were filling the ice-houses with provisions—beef, veal, pork, poultry, pale suckling pigs, calves heads, and fresh garden vegetables for the rich passengers who could afford the fancy new steamships.

All that food, Kara thought with bitterness, remembering the anguish, the pain, of these past four years, with Ireland devastated by the potato famine. Three quarters of a million dead of starvation and disease—every family in Ireland hit.

Where the Sean Thomas family had been six, in the thatched, whitewashed cottage at the edge of six acres, there were only two—Papa and Kara—when the famine subsided. Its three rooms, once bursting with love and joy, became a wasteland harboring father and eldest child.

She had survived those years of standing by helplessly, watching them die, one by one. Her sister, then her brothers, and finally her mother. Dying in her arms, not understanding why. She had survived her father's turning to drink, wishing himself dead—and who could stand there and lay blame upon him? But Kara wanted to live.

Between them, she and Papa had managed to get together the money for her passage. Because of the stories about how Irish girls were finding jobs in New York as maids in the big, rich houses. She was eighteen and pretty—some called her beautiful—but she'd turned a cold face to the lads who'd come courting.

No more of farming, Kara told herself fiercely. No more starving because crops failed and what food there was, shipped off to the city to be sold. Never would she see her children die—with bloated bellies and cavernous eyes—because boiled oatmeal was not enough to sustain the spark of life in pathetically wasted bodies.

"This way. This way," a ship's officer ordered, almost with contempt. But then a deferential smile, a bow, for those of more affluence. "The corridor here, sir. Careful of the stairs, ma'am."

So many fine people making this trip. Kara gazed at the dresses of the ladies, the delicate worsteds, silks, taffetas. Their mamelouk sleeves semiconcealed by mantillas. But there were also others, like herself, modest of dress, clutching their carpetbags and boxes with anxiety as they clambered up the gangplank.

Kara descended below deck, stealing curious glances at the tiny cabins, each with a washing slab, two shelves for sleeping. Everywhere, people swarming with baggage, bumping into one another, moving mistakenly into already occupied cabins, shuffling along the corridors. And then at last, far from the open decks, Kara came face to face with the room—deep within the entrails of the ship—set aside to hold passengers who had steerage tickets, such as hers.

Kara strived to conceal her shock as her eyes swept about the room. Probably seventy-five feet long, twenty-five feet wide. No more than five and a half feet high. If she stood up tall, in her shoes, she'd almost brush the ceiling. She walked down the narrow aisle that divided the room. Wooden partitions reached from floor to ceiling. Within the partitions, two decks of bunks, each five feet long, ten wide, less than three feet high. Here, anywhere from six to ten passengers must live for the duration of the voyage.

Kara's eyes became accustomed to the dimness. She saw a pair of community cooking stoves, a few tables. At either end of the room were carelessly concealed water closets, marked for the women passengers; the men must go above.

"All right, everybody find your places," a male voice said brusquely. "Now you'll be gettin' a ration of water every day, and when the weather is good you'll be allowed up on deck each day for an hour. The captain's good about that. Any family runs out of food, the captain sells supplies."

Papa had been right not to believe what they said about food being supplied daily. She was glad for the rations she'd brought along. She wasn't spending the seven dollars she had to see her through until she found a job.

Kara found her way to the cubicle where she was to spend the days and nights of the voyage. People of all nationalities filed away in their shelves. Heavy-featured, silent Germans; gesticulating French; garrulous Irish; a neatly bearded Sephardic Jew from Turkey who sat praying silently amid the hubbub as though he were alone; a family of Scandinavians, fair-haired and meticulous, the children well behaved even under such trying circumstances.

Already the air was growing fetid. Babies cried, seeming to sense the stress that lay ahead. An elderly woman wept silently, while her husband hacked with a near-constant cough that was to endure until the ship reached its destination.

"You be goin' to a sister?" the sturdily built woman with

three small ones clinging to her skirts asked Kara with a determined smile. "They call me Meg."

"I'm Kara. From the farm country to the north of Cork."

"You don't talk like one from near Cork." The woman looked at her curiously. "More like from London."

"Mr. Watterson, the schoolmaster," Kara explained as they sat there in quiet conversation amid the babble that surrounded them. "He took a fancy to me, and to Papa," she added swiftly, lest Meg develop improper ideas. "He would sit at night with Papa and me, and teach me to talk the way the ladies talk in London, and then Papa and he would drink until they fell asleep in their chairs. Sad he was, about all the dying. And angry. You never saw a man grow so angry!"

"I was three months' with this one," Meg gently touched the toddler, engrossed in demolishing a biscuit, "when my husband went." She closed her eyes, sighed deeply as she crossed herself. "Even then I knew I must leave. It took a while." She began to weep silently. "I'll never see Ireland again. I'll never see what's left of my family."

"You have the small ones to think about," Kara said. "This is the most important thing." She forced a smile. "Do you know, I heard somebody say on the wharf that a steamship arrived at the harbor in New York in only ten days and four hours out of Liverpool?"

"I heard too," Meg blew her nose. " 'Twas the S.S. *Pacific*, of the Collins line. I read it myself in the newspaper. But not for us such fine doin's," she added grimly. "With the sailin', with everything dependin' on the wind, you never know when you'll be dockin'."

"They told us when we bought the ticket that it would be thirty days. Papa said we'll be lucky if it's no more than forty." She shuddered involuntarily. Forty days pressed together in such closeness. Already the pungent aromas of

Scandinavian cheeses, German salamis, smoked fish, somewhere a small keg of herring, blended together into a stomach-turning mixture.

"In New York," Meg said firmly, "you'll come with us to my sister's. She'll help you find a job. She warned me to have no truck with anybody at the landin' places. They be crooks and thieves. But Viv will help us find jobs. She knows all the places to go, how to manage these things," Meg beamed with pride. "Now don't say a word against it," Meg insisted when Kara opened her mouth to object. "Always room at Viv's for one more. Especially when it's a young lass with no one else to turn to."

"Mama, why don't we leave?" a high, clear young voice with a touch of Cockney demanded impatiently.

"Ssssh," her mother said gently. "We'll be leavin' when the mailbags come aboard. Soon. Soon—"

Above, the captain shouted orders through his speaking trumpet. The timbers creaked with activity. The vessel throbbed with life. And the ship moved majestically through the foaming water, her sails unfurled, her flag blowing in the breeze.

For a brief period their first day out, the steerage passengers were herded onto the lower deck for air, like animals left out to graze. They clung to the railing, sniffing nostalgically. On the second day the airing period was overlooked; the crew was too busy for such niceties.

On the third night they hit heavy seas, with a fearfully strong head wind. The passengers in the steerage listened apprehensively to the roaring water which thrust the ship from side to side. The wind howling in the night. And then the fury of the beating rain. Lights flashed about from up above, visible through the tiny portholes when the ship rose high above the belly of the sea. Despite the drop in temperature outside, the steerage quarters were uncomfortably close. Aromas which had been mildly annoying earlier became oppressively sickening.

Tables careened about the floor. Bundles, carpetbags, and portmanteaus slid about as though weightless. Every plank of wood built into the ship creaked ominously.

"We'll drown for sure," Meg whispered, clinging to her rosary beads, as night gave way to dawn with no lessening of the storm. "It was wishin' too high, to think we could find a home in the new land."

"We're not going to drown," Kara insisted resolutely, cradling Meg's smallest in her arms. She was determined to appear calm in the midst of all this turmoil. "This is a big ship, she'll make it out of the storm. You'll see."

"We're all alone out in the middle of the ocean," Meg cried. "Oh, pray, Kara! Pray the Virgin Mary brings us through this safely!"

"Pray the captain knows his business," Kara suggested with wry practicality. "And that I'm sure he does.

"One thing sure," Kara said with an attempt at humor, "the fine ladies and gentlemen up above aren't bearing the storm any better than us. For all the big money they paid for their tickets."

Up above, the furniture was flying, glass and crockery smashed everywhere, and shrieks came from those foolhardy enough to try the decks.

"Will it get worse?" Meg asked, white and trembling.

"It cannot get worse!" Worse, and Kara knew they'd be at the bottom of the sea.

The children were the first to become ill. Kara moved among them, crooning sympathy, cuddling small, anguished bodies, washing faces with swatches of cloth provided by the Sephardic Jew who was going to America to become a "traveling merchant." By the end of the second day of the storm, well over half the passengers of varying ages were plagued with seasickness.

Kara, despite her youth, her seeming fragility, organized those who were well into a committee to clean the room, to remove the unbearable stench of the vomit, to make the ill-ventilated area at least endurable.

By the end of the fifth day, with the storm not yet subsided, only a handful remained vertical for any period of time.

The fearful, certain that death lay just ahead, required comfort. The Sephardic Jew moved with a beautiful serenity among the afraid, managing to communicate in his heavily accented English. Speaking a kind of German dialect—Yiddish, someone told Kara—with the German families. Seeming to soothe by the touch of his slender, graceful, faintly yellowed hands that looked like aged parchment. Resembling, Kara thought, one of the old men in the pictures Mr. Watterson used to show her, by a Dutch painter named Rembrandt, who lived two hundred years ago.

And then the storm built to an unbearable intensity. The timbers of the ship creaked as though it were a mere toy cast about by the heaving waves. The hostile winds rose to a frenzy. Water splashed everywhere as the sea seeped into the steerage quarters. Rags, cloths, paper were hastily brought forth to sop up the water.

"We'll drown!" Meg predicted, her voice high with fright. "We don't have a prayer of a chance against that ugly sea!"

"We'll make it," Kara insisted.

"We're going over on the side!" a woman screamed, as tables, boxes, carpetbags slid precariously, along with startled passengers.

Voices called out in the darkness, warning against panic. A woman prayed. The Sephardic Jew intoned the prayer against storms in a high singsong voice that was oddly calming. And then, quite suddenly, the ship moved out of the storm. The sea was gentle again.

Gradually the passengers brushed off their tension and relaxed again, as much as one could relax in the prison of such quarters. The next evening brought sounds of conviviality from the upper decks. Dinner was being served to the first-class passengers. The aromas of roasting beef, a savory stew, bread rising in the ovens floated down to tempt stomachs that were just losing their queasiness. A new lilt laced the voices of the crew as they called out to one another up on the deck. All rejoicing that the storm had been safely hurdled. Full speed ahead!

Those in the steerage settled down into a kind of vacuum, waiting anxiously each day for the period when they were to go on deck. Sometimes, the captain was too busy to be bothered and those below cursed him. Sometimes, it rained.

The tenth day out, a woman died. An elderly woman who had hoped to finish out her days in a free land. The family was Orthodox Jewish. The Sephardic Jew, impressive in prayer shawl and skullcap, said the service for the dead as the body splashed into a dark, night ocean. For seven days the woman's family mourned, as was the tradition of her people.

By the third week, there were some who ran out of potatoes, and they made reluctant deals with the captain. The water tasted more and more of vinegar, added to the daily ration to conceal its foul odor. The ration was shortened. There were those who were sure the captain had sent back casks of water via a tender when the ship was already at sea, and the inspector satisfied that the quota was on board.

Wild rumors raced among the steerage passengers about a longer trip than anticipated. Quarrels broke out. At the end of the third week, the night slumber was pierced unnervingly by the sudden shrieks of a woman in labor.

Kara rose swiftly, slid from her cubicle to find her way in the dark, following the anguished sounds.

"It isn't time!" the woman gasped, as Kara leaned over. Between the pains, the woman in labor gazed at Kara. "You're but a child yourself. Call someone older."

"They're here," Kara whispered. "Taking care of your children. I was with my mother with her last two. If there's trouble, I'll ask for help."

"I'm puttin' up water," Meg whispered. "How far along is she?"

"Soon, I think," Kara said. "The pains are one on top of another."

A frightened child wailed nearby. The woman bit her lips to stifle her cries. She reached for Kara's hand; clung.

Meg talked to another woman at the stove, returned to the partition, leaned toward the woman.

"You should be seein' the head by now, the way the pains are comin'," Meg said worriedly to Kara, then turned to the woman. "Are you bearin' down?" she asked. "We should be catchin' the wee one by now."

A tall, bulking brute of a man thrust his way into the candlelight the women had provided. Quickly Kara tried to conceal the woman in labor.

"What would you be wantin'?" Meg demanded. "Have you no decency in you?"

"I cared for the animals on the farm back home," he said with unexpected gentleness. "The way she's carrying on, I wouldn't be surprised but that the baby's coming the wrong way."

"It's nothin' for the likes of you," Meg began, but Kara prodded her into silence.

"Can you help?" Kara asked quietly. The woman would die, and the child as well, if the position wasn't righted. She was helpless in this. From Meg's alarm, she knew Meg, too, was unable to cope. "Can you do something?"

"I can try," he said. "I done it with a calf coming wrong."

"Please try," Kara said. He was right. It had been going on too long.

"First, let me wash up. You," he said to Meg, "come help me."

The woman's face was drenched with sweat. Her body hard with pain. No sight of the head. Then Kara saw a tiny foot emerge.

"Hurry," she called out anxiously. "It's coming foot first!"

The man reached gently with his oversize hand and repositioned the baby.

"It's going to be all right," Meg whispered, leaning beside Kara.

The head, swollen and misshapen from its ordeal, moved into view within minutes. Meg received the baby, wrapped it in a clean yard of flannel, crooning tenderly. Kara stayed with the man while he waited for the placenta, then did what cleaning up was needed. And in the quiet, the cries of the newborn echoed through the room. They had spanned the cycle from death to life.

The women were drawn together by the newborn. Even the children shared a pleasure in the new arrival; they took turns viewing the small bundle, playing little nursemaids. But among the men tempers grew short. Twice, flailing fists had to be stopped, and the sheepish combatants retired to their own confining quarters.

Slightly past the fifth week, word came through that they would soon be approaching land. Instantly a fresh optimism swept through the steerage. Clothes were hastily washed, though it might be days before they would actually set foot off the ship. The children scrubbed themselves into cleanliness and were changed into fresh clothing. A new vitality replaced the hopelessness of the past weeks.

Most steerage passengers were alarmed when the ship docked not in New York but in what was called Fairfield, Connecticut. The word came down from a garrulous member of the crew that they were landing here first, to put off certain passengers.

"It don't do to take in passengers with no cash on 'em, who might have what looks to be a contagious disease, or come from jails or almshouses. So the captain steers away from trouble, puttin' 'em ashore 'ere. Come along now, move quick!" he called out loudly to the designated passengers, and leaned toward Kara with bold eyes. "You 'ang around when we land, and I'll take you 'ome with me."

"No, thank you!" Kara said, anger in her eyes.

"An 'ot-tempered colleen, are you?" he jeered. "You change your mind, you call for Jeb!"

"What will these people do?" Meg asked fearfully. A woman was near hysteria.

"Oh, they might have a long walk to New York," the seaman conceded with a raucous laugh. "Fifty-one miles to walk or ride by coach if they have the fare. Fifty miles out, the captain don't have to pay head tax." He winked knowingly.

The disembarking was completed. Down below, the steerage passengers waited restlessly, their luggage within hand's reach. Another twenty miles closer to New York and they were allowed on deck.

In the soft wind Kara stood with her carpetbag at her feet. Trembling. Waiting for the first glimpse of America. A whole new life ahead of her.

"They'll be holdin' us at quarantine for a while," Meg warned. "They don't let everybody into the country. Even those that get this far."

Chapter Two

Kara stared with veiled distaste at the two-room, dirt-floor shack that must sleep Viv, her husband, Pat, their four kids, Meg and her three, and Kara. Not to mention the pigs, Kara thought with a flash of humor. In comparison, the whitewashed cottage back home was a palace.

"Inside with you all," Viv called out. "I'll be havin' food on the table in minutes."

"So this is the Empire City," Meg said, gazing avidly about. Not even distrustful when a rambunctious pig darted out of the front door, as though he were a rightful member of the household.

"Go on with you!" Viv scolded the squealing pig, and gestured everyone indoors.

Despite her discomfort, Kara sat down with relish before the plateful of potato pancakes and the tall, cracked mug of steaming hot tea. This was Forty-second Street, and no more than two miles below lay the fascinating city that people all over the world were talking about. So much to see! And Kara yearned to see all of it!

"Viv, plenty of jobs, you wrote me," Meg leaned forward earnestly. "We'll be havin' no trouble?"

"No trouble at all," Viv reassured her. "A hardworkin' girl can pick up as much as two dollars a week workin' as a maid, though there'll be those who'll try to get by for a dollar. But you hold out, Meg." Then Viv's optimism seemed to retreat into a veiled caution. She glanced uneasily at Pat. "Some folks here in New York are gettin' worried, though, the way them free niggers are comin' in and working for nothin'. Just to have a place to sleep and food in their bellies."

"Hate 'em," Pat said intensely. "Comin' in, messin' up things for honest white folks. They be ruinin' jobs for the likes of us. We're gonna have to organize against 'em, wait and see!"

"We'll find jobs, won't we?" Kara asked, slightly alarmed.

"You'll be havin' no trouble," Pat promised with a chuckle. "A beautiful colleen like you will be pickin' herself off a husband before she's workin' three months."

"Eat!" Viv snapped. "You need yer strength to be puttin' in a day's work."

Meg and Kara walked with wonder along the streets of New York. What color everywhere! The ladies' fine dresses, the parasols, the elegant clothing of the men! Even the uniforms of the coachmen were intriguing, with their variations that spoke of many nationalities.

They strolled along Fifth Avenue, where it was paved below Twenty-third Street. They stared at the impressive brownstone mansions that belonged to New York's wealthier families.

"Why do they make all the houses so much alike?" Kara asked and giggled. "Why, a man comes home indisposed from tilting the bottle, and he could find himself going into the wrong house without knowing it!"

They walked, forgetting jobs for the present, eyes wide with admiration and curiosity. All the way down to Astor Place. Too conscious of their meager finances to venture aboard the gleaming, gaudily painted omnibuses that threaded their way through the heavy Broadway traffic.

"My, just look at 'em!" Meg nodded toward the lineup of buses belonging to competing companies. The "Original Broadways," the "Yellow Birds," the "Red Birds." All seats occupied, and with passengers standing in the aisles. "I'll bet they hold thirty folks or more."

"Meg, look at that." Kara pointed to the "bulletin wagon," its sides plastered with ads of a current play, a cream guaranteeing a crop of whiskers in six weeks, Barnum's museum, which boasted such sights as "the world's most celebrated midgets."

"Kara, did you ever see so many people?" Meg seemed uneasy about their being jostled each time they stopped to inspect the sights. "Why, it's takin' your life in your hands to try to cross the streets here!"

"Let's walk farther down," Kara said coaxingly, and Meg agreed, though grumbling about her feet.

"Pat was tellin' me last night he's goin' to have a fine job workin' on the World's Fair that's planned to open up next year. They're buildin' somethin' there to look just like the Crystal Palace in London. It's going to be near the Croton Reservoir, there on Forty-second Street, about a quarter mile from Dutch Hill."

"Meg, are you hungry?" Kara asked cautiously, glancing about.

"I'm starvin', that's what," Meg announced flatly, her eyes scanning the area. "That looks good," she said, pointing to a girl street vendor. "What do you think?"

"Corn," Kara declared with interest. "I never ate corn, did you?"

"No," Meg admitted, "but I'm willin' to give it a try."

"Here's your nice hot corn! Corn smokin' hot, just from the pot," the girl called out at the curbstone, smiling encouragement to them.

"How much?" Kara inquired. Seconds later, she was handing over the necessary pennies in exchange for the butter-brushed golden ear.

They ate with gusto as they strolled along the crowded sidewalks, stopping at intervals to inspect the shop windows, ignoring remarks of passersby who were annoyed by their leisurely gait.

"Meg, look!" Kara gaped in ecstatic wonder at the six-story, white marble building that occupied a full block along Broadway. "Did you ever see the likes of that?"

"That's Stewart's Department Store, lassie," an eager-to-be-friendly male passerby explained. "You gotta be rich to buy in there."

Meg ignored him pointedly. Kara's initial reaction had been to reply in friendly tone, but Meg dug meaningfully into her ribs. The man shrugged and moved on.

"Look at all the windows. Did you ever see shop windows so big?" Meg was busily counting. "Fifteen!"

"Someday," Kara murmured softly, "I'm going in there and buy myself a dress. The prettiest dress ever."

"Well, even a mangy cat can look," Meg jibed.

"I guess we've been doing enough looking," Kara said. "Now we'd best be asking about work."

Two hours later, Kara and Meg having gone their separate ways, with each telling the other about how to get back home, Kara stood in the downstairs kitchen of a fine brownstone mansion on Twenty-third Street between Lexington and Fourth avenues. Mrs. Elvira Johnston, tightly corseted and double-chinned, quizzed Kara in a formidable voice about her capabilities, her sense of responsibility on the job.

"You'll be off every other Sunday afternoon, and your uniforms will be supplied, as well as a room of your own and all your meals." Mrs. Johnston said this with a faint air of condescension, while the cook pretended to be deeply engrossed in the savory stew that bubbled in a black pot on the stove.

"And the wages, ma'am?" Kara asked politely.

Mrs. Johnston appeared startled, cleared her throat, spoke sharply to the woman at the stove.

"Molly, go up to my bedroom and bring down my morocco gaiters. They need cleaning."

"Yes, ma'am." Molly put aside the stirring spoon, perched the lid at an angle on the stew, and walked vigorously from the room.

"About your wages," Mrs. Johnston picked up, as though this questioning were an affront to her honesty, "you'll be paid a dollar a week." She hesitated, seeing the disinterest on Kara's face. "A dollar and a half," she corrected. "And in a year, if you behave yourself, you'll be raised to two."

"Yes, ma'am," Kara said, docile on the surface. Inwardly, her Irish pride bristled before the condescending air of mistress toward servant.

"When can you start?" Mrs. Johnston asked.

"Tomorrow?"

"Now," Mrs. Johnston decreed. "Silas will drive you to where you live, to pick up your luggage."

Kara glowed with the pleasure of such August traveling accommodations. She leaned at the window of the magnificent Johnston carriage, behind as fine a pair of horses as she'd ever seen, and stared at the grandiose mansions that lined the road. At the other carriages bound for the suburbs, like Yorkville and the area to the east, where the country estates of the Rhinelanders, the Astors, the Gracies were situated.

The carriage moved out beyond the city, the traffic thinning now. Kara was nervous, agitated, as they pulled up before the dismal hovel that had been temporarily home. She moved quickly from the carriage, humiliated by the glint of distaste in Silas's eyes as he viewed the sprawl that was Shantytown.

The cluster of children hovered outside the shack, peering avidly at the impassive Silas as he waited for Kara, appearing not to see the surroundings. Her color high, blue eyes aglow with triumph, she emerged from the shack, with Meg following her quick, small steps, wishing her luck, exhorting her to keep in touch.

Meg had not yet found a job, was a bit apprehensive, despite Viv's insistence it was a matter of days. The Irish would one day rule this city, Viv had predicted brashly. Why, by 1860, folks said, New York would be the largest Irish city in the world! Wasn't that grand department store, six stories tall and covering a whole block, owned by an Irishman named Alexander T. Stewart?

When the Johnston carriage drew to a halt before the brownstone mansion with its double stoop, its mansard roof, Kara inspected the house with fresh interest. Her first real home in New York. Papa would be astonished if he could see this magnificence!

Molly, whose corpulence attested to the cuisine, showed Kara to her room, on the attic floor. The room, hardly larger than a good-size closet, with one tiny window, contained a narrow bed, a washstand, and a pole on which, Molly pointed out, Kara could hang her clothes. The walls were roughly painted, the wood floor bare, in sharp contrast to the attractively wallpapered halls and lushly carpeted stairs of the curved stairway Molly and Kara had just ascended.

"Don't be wastin' the gaslight," Molly warned, still panting from the exertion of climbing five flights. "And mind your manners around here, girl. The mistress ain't one for puttin' up with airs. And watch out for Miss Denise, she's a hot-tempered one, she is. When she calls, you jump lively."

"I will," Kara promised.

This was part of the price of coming to this wonderful new country. But she wouldn't always be a maid. Mr. Watterson had said she was bright; use her head and she'd get on in the world. And Kara had every intention of fulfilling the schoolmaster's prediction.

She had hardly hung away her meager possessions when another maid, Peggy, banged on the door to tell her Miss Denise required her attentions. Kara opened the door to find a plump, pleasant-faced girl before her.

"Where's her room?" Kara asked.

"The door at the head of the stairs, the floor below," Peggy said, and thrust a black uniform at her. "Put this on first. Mrs. Johnston is strict about all the maids being in uniform," Peggy stood there, avidly inspecting Kara.

"It's big," Kara pointed out dubiously. "Should I take a quick seam? I have black thread and a needle."

"With her waitin' below?" Peggy lifted an eyebrow in reproach. "Hop down there and do what she says. There's been five girls here in the last five months, none of 'em would be takin' her high-handed ways. But then, like Mrs. Johnston keeps complainin' about," Peggy continued humorously, "Irish girls aren't like them Negroes. They got this way of bein' independent, givin' themselves airs." Peggy, too, was Irish.

"You said the first door at the head of the stairs?" Kara was struggling for a show of nonchalance. She wasn't going to be driven away by Denise Johnston. This was where she stayed put, until she learned her way around, had a few extra dollars ahead. You kept your silence when it meant money in your pocket.

"Come along, I'll show you." Peggy was apparently

pleased at Kara's presence in the house. "Now, when her ladyship starts up, just smile politely and don't let on you're mad. That'll cool her off. She's in a real tizzy tonight. Some young man is comin' for dinner. He's from one of them cotton plantations down in Louisiana."

"Where's that?" Kara asked, falling into step beside Peggy.

"Oh, down South somewhere," Peggy said vaguely. "Toward the west. New Orleans is down there." She rolled her eyes expressively. "Oh, la, la, that's a wicked city."

"She interested in marrying him?" Kara asked.

"She'd better be," Peggy said ominously. "She's gettin' on almost twenty, and the old lady's worried, what with her temper and all. She's scared she's so independent and particular she'll be left at the startin' post." Peggy giggled infectiously.

"Peggy!" A high-pitched voice yelled imperiously from down below. "Where is that girl?"

"She's comin', Miss Denise," Peggy called back, as she pantomimed for silence from Kara. "Be right there."

Kara followed Peggy to the open door, stared in at the large, square, wallpapered bedroom with its high ceiling, its tall, narrow windows, the figured Turkish rug, the rosewood carved furniture.

"Iron this!" Denise Johnston's voice shot forth from the side of the room.

Startled, Kara caught the armful of white water silk tossed at her. Color flooded her cheeks as she exchanged glances with Denise Johnston.

"Yes, miss," Kara said with pained politeness. So this tall, arrogant, dark-haired beauty was the daughter the mistress feared would be left at the starting post.

"Don't stand there," Denise chided impatiently. "Go

down to the kitchen and iron it. And don't scorch it, I have to wear it tonight. And hurry with the ironing!"

"Yes, miss," Kara repeated, and fled behind Peggy.

"Mama!" Denise screeched at the top of her lungs. "Mama, do come here!"

Kara followed Peggy down to the basement kitchen, where the stew simmered with a savoriness that elicited a grumble of hunger from the pit of her stomach. The ear of corn had been a light, inadequate lunch. Fresh bread browned in the oven.

"Here," Peggy said, handing over an iron and board. "I'll have to be settin' the table for dinner."

Kara ironed the delicate silk with care, watching Peggy move in and out between the kitchen and the dining room which was to the rear of the basement. With the dress ironed, Kara walked to the dining room, admiring its elegant furniture, the oriental carpet, the small crystal chandelier which would be gas-lit later when dinner was served.

"You see the garden?" Peggy asked with proprietary pride as she stood at the open French door. "Come have a look."

"Oh, it's pretty," Kara said, admiring the small square area with its pair of trees.

"That's an ailanthus tree," Peggy explained. "It's called the 'tree of heaven.' It's about the only kind that grows in these here gardens. They were brought over from some country I don't know just which."

"Birds, too!" Kara exclaimed. "Even here in the city!"

"They be English sparrows." Peggy pointed to the clusters of brown-gray birds, chattering noisily on the branches. "Brought over to this country just a while back, to kill off the insects. Her Royal Highness complains they make too much noise," Peggy said disgustedly.

"I'd better get upstairs with this," Kara said, just as the

door knocker sounded sharply at the stoop above.

"I'll get it," Peggy said quickly and hurried off to the stairs.

"That'll be Mr. Johnston," Molly said. "It's him I feel sorry for," she added piously. "Workin' all day at the bank and comin' home to them. The older daughters are both married, livin' up in Boston. But this one . . ." She clucked her disapproval.

"Where shall I put the iron?" Kara asked, with a show of respect for Molly's position among the staff.

"Leave it. I'll put it away. Go on up with the dress before she starts yellin' her head off again."

Kara plowed up the four flights again, faintly out of breath upon her arrival. The door to Denise's room was half open, but Kara cautiously knocked.

"Come in." Denise's voice was sullen.

Kara brought in the dress, walked to the bed with it. Mrs. Johnston was squinting at her daughter, who posed in the middle of the room in cambric pantalettes and handmade corset.

"Papa has bought tickets to the theater. Edwin Forrest is playing tonight, I believe," Mrs Johnston said cajolingly. "Papa will offer the tickets to Mr. Rankin. Of course, he'll ask you to attend with him."

"If he's ugly and dull, I won't go," Denise said, her dark eyes flashing. "And don't tell me again how old I am!" She swung around to Kara, who was carefully spreading the dress across the bed. "Polish my black kid shoes," she ordered, pointing to the pair that sat beside the bed. "Ask Molly for polish. Silas did an impossible job."

"Yes, miss," Kara said politely, stooping to pick up the pointed, black kidskin shoes.

"Yes, Miss Denise," she corrected coldly. "You're not working in a hotel."

"Denise, you'd better mind your manners." Elvira Johnston's voice followed Kara out the door. "Sometimes, you act as though you thought you were Queen Victoria. Papa says you start behaving or he'll send you off to that female seminary he heard about out in Sparta, New Jersey."

"Mama, at my age!" Denise's voice rose to an offensive shriek.

Kara found the shoe polish in the kitchen and settled down to her task. Molly was annoyed about the dinner guest.

"Why didn't they ask him for after dinner?" Molly fumed. "Just give him a shot of whiskey and send him off to the theater with her. He don't want to sit here listenin' to Mr. Johnston go on, so long-winded, about business, and Mrs. Johnston carryin' on about how everybody is in love with Denise. She's mad," Molly said with satisfaction. "Denise, I mean. He's been here in New York almost a week, and put off callin' until tonight."

"They're going to see Edwin Forrest," Kara said with wonder in her voice. Mr. Watterson had talked much about stage folks, both in England and New York. He's even read plays to her, in that melodious, wide-ranged voice of his.

"She's a play all to herself," Molly said grimly.

"Molly," Elvira Johnston called down from her third-floor bedroom. "You make sure you listen for Mr. Rankin, you hear?"

"Yes, ma'am," Molly yelled back, and sniffed quietly. "You'd think it was the Prince of Wales himself arrivin', now wouldn't you?"

Both Kara and Molly started at the sound of the knocker above.

"Answer it, Kara," Molly said, busy at the stove. She frowned at Kara's stare of consternation. "All you have to do is let him in and take him in to the front parlor," Molly explained. "Then run upstairs and tell Mrs. Johnston he's here. And don't talk to me about all the runnin' up and down the stairs, that's part of workin' in houses like these."

Kara hurried up the flight of stairs, down the corridor to the front door. Rehearsing in her mind the words that must be said. She pulled the door wide.

A tall, dark-haired, hazel-eyed man with a storybook handsomeness smiled politely in the doorway.

"I'm Tim Rankin," he said in his slow, rich southern voice. "I'm expected."

"Yes, sir." Kara stood aside. Color brushed her cheekbones. How handsome he was. How elegant. "Please come in, sir."

Chapter Three

Kara walked with her small, graceful steps across the corridor to the mahogany double doors that led to the front parlor. Painfully conscious of Timothy Rankin's presence.

"In here, sir," she said softly. Her eyes met his for an instant.

"Thank you." He strolled into the room. Walked across to look at the fine Coromandel screen that reached all across the tall, narrow front windows of the parlor. Turned, saw Kara still standing at the entrance, smiled faintly. Kara colored, spun around, fled hastily up the stairs.

Mrs. Johnston was still in Denise's room. Kara could hear the two talking in their high-pitched, strained voices. At Denise's door, slightly ajar, Kara knocked lightly.

"Come in," Denise said impatiently.

Kara opened the door, stood there hesitantly.

"The gentleman has arrived," she said quietly. "He's in the front parlor."

"Well, bring my shoes!" Denise shrieked, but there was a glint of anticipation in her eyes as she stood there, statuesque and resplendent in her silk dress. "I can't go downstairs like this."

"Yes, Miss Denise." She turned to go.

"Wait a minute, Kara. Mr. Rankin," Denise said with liquid demureness, "is he handsome?"

"Oh, yes," Kara said earnestly, and felt herself coloring again. Furious with herself. "The gentleman is quite handsome." Trying to be calm.

Kara moved with compulsive haste down the stairs to the kitchen, collected the polished shoes and returned them to Denise, her legs beginning to protest the constant ups and downs.

In the kitchen, Molly put Kara to work washing pots and pans. They'd be sitting down to dinner right away, Molly surmised aloud, while they heard Mr. Johnston and Tim Rankin exchanging pleasantries in the parlor. Obviously, Kara realized, the servants wouldn't eat until after the family had dined. But Molly was complacently biting into a slice of thickly buttered, fresh-from-the-oven bread, whose aroma permeated the kitchen.

"Go on, help yourself," Molly offered.

Word came through to serve dinner. At the exact moment Peggy was overtaken by an attack of coughing.

"Oh, Lord, don't do that," Molly said. "Mr. Johnston will be sure you're comin' down with consumption." She reached high on a shelf and pulled down a bottle of Cherry Pectoral, spooned out a dosage which Peggy obediently swallowed. "All right now, take in the turtle soup," she said while Kara sniffed curiously at this exotic first course.

Peggy moved with her sturdy heavy-footedness from the kitchen into the dining room. Kara listened eagerly to the table conversation in the other room. Mr. Johnston was inquiring about the state of this year's cotton crop, and Tim Rankin was politely responding. What an interesting way of talking, Kara thought. So soft and gentle.

Peggy sauntered back into the kitchen with a triumphant glint in her eyes.

"I tell you, there's gonna be a weddin'," she predicted

with relish. "We'll be seein' the end of Her Royal Highness. This one is rich *and* good-lookin' and she figures she can wind him around her little pinkie." Peggy inspected the tray of stuffed clams with interest, reached out an exploring finger. Molly smacked her smartly. "No clams for the likes of us." Peggy shrugged. "Only for them. And the stew's goin' to be watered down, like the soup."

"You eat better'n you ever ate in your life," Molly grinned. "Anyhow, we got our little ways of makin' up." She winked conspiratorially at Peggy. "Now go in there and bring back the soup plates."

Kara scrubbed at the pots, listening avidly to the conversation going on in the dining room. Sopping up words, impressions, undercurrents. Glowing with an inner excitement at being part of this glamorous new world.

"I tell you, Tim, the clipper ships will soon be driven off the seas," Mr. Johnston declared heavily. "How can they compete with the steamship lines? Why, the day'll be coming soon when the Cunard line will be making it from Liverpool to New York in ten or eleven days. And the prices of tickets are dropping. They can't fight big business, they'll learn that lesson the hard way."

"Tim, how far is Manoir from New Orleans?" Mrs. Johnston was kittenish with admiration. "I hear it's such a fascinating city."

"Oh, we're no more than an hour and a half by coach," Tim said casually. "New Orleans is the largest city in the South, you know, and so cosmopolitan. Mama finds it quite attractive, for visits."

"I'd love to see it someday," Mrs. Johnston pursued.

"You must be our guest," Tim invited politely.

Mrs. Johnston had deliberately switched the conversation to New Orleans to reassure Denise that she wouldn't be stranded on a plantation if she married Tim. Elvira Johnston was nervous, despite Peggy's predictions. This would be a wedding of cotton money and New York banking money, and both families should be delighted.

Peggy, enjoying the drama being enacted in the dining room, moved in and out between the two rooms with an air of smug secretiveness serving the stuffed clams, asparagus, the savory stew, deep-dish apple pie with sweet cream, strong black coffee.

The three in the kitchen listened attentively while Mr. Johnston casually mentioned the pair of tickets to the Edwin Forrest play, and as expected, Tim gracefully accepted and then invited Denise to attend the performance with him.

"Listen to her!" Molly whispered. "She's carryin' on about not bein' sure she wants to go, when she knows her papa bought those tickets just so she could go out with him."

"She's gotta be the boss," Peggy whispered back. "And she's lettin' him know that, right from the beginnin'."

Kara settled easily into the household routine, though the back of her legs ached from all the running up and down the stairs, and her feet burned by the time she tumbled into the narrow bed in her tiny room each night. She was acutely conscious of the air of expectancy which permeated the house, because nightly Tim Rankin was a dinner guest, and nightly he took Denise off for outside entertainment. Peggy reported that they had gone to see the public demonstration by the Fox sisters, who claimed to be able to communicate with the spirit world.

"My gentleman friend and me, we almost walked right into 'em when we came home," Peggy giggled.

"Peggy, aren't you scared they'll catch you goin' out at night?" Kara asked uneasily. Knowing all about Peggy's

German "gentleman friend" and the left-open kitchen window through which Peggy returned late in the night.

"Molly or you cover up for me," Peggy reminded her. "And nobody's the wiser. Besides, the missus is too anxious to hold on to her help to start up."

"Did you hear the ruckus when the day girl quit yesterday?" Kara said. "Mrs. Johnston was telling her husband, one more upset like that and she was closing up the house and moving into a family apartment at one of those new hotels."

"He won't let her," Molly said complacently. "He believes like I do, it's immoral, the way them women sit around all day, doin' nothin'. He's worried about the loose morals of the young people these days, the way they don't listen to their elders. No, they won't be movin'," she promised emphatically. "He's a man who speaks his piece just once in a while but when he does, he means it."

"That young man better speak his piece soon," Peggy chortled. "How long's he hangin' around here. Or maybe," she said slyly, staring at Kara, "he can't make up his mind. Maybe some folks don't notice, but it seems to me he's lookin' at others besides that Denise."

Kara turned scarlet. It was impossible for her to talk about Tim Rankin without falling apart within. Each evening she listened eagerly for his approach, to be the one to admit him. And each night, before going to sleep she reenacted the brief encounter, the meeting of eyes, the unspoken words.

She stood at the window, polishing silver with eyes fastened to the street beneath the high stoop. Seeming to be concentrating on the job, but her mind running helter-skelter on romantic ideas that she would have died rather than admit.

Kara stiffened. A coach was pulling up. She dropped the cloth from her hand, sped toward the door.

"Now don't be leavin' half the silver unpolished," Molly

jibed good-humoredly after her. "You be gettin' yourself right back."

Kara moved over the foyer just as the knocker sounded. She reached for the knob, pulled the door open. Blue eyes aglow. Delicately pink lips parted from the exertion of running up the stairs.

"Please come in," she invited, her voice uneven. "It's a lovely evening." Startled at her own brashness.

"Yes, it is." His eyes held hers. His voice dropped to a caressing whisper. "You're lovely, Kara."

"Thank you." Her eyes widened. Her heart pounded.

"For days I've wanted to talk to you." For a second, his gaze swept cautiously past her, down the empty corridor. "There's been no chance until tonight. Kara, Kara, meet me at the far corner tonight. After I bring Denise home from the concert."

"But I—" She wavered, trembling.

"Watch for the coach. About eleven," he said, his eyes pleading with her. "The far corner."

"Tim?" Mrs. Johnston appeared at the landing on the floor above. "Oh, I'm glad you're early. I'm certain we're going to have a thunderstorm later, even though it seems fairly nice now. My arthritis never misses."

"Good evening, Mrs. Johnston," Tim said with a show of warmth, striding toward the front parlor.

Kara, eyes downcast to conceal her distress, hurried downstairs to the kitchen. Mrs. Johnston would throw her out of the house if she found out. What was she to do? Papa had said you always had to be ready to make important decisions, that your life could change completely in a minute. With Tim?

"Finish the silver," Molly interrupted her thoughts a little sharply. "What are you day dreamin' about now?" But her eyes softened. "Don't you be lookin' so hard at him, you hear? Can't you see the handwritin' on the wall? He'll be marryin' her, the way his folks want, and they'll go off to live on his fancy plantation."

Mr. Johnston was home now. Kara heard him talking with Tim in the parlor. Complaining about all the traffic coming up from the bank, down on Bowling Green. They'd sit there talking until Silas would go up to tell them Molly was ready to serve.

Kara peeked in at the dining-room table, resplendent with its fine Irish linen cloth and Mrs. Johnston's best china. Peggy was humming under her breath while she laid the silver.

"Peggy," she whispered, anxious that Molly not hear her, "you're sure now, it's all right to be sneaking out late?" Mrs. Johnston was quick to remind them that a good night's sleep was part of what was coming to her, because they couldn't put in a day's work if they were carousing in the evening.

"Sure, it's all right." Peggy's eyes brightened with curiosity because Kara hadn't said who she was meeting. "Him?" she asked cautiously. Kara nodded. Peggy pantomimed her respect for such a conquest. "You're doin' all right, for one fresh off the boat. But don't worry about her catchin' on. She's sure we're tucked in our beds by nine thirty, with our supper eaten and the dishes washed. After all," she drawled, "don't we have to be up and in the kitchen before six? And if somethin' happens and somebody sets up a call, I'll answer. I'll say you're in bed with cramps or somethin'." She winked complacently.

"Peggy, stop bein' the fancy lady. Hurry up with the silver," Molly called from the kitchen. "This lamb is ready to be sliced. And Kara, I need your help too."

For the next hour Kara moved about the kitchen, automatically doing Molly's bidding; but her ears were alert to the conversation in the dining room.

"Oh, you should have been in town year before last," Elvira Johnston gushed. "When Jenny Lind sang at Castle Garden."

"He should have been here last year," Mr. Johnston corrected drily. "When Lola Montez appeared at the Broadway Theatre."

"Mr. Johnston!" Elvira was shocked. "How dare you mention that woman's name in the presence of your wife and daughter!"

Tim tactfully intervened to ask questions about the coming World's Fair. And dinner went off with its usual accompaniment of slightly tense table conversation. Tim and Denise took off for the performance by the Philharmonic Society. Mr. Johnston retired to the rear parlor, to fall asleep over the *Daily Times*. Mrs. Johnston, fearful that the servants would hear his snoring, woke him up and suggested they retire. In the kitchen the domestic staff was complacently eating roast lamb and potatoes. Kara ate without tasting, though normally she found sensual pleasure in the near-gourmet meals served in the brownstone.

As usual, Kara and Peggy stayed behind to clean up, then climbed the narrow, winding flights of stairs to the top floor. Peggy was not meeting her gentleman friend this evening and was looking forward to a chance to sleep.

In her dimly lighted, narrow bedroom—uncomfortably muggy in the first heat wave of the summer—Kara changed from the uniform to her one good dress, brought out her cashmere shawl. Not that she'd be needing it in this heat, Kara thought, but like Mrs. Johnston said, it just might rain before the night was over.

She settled down to read yesterday's copy of the New York

Daily Times, which Silas saved for her since she'd expressed an eagerness for news of the city. Anything, anything to keep her mind off what was to come later.

She started at the first flash of lightning through the small attic window. Sat immobile, listening while thunder rumbled ominously. A late storm, to wash the hot, uncomfortable city. A spectacular show that both terrified and fascinated her.

In minutes the rain was pounding on the mansard roof. Kara stood at the window, relishing the clean, fresh rain that swept her outstretched face. Feeling a faint wave of homesickness as she hovered there, her face tilted toward the pink sky. So far away from Papa! So very far.

Yes. She must write to Papa. She sat at the edge of the bed. Squinted in the dim gaslight as she carefully formed the letters on the sheet of ruled paper. Papa liked her handwriting to be pretty. Usually, it was a fast, impatiently formed scrawl, with her quick mind outrunning her fingers.

The rain was letting up. She almost wished it weren't. Just one of those fast, noisy summer storms. But at least the air was less humid. There was a lovely outdoor freshness now. She stood before the window again, inhaled the after-the-rain sweetness. Remained to inspect the sparse traffic below.

Her gaze sharpened. A carriage turned down the street. It came to a stop before the Johnston stoop. Kara's heart beat wildly. Tim emerged. Then Denise. Kara quickly pulled her head back inside the window.

She heard the sharp slam of the front door. Denise was in a foul mood. Kara moved in bare feet to her door, cracked it, listened to Denise stamping up the stairs to her room. Heard the door opened, then shut.

Kara reached for her shawl. Sneaked a glance at herself in the tiny, faintly distorted mirror that hung on the wall at the foot of the narrow bed. Shoes in hand, she started the long climb down to the kitchen. Hearing, when she arrived at the landing below, the low-keyed, tense voices of Denise and her mother.

"Mama, he doesn't say a thing!" Denise hissed indignantly. "I'm not sure I care any more."

"Quiet, Denise," Mama cautioned. "I'll talk to Papa tomorrow. Maybe the young man's nervous."

"About talking to Papa?" Denise demanded scornfully.

Kara moved noiselessly down the stairs, confident the other two were unaware of her presence. She heard the regular snoring from the master bedroom on the floor below Denise's. He'd hear nothing until morning.

In the kitchen Kara paused to pull on her shoes. She approached the kitchen window adjacent to the stoop. Took a deep breath, glanced up at the sliver of moon that was determinedly pushing past a cloud.

The street was deserted except for a tall, slim figure down at the far corner. Tim. Kara half ran joyously in his direction.

"Kara—" Tim moved eagerly toward her, a hand outstretched. "You came—"

"I said I would—"

Chapter Four

Amory Rankin rode his Arabian stallion slowly through the avenue of pecan trees, glad to have left the fields behind for the day. The noon sun was broiling, with summer barely launched. But the cotton was in, thanks to Charles, and with luck it might bring eleven cents a pound.

He ran a hand through his gray-sprinkled fair hair, tugged at the shirt stained between his shoulder blades. He'd be glad for a shot of bourbon and the shade after an hour out there in the fields.

Sometimes he felt guilty about Charles's filial solicitude for his health. Ever since his heart attack six years ago, Amory gave in to Charles's insistence that he not concern himself with the problems of running the plantation. Charles was capable, give him that.

Hell, Doc Scott was out of his mind, trying to treat him like a semi-invalid! He was as strong as he ever was. A wry smile crossed his face, still handsome at fifty-two. He'd be a first-rate ass to contradict the doctor's orders to take it easy. All these years of managing Manoir had left a bad taste in his mouth. The South was a sick society.

He rode to the rear of the brick-and-cypress mansion, to the stables. Turned the horse over to Jupe, who harbored such love for the animals, gave them the care that made the Rankin stables the finest in this part of the state.

As he walked toward the house, the sound of piano music came from the front parlor. Even at the piano, playing Debussy, Annabel could contrive to seem prim.

Above the music, his wife's deceptively sweet, airy voice prattling on about some imagined complaint. "Annabel, I don't know why some folks just go out of their way to hurt me. It seems they can't stand to see me happy."

Fate was an ugly old man, in minutes changing the whole course of a life. How old was he when he met Emilie? Twenty-two, and all but engaged to another girl. Taking one look at that fragile beauty, barely sixteen and at her prime, and thinking only one thing. Less than six weeks later, her folks, the very wealthy Butlers, were preparing for the fanciest wedding anywhere around for fifty years.

Emilie gave him two sons, he thought with ironic humor, and considered it a favor that she'd let him touch her. God, what a chunk of ice she was from the beginning! And she remained so. The same way, every time from their wedding night until six years ago.

Once he had the heart attack, she wouldn't let him near her again. It was all the excuse she needed. He wasn't without, of course. He'd never been without, even those long months, from time to time, when Emilie took it upon herself to deny him. What a strong-willed, domineering example of southern womanhood she was, beneath the wide eyes, the still-slender body, the tiny hands and feet, about which she was so inordinately vain.

Damn, he shouldn't have allowed her to bring Charles home that way, after only two years away at college. Charles had a splendid mind, it should have been put to better use than running Manoir. And her keeping Tim under foot, with no college at all, just those few months of studying painting in Paris. At least Tim found out he was good enough to play at painting, not good enough to make a living at it.

Amory stopped off at the kitchen to tell Octavia to send a pitcher of ice to his study. Best thing he ever did, he thought complacently, buying that icebox. A shot of bourbon to start him off, then a string of juleps to spell him through the hot afternoon while he settled down to reread Plato or Aristotle.

Octavia wouldn't ask questions. She'd bring him a plate of cold chicken and fresh biscuits. Knowing he hated sitting down to the noonday meal with Emilie and Annabel. Charles ate out in the fields with the hands.

"Octavia, some ice," he ordered with mock sternness. "That sun out there is enough to burn a man to a crisp."

"Ah bring it to yuh in de study," Octavia said, unruffled.

Twenty-five years ago, Amory Rankin had brought Octavia to his bed, between frustration bouts with his wife. Octavia had been slim then. Small-breasted, narrow-hipped, and passionate. She had long since gone to fat, her baby-doll prettiness dissipated. But there was a friendship between them, of which Amory was proud. Octavia would give her life for him.

"Make it quick with that ice," he jibed.

"Ah make it fas' enuf," she promised. "When dat boy comin' home anyway? Seems lak him be gone too long."

"Soon," Amory promised. "Maybe with a bride."

Octavia's deep brown eyes went secretive. He frowned in mild annoyance. Octavia had wet-nursed Tim, at the same time she had Jupe at her breast. She was after him enough to choose a wife for Jupe.

"Ah bring de ice," Octavia said softly, her voice trailing after him as he left the kitchen wing and headed for the study.

For a while he had been nervous about Jupe's being his own issue, until Octavia, with that ageless intuition of hers, understanding his concern, pointed out that this child could not be his because of the time element. When Emilie had become pregnant the second time, he had abstained from lying with Octavia out of some false sense of loyalty. Octavia had become pregnant by one of the field bucks, and he'd never touched her again.

After Tim, he'd made up his mind not to scatter his own issue about the plantation. He'd become impatient with the habit of plantation owners to lie with a dozen wenches, to watch with amusement or concern the carbon copies of themselves under dark skin.

Jasmine, that new girl. He felt desire stirring in him every time he thought of her. He'd bought her in New Orleans two weeks ago. If she had been two shades lighter, she could have passed for a quadroon, might have been set up by some New Orleans gentleman in a cottage along the rue des Ramparts, to live the fancy life of the *placées*.

He'd snapped her right up off the auction block at the Saint Charles Hotel, after a whispered conference with the auctioneer, a long-time friend. All the way from Sea Island, Georgia, she came, by way of Haitian parents. He hadn't touched her. Not yet. He'd brought her to be Annabel's maid. No more than fifteen, still scared every time anybody looked hard at her. The auctioneer friend swore she was a virgin. She was eating well in the kitchen. Filling out.

Already Octavia was developing ideas in her head. Guessing this one was to be his private stock. And no babies with this girl, he reminded himself with satisfaction. This one couldn't conceive.

The auctioneers down in New Orleans were smart, out to please the steady customers. He'd told his friend to be on the lookout for a pretty piece that wouldn't be dropping babies every year. Saying this would be a nice gift for his daughter-in-law. A maid who wouldn't be walking around half each year with a swollen belly. An affront to Annabel, who could not conceive. *Would* not conceive, after five miscarriages. Tough on Charles, who swore he never touched the plantation wenches. Charles was strange that way.

In the study he settled himself by the tall, lace-curtained open windows, poured from the bourbon bottle, swung down the shot neatly. Warmth in his belly, heat in his loins, he thought humorously. Not bad for fifty-two.

What about Tim? Would he marry the Johnston girl? Emilie was determined to bring that off, and she was a tough one to stop once she set her mind on something. She'd called on the Johnstons when she was visiting up in New York last summer, because they'd been doing business with Johnston's bank for close to twenty years. Banking money and cotton money, a fine combination, Emilie was thinking.

The girl was supposed to be a beauty. But high-strung, demanding. Another Emilie, he thought uneasily. He wanted better than that for Tim. Tim would have a rough time coping with a strong woman.

He'd never been as close to Tim as he would have liked. Tim was Emilie's child. Her baby. She spoiled him impossibly, and made impossible demands. That long string of tutors because she couldn't bear to let Tim go off to college. She'd carried on those few months he was in Paris at the art school. All the pretty young things she dangled before his eyes, but never completely satisfied with any one of them, and Tim knew.

Amory straightened to attention, hearing horses hooves clomping through the grove of live oaks and pecans. Probably a slave from one of the neighboring plantations, with a note for Emilie. For all she complained about being cut off from civilization, all the way up the river from New Orleans, she still managed an active social life. He reached for his book, relaxing in the deep chair again.

Octavia, graceful despite her girth, moved noiselessly into the study, put the pitcher of ice on the oak commode, japanned in gold on a black background, where Amory kept his liquor supply. She pulled up a small table beside his chair, to hold the platter of crisp fried chicken and hot biscuits, then left without a word. The curtains moved slightly in the unexpected breeze. The scent of honeysuckle, blending with magnolias, was sweet into the room.

"Celestine, call my husband!" Emilie ordered sharply, her voice carrying through the whole lower floor. But Amory didn't move. Savoring these few minutes before slow-moving Celestine would track him down. He was notoriously deaf to outside voices when he was deep in the Greeks. "Tell Mr. Rankin to come right here, you hear me?"

Amory reached for a succulent drumstick, bit into it with relish. Refusing to be baited by the excitement in the front parlor. Annabel was trying vainly to soothe her mother-in-law. After seven years at Manoir, Annabel still didn't know that nobody could stop Emilie once she was launched. Celestine would look for him by way of the kitchen, to report whatever gossip had brought on Emilie's outrage.

Amory crossed to the commode, mixed himself a drink. When Emilie was on a tear such as this, he fortified himself. Charles worried that he fortified himself too frequently.

"Oh, der yo' be," Celestine clucked dramatically at finding him, though she knew he was in the study each day this time. "Ole Miss wish yo' come to de parlor real quick."

"Tell her I'll be there directly," Amory drawled, amused by her simulated consternation that he didn't hop right out of the room. Celestine was Emilie's personal maid, well versed in Emilie's tantrums, her convenient headaches, her attacks of nerves. Celestine was also the house gossip.

Celestine hurried out with her awkwardly mincing steps,

calling out to Emilie as she approached the front parlor. Hell, he might as well go in and have it over with, Amory decided, relinquishing the drumstick but clinging to his julep.

Emilie was agitatedly pacing up and down the prized oriental rug that had been her late father's wedding present to them. She was talking feverishly to Annabel, who sat at the piano, her hands idle in her lap, her eyes distressed.

"All right, Emilie, what's happened?" Amory asked matter-of-factly.

"This is what's happened, Amory!" She waved a sheet of paper beneath his eyes, with the air of a matador goading a bull. "We've had a telegram from Elvira Johnston. A man just brought it out from the New Orleans office."

"Tim?" A knot tightened in his stomach. "Is Tim all right?"

"He's lost his mind, that's what!" Emilie's voice soared nearly out of control. "He's run off and got married!"

Amory let out a deep sigh of relief.

"Well, now you won't have to worry about a fancy wedding," Amory said. Emilie had it all planned that Tim and the Johnston girl would be married here at Manoir. "So the boy rushed things a bit," he chuckled. "You can give a ball to introduce her." Emilie grabbed at any excuse to give a ball, which was one reason why he hoped cotton would go up to eleven cents a pound this fall.

"A ball?" Emilie shrieked. "To introduce the Johnston's maid? An immigrant fresh off the boat from Ireland?" Her blue eyes almost black with rage, she spun about to Annabel. "Send for Charles! Have him come up to the house!"

"No," Amory intervened with quiet strength. "If Tim's married, there's nothing Charles can do about it." So the Johnston woman was up in arms because the young whelp walked out on the daughter for the maid. Probably a beautiful little piece, with plenty of fire. The Irish were strong on humor and temper. "Emilie," he spoke sharply, "don't get hysterical. That's not going to change anything."

"You'll be sending for Doctor Scott before the night is over," Emilie warned, her voice cracking. "I know I'll have an attack of nerves over this. My heart's pounding like mad already."

Amory reached out a hand, refusing to relinquish his calm. "Let me see the telegram."

Amory took the telegram, read it slowly. So Tim took a long look at the Johnston girl, and wasn't having any. It required guts to turn his back on his mother this way, when they were thick as thieves most of the time.

"It seems to me, Emilie, we'll be welcoming a daughter-in-law," he said casually.

"Amory, an Irish maid!" Her voice wavered out of control again. "How will we ever face folks?"

"You don't go around advertising she was a maid," Amory said quietly. "You'll welcome her, polite as though she were royalty." He was thoroughly in command, for the moment. "And when they've had time to rest up from their trip, you'll give a ball to introduce her to the local society."

"Oh, Amory, how can you stand there and speak so calmly about this?" She swung from Amory to Annabel, who lowered her eyes unhappily. Annabel wasn't one to take sides publicly. She'd probably have plenty to say later.

"Because this thing is done, and we must accept it, Emilie." He felt almost sorry for his wife at this moment. But damn it, who were they to turn up their noses at Irish immigrants? A hundred years ago their ancestors were immigrants, in a country not yet formed. He loathed this intolerance, bred in the family, passed on to succeeding generations. All except Charles. Charles was like him, he thought with passing satisfaction. Charles looked hard into people. “Emilie, I’m looking forward to meeting Tim’s bride,” he pursued calmly. “Maybe after a while, we’ll have some grandchildren to liven up the place.”

Damn, he shouldn’t have said that! Annabel had taken it as a personal affront. She turned white.

“Oh, Amory, it’s going to be awful!” Emilie wailed. “To have to face folks all around here, with an Irish servant girl for Tim’s wife, when he’s so handsome and bright and talented. Amory, how will we live with it?”

“We’ll live with it,” Amory promised.

There would be two camps in this house when Tim crossed the threshold with his bride. Amory Rankin, for what that was worth, would be on the side of his brand new daughter-in-law.

Chapter Five

Kara awoke early in the small tavern bedroom in New Jersey, with a river breeze softening the hot morning sun. Instantly, aware of her surroundings. The poignant memory of the hurried wedding ceremony last night, performed by the disapproving minister. Their flamboyant wedding dinner at Delmonico's, where Tim was inordinately proud of the glances of admiration cast at their table. The champagne, though, to be honest it hardly tasted more exciting than a glass of sherry. She must develop a taste for champagne. And for oysters and snails and fried frogs' legs.

She started at the faint knock at the door.

"Yes?" Her voice eager. Knowing, of course, that this was Tim.

"Dress and come down for breakfast, Kara," Tim said, clearly in high spirits. "The coach leaves in forty-five minutes."

"Five minutes, Tim," she promised, already thrusting aside the light blanket.

How sweet of Tim to take two rooms for them this first night! Knowing their courtship was shockingly brief; this modest tavern hardly a honeymoon site. The tavernkeeper had stared oddly at them when Tim asked for two rooms. But they had been so tired yesterday, shopping all day for a trousseau for her. And then the wedding last night. On the ship they would have a fine cabin of their own, and their married life would begin.

It was like a dream. For a whole week now, she had lived, breathed, walked on a cloud. Each day going though the household chores, thinking only of Tim, waiting for the evening to come. Tim always so kind, always treating her like a lady.

Breakfast was served in practised haste, with an eye for the coaches' departure schedule. Five of them waited outside, in varying stages of readiness. Four horses to pull each coach. Kara and Tim were the first of the passengers to show up and were asked grandly to stand by. Luggage was brought forward in wheelbarrows that creaked and squeaked, threatening to collapse under their burdens. Some of the horses were impatient, stamping at the dirt.

The coaches were roofed, curtained with painted canvas. Kara inspected their mud-covered exterior with covert distaste. They appeared not to have been cleaned since they were built! The Negro drivers wore suits with darns and patches, particularly at the knees, a situation with which Kara was familiar. How many pairs of trousers she had darned for Papa! The driver of the first coach wore trousers that were absurdly short, and a pair of mismatched gloves, but his face shone with pride in his job.

The passengers had started to board. Kara viewed the single step, three feet from the ground, with consternation.

"This way," Tim chuckled, and reached forward to hoist her competently inside.

The coach was designed to hold nine passengers, the capacity provided by means of a seat across from door to door. One passenger sat outside, up on the box. The luggage was strapped both on the roof and on a tray behind.

A man stood forward, and in a jovial Irish voice cried out, "All right!" and all five coaches started off with a dramatic flourish. Kara leaned back, trying not to advertise to the other passengers that she and Tim were on their honeymoon, yet she suspected this shone from her.

In Philadelphia they left the coach to board the railroad. Kara's first experience with such a contrivance, and her curiosity made the occasion an exciting one. Not that the surroundings were elevating, she told herself with wry humor. Each car looked like a long greenhouse, with two rows of seats that accommodated two persons each, with no room to spare, and with an aisle that would be a squeeze for anyone of corpulent dimensions.

Tim settled down to read a newspaper. Kara looked avidly around at the other passengers. About a mile outside Philadelphia, they crossed a bridge over the Schuylkill. Tim stopped reading to tell her the name of the river, then returned to his newspaper. Kara was too keyed up to read, though normally she found American newspapers fascinating.

The railroad cars moved over tracks laid in flat, low meadows, skirting the Delaware, this time of year rampant with greenery. They passed through Wilmington, crossing the Brandywine, where Kara pulled Tim away from his reading to enjoy the magnificence of the scenery.

At two thirty in the afternoon they arrived at Baltimore. They had sufficient time for a meal before beginning the train trip to Louisville which, Tim warned, would be interrupted because of incompletion of the railroad tracks. For these in-between stretches, they would travel by coach.

It was on this section of the journey to Manoir that Kara became aware of the poverty, the decay, that was part of the South. She stared out the windows with misgivings, taking in the barns and outhouses that were sagging with neglect, the squalid log cabins, pitifully small, the sheds that were patched and half roofless. How different all this was to what Tim had told her about Manoir!

Kara's throat tightened at the sight of the near-naked Negro children who played before the cabin doors, with dogs and pigs running among them. There was no spirit of joy here. Gloom, dejection, acceptance, even from the children.

They stopped at one miserable railroad station after another. A car was added on at one station while the engine was being supplied with fuel. A car full of just-purchased slaves. Some of them wailing at being torn apart from families, others crying out of fear of a new master. A look of resignation on glistening black faces. Kara felt faintly sick. She had seen that look in Ireland, during the famine.

The boat they boarded at Louisville was modest, with Tim making earnest apologies for its lack of pleasant accommodations. The cabins were tiny, with two berths, one above the other, and a washing slab.

"Nothing smaller was ever made for sleeping, except coffins," Tim grumbled as they changed into their night clothes. He grinned apologetically. "We'll be able to live like human beings on the ship down the Mississippi. Now *that,* Kara," he boasted lightly, "is the way to live."

At the junction of the Ohio and Mississippi Rivers, they changed ship. Kara wide-eyed with awe when she saw the queen of the Mississippi, the *Crescent Queen,* which was to transport them to New Orleans. Tim holding her arm tenderly as they walked up the gangplank.

"See how calm the river is?" Tim pointed out. "But come the rainy season and this low land around is flooded; sometimes, all you see of the houses are the roofs."

"How awful for the people who live here!" Kara sighed, losing her high spirits.

"How do you like the ship?" Tim asked.

"Tim, it's beautiful."

Kara looked at the ornamented white wooden steamer with renewed interest. Her eyes skimmed the double stacks, which towered imposingly above the decks, the pennants waving proudly in the summer breeze, the horde of passengers moving importantly about the decks. Perhaps two hundred passengers.

They were shown to their lavishly appointed cabins. Tim and Kara stowed away their luggage, and Tim eagerly prodded her out to see the velvet-hung saloon. The bar, many feet long, was served by smiling bartenders.

"There's an orchestra for dancing later," Tim whispered, enjoying her delight. "And wait till you taste the food. Not a restaurant in the world can top it!"

The engine steamed. The vessel slid away, down the river toward New Orleans. The saloon was filling up now with men seated at the tables, intent on card playing to while away the hours. Expansive planters and quiet, sharp-eyed professionals. The women, gay and attractive, undaunted by disapproving glances from plantation ladies. On the decks, river boatmen sprawled, drinking and joking. And from down in the entrails of the vessel came the strange, sad songs of the Negroes who stoked the engines.

That night, in the luxurious cabin, Tim took Kara to bed. Her eyes filled with tears of happiness because her husband was so gentle, so tender, so considerate. For herself, she was astonished at the fire of her response. Had she been too forward, she wondered uneasily, later, when she lay sleepless beside Tim. Was it wrong, unladylike, to enjoy this side of marriage?

The days along the Mississippi blended one into another. The ship adroitly skirting floating timbers, stopping to avoid snags, or the hidden trunks of trees that have their roots below the tide. At night, if the moon were in hiding, a lookout was stationed at the head of the ship to watch for danger, the rippling of the water alerting him. At night in their cabin, Kara and Tim could hear the warning bell, the signal for the engine to be stopped.

For Kara, the most beautiful time of day was sunset. The sky a spectacular splash of golds and reds. The river, so immensely wide, a muddy gold, taking on the changing hues of the sky. The sun sinking lower, until it hid behind the bank, with every blade of grass taking on an individual light. The glowing colors of the day paling slowly into full night.

On the morning they were to arrive in New Orleans, Kara approached the deck with a kind of nostalgia. These days along the river had been special. Yet she knew Tim so little, Kara acknowledged, stealing a glance at his handsome profile.

Tim grew more and more introspective as home grew close. But he was warm, as solicitous as ever for her comfort! He was proud of her, too, when others looked admiringly upon her. Yet, some nights she lay with Tim, and he wasn't there at all.

"Tim, you're sure your family has received the letter by now?" She'd asked him that a dozen times already!

Tim turned to her with a smile.

"You distrusting the U.S. mails?" he jibed. "I mailed the letter before we left New York."

Tim tried to be amused by her uncertainties. She knew he was disturbed. His parents had expected him to marry rich and beautiful Denise Johnston, and here he was coming home with their Irish maid.

The Irish maid would not disgrace him, Kara promised herself, head high with determination. She knew how to handle herself, thanks to the years of Papa's friendship with Mr. Watterson—this was her one vanity. But it was going to take some doing for her to understand Tim's way of living. The South's way of making the Negroes a master's possession.

New Orleans was coming into sight. Tim's hand tightened about hers. He glowed with the fervor of a man glad to be home again. Ships everywhere! Ships of all sizes, all nations. The levee bustling with the vessels and the rush of business evoked by their arrival.

The sweet aromas of molasses, the pungent scent of spices, coffee, salted meats, and rum permeated the air. Cotton everywhere on the wharves, bales piled to frightening height, advertising to all that here cotton was King. The noise deafening as people surged along in competition with the drays, cumbersome, clattering vehicles, each with two mules in tandem.

"Tim, it's fantastic!" Kara's eyes moved avidly as she sought to take in everything in the vast panorama before her, the color, the sounds, the scents, the enormous vitality everywhere!

The ship was being made fast at the wharf, but even before this was accomplished people were already rushing aboard to greet the arrivals. Kara and Tim shoved their way through the jostling hordes. Tim found a carriage for them, bargained with the driver, who spoke a French *patois*. Around them, the multilingual voices—French, German, Spanish, Italian. The faces of Irish workmen, in long-tailed blue coats with bright buttons and drab trousers—the ones who would dig and labor under the sun.

Tim helped her into the carriage, and they were on their way. Past the tin-roofed stores that catered to the sailors' tastes, past the grogshops, the oyster stands, native hawkers, blind men playing fiddles, children jigging for pennies. Graceful Negro women, with coffeepots in their baskets, eager to pour for any customer.

Kara and Tim left the city behind, moving higher up the river, where well-to-do Americans had erected fine new homes in the midst of wide, carefully tended lawns. Huge oaks, fragrant magnolias, pecans and palms everywhere. The pink blossoms of crepe myrtles, rose bushes, fig trees, and sweet olives growing magnificently in the rich soil.

The carriage rumbled on, leaving behind the well-maintained houses that ranged from Greek Revival to Georgian. Open land now on all-sides. Cotton thrusting itself through the light brown earth, the cream of America's valley soil. Farther along a sugar plantation, the cane growing tall in stately rows; in the background a sugar mill.

"Tim, how far is it?" Kara asked finally, tense with anticipation. Her throat tight as she contemplated greeting Tim's family.

"Another forty minutes," Tim forced a smile.

The carriage turned into a narrow side road. Tim seemed faintly nervous. Kara sat beside him, realizing they were approaching Manoir.

"Tim, how many acres?" Kara asked.

"Twenty thousand, Papa figures." Tim smiled, knowing she was impressed. "With slightly over a hundred slaves."

Twenty thousand, when in Ireland a man considered himself well fixed with six! Kara leaned forward, her eyes skimming the avenue of towering trees. Awaiting eagerly the first sight of the house.

"My grandfather spent four years selecting, cutting, and seasoning the timbers for Manoir," Tim said reminiscently. "Years in building the limekiln and brickwork. The house is built of Louisiana cypress, and the bricks were fired by the slaves here on the plantation." Tim was proud of his ancestral home.

And then it rose before them. Manoir. Majestically tall, with eight massive Doric columns to support the front galleries. A gabled roof and wide attic, an avenue of tall, narrow windows across the front of the house. The house elevated from the ground with an imposing flight of stairs leading to the main entrance.

Aspidistra edged both sides of the path to the house. Azaleas and camellias vied with glowing oleanders across the foundation. Yellow butterfly lilies and mimosa trees.

"Oh, Tim, how beautiful." Kara's voice a hushed whisper.

The carriage pulled up before the mansion. Tim leaped down, reached up to help Kara, then moved forward to pay the driver.

"Go around to the kitchen for a bite to eat before you drive back to New Orleans," Tim said to the driver.

"Marse Tim!" A joyous, rich, young voice, male, liquidly melodious. "Marse Tim! They be expectin' yo' for two days now!"

A tall, slim, ebony young man, strikingly handsome, darted forward.

"Jupe!" Tim, happy to see him, moved forward with a wide smile. "Have you been behaving yourself while I was away?"

"Oh, yessuh!" Jupe grinned broadly, his eyes moving shyly to Kara.

"Kara, this is Jupe. Jupe and I grew up together here at Manoir. His mama, Octavia, spanked the two of us many a time, for sneaking into the wrong pots in the kitchen." Tim took a deep breath, seeming to gear himself for what lay ahead. "Jupe, this is my wife," he said quietly, pulling Kara's hand through his arm. "I guess she'll be Little Missy."

"Yessuh," Jupe nodded. "Welcome, Little Missy."

"Where are they, Jupe?" Tim asked.

"In de front parlor, Marse Tim," Jupe said. Quickly, he bolted up the graceful flight of stairs, hurried across the gallery to open the paneled cypress door.

In the foyer walked a small, plump mulatto woman, her eyes focused on the glass-laden tray in her hands.

"Celestine," Tim said softly, and she swung around to face him, brown eyes wide with surprise.

"Marse Tim!" she squeaked delightedly. "Yo' mama be so glad yo' home!" She darted forward with such swiftness that Kara feared she would drop her burden. "Ole Miss! Ole Miss!"

Tim chuckled.

"Don't be alarmed by the titles," Tim warned. "Mama is Ole Miss, and Annabel is Young Miss, and now you'll be Little Missy."

On Tim's arm, Kara walked across the marble floor of the foyer. Small oriental rugs cushioned sections of the floor. Lush velvet hangings and oil paintings from Europe hung on the walls. A magnificent, curving marble stairway rose from the far end. Hanging high from the eighteen-foot ceiling was the most exquisite crystal chandelier.

Her face etched with a tight, reluctant smile, Emilie Rankin sat beside her cold-faced daughter-in-law on a tapestry-covered Hepplewhite sofa in the front parlor. From the thinly veiled disdain in Emilie Rankin's eyes, Kara knew that word, other than Tim's letter, had preceded them to Manoir. Intuitively, she knew that Elvira Johnston had vented her rage with a full description of the new Mrs. Tim Rankin's background. Kara stood at the entrance, her face white, her hands ice cold.

"Tim!" Amory Rankin came forward with a smile of pleasure, arms outstretched.

Tim stood tensely beside Kara.

"Mama, Papa, Annabel," he said with stiff politeness, "my bride."

Chapter Six

"Tim, you didn't tell us she was so beautiful." Amory leaned forward to kiss Kara lightly on the cheek, while Tim dutifully crossed to embrace his mother and sister-in-law.

"Do sit down," Emilie invited, her inner fury flimsily masked.

Kara, self-conscious, sat down and looked around her. There was an uncomfortable moment of silence. Kara examined the elegant piano, the marble-faced fireplace, the oriental rugs with their intricate patterns. Avoiding Emilie Rankin's cold stare.

"Celestine, don't stand there like that!" Emilie admonished sharply because Celestine's eyes were alive with curiosity. "Go bring lemonade for Mister Tim and—" a barely perceptible pause, "—and for his wife."

"Did you have a good trip?" Annabel asked with perfunctory politeness, after an exchange of glances with her mother-in-law.

"It was lovely." Kara's face lighted up reminiscently. Briefly. She was inwardly aware of the reluctance of the women to offer even a façade of welcome. She hesitated, then looked directly at Emilie. "It was certainly a great improvement on my trip from Ireland." She smiled determinedly. She had obviously rocked them with her candor. She swept on. "I'd been living in New York a very short while when I met

Tim." She paused, faintly breathless, turned to Tim for encouragement. He appeared discomforted.

"It was bad in Ireland for a while." Amory rushed to fill the sudden silence.

"Nothing like that must ever happen again." Kara's eyes flashed. "How could the government allow seven hundred and fifty thousand people to starve to death? It's on the politicians' souls!"

"We in America stood by and let it happen," Amory conceded somberly. "We haven't yet learned that humanity is one."

"Amory, please." Emilie shuddered slightly. She considered starvation an unladylike subject. Die under wraps with her sensitive nature. "Tim, did you have a chance to show Kara—" Emilie stumbled over the name, seeming to find it difficult to voice. "Did you have a chance to show her much of New Orleans?"

"Just what we saw from the carriage driving through town." Tim stared miserably at the rug.

"Kara is an unusual name," Amory remarked, his tone making this a compliment.

"It's Gaelic," Kara explained. She liked Tim's father. On sight, she liked him. How different from his wife and daughter-in-law. "It means 'dear little one,' " she explained.

"Annabel went to school in London for a year," Emilie stated with pride. "She visited Dublin."

Kara felt the hot color stain her cheeks.

"I've never been to Dublin, nor London. I went to a village school sixty miles from Cork. That and the books the schoolmaster used to give me to read made up my education." Her voice wore a lilt. She would not let herself feel inferior to these flowers of southern womanhood.

"I'm a reader myself," Emilie said with an air of disbelief

in Kara's leanings in this direction. "Have you read *Ivanhoe*?"

"Yes, I've read all of Scott's novels," Kara said serenely, relishing the older woman's look of astonishment. "I like the poems best. *The Lady of the Lake* was my favorite."

"Well, Emilie." Amory's voice was faintly ironic. "Now you have someone to talk to about your novels." Emilie stiffened, her mouth betraying her annoyance. "My reading is rather heavy," he drawled, turning his attention to Kara. "It bores my wife to discuss such dullness."

"You must be exhausted from that long trip," Emilie said, as Celestine returned with tall, frosted glasses of lemonade for Kara and Tim. "When you've quenched your thirst, you'd probably like to go up to your rooms and refresh yourself."

Kara was puzzled by the tightening of Amory's face as he stared suddenly at his wife.

"Emilie, they're probably famished." Amory was brusquely reproachful. "It's almost an hour-and-a-half drive from New Orleans." He turned to Tim, "When did you eat last?"

"We ate just before the ship came in," Tim stammered. He tried for a convivial note. "You know the meals aboard those steamers, every one a feast. Lemonade will be fine until we sit down to dinner. Right, Kara?"

"Oh, yes," Kara said politely, sipping the frosty lemonade.

"Jasmine can do for you," Emilie said sweetly, "until Amory brings a girl into the house for you. Jasmine is Annabel's maid," she explained. "She's quick and polite, and I'm sure you'll be pleased with her." Emilie Rankin was suddenly spilling over with southern charm. "I've put you in the room at the north corner, right near the magnolias."

Again, a charged exchange between Emilie and Amory, which Kara intercepted without understanding.

"Just let Jasmine iron and put away everything for you,"

Annabel said airily. "She can do it when you come down to dinner, without disturbing you."

Kara listened with a blend of awe and distaste. She was perfectly capable of ironing her own clothes. The prospect of having a slave "do for her" made her uneasy.

"Kara," Amory began, "Tim, you and I will go into New Orleans later in the week. We'll buy a girl at the Saint Charles auction for you. Your own property. Our wedding gift to you, Kara," he said with a courtly bow. An enigmatic glow in his eyes.

"Amory, how can you take your son's wife into that kind of atmosphere?" Emilie demanded angrily. "What will folks think of you?"

"I long ago gave up caring what folks think of me," Amory smiled with malicious pleasure. "I'm sure Kara would enjoy some local color. Not even Ireland offers anything quite so exotic as our slave auctions." He looked at Emilie, his eyes mocking, baiting.

Emilie uttered a low sigh of impatience, swung to face her older daughter-in-law. Her small hands lacing and unlacing themselves in her lap.

"Annabel, do play for us. That piece by Debussy, I so enjoy that."

"Tim will be in the room right next door," Emilie said sweetly to Kara as she turned the silver-knobbed cypress door. Kara's eyes widened in shock. Tim and she were not to share a room? Involuntarily her gaze swept to Tim. She saw his astonishment. But he wasn't objecting. "I do hope you like your room, Kara" Suddenly Emilie was all concern, the anxious-to-please mother-in-law. "Celestine sewed new draperies and curtains for you because she's so devoted to Tim." Emilie shot an arch glance at him.

"It's very pretty." Kara, her throat tight with dismay, walked into the spacious corner bedroom. "What a beautiful bed," Kara exclaimed, sensing some vocal admiration was required of her. She gazed intently at the delicately canopied Chippendale bed, without seeing it.

"That bed belonged to my great-grandmother on the Butler side," Emilie said. Evidently the Butlers were important folks, Kara decided. "Half a dozen young Butlers were born in that bed," Emilie added.

"It's a beautiful room," Kara said, afraid Mrs. Rankin might realize how little she knew about furniture and such things.

"Jasmine will be up presently to unpack for you. Rest until dinner," Emilie said. "I'll send word up when it's to be served." She turned to Tim, linked an arm through his. "Now I'm going to take my boy away for some mother-son conversation," she said with cloying sweetness. "I haven't seen Tim for all these weeks."

With the door firmly closed, Kara stood in the center of the room. Emilie Rankin hated her. Because she was not Denise Johnston. Because she was not Emilie Rankin's choice for Tim's bride. He'd had the brass to select his own, and his mother wasn't accepting that.

Impatiently, Kara crossed the room, fighting against a wave of claustrophobia. Frowning, she pushed aside the curtains, opened the long, narrow windows, pushing back the shutters that had been closed against the afternoon sun. The air was hot, humid, heavily fragrant. In a rush of bravado Kara moved about the room, opening windows, pushing aside shutters. Relishing the odd sense of freedom this action provided.

Suddenly Kara stiffened, her ears assaulted by the faintly strident voice of Emilie Rankin emerging from behind the closed windows in the next room. Tim's room.

"Tim, how could you do this to us? Humiliate us this way! Paying court to Denise Johnston like that. Her mother was certain you were about to propose any evening. She was just distraught when she found out, from the servants"—contempt laced her voice—"that you'd run off with one of the maids. She telegraphed us immediately. I was embarrassed that the telegraph company office in New Orleans had to know. It's probably all over the county by now!"

"Mama, please," Tim pleaded unhappily, while Kara listened at the window, too sick at heart to move.

"Oh, I understand," Emilie Rankin's voice soared scornfully. "This girl looked at you adoringly, as though you were the most important thing in the world, and you, of course, were taken in."

"Mama, don't talk like that," Tim protested, his voice strengthening. "Kara is going to be the best thing that ever happened to me. With her, I'll be all right. Mama, I know I will."

"Tim, an Irish maid!" his mother threw back at him. "How do we introduce her to our friends?"

"Mama, you're clever about these things, you know how to train Kara. She's so pretty, and she's bright, you'll make her into a fine southern lady."

Kara recoiled. Her face hot. Churning within. Stung by Tim's words. Nobody had to train her to be a lady! She glanced at herself in the mirror. What did Tim mean when he said he'd be "all right"? Had he been too loose with the girls in New Orleans? It was easy to see that this was a town where a man could easily satisfy himself that way. Was Emilie Rankin nervous about Tim's getting into trouble with a girl? Why, he'd never even kissed her until he'd asked her to marry him!

Kara started at the knock on the door. A timorous knock. She hesitated a moment, fighting for calm.

"Come in."

The door opened. A tall, exceedingly slim girl, no more than fifteen, with faintly swelling breasts and narrow hips, her features small and even beneath a golden brown skin, walked into the room with an unknowingly sensuous grace.

"Ah'm Jasmine," the girl said softly. "Ah unpack fo' yo', do de ironin'."

"Thank you, Jasmine." Kara smiled encouragingly. The girl appeared scared and nervous. "But I haven't even opened my portmanteau."

"Ah do," Jasmine said eagerly, and suddenly she smiled. Recognizing the honesty of Kara's efforts at friendliness. "Yo' res', yo' heah?" she said, capably lifting the portmanteau across a chair. "Lay yo'sef on de bed," Jasmine folded back the elegant bedspread, arranged the downy pillows. "Res' afo' dinnuh. Dat way yo' 'preciate Octavia's cookin'. Her de bes'."

Kara didn't expect to fall asleep. But with the heavy scent of magnolias invading the room, with the lulling sound of Jasmine's voice singing softly as she unpacked, Kara drifted off into slumber.

She came awake slowly, to the sound of rain slanting heavily against the house, to the scent of freshly pressed clothes. Weighed down by a sense of unreality, Kara opened her eyes. A delightful coolness filled the room. Without moving, she swung her eyes to the windows. Jasmine had closed them.

"Feel bettuh?" Jasmine shot a dazzling smile at her from across the room.

Kara smiled, pulling herself into a sitting position.

"I feel fine," she said.

"De rain hep wash away de heat," Jasmine said contentedly. "It stop soon but stay nice all night." Her amber eyes were liquid with admiration as she surveyed the array of dresses, not knowing that such luxury was strange to Kara, too. "What yo' weah to dinnuh, Li'l Missy?"

"You pick, Jasmine," Kara said, and laughed at the reaction of astonishment and delight that shone in Jasmine's eyes.

On impulse, while Jasmine deliberated among the dresses, Kara crossed to the mahogany chest of drawers and opened a small tin box which once had contained English tea biscuits. It now held Kara's few cherished trinkets from home.

"Would you like these, Jasmine?" She extended the splash of colored glass.

"Me?" Jasmine stared in disbelief. "Fo' me?" Her eyes searched Kara's.

"Yes. If you like them."

"Oh, ah like!" Jasmine's smile was beautiful.

With childlike wonder, Jasmine draped the brilliantly colored beads about her neck. Then, with a wise glint in her eyes, she slipped the beads within the neckline of the flimsy cotton dress that was her entire attire, so that they were fully concealed.

"Ah thankee, Li'l Missy. Thankee, yes!"

Jasmine helped Kara dress for dinner. All the while, Kara listened for the sound of Tim's voice. Her face lighted when a knock sounded briskly on her door.

"Come in."

The door swung open. Annabel, tall, cold, annoyed, hovered in the doorway.

"May I borrow Jasmine now? I really must dress for dinner." Her attitude imperious, condescending.

"Please do," Kara said politely. "Thank you, Jasmine." Her eyes grateful.

Kara stood alone in the center of the room, beset by conflicting emotions. Hurt, angry, defiant. Was she supposed to wait here, like a caged bird, until sent for? No. She would not live that way!

Head high, blue eyes flashing, pink staining her high cheekbones, Kara left her room and walked slowly down the staircase. She could play the lady as well as any of them.

Kara hesitated at an open door, hearing men's voices, gazed inside. This was the library. With a blend of awe and pleasure, her eyes skimmed the row upon row of leather-bound books that rose from floor to ceiling on two walls. In one corner, before a tall, open window, stood Tim, his father, and a third man, his back to Kara, engrossed in conversation.

"I tell you, until we get clean government in this state all we'll have is a false prosperity that'll blow up in our faces," Amory said. "All the people, no matter what their roots, deserve a voice in what's happening." He picked up his ice-laden glass, then spied Kara, standing there in the doorway in nervous indecision. "Kara, come in," he invited, his eyes affectionate.

Tim swung about as though startled by her presence. As though, she mocked herself, he'd forgotten for a moment that he had a wife.

"Kara, you must meet Charles," Tim said, striding toward her.

Kara looked up into the warm brown eyes of a man who was undoubtedly Tim's brother. The features the same, except that in Charles they were less finely chiseled, not quite attaining Tim's Knights-of-the-Round-Table handsomeness. He smiled.

"Welcome to Manoir, Kara," Charles said, his voice resonant, sincere.

"Thank you."

"Would you like a drink, Kara?" Tim seemed to relax beneath Charles's approval.

"Thank you, no," Kara said politely, grateful for the years of being molded by Mr. Watterson and her father. They had seen to it that she was a lady, even on a tiny potato farm in Ireland. Her father, she thought with Irish pride, could hold his own with any of the men here, despite the fact that his schooling had stopped when he was thirteen.

Kara allowed herself to be seated on the small, tapestry-covered sofa that flanked the fireplace. Tim deposited his empty glass on the mantelpiece and sat beside her, his eyes moving compulsively to the door. Steeling himself for his mother's arrival.

"Look what's happening up in New York," Amory pointed out with a show of indignation. "The gambling that goes on there, you must have seen that, Tim. The corruption, that you couldn't see! I tell you, Tweed is wrapping Tammany Hall around his little finger, and the people are paying for it."

Emilie Rankin joined them, surprised at Kara's presence. She sat in a chair close to the window, indicating her wish for fresh air. Kara concentrated on the discussion, as ever taking in everything she heard. Emilie seemed bored, only brightening when Annabel appeared in the doorway.

"Did you have a good day, Charles?" Annabel asked her husband with a perfunctory smile.

"Yes," Charles replied.

He seemed so much older than Tim. Because of his air of authority, of a man used to commanding. But Charles, Tim had told Kara, was only twenty-seven, four years older than Tim.

They lingered in the library until Celestine arrived to announce dinner. Kara was relieved that they were going in to the dining room. Charles had a charming way of including her, by glance, in their conversation, perhaps because her face indicated an avid interest. Annabel had noticed, and was annoyed. Kara felt a tremor of anxiety.

The six of them sat down at the long, beautifully laid dining-room table, beneath an impressive wrought-iron chandelier. Wall sconces added additional lighting. Annabel on Amory's right, Kara at his left, Charles and Tim flanking their mother.

With the arrival of the vegetable soup, seasoned deliciously with hambone, Emilie Rankin launched into a lively discussion about the ball that must be given to introduce Kara to their friends. Amory seemed relieved that his wife was on that path. He exchanged a knowing look with Charles, chuckled.

"Emilie is never happier than when she's planning a party," he jibed good-humoredly.

Kara lowered her eyes, a little nervous at the prospect of the coming ball, which her mother-in-law described in such fulsome detail. There would be hundreds of people, from all over the state! Glancing up, feeling the weight of Emilie Rankin's gaze, Kara realized her mother-in-law anticipated and relished her discomfort.

Kara concentrated on the food. Celestine and Horatio served the sumptuous meal. Trout, covered with melted butter and slivers of almonds. An oxtail ragout that was savory and tender. But Charles did not seem to have much of an appetite.

"Pecan pie to welcome you home, Tim," Emilie said in the slightly flirtatious manner that set Kara's teeth on edge. "Octavia knows you just adore it."

Tim grinned.

"Never could pass up anything Octavia bakes. Particularly pecan pie." He dug into the wedge with relish.

"Do you like music, Kara?" Emilie asked with ostentatious cordiality. "We all went down to hear Jenny Lind when she was in New Orleans last year."

"Yes, I like music," Kara said politely, and lowered her eyes quickly to her dessert plate.

She knew nothing about music, which was the reason Mrs. Rankin had asked the question. Annabel, of course, played the piano. Annabel spoke French and did needlepoint. Like Denise Johnston.

"The fuss they made over that woman," Amory reminisced with amusement. "Half the town took leave of their senses. Thousands flocking to the levee to welcome her. Shopkeepers were suddenly selling 'Jenny Lind shirts' and 'Jenny Lind ties.' That same night, about eleven o'clock, there was a torchlight parade and all those thousands of folks sang to *her*." Amory shook his head in incomprehension.

"We went to the opening performance," Annabel contributed. "It was very exciting."

"She's a rather cold woman for my taste," Charles admitted, and his wife stared as though this were an obscene remark. "Like an alabaster statue."

"You didn't say that when she sang the 'Casta diva' aria from *Norma*," Annabel pointed out with vindictive triumph. "You were as enthusiastic as the rest."

"I kept to my seat, though," Charles said humorously.

"Charles, do you ever see that friend of yours who used to work on the *Crescent*?" Tim asked. "That Walt Whitman?"

"He's moved on up to New York again," Charles reported. "He's determined to astound the city with his poetry." His smile was gently joshing.

"From what you've said, it's hardly suitable for a lady's ears," Annabel shot back with disdain.

Kara silently concentrated on the extravagantly rich triangle of pecan pie with a growing awareness of her deficiency in small talk. Amory, sensing Kara's discomfort, drew her into the conversation with questions about the boat trip from Louisville.

Coffee was served to the ladies in a small sitting room across the corridor. The men retired to the library, their voices raised in good-humored argument. Tim's voice, Kara noted, contributed little, which was natural enough because the other two were talking agriculture, which held no interest for Tim.

Kara sat on a sofa beside Annabel. Wearing a stiff little smile, she pretended to listen politely while Emilie and Annabel discussed the coming ball. The prospect was a nightmare. It was a relief to Kara when Emilie, with an inscrutable glance at Annabel, suggested the ladies retire to their respective rooms.

"Good night, Mrs. Rankin," Kara said politely at her door. "Good night, Annabel."

To her mother-in-law and sister-in-law, Kara thought furiously behind the closed door to her bedroom, she would forever be the Irish maid Tim was stupid enough to marry. Rebellion raging in her, she prepared for bed. Listening carefully for a sound of Tim's approach. She hadn't even said good night to him!

Kara dawdled over her night preparations, as though this would stave off the moment when she must climb into the solitary double bed. Last night she had slept in Tim's arms. She yearned for that closeness now. Felt color stain her cheeks because she was remembering his tender lovemaking. Wishing for his arms around her again. Wishing for the exquisite pleasure of receiving him.

Kara slid beneath the cool sheets, glad for the breeze that infiltrated the large, square bedroom. Waiting for Tim to come to her. Waiting, painfully awake, until tiredness rode over her, and she gave way to solitary sleep.

Chapter Seven

In the library Amory yawned, though Charles was certain his father would sit here, slumped over his books and sipping at a forbidden tumbler of bourbon, until dawn streaked the sky. Tim sprawled moodily in a chair beside his father, drinking more heavily than usual.

Charles pushed his chair back, cleared his throat.

"I have some things to take care of," he excused himself casually, and caught his father's quick, knowing glance.

"A long ride this hour of the night," Amory drawled.

"I know," Charles conceded. Not caring at all. He frowned at the way Tim's eyes shot to him, with curiosity. It used to be Tim who took off at odd hours for New Orleans. Despite the distance. "Good night, Papa. Good night, Tim."

Charles strode from the library, down the corridor to the rear of the house, to the door that led outside, to the stables. He'd told Jupe to have a carriage ready to go to New Orleans tonight. Jupe understood.

The knowledge of Tim's marriage had been the catalyst that had propelled him into "the arrangement," though the idea had been in his mind for months. Seeing Kara, suspecting the passion beneath that delicate loveliness, he was aware of his maleness, of the nights he wished to turn to a wife, who kept him out of her bed. Three years now.

Five miscarriages in four years, and she'd declared she

would have no more of that side of marriage. He had been ostracized from his own bedroom. How could he object, when the doctor was on Annabel's side?

Even on their honeymoon Annabel had been cold, though submitting to his demands. Never participating. Providing the body because the marriage contract demanded it. Each time she miscarried, early in pregnancy, the unspoken accusation that he had given her a "bad seed," because Dr. Scott had said a miscarriage was nature's way of disposing of a defective child before birth.

Charles walked out into the night, feeling a surge of anticipation that was rare. Not minding the long ride into New Orleans, when he considered what waited at the end of his journey. Papa was philosophical about the "arrangement." A French custom the Americans in Louisiana had adopted with alacrity.

When he had left the insufferably dead ball at the Andersons last month, Annabel had believed he'd gone off to gamble with Gabe Anderson. Gabe wanted him for cover because his wife grew hysterical every time he took off for one of the quadroon balls, admittedly more amusing than the society balls.

They had been at the ball, on the second floor of the handsome Salle d'Orleans, when Charles's eyes had lighted on the girl, and remained there. Small but beautifully rounded. An incredibly tiny waist. Features delicate, head high. A mass of honey-colored hair above a peach-tinted skin. The eyes an unexpectedly deep blue. Sixteen or seventeen, already trained in the art of being a *placée.* Virgin, he could be certain. A girl was kept intact until she became a *placée.*

As he had stood there four feet away from this girl, all the dissatisfaction in his mind, the conjectures which had floated, heretofore, aimlessly about, congealed. He could not endure the celibate life that Annabel imposed on him any longer. His pulse racing as though he were a stripling, he had approached the girl. Odette. Knowing how these things were to be arranged.

Odette's mother had been delighted. Manoir was one of the finest plantations in Louisiana. She couldn't have wished better for her daughter. Odette would have her little house along rue des Ramparts, with a maid to care for her. It was agreed, on businesslike terms, that the relationship would continue for a minimum of two years. If monsieur desired to terminate the relationship earlier, he would settle two thousand in cash on Odette.

In the carriage, with Jupe coaxing the horses to pick up speed, Charles thought about the effect of his "arrangement" on Annabel. She'd be upset if she found out. But she had asked for this, damn it!

He would be as discreet as possible. Of course, these things had a way of being rumored about. Gabe's wife knew about his *placée.* She'd carried on so badly he'd settled money on the girl to set her up as a dressmaker, and remained faithful for almost a year. But now, again, he was making the journey, two or three times a week, to rue des Ramparts.

Charles leaned back in the carriage, envisioning Odette in his mind. Three times he had seen her. Always with Mama in attendance. But tonight she would be alone in the modest white cottage he had rented and furnished as befitted a wealthy plantation owner.

Odette was trained by Mama in all the things to do. A hot supper would be kept waiting for his arrival. After they had eaten, the maid would be sent away. He felt a surge of warmth in his loins. Odette would not turn him away. She would not be cold.

★ ★ ★ ★ ★

Charles straightened up as they approached the irregular row of small, white one-storied houses, with their wrought-iron railed porches. Modest cottages behind which dwelt passion, arranged and available.

Jupe pulled up before the house, his eyes moving with curiosity along the rows of discreetly closed windows.

"Send Lucifer to pick me up at five sharp," Charles said. "Tell him not to dawdle."

"Ah be here," Jupe said firmly. "No need fo' dat no-good Lucifer." Jupe, christened Jupiter, had a taste for New Orleans. "All right, suh?" he asked anxiously, as though he might have overstepped his bounds.

Charles laughed.

"All right, Jupe, but you take care of the horses."

Jupe grinned, relishing an evening in New Orleans.

"Ah do," he promised. "Pick yo' up at five sharp, suh." Charles strode to the small white house, mounted the stairs, crossed the porch. As he reached for the door, it swung wide in welcome. Odette stood there. Slender, beautiful, desirable. Appearing faintly uneasy, fearful. Afraid of not being able to please him.

"Come in, monsieur," she invited demurely, standing to one side.

Charles walked into the foyer with its handsome wall hangings, personally chosen by him, the glittering girandole, the oriental throw rug on the floor. Lavish interior in comparison to the humble outer appearance of the cottage.

"It's late," Charles said apologetically, his eyes drawn to the beautifully rounded breasts, outlined by the delicate silk of her gown.

"I expected you," she said with a smile. "Supper is ready."

He followed Odette into the sitting room, where a table

was laid with lavish attention to detail. She gestured him to a chair, picked up the silver bell that sat at one edge of the table, shook it gently.

"Supper," she said softly when the small, rotund mulatto woman arrived.

With swift, silken glides, despite her bulk, the maid served them. Charles hadn't expected to be hungry, but the calves' feet la vinaigrette, the bouillabaisse served on small squares of butter-fried toast, and the red beans with boiled rice enticed him into eating.

Odette ventured no conversation except whispered consultations with the maid from time to time. Responding with musical softness when Charles's conversation required an answer.

With the pecan pralines, the maid brought Creole café au lait, and Charles leaned back in his chair with satisfaction. In this setting, with the excellent food settling warmly in his stomach and the caressing candlelight sending attractive patterns of illumination about the room, Charles relaxed. The perpetual tenseness about his shoulder blades grew less painful. He smiled. Odette seemed pleased.

"I won't be able to stir for hours," he predicted, and Odette laughed delightedly. But their eyes collided and he saw the wise, almost expectant acceptance that he would, indeed, stir.

When the table was cleared, Odette dismissed the maid for the evening. She sat on the edge of her chair, like a marvelously wrought porcelain figurine, waiting for the time when he would push back his chair and take her into the bedroom. Because to the *placée* there was beauty in a man and woman coming together. It was natural.

When he had taken Annabel, she had cried bitterly afterward. Her back to him, her body drawn together beneath the blankets in a tight, small ball, as though she had been violated. He had never gone to any of the Negro women, though the signs were unmistakable, from time to time, that some would welcome him. It didn't seem sporting, no matter what the southern custom, to take a woman to bed, when she didn't have the choice of refusal.

Damn, Annabel didn't have to marry him! She'd been glad enough, until he took her to bed. To a woman like Annabel, a woman like his mother, that side of marriage was disgusting, ugly.

"You're beautiful," he said to Odette. Excitement charging through him now.

No man had ever been there before. He would teach and she would respond. His tongue moved about his lower lip, his thighs tightened as his mind raced ahead. His eyes held hers, revealing his passion.

"Let's go inside, Odette."

"*Oui,* monsieur." Her eyes downcast, but not before he'd caught the look of quivering expectation.

"*Oui,* Charles," he amended.

"Charles," she repeated, lending it the French touch.

They rose together from the chairs. He took her hand while they walked together into the small bedroom. Despite its size, the room wore an air of elegance. Handsome draperies at the windows, small oriental throw rugs on the floor.

"You don't know how I've been waiting for this, Odette," he whispered, drawing her to him, removing her gown.

"The candles, monsieur." She frowned in apology, "Charles. Shall I blow them out?" Her breathing uneven now.

"No. I want to see you."

She stood still, an ivory statuette threatening momentarily to burst into life. Small, high breasts with nipples that stiffened at his touch. Her eyes fluttered shut. He heard the low, startled gasp in her throat when his hands rippled over her body.

He dropped her across the width of the bed, stood there thrusting off his own clothes. Pleased at the way she watched, with admiration, expectation. Part of it the training of the *placée.* Part of it. Glad for his tall, flat, muscular body, tanned to the waist from the hours he spent each day in the fields. Tanned to a mulatto darkness.

"Don't be afraid," he said softly, lying beside her.

"I am not afraid." Her voice startlingly clear, almost happy.

His mouth dropped to hers. He felt the tremor of response in her when his fingers stroked her breasts, moved down to the delicate swell of her belly. He felt a rush of pleasure at the faint, astonished sound of excitement that escaped her.

His mouth moved about her breasts, down the slender frame. Her eyes shut, her mouth open in desire, her body straining toward him.

He lifted himself upon her, drove between the slender thighs. His eyes fastened to her face, enjoying the sight of her passion. Her face glistening, mouth half smiling. Her hands caressing him, wanting it to be right for him.

In the carriage Charles dozed, not waking until the horses turned into the private road that led to the house. The sun strong now, dappling the rows of pecans and live oaks with gold. Charles felt himself relaxed, pleased with life. A whole man.

Jupe deposited him at the front door, rumbled off to the stables. Whistling under his breath, Charles walked to the dining room. Kara was sitting there, engrossed in a book while she waited for breakfast to be served.

"What are you doing up at this hour?" Charles asked, astonished.

Kara gazed up at him, startled for an instant, then smiled.

"I was never one for staying in bed half the morning. I couldn't sleep," she admitted honestly, "and since I was famished I figured the best thing was to come downstairs."

"What are you reading?" he asked curiously, sitting at right angles to her.

"I found it in the library. A book by a woman writer." Kara looked at him, almost defensively, as though expecting a reproach for such a choice. "*Domestic Manners of the Americans*," she read the title, "by a lady named Fanny Trollope. I don't think she was highly impressed," Kara confided with an elfin smile, "but of course, I've read only a few pages."

"That would be one of Papa's books," Charles guessed. "He's fascinated by what Europeans think of us."

Celestine swept into the dining room with a coffeepot in her hand.

"Mawnin', Mistuh Charles," she greeted him briskly. "What yo' be havin' for breakfus?"

"What are you bringing Little Missy?" he asked good-humoredly.

"Grits and eggs, with some nice fried bacon on de side. Fill her out some, me be think'." She grinned admiringly at Kara while she poured coffee for the two of them.

"Bring me the same, Celestine," Charles said.

"I thought after breakfast, maybe I'd go for a walk," Kara began when Celestine left them, and hesitated at the startled glance Charles shot in her direction. "Is that all right?" All at once she seemed insecure. Vulnerable.

"Certainly it's all right," Charles said, aware of her puzzled stare at his silence. "What did you have in mind? The gardens? Mama's very proud of them, you know."

"The slave quarters," Kara said, her face coloring. "I've never seen a plantation before."

"And that's the part that most interests you?"

"I'd like to see the quarters for myself," she said candidly. "I've heard a lot." She didn't elaborate.

"I'll show you," Charles offered, almost brusquely.

Faintly ill at ease with him now, Kara laid aside her book and flashed her eager-to-please smile that somehow brought Odette skimming back into his thoughts, though the two were very different. Kara would never be one to understand the philosophy of the *placée*. Kara was an Irish scrapper. Unexpectedly, a tenderness surged through him as he looked at her. His brother had done better for himself than any of them had expected.

But Odette returned to his thoughts. Annabel would be furious if, when, he acknowledged philosophically—because how did you hide these things?—she found out about Odette and the house on rue des Ramparts. His "serpent woman," as the local ladies liked to refer to the *placées*. He frowned unhappily.

"How do they feel about slavery in Ireland?" Charles asked, realizing Kara was watching him.

Kara hesitated.

"They don't like it," she said honestly. "It seems a sin against God to enslave other human beings. On the train, we saw a car of just-bought slaves. It broke my heart, the way some of them carried on. Families being broken up, I understand, with no thought for them at all."

"Papa and I never split up a family when we sell."

But they bought slaves from the block, who had been separated from families. Papa and Kara would have much in common, he thought drily. Papa hated slavery, even while he lived from it.

And there were other people who raised their voices in

condemnation of slavery, and the voices were becoming louder. Mostly, there were people living in the North, knowing nothing that was fact.

At least the slaves ate, Charles reminded himself defensively. Damn it, slavery was the way the South existed. Their way of life! Here at Manoir the slaves had a fair time of it, as well as the poor whites working in the fields from sunup to sundown with little to show but food and their cabins. In Ireland, three-quarters of a million people starved to death. This didn't happen in the South.

Celestine arrived, slid steaming platters before them, hurried back into the kitchen wing to return with a bowl piled high with fluffy, golden-brown biscuits and a dish of freshly churned butter. Kara and Charles dug into breakfast with mutual gusto, content to abandon conversation except for occasional comments.

Charles approved of Kara's appreciation of good food. Annabel had a delicate stomach, or so she claimed. To show a hearty interest in food was a gross quality in his wife's eyes. His mother was one to be petty even about Octavia's unexcelled cuisine.

When they were finished with breakfast, allowing Celestine to coax them into extra cups of coffee, Charles leaned back with an air of satisfaction.

"I'll have a carriage brought round and take you down to the quarters," he offered.

Kara glanced up, her face bright with interest.

"How far is it?"

"About a quarter of a mile."

"Then let's walk," Kara laughed, "A carriage on a lovely morning like this, for a quarter-of-a-mile trip. Oh, you should have seen the way I walked about in New York!"

"Let's walk," he said. "I do it every morning."

Chapter Eight

Kara and Charles left the house and walked in silence out into the still early morning sunlight. The air washed out sweet by the breeze from the river, perfumed by the profusion of honeysuckle blossoms, jasmine, camellias. Birds chirped noisily in the oaks and cypress, draped with their shawls of Spanish moss.

Tim had said the house slaves, like Octavia and Celestine and Jasmine, lived high on the hog. They ate from the kitchen, wore hand-me-downs from the family, were spoiled and pampered.

Kara smiled wryly. Hadn't Mrs. Johnston boasted that she spoiled her servants? They, like the slaves, worked fourteen hours a day, took their meals in the kitchen. With none of the luxury tidbits served at the dining-room table, to be sure. But they were free. To quit at will. To dream. Paid, shabbily, yes, but money in their hands for this labor.

"We turn off here," Charles' voice intruded on her thoughts. "This footpath here."

"Am I keeping you from your work?" Kara asked.

"I don't have to be out in the fields every morning," Charles said with a slow smile. "We have an overseer. It's a kind of compulsion with me to make sure, personally, that everything is rolling properly. Actually, I should be concentrating on the paperwork."

"Tim said there was over twenty thousand acres here,"

Kara said, her voice brushed with wonder. "You know, it's hard for me even to visualize that much land."

"It's a lot of land," Charles conceded. "I'm not sure we're using it in the best way."

"What do you mean?"

"I feel we ought to vary the crops, not follow this complete insistence on cotton or sugar."

"Oh, one crop is wrong," Kara agreed with sudden intensity. "Look what happened in Ireland! Everything given over to potatoes, and then the blight and the starvation." She shuddered, hurtled back mentally to the small, whitewashed cottage near Cork. Remembering the small, wasted bodies in her arms. The anguish, the helplessness. "What happens to a cotton grower when there's a blight?" she asked. "At least you eat. But with no cotton to sell, there would be money troubles, wouldn't there? Perhaps not for the big planters, but what about all the small farmers?"

"I doubt if they'd eat," Charles said grimly. "They put every acre into cotton. It's happened already, there have been bad years. Nothing like in Ireland, but bad enough to hurt."

Suddenly, high-pitched, argumentative voices of children at play pierced the early morning air.

"Yo' don' do dat, yo' heah?" a child's voice squeaked. "Yo' do, an break yo' haid!"

"The quarters are just through there." Charles pointed to a path that cut through a tall avenue of pecans, then ran one hand through his rumpled fair hair in a gesture of restlessness.

They followed the path for a few feet, emerged to a wide clearing. A dozen cabins sprawled in two unprepossessing rows, with a dirt "street" between them. The cabins evidently no more than single rooms, about twelve by fifteen feet. Here and there a neat garden patch behind a cabin. At the far end a larger house of whitewashed wood, two stories high.

The children discovered Kara and Charles and abandoned their play to dart forward with bright-eyed curiosity, yet shy before Kara. Their bright, shining eyes covertly inspecting her. Fourteen of them, Kara counted, smiling. Their skin varying from ebony to gold, ages from infant-in-arms to about ten. The older children, capably balancing the babies in their arms. All of them barefoot, near-naked, but with woolly heads bound in many layers of cloth.

"Here, you young scalawags." Charles chuckled, bringing a handful of hard candies from his pocket. It was probably a daily ritual and they'd been expecting it. Charles tossed the candy. They rushed forward, squealing delightedly, scrambling for the small, paper-wrapped confections.

"Where do the other slaves live?" Kara asked, stooping to pick up a particularly winsome toddler, with pert features and glowing eyes, who was uncertain about this attention but fearful of crying. How lovely these children are, Kara thought as she nuzzled the little one in her arms.

Charles searched around in his pocket for another candy, gave it to the toddler while Kara waited for an answer to her question. Charles' eyes were opaque, his smile impersonal.

"All slaves live here, Kara. Two families to a cabin. The house slaves sleep in the kitchen wing." He stared stonily ahead.

"Could I go inside one?" she asked politely. A *hundred* human beings lived in these twelve cabins? "Oh, what is the big house down there?"

"That's the infirmary." Charles' voice was terse. "Yes, you can go into a cabin if you like. Nothing much to see," he shrugged. "They're all out in the fields now, except for whoever is sick and in the infirmary."

At a nod from Charles, Kara walked onto the rickety porch

of the best tended of the cabins, though even here the windows were unglazed, open to all the elements. The main room offered a pair of tiny cubicles, each of which held a bedstead, with moss piled beneath a blanket to substitute for a mattress. The blankets strangers to soap and water.

Kara stared in disbelief while her mind coped with the mathematics. An average of eight humans were stuffed into each of these cabins, four to a bed!

"The cabins are dirty this late in the week," Charles said stiffly. "They do their cleaning on Saturdays, when they're not in the fields. Saturdays they only do light, essential work. Sundays, of course, they're off." He was speaking with a sort of inner anger that captured Kara's attention. "Come along, I'll show you the infirmary."

In comparison to the cabins, the infirmary appeared large. There were four fairly large rooms. Two downstairs, two upstairs. The windows on the downstairs rooms were glazed but encrusted with dirt; the upper windows were unglazed and had shutters closed tightly against the morning sun.

Charles paused to talk gently to an old man lying on a bed. White-bearded, palsied, eager to confide his aches and pains, to which Charles listened with attentive, sympathetic interest. Nearby, a black buck with a broken leg stared sullenly at the ceiling.

"How're you doing, Merc?" Charles asked casually.

"All right, suh," he acknowledged cautiously, but Charles frowned when the buck covertly stared at Kara. "Jes' hafta lay heah till him heal."

A woman appeared at the top of the shaky stairs. Toothless, rotund, commanding of stature.

"Mawnin', Marse Charles," she greeted him effusively. "Look lak dat Rebecca be droppin' her sucklin' couple hours now. Lawd!" she frowned at an outcry from the upper floor, "her carry on lak her be white."

"Rose!" a young, scared voice cried out. "Rose, him comin'! Ah know him is!"

"Don't fret, child," Rose called back calmly. "Yo' got a while yit."

A sudden, wild shriek rent the air. Charles tensed.

"Let me go up," Kara said.

Before Charles could stop her, she was swiftly climbing the rickety stairs. In the room to the left, a young mulatto, barely sixteen, lay on a makeshift bed. Belly distended, a shabby cotton dress hiked above her flexed knees as she strained in labor. Kara rushed to her side and sat at the edge of the bed.

"It's going to be all right," she whispered softly. "Soon now," she guessed, while the midwife moved back to inspect, pleased by Kara's interest.

Kara rose to her feet, crossed to the window to push open the shutters and allow in the sunlight.

"Her be young," Rose said matter-of-factly. "Built small, her. Hard, de fus' 'un."

A shriek erupted from the girl. Kara took her hands. The hands clung while perspiration glistened on her golden skin and she braced herself for the next contraction.

"I'll be right back," Kara promised, gently tugging her hands free. "Right back." She hurried to the stairs. Below, Charles waited, frowning. His eyes restless. "Charles, I'm going to stay with her," Kara called down. "I'll find my way back to the house." She swung away before Charles could protest.

Kara went again to the girl, clutched tightly at her hands, murmuring encouragement. The contractions coming one on top of another now. Cries escaping the tortured mother as she threshed about on the narrow bed.

"Him comin'," the midwife announced with satisfaction a few minutes later. "Haid fus' lak him belong."

Kara soothed the pain-wracked girl. So young, too delicately constructed for the task of delivering life. Another slave for the plantation. Another pair of hands to work in the fields.

"Boy," Rose murmured complacently, as though personally responsible. "Marse be pleased."

Kara took charge of the tiny, squealing bundle while Rose waited for the girl to expel the placenta.

"Her be all right quick," Rose prophesied. "Her be back in fields tomorrow."

"Oh, no!" Kara stared in disbelief.

"Marse say three days no fields," the girl whispered, exhausted from her labor. *"Marse say."*

"Him too easy," Rose scoffed. "Ah drop my sucklin's, same day ah be choppin' cotton."

Kara remained until the baby and the mother were respectably cleaned up and sleeping, with the shutters adjusted to allow a little light and air into the room.

"Dat Marse Tim, him got hisself a fine lady," Rose announced with satisfaction.

Kara walked slowly into the house. Hating the whole institution of slavery. Sickened by the contrast between the elegance within these walls and the plight of eight humans pressed into a cabin with two beds to serve them. The grove of tall pecans, shielding the delicate eyes of the Rankins from what lay beyond.

"Kara, come in."

She started at the sound of Charles's voice. He was seated at the dining-room table, drinking from a tall coffee mug. A pot on a trivet before him.

"I found my way back," she said with an effort at humor, walking into the dining room.

"I decided to come back for more coffee. Everyone else is still in bed." He leaned back in his chair and shouted lustily. "Celestine! Celestine, bring a mug for Little Missy." He smiled at her. "So now you've seen the picturesque plantation life. I gather Rebecca dropped the baby?"

Kara nodded defensively. "A boy."

"I was afraid she'd have a hard time," Charles said quietly. "Too young. She wasn't meant to mate for another year, but one of those hot-blooded bucks caught hold of her."

"Rose was ready to send her back into the fields this afternoon," Kara accused.

"She won't dare," Charles said firmly. "I have established a rule. Not for three days, at least. No point in sending them out before they've healed properly. It only makes trouble later."

"Bad business?" Her eyes faintly defiant.

"Bad business."

They were silent while Celestine ambled in with a mug for Kara.

"Charles," she ventured, while he poured coffee for her. "Could I help some way down in the quarters?"

Charles looked up sharply. "You in the quarters?"

"I could help in little ways," she stammered. "I could show them how to take care of the little ones. All those head wrappings on the babies. My goodness, they have enough hair of their own!" Uneasily, she joined in with Charles's laughter. "Maybe I could teach the ones who're old enough," she suggested. "To read, I mean."

"There's a law," Charles said tersely. "No one may teach a slave to read."

"Oh!" All of Kara's incredulity, her revulsion, her condemnation ricocheted in her voice.

"Reading would be rather useless," Charles said unhappily after a heavy silence between them. "Where could it lead them? To dissatisfaction with their lot, which isn't going to change. The whole economy of the South is tied up with slavery, as well as much of the northern banking money. We can't change that, Kara."

Again, a silence fell between them.

"I'm going to have a lot of time on my hands," she said softly, after a while. Discomforted, suddenly at this prospect. Not until this morning had she emerged into reality. "I'm not one to sit around all day doing needlepoint and such," she said with candor, and suppressed a shudder at the vision of being closeted interminably with Emilie Rankin and Annabel. "Could I go down to the quarters for an hour or two each day, to tell them stories, teach them songs we sang in Ireland?" She smiled persuasively. "It would be something for me to do, and I think it might give them pleasure."

"If you wish to do that. Only the small ones are in the quarters during the day, so no harm could come to you. But you'd better discuss it with Tim first," he cautioned.

"Oh, I will," Kara promised.

"Well, do my eyes deceive me?" Amory drawled from the doorway. "A young lady to honor us at the breakfast table." His smile was warm, welcoming. "Celestine!" he yelled over his shoulder. "Breakfast."

"I'm not used to lying in bed late," Kara said. "There's always been something that had to be done." But color edged into her cheeks because she remembered the weeks as a maid in the Johnston's house, and remembered Emilie Rankin's scathing opinion of her. "Besides," she said with a touch of defiance. "There's too much to be seen to sleep away the morning."

"A pleasure to have a pretty face across the table at breakfast," Amory pronounced gallantly. "My wife and Annabel are accustomed to having breakfast in their rooms." Good-humored irony laced his voice. "To prepare for their strenuous days of planning balls." He lifted an eloquent eyebrow at the sight of nothing more substantial than coffee before her. "But you're not one of those ladies who breakfast on coffee alone? I took you for a lass with a relish for good food."

"That I am!" Kara laughed. "I ate like a field hand. Much earlier."

"Kara's been sight-seeing down at the quarters," Charles said, exchanging a loaded glance with his father. "She even lent a hand when Rebecca dropped the baby."

"The girl all right?" Amory leaned forward with solicitude. "The build on that one made me uneasy, and she's so young."

"She had a rough time," Kara told him. "But she's all right. It was a boy. He's fine, too." She smiled, remembering the tiny dark bundle with the lusty voice.

"I don't know how fine he'll be," Amory said drily. "No luck, coming into the world a slave. One more hand to work in the fields."

"Papa, we're good to our slaves," Charles frowned, his voice defensive. "We've never once had an uprising here. There's never been a question of it! All the milk they can drink, all the bread, greens, pot licker, hominy, molasses they need to fill their bellies. They raise enough chickens and ducks to eat poultry every Sunday. Yard goods twice a year. A little something special at Christmas."

"You satisfied with that Dent fellow?" Amory asked, his eyes narrowing.

"His references were the best. He handles himself well, as far as I've seen."

Charles and his father discussed the overseer question at length. Kara guessed that both men were conscientious about whom they put over the slaves. But Charles was withdrawing again. For all his protestations about how well they treated their slaves, Charles Rankin bore the covert guilt that troubled many a slave owner. He disliked slavery; but he didn't know how the South could exist without it.

"Your mother likes Fred Dent well enough. When she invites an overseer into the house, you know damn well Emilie likes him." Amory chuckled. "We never had an overseer with parlor manners like this fellow. A real ladies' man, this one." Amory turned to Kara. "Well, young lady, you think you're going to be able to take living at Manoir?"

"It's the most beautiful place I've ever seen," Kara said enthusiastically. "As beautiful as Ireland," she declared.

"As long as you ignore the quarters," Amory said. "The fields where they work. As long as you forget how we keep the beautiful South in existence."

"Papa, what's the use of all this?" Charles demanded with exasperation, yet Kara knew this was a daily needling on the part of his father. "There's good and bad in everything."

"There's no good where human beings are oppressed," Amory growled. "And the day will come, mind you, not in this decade, perhaps, but in the next, when there'll be no slaves. When the plantations will hire their labor, for pay. And *we'll survive,* Charles."

"Good morning." Tim strolled into the room with a tentative smile, hesitated, then took the chair beside Kara. Aware that his father's eyes were hard upon him. "Kara, you're looking beautiful."

"Thank you." Kara's face lighted up. It seemed such a long time since she'd seen Tim. The first night at Manoir, and they'd slept apart. How many times had she awakened to the emptiness beside her? But now she glowed at his closeness.

"Celestine!" Amory yelled again and chuckled. "Emilie will be tearing in here, complaining I'm carrying on like a slave trader." He stared disdainfully at the bell kept at the table to summon the house slaves. "Celestine, tell that Octavia to get moving!"

"I'd better get out to the fields." Charles pushed back his chair. "Dent is still new to our ways."

"Why don't you wait and take Tim here out with you?" Amory winked at his younger son. "New interest now in Manoir, when you'll be raising a son of your own one of these days." Kara quickly dropped her eyes to the table. Tim appeared startled. "That'll settle your mama like nothing else," Amory said firmly. "A grandson to make a fuss over."

"I'm going riding after breakfast," Tim said tightly, with a polite, impersonal smile, then turned to Celestine, who hovered in the doorway. "Breakfast, Celestine," he said carelessly. "Whatever's ready."

Kara sensed the uneasiness between Tim and his father. Tim loathed the prospect of being involved in running Manoir. He'd made this clear to her before. That was Charles's responsibility.

"Yes, riding is one of the things you do well." Amory's voice was edged with sarcasm. "That, and dancing, and charming people. And painting, of course. Kara, did you know Tim studied painting in Paris for six months?"

"Yes, he told me."

"Excuse me." Charles rose to his feet now, impatient with the byplay between his father and Tim, and stalked from the dining room.

"Tim, why don't you paint a portrait of Kara?" Amory prodded. "Instead of some of those outlandish paintings you do. I'm sure your mother would find a place for that in the parlor."

"A place for what, Amory?" Emilie asked from the doorway. "Good morning, Kara." The name still seemed to come from her with difficulty. "Tim, dear." Her eyes skimming Kara with perfunctory politeness, coming to rest dotingly upon Tim. "Whatever are you talking about, Amory?"

"A portrait of Kara," Amory drawled. "I think that would be a project worthy of Tim."

"Amory, you don't force a creative person into something until he's ready for it," Emilie said crossly, settling herself at the end of the table. "That's something Papa always understood," she said with nostalgia. "He understood the creative individual. It's a pity Tim was so young when Papa died, but Charles was old enough to remember him. Papa and I were always so close, of course." She laughed girlishly. "I could always twist Papa around my little finger. I was his baby girl, and he just adored me. Tim is the image of Papa."

"Kara, do you think you'll be rested up enough to go into New Orleans by Friday?" Amory asked. Obviously, he'd long ago had his fill of stories about Emilie's "Papa."

"Oh, yes." Kara glowed at the prospect of a day in New Orleans.

"Good," he said with satisfaction. "I'm scheduled for my checkup with Doctor Scott then. We could make a day of it. Tim, you take her to Antoine's for *Dinde Talleyrand* while I'm with Scott."

"What's that?" Kara asked eagerly.

"Turkey," Amory explained with a glint in his eyes. "Perpared as you've never tasted, with a seasoning that's a family secret. Since Antoine's opened up in New Orleans twelve years ago, there hasn't been a restaurant that can touch it."

"Oh, Amory!" Emilie frowned. "How can you think of dragging Kara and Tim into New Orleans this time of year?"

"They're young enough not to mind the heat." Amory suppressed a smile as Emilie bridled at the inference that she was no longer young. "And if it rains, it won't bother them. I promised Kara a maid for herself for a wedding present, and she's to make her own choice. A lady of property, Kara," he joshed. "How are you going to like that?"

"It's a very handsome present," Kara said politely, not at ease with the situation.

"Amory," Emilie's voice was laced with fury. "You haven't yet given Annabel the papers for Jasmine." Her eyes clashed with his.

Amory scowled, dug into the thick slice of ham steak on the plate Celestine had just slid before him, as though he were sublimating a wish to inflict bodily injury upon his wife.

"Annabel will have the papers in time," he said testily. "She's got herself a maid. What's the difference?"

But the difference, Kara realized, was that Amory Rankin was gifting Tim's wife of his own free will, complete with papers.

Chapter Nine

Kara sat at the breakfast table, her eyes downcast, fighting to conceal her impatience with Emilie Rankin.

"Amory, I think it's absurd to drag them into New Orleans today," Emilie protested. "It's going to be one of the hottest days of the summer, and just look at that sky. I know it's going to pour." Emilie turned solicitously to Tim. "Tim, are you getting enough sleep? You look tired, dear."

"I'm fine, Mama," Tim said unhappily.

"I know you haven't been eating properly," Emilie insisted. "You always did have a finicky appetite."

Why must Mrs. Rankin constantly nag at Tim this way, Kara asked herself for the tenth time. Why couldn't Tim and she have a house of their own somewhere, even a tiny house, without the fancy trappings of Manoir! Maybe then, she thought with wistful irony, Tim would sleep with his wife, where he belonged. Not since they'd been at Manoir had he come to her room at night.

"We have all the invitations out for the ball," Emilie announced with triumph, then frowned slightly. "Perhaps we should have postponed it another two weeks, until Tim recovers from that strenuous time in New York."

"Emilie, let up on Tim," Amory growled, with an apologetic glance at Kara.

"Tim's still my baby," Emilie insisted with a cloying smile, "even if he is a grown man. And married." A fleeting glint of reproach in her eyes which Kara didn't miss.

Emilie Rankin was jealous! Her mother-in-law would have resented even Denise Johnston, if that marriage had come off, because someone would be more important to Tim than she was. Emilie Rankin didn't want any woman close to Tim except herself. Kara laid down her fork, the fluffy omelet half eaten. His mother would not rule Tim, Kara promised herself. Tim was a husband first, a son second. And that was the way it would be.

"Call Celestine for more coffee," Amory told his wife, with a conspiratorial grin for Kara. "Another cup and we'll hop into the carriage and head for New Orleans."

Her small mouth pursed with annoyance, her fading blue eyes reflecting her dislike for the day's plans, Emilie delicately jangled the bell.

"Coffee, Celestine," Amory ordered when she moved leisurely into sight. "And tell Octavia to send in some of those pecan pralines to go with it."

"The only time I truly want to go into New Orleans," Emilie said emphatically, "is for the Mardi Gras. Or to attend the theater or the opera. I do so love the arts."

Emilie lapsed into a reproachful silence while she sipped her café au lait. Tim, too, was somber. Amory smiled at Kara, then launched into a series of anecdotes about the past Mardi Gras season.

"The year 1852 will go down in the annals of Louisiana," Amory proclaimed in high good humor, "as the year of the Great Mardi Gras. Of course," he recalled with a chuckle, "before Mardi Gras the press had set up a great hue and cry against the masks, condemning the public celebration, but afterward they all praised it to the heavens. You'll see next year's, Kara."

"Amory, don't you dare touch another praline," Emilie said sharply, "or you'll be complaining about heartburn all day long."

Kara sat between Tim and Amory, brushing damp tendrils from her forehead as the carriage rumbled along at a steady pace through the stately Garden District. Despite the sweltering heat, she gazed with lively curiosity at the wide-galleried houses, with their columns, their ornate grillwork, their dormer windows. Rising in privacy behind brick walls, but here and there a good gate open on gardens where people sat fanning themselves.

Tim and his father were discussing the coming World's Fair up in New York. How different Tim seemed away from Manoir! Away from his mother. Relaxed. Alive. Kara was content to sit back and view the passing scene while the men engaged in animated conversation.

She was pleased about her morning activities in the quarters. Tim had seemed surprised when she brought up the subject, but responsive. And Charles was allowing her to go to the quarters every morning to spend time with the children. It was a tacit arrangement, not discussed with other members of the family.

Charles was a difficult man to understand, Kara mused, as always fascinated by the complex individual. He spoke with such heat about the necessity for slavery, as though the South couldn't exist without it. Yet his eyes were troubled when he moved about the quarters. She'd seen him more than once, pick up a small black youngster, and walk about with the delighted child in his arms. He was a man with a need for children. It shone from his eyes when he cuddled a dark-skinned toddler in his arms.

The carriage rumbled through the Garden District, onward toward the business district of New Orleans, a few miles below.

"That's the New Basin Canal there," Amory pointed to the canal parallel to Shell Road. "It's a waterway for the melon schooners from Mobile, the ships that bring in wine and fruit."

"It was a long time being built," Tim added.

"Kara, you wouldn't believe what went into building that canal," Amory said heavily. "Built I might add, by your countrymen." He smiled at her look of astonishment. "Oh, life was hard in Ireland even before your time, and when the word went out that jobs were available here in New Orleans, the Irish came running. I remember that actor Emilie set such store by, Mr. Tyrone Power, saying one night at supper that he'd never seen men laboring under such a fierce sun and in such a pestilential swamp, with the contractors wringing profits 'from the men's blood.' He said the women were as worn out as the men and must be remembering Ireland where the valleys were green and the brooks sparkling, no matter how bad the times. But they stayed on, even until today, through the terrible epidemic of thirty-three." He sighed. "That was a bad time, with thousands dying. The work stopped. Bodies lying along the banks, rotting in the sun because they piled up too fast to be thrown into the ditches. Nobody expected the canal to be finished, but it was, after almost seven years of labor."

"I didn't know there were Irish in New Orleans," Kara said with wonder. Pleased. Feeling, somehow, closer to home. She must write Papa and tell him this. "I knew there were French and Spanish, but not Irish!"

"Didn't you now?" Amory joshed high-spiritedly. "Why come Saint Patrick's Day, and the Irish parade, no matter if New Orleans is temporarily a lake. They lay a line of boards right down the middle of the street, and there they prance, proud as you please."

They were driving through the hustle and bustle of New Orleans proper, vying with the ever-present drays and cabs on the cobblestone streets.

"You'll be pleased to know, Kara," Amory told her, "that it was an Irishman named Gallier who was the architect for the Saint Charles Hotel, where we're going for the auction."

"It's quite a building," Tim contributed.

"This isn't the original Saint Charles," Amory said, determined to be exact in his information. "It burned to the ground last year and has just recently been rebuilt, with some variations. There used to be an open turret atop a dome, which offered the highest view of the city. But there's the hotel, just ahead."

"Oh, it's beautiful!" Kara leaned forward eagerly as her eyes inspected the immense, imposing building with fourteen large fluted pillars.

The street floor was occupied by shops, and there was a large tavern located in the center of the building. On either side of the tavern were flights of stairs that led to the main entrance to the lobby.

"This is considered one of the major social centers in New Orleans," Amory said as they got down from the carriage. "It accommodates a thousand guests. The shops include confectionery and cigar establishments, a telegraph station, a steam bath, a barber shop, a baker, a laundry."

"Papa," Tim protested laughingly. "You sound like a tourist guide!"

"This is a prime spot for tourists," Amory conceded with a leisurely grin. "They never miss the Saint Charles. People from the North," he said drily, "usually want to see the slaves go on the auction block, on the rotunda inside." His face was suddenly somber. "Summer, however, is the slowest time; there won't be as much action as there is in the winter."

"You should see the slaves promenade when they're being brought to market," Tim said. "Marvelous, the way the owners dress them up. The men in their tall hats, the women in colorful kerchiefs. Everybody wearing a riot of color, gold, red, pink, white, usually with a handsome buck strutting at the head of them. All this to attract the attention of the prospective buyers. I've been trying to get that on canvas for six years."

"We go up these stairs," Amory said, a hand at Kara's elbow. She caught the glint of distaste in his eyes as he guided her up the elegant flight of stairs.

In the center of the large lobby eight Corinthian columns supported a huge dome, from which was suspended an imposing chandelier. The columns also supported the gallery which ran on three sides and which led to the second-floor rooms. The rotunda floor was a splash of color, a hubbub of activity, the noises deafening.

On a platform the bilingual auctioneer stood shouting, striving to be heard above the animated conversation of the wholesalers, the commissioner merchants, the sugar brokers and other businessmen who used the huge lobby as a business forum. Hotel guests pushed their way through the hordes. Hotel employees elbowed their way through with smiles of apology. Both repelled and fascinated, Kara watched the sale of the slave on the block. The auctioneer complimented the new owner in extravagant terms as the slave was led away.

An elderly slave, white-haired, toothless, stooped, was helped up on the block.

"And now, gentlemen . . ." The auctioneer's eyes lighted, astonished, on Kara. "And young lady," he acknowledged with a courtly bow. "Here we have Jim. A fine butler, a good house servant. Only trouble, he's what is known as a hypochondriac. Always thinks he's sick. What am I offered? A hundred dollars to start?"

Two prospective buyers crossed to the slave on the block; poked him experimentally in the ribs. One leaned forward to ask a quiet question.

"Nawsuh, me not well," the elderly slave replied, loud enough to be heard by the gathering. "Me got bad cough." He demonstrated weakly at that moment. "Pain in de back, suh, killin' me."

"Give him a few lashes from the cowhide and he'll work," the auctioneer intercepted smoothly. "Speak up, gentlemen. Here's a bargain for you. One hundred dollars?"

For Amory, it was a kind of self-inflicted torture to watch the proceedings. As for Kara, it turned her stomach to see human beings auctioned off as though they might be furniture or livestock. Tim stood beside her, impassive, listening intently.

A towering black buck was brought to the block. The auctioneer straightened up with interest, picked up considerable steam as he expounded the slave's virtues. Kara listened, disgusted by the spirited bidding. A prospective buyer moved forward for a whispered consultation with the auctioneer.

The auctioneer threw back his head, burst into ribald laughter.

"Take him off and see for yourself, sir. He'll be a prime stud for you!"

The black buck, his eyes faintly arrogant, wary, pleased at the high price he was about to earn for his seller, stalked off to be examined privately. Tim's eyes followed the two men and the buck.

"He'll be bought," Tim prophesied. "Nothing wrong with that one."

Next, a tall, stern-faced woman, about thirty years old, was prodded onto the block. She stood there, stiffly erect, eyes lowered, still except for her hands that nervously soothed the infant in her arms. Terrified, but determined not to show it.

"Kara, look at this one," Amory said softly.

"Daphne and child," the auctioneer began. "Two for the price of one, and the mother is a prize. Does fine sewing, trained for it for years. Six hundred to start, gentlemen? What am I bid over six hundred?"

"What about her teeth?" a corpulent planter in a broadbrimmed hat called out, striding forward for a closer inspection.

"See for yourself, sir," the auctioneer said, his hand in the woman's mouth, putting on display two rows of perfect teeth. "This one is bright, experienced, she wouldn't be for sale if her master hadn't fared badly at the gambling tables." A titter arose from the spectators. "Look lively, gentlemen, this is a good buy."

"Six hundred!" a dry voice called out from the rear, "and that's as far as I go."

"This one is old enough to have learned some," Amory whispered. "But perhaps you'd prefer one of the younger ones."

"Daphne," Kara said quickly because the prospective buyer was bidding against another now. Though the woman's face remained impassive, her hands about the bundle in her arms were trembling.

Amory Rankin calmly joined in the bidding. The price skyrocketed as the auctioneer dramatically extolled Daphne's abilities as a seamstress, as a ladies' maid.

"Seventeen hundred," Amory called crisply, and there was a low sound of astonishment about the room as he had topped the previous bid by two hundred.

The other bidders retreated, one vocally chagrined. The bidding was obviously over.

"Going, going, gone! For seventeen hundred!"

Kara Rankin owned a woman slave named Daphne.

"A handsome present for you, Kara," Tim whispered with surprise at the price his father was paying. "Papa certainly likes you!"

"I'm very fond of your father," Kara said with honesty. "And that has nothing to do with the gift."

"Come, Kara," Amory said, leading her to the bar rooms. "Let me show you a little more of this famed hotel of ours."

Kara walked by his side. Outwardly displaying the awe this tour of the hotel demanded. Inwardly upset by the action. By her acquisition of a personal slave. But she was a Rankin now. She must live as her husband lived.

"Here, Kara, is the politicians' domain," Amory said with lively interest. "In these rooms deals that affect the whole state of Louisiana are made. See that fellow standing by the table there," Amory pointed to a tall, eager-faced man hovering above a group at a nearby table. "He's a newspaperman, looking for new items. He knows that news is made at these tables." His eyes were suddenly cynical. "Politics get dirtier by the year in New Orleans.

"There are those who complain," Amory chuckled, taking her by the arm again, "that the grates in the rooms are only a foot wide—to save on fuel consumption. Still, it's one of the finest hotels in the world. Even compared to those in Paris, right, Tim?"

"Yes, sir," Tim responded absently. Bored with the sightseeing.

Outdoors again, the sweltering summer heat assailing them, they found Jupiter, ascended into the carriage to drive to the fanciful French quarter, at Amory's orders. Amory bought trinkets for Emilie and Annabel, chose a handsome scarf for Kara, with which she was delighted.

"I didn't buy much in New York," Kara said, "but, oh, the prices were so much lower!"

"That's the trouble in the South, Kara." Amory shook his head unhappily. "We import so much. Everything we use, everything we own, comes from the Yankees. We wear Yankee-made clothes, live with furniture made by Yankees, ride in Yankee-manufactured trains, travel on Yankee-made steamboats. It seems we can't do anything for ourselves but raise cotton and cane, and there, Kara, lies the downfall of the South."

Jupe drove Amory to Dr. Scott's house, depositing him before wrought-iron gates with Amory promising to join Tim and Kara at Antoine's as soon as the doctor dismissed him.

Tantalizing aromas of seafood, roasts, herbs simmering arose as Kara and Tim walked into Antoine's. Twelve years ago, Antoine had deliberately adjusted his kitchen shutters so that appetizing smells could waft out to intrigue fashionable New Orleans into dining there. And he had succeeded.

Although the hour was shockingly early for fashionable dining, several of the immaculately clothed tables were already occupied. Within an hour, silken-gowned, bediamonded ladies with their escorts would be waiting eagerly to be seated. Again Kara was aware of Tim's pleasure at the attention she was attracting.

"I should have worn my hair up," Kara murmured apologetically to Tim as she looked around her at the elegantly gowned ladies with their hair in tight curls about their heads.

"No, always wear it that way," Tim said, his artist eyes pleased with the cascade of silken, dark-auburn hair that fell to her shoulders.

It was astonishing how Tim blossomed beneath attention. His smile was brilliant, charming, as if he were giving a performance for an admiring audience. How marvelous he would have been as a stage actor, Kara thought, but no Rankin would appear on stage, of course.

This was the Tim Kara had known in New York, and she glowed. A waiter attended them as though they were royalty. Tim was not unknown at Antoine's. Kara was beginning to see the importance of the Rankin family in New Orleans. Probably, one of the most important American families.

While they were enjoying their pompano *en papillote,* Amory arrived, jubilant at having received a clean bill of health. There was a rare closeness between Tim and his father tonight. Usually, Tim regarded his father with a kind of wariness that appeared to baffle and frustrate his father. Charles was Amory's son, Tim his mother's, though not without reluctance on Tim's part.

In the carriage Kara was uncomfortably aware of Daphne, sitting atop with the baby in her arms. It would be a long drive for Daphne, yet there was no alternative. In the South a slave would not share her mistress's carriage. Kara felt responsible toward Daphne, frustrated because there was so little she could do to better Daphne's way of life. The baby would grow up in the quarters, mothered by a nine- or ten-year-old "nurse," but at least Daphne would see the child. She would sleep in the kitchen with the other house slaves. She would wash and iron and sew for Kara, and fill in as an extra hand about the house. A far better existence than a field slave.

The carriage moved to the edge of town, past an irregular row of small, white one-storied houses.

"Why, there's Charles!" Kara said in astonishment, and leaned forward to call him.

"No!" Amory's voice stopped her sharply, and she turned

round to face him questioningly. "Charles is making a business call," he explained uncomfortably. "We'd only delay him."

Kara settled back in the carriage again, puzzled by the strange hour for making business calls, but then, New Orleans was a strange, exciting town. She stifled a yawn, struggling to keep her eyes wide. But for the last half of the drive to Manoir she dozed, her head on Tim's shoulder.

Kara came awake slowly, eyes still shut.

"Tim, I know it's been hard on you all these years," Amory was saying quietly. "But that's the way your mother is, all nerves, all anxiety. And you're her baby."

"Papa!" Tim said with a sigh. "This can't go on forever."

"Give Kara a child, Tim," his father said softly. "And your mother a grandchild. She'll let up on you. She'll have somebody new to spoil. Give Kara a child, Tim!"

Jupe halted before the entrance to the house, and the three scurried through the rain to the gallery. Kara stood for a moment watching the carriages roll off. Daphne was bent over the small bundle in her arms, trying to protect the baby from the rain with her own body.

Amory insisted they all go to the library for a drink, bourbon for the men, a cordial for Kara. She sat back in the chair while Tim lit the fire that was always laid in readiness.

"Drink up and go on up to bed, Kara," Amory said gently. "You're tired."

"I am sleepy," Kara admitted with an apologetic smile, and hesitated, "What about Daphne and the baby? Will they stay in the quarters tonight?"

Amory nodded.

"Don't worry, they'll be all right there. Daphne will come to you in the morning. Train her properly, Kara, and she'll serve you well."

Kara went up to her room and prepared for bed. Suddenly awake as she lay back under a light coverlet and reran in her mind the events of the day. Still not at ease with Amory's gift. She started at the light knock on her door.

"Yes?" Thinking, at first, that it was Daphne.

"It's Tim," he called out quietly, then opened the door. "It's going to rain all night. You might like a fire lit."

"That would be lovely." She smiled, her heart beating fast. The first time Tim had set foot in this room since it had been hers.

The slanting rain pounded against the house, sounding as though it would never let up. A shutter, unloosened by the sharp wind, banged repeatedly against an outer wall. Tim looked at her, his handsome face flushed with the glow of the flames. He crossed to the bed, pulled off his robe, bent to blow out the candle on the table close by. Her mouth parted with sweet expectancy. Her eyes fluttered shut as he lifted the coverlet and slid beneath with her.

"You're cold," Tim said gently.

"I won't be with you," she promised, trembling.

His mouth was on hers. Her arms closed in about him with welcome, her body moving in to his. His hands moved about her. He took her gently.

"Oh, Tim!" she cried. "Tim!"

Chapter Ten

Kara stood before the mirror. She tried to concentrate on her reflection, but one thought monopolized her mind. In a few moments she must leave the sanctuary of this room and descend to the lower floor to become part of the ball being given to introduce her, as Tim's wife, to the New Orleans' American society.

All week long, the closed-up wing of Manoir, which contained the ballroom and the huge dining salon, had been subjected to cleaning, polishing, painting. For days the slave orchestra had been rehearsing for tonight. For days the banquet had been in preparation.

Octavia had pounded refined sugar brought all the way from New York, so that it could be used in making the pastries and cakes Emilie had ordered. Field hands, those with the most impressive brawn, had been brought up to the house to take turns at churning the ice cream. Charlotte russes and sherbets had been prepared. Turkey, venison, goose, and wild hog had been roasted in the fireplace in the kitchen. Even now, soups and gumbos simmered.

Emilie and Annabel had bought perfumes and rice powder in New Orleans, complaining mightily about having to endure the heat of the city. Both had usurped Daphne for hours each day, to fit the Parisian gowns they had purchased on Chartres Street, and about whose cost Amory grumbled. Tim insisted Kara wear one of the gowns he'd bought for her at Stewart's in New York.

Kara sighed. She mustn't dawdle another instant. Soon the carriages would be arriving. She would have to stand in line beside Tim and be presented to their friends. For a poignant moment she thought about papa. His Irish humor would run wild if he could see that scene! Over a hundred people coming tonight. New Orleans' American society.

She ran slender fingers over the gleaming cascade of hair about her shoulders. The yellow satin gown brought out the highlights in her hair, lent a glow to her skin. She took a deep breath and walked with quick, compulsive steps to the door.

With her hand on the bannister, Kara stopped dead, her attention snared by the heated conversation emanating from Annabel's room.

"Annabel, I can't bear it," Emilie was declaiming dramatically. "All these people here in the house to meet Tim's wife. What happens when they find out she was a housemaid in New York?"

"Mama, no one will know," Annabel soothed in her monotonously proper voice. "She's not so stupid that she'll announce it."

"They'll know she's Irish!" Emilie insisted contemptuously. "The hair, the face. Who are the Irish in New Orleans? The waterfront laborers, the cabmen, the 'screwmen.' They drive the drays and trade on a flair for low politics. Who receives them in their homes?"

Kara walked down the wide staircase, her face aflame. So that was Emilie Rankin's opinion of the Irish! But an Irish architect had drawn the plans for the great Saint Charles Hotel, and for many of the finest homes and buildings in New Orleans. Amory Rankin said the Irish built the canal, that they had an important hand in much of the construction in the city for the last twenty years.

The crystal chandelier in the wide foyer was ablaze with a hundred candles, a hint of the magnificence of the ball. Mahogany dining-room tables had been joined together to form a horseshoe in the dining salon. In the ballroom the slave orchestra, with a predominance of violins, was engaged in a last-minute rehearsal.

The wide hall was resplendent with summer flowers. Masses of camellias, lilies, roses everywhere. Slaves moved importantly about, performing small chores. Daphne and Jasmine stood beside the foyer door to help receive the ladies' wraps. Jupiter, darkly handsome in new livery, hovered in readiness for his appointed task of announcing the guests. An assignment given to him because of his ability to read. An ability surreptitiously acquired when he briefly shared Tim's tutor when both were very young.

Kara walked down the hall toward the door that led to the ballroom and dining-salon wing. She hesitated at the doorway. Amory was singing high-spiritedly while busily arranging the wines and liquors on a side table. Slaves stood by to do his bidding.

Tense at the prospect of the ordeal before her, feeling a staggering aloneness, Kara returned to the foyer. Her pulse racing. Carriages were coming. She could hear the rumble of wheels well down the road. The footmen were outside, standing by to open the doors, while other slaves would take the coaches away to the stables, care for the horses.

Nervously, Kara glanced up the stairs. Tim was descending. How handsome he was! Emerging from the room at the head of the stairs were Emilie and Annabel.

"Jasmine!" Emilie called sharply. "Tell Mister Rankin and Mister Charles to join us in the foyer. I hear guests arriving."

Tim approached Kara with a reassuring smile.

"Nervous?"

"Yes." She returned his smile. For an instant feeling close to her husband.

"You needn't be. You're beautiful." His eyes admiring as they rested on her.

"Kara, I do think you should wear a lace mantilla with that gown," Emilie said fretfully. "It's cut much too low. Daphne," she ordered sharply, "go up to my room and—"

"No, Mama," Tim said firmly, but Kara saw the color staining his throat. "Just the way she is. She's perfect."

Emilie flinched, as though Tim had slapped her smartly across the face.

"Never mind, Daphne," Emilie retracted coldly, and turned to speak to Annabel.

Amory came striding down the hall. Charles emerged from the library, sheepish because he had been dozing. The family took their places. In a semitrance Kara stood beside Tim in the receiving line. Voices rose to a crescendo outside. A convivial burst of voices in the foyer as guests poured into the house.

Kara smiled, listened attentively to each name, though she knew she would never remember so many. The men were openly admiring of Kara's beauty, and Tim gave all the indications of being a smug young husband. The women were polite but reserved, saving their effusive greetings for Emilie and Annabel; there had been much talk around New Orleans about Tim's wife.

Kara danced with all Amory's friends, flattered by their interest, demure before their banter. Her eyes invariably moving about the room to find Tim. He seemed to be enjoying himself. His boyish politeness, his air of sincere eagerness to please, delighted both the ladies and the gentlemen guests. Charles appeared restless, ill at ease in this atmosphere, impatient with the levity.

At midnight, everyone strolled, amid lively chatter, into the flower-festooned dining salon. Elaborately costumed Haitian twins of about twelve were stationed at either side of the room, beside the silken ropes that controlled the enormous fans. For one private moment, Tim's hand squeezed Kara's in encouragement as they took their places at the head table. Emilie's smile was strained; she was annoyed at the ribald jokes Amory was recounting to a neighbor.

Slaves streamed in and out of the dining salon with an impressive procession of food. Others moved with wine bottles, filling each glass before it could be fully emptied. Kara abstained, intoxicated already by the festivities.

Mr. Tatum of the neighboring plantation was much taken with Kara, who listened earnestly to his lengthy discourse on the advantages of investing in the railroads. His wife and two rather plain daughters seemed annoyed that he was evincing his interest so plainly.

"And now that Tim has such a beautiful bride," Mr. Tatum said fatuously, "is he going to settle down and help Charles run Manoir?"

Kara smiled at him, her eyes moving fleetingly to Tim, and simultaneously encountering the glint of dislike in Emilie Rankin's eyes. Emilie was furious at Kara's success tonight.

"Oh, I don't think Tim will help with Manoir. Charles does so well himself." Kara's voice was deliberately loud and clear. "I'm trying to persuade Tim to go into politics. I'm sure he has a flair for that."

There was a sudden, very pregnant silence at their table. Eyes brightened with curiosity. Kara immediately realized the impression she'd made. The men here, all influential, important men, friends of Amory Rankin, were taking her seriously.

"Amory, why are you keeping this a secret?" an officious-looking guest demanded, his mustache bristling with enthusiasm. "We need young blood in politics. The corruption is shocking! Why, at the last city election, there were voters who went from one precinct to another to cast a ballot. A device that was arranged. Too bad the ladies can't vote," he chuckled unexpectedly. "You'd have Tim Rankin as your mayor in five years."

"All this has been a secret to me, too," Amory said quietly. His eyes moved from Tim to Kara, questioning. "Young folks today aren't much for confiding in their elders."

"Kara and I were just casually talking about the political scene in New Orleans," Tim explained uncomfortably. But Kara saw a rising awareness in him of where this road could lead. "I have no serious plans. Not yet—"

"Tim, you couldn't possibly allow yourself to become involved in politics," Emilie said with a brittle smile, her eyes flailing Kara. "That's all so dirty."

"Tim could rise above all that." Kara's voice was rich with enthusiasm. "He could do a lot for New Orleans, if he put his mind to it." Kara surged with a needy triumph because all these folks at the table were looking at her with such respect. "Someday Tim might be governor." For one ugly instant, so brief that only Amory Rankin intercepted, Kara's glance clashed nakedly with her mother-in-law's.

Kara listened to the enthusiastic conversation generated by her impulsive remarks. Only Emilie appeared contemptuous. Charles was hardly listening. He kept pulling out his watch and gazing at it. She wasn't surprised, when the guests left the dining salon to return to the ball for more dancing, to see Charles quietly sneaking away. Listening attentively, she heard the paneled cypress door thud shut.

In the ballroom the orchestra was playing again, filling the night with music. Annabel danced little. Her face was stony and set as she talked with the other ladies. Emilie bustled about, smiling, playing the grand hostess.

Dawn was streaking the sky before the musicians finally laid aside the borrowed instruments, and the guests were served steamed bowls of gumbo and thick black coffee. It was with exhausted relief that Kara saw the last guests leave Manoir, and she was, finally, free to go to her room.

"Kara, you were a huge success," Amory said gallantly. "They'll be talking about Kara Rankin all over New Orleans, all over the parish, tomorrow."

"Amory, stop being so extravagant," Emilie snapped impatiently. "And I don't want you adding fuel to this nonsense about Tim's going into politics."

"Emilie, the boy could do worse," Amory said gently, and an ironic smile touched his mouth. "Better than spending his time with a paint brush in his hand. As Kara said, he does have a flair for mingling with people, winning their approval. Definite assets in politics."

"I don't want to hear any more about it!" Emilie's voice rose hysterically. "Tim, dear, there you are," she smiled at him as he strode into sight. "Please go upstairs and bring down my nerve medicine; *you* know where I keep it." Her voice was a tired caress. "I'm so exhausted from this ball I just know I'll have an attack if I don't take my medication this instant."

"You're going to be fine, Emilie," Amory said firmly, but he shot a warning glance at Tim, who started uneasily up the stairs.

"My heart's pounding like mad already. I *knew* this ball was going to be too much for me." Her voice faded. "Kara, find Octavia. I'll want her to sleep in my room tonight."

"Yes, Mrs. Rankin," Kara whispered politely.

Emilie Rankin's voice rose to a sharp crescendo as Kara left the room. "What is she doing to my son, Amory?"

Chapter Eleven

Kara came awake slowly, conscious of the lulling symphony of the steady rainfall outside. All through the early morning lightning had zigzagged across the gray sky. Thunder had clapped continuously. Hardly a day or night passed without a downpour during these summer months.

She smiled faintly without opening her eyes. Thank God for the rain. It would relieve the awful heat. Amory had said this was a semitropical climate, that the heavy rains were part of the summer, and they should be grateful because the rain put to rest the dust that choked, that lay on everything.

Kara stirred slightly beneath the light coverlet, opened her eyes to stare up at the mosquito netting.

She'd slept late, she realized guiltily. The little ones down at the quarter must be waiting for her, with their shining dark eyes and their eager smiles. She tossed back the coverlet and hurried to dress. Glad that Daphne had not appeared to help her. Daphne disliked her. She felt more comfortable with Annabel. Annabel was predictable.

Celestine responded immediately to her gentle ring at the dining table. A yawning Celestine, obviously tired from last night's exertions but jubilant about the success of the ball, appeared to take her breakfast order and to gossip about the guests.

"Li'l Missy, yo' de prettiest li'l thing der las' night. Marse

Tim, him proud 'nuf to bust."

Celestine overruled Kara's insistence that all she cared for this morning was a biscuit and coffee. She went back to the kitchen wing, to return with a plate piled high with buckwheat cakes and surrounded by mahogany-browned sausages, a pitcher of molasses and coffee. Kara sniffed appreciatively and realized with astonishment that she was hungry.

Amory, yawning uninhibitedly, his eyes bloodshot, stood in the doorway.

"Damn it, I'd made up my mind to sleep late, but you can't beat down the habits of a lifetime." He inspected her with narrow-eyed sharpness. "I thought you and I were friends," he said, sitting beside her. "You never said a word to me about pushing Tim into politics."

"I never thought about it till the words popped out," Kara confessed, the familiar color staining her cheeks. "But I do think Tim would be fine at it."

"Kara, you're an astute young lady," Amory said approvingly. "Now let's see if you can prod Tim in that direction." His eyes were quizzical. "I know Tim wants no part of managing Manoir, we've been through that. He hasn't the drive to be a professional artist, though he has some talent. But not enough to make a success in that field. Maybe, with you behind him, Tim could carve a spot for himself in politics."

"Why not?" Kara's eyes glowed with the challenge.

"We'll work at it," Amory said firmly. "God knows, Tim has the charm for it, a way with folks. When Emilie gets used to the idea, she'll be for it, too." He smiled wryly. "Right now, things are moving a bit too fast for her. After all these years of keeping Tim under her thumb, she's lost control, she's been kicked out of the driver's seat."

"We'll have to take it slowly with Tim," Kara cautioned.

"Not push him too hard." If they did, he would balk.

"Well play it slowly," Amory agreed. "You take the lead, Kara."

They abandoned serious conversation for more casual talk, but both were pleased with this alliance to lead Tim into politics. Kara drank down her coffee, pushed back her chair.

"You'll excuse me, won't you?"

"What's the matter?" Amory clucked mockingly. "You can't stand the old man's company a while longer?"

Kara hesitated.

"I'm expected down at the quarters," she replied. "I have a project with the children. Charles knows."

"What kind of a project?" Amory eyed her intently.

"Something to keep me busy mornings," Kara explained lightly. "I play with the children, teach them songs and games, try to teach them how to keep the cabins a little neater, and themselves, too."

"Kara," Amory said with quiet pleasure, "you are a lady. Now you have one more cup of coffee with me, and I'll let you go." He shot her a conspiratorial smile. "And we won't mention your project to the ladies."

Kara finished the second cup of coffee and hurried from the house. She saw Tim, in riding clothes, stalking toward the stables. She pressed down an impulse to call out to him. He hadn't even stopped for breakfast, he must be eager to ride this morning. She was hoping last night that he would come to her. Not merely because she wanted the comfort of his arms, but to be able, in the darkness, to talk about the ball. That was part of marriage, too, to share experiences.

A daily pattern had set. After breakfast Kara went to the quarters to play and sing with the young brigade there. A midday meal with Emilie, Annabel, and Tim. The first time each day that she saw Tim, who seemed to make a point of avoiding breakfast. In the afternoon, everyone except Charles returned to their rooms to rest in the semitropical heat.

The entire household met at the evening meal, though Charles, appearing exhausted from the long, hot summer, often excused himself while they were still at dessert. For a little while they'd all sit together on the gallery. Kara would go up to her room early. The unfamiliar heat was taking a toll of her strength, she was tired and sleepy long before the normal time.

For a little while Kara would stand at a window in her bedroom, welcoming any faint breeze from the river, while Emilie and Annabel rocked away on the gallery and fought off mosquitos with their fans. Amory drank and read in the library and Tim painted in his room.

Occasionally, Tim called her into his room to pose for him, but he never made love to her then. Tim was so angry with himself because his talent wasn't enough to do what he wished. Kara waited wistfully for those rare nights when Tim came to her room. He promised that, when the heat let up, they'd go down to New Orleans for a couple of days, stay at the Saint Charles. Away from Manoir, away from his mother, perhaps he would be the Tim she'd known in New York, or on the long trip to New Orleans.

By mid-September, the rains ceased. The sun was less intense. New Orleansians who escaped to plantations for the summer were returning to their city houses again. But Kara found herself still tired, still very sleepy, as though the semitropical summer was still upon them.

Kara rose early this morning, as usual, still exhausted, went downstairs for breakfast, now shared regularly with Amory. He was sitting at the table, absorbed in the *Daily Picayune.*

"You look tired," he said, looking up. "Sitting up half the night reading, I'll wager."

"I fell asleep over the book," she acknowledged wryly. Amory chose books for her from the library, which they both discussed with enthusiasm after she'd read them. "Not that I wasn't interested. I was."

"Maybe we ought to ask Doctor Scott to give you a tonic," Amory said, a little worried.

"Oh, I'll be fine now that the hot weather is past."

They finished breakfast leisurely, and Amory went off to his morning rendezvous with the library. Kara went out to the kitchen and asked Octavia for half a dozen bars of soap. Octavia, aware of where Kara spent her mornings, chuckled indulgently.

"Li'l Missy, yo' ain't gonna make dem kids keep deyself clean, don't yo' know dat yet?"

"We'll try, Octavia," Kara said softly, smiling.

"Yo' wait a minute," Octavia said with a wide grin. She wrapped a dozen pralines left over from the night before in an old newspaper. "Ah'm gittin' too old fo' dem sweets, an' de odders don' be needin' 'em."

Kara hurried down to the quarters, delighted to be bringing a treat. It would be a bribe, to persuade them to do the washing she planned for this morning. All the blankets covering the moss on the beds must be washed and dried in the sun by the time the field hands returned to the cabins tonight. They would make a game of it together, she and the children.

The children met her with their customary excited squeals. Midmorning, Charles showed up, to watch their efforts with signs of goodhumored dismay. But Charles approved of her interest in the children, Kara realized with pleasure. With the blankets eventually hoisted on a line to dry, the children happily nibbling away at scrupulously divided pralines, Kara returned to the house.

"What do you mean, you gave six bars of soap to Miss Kara?" Emilie was demanding indignantly in the kitchen. Kara froze. "Octavia, don't start lying to me after all these years! I want to know where that supply of soap is, and I want to know this minute!"

Face aflame, Kara hurried into the kitchen.

"Mrs. Rankin, Octavia isn't lying," Kara said quietly. "I asked for the soap." She'd forgotten about Emilie's periodic inspections of the kitchen. Emilie was always suspicious of the house slaves' stealing.

Emilie stared at her in shock.

"Whatever for?"

"I took them down to the quarters," Kara hesitated. "I go down there for a while every morning, to spend time with the little ones."

"You go to the quarters?" Emilie's voice broke in, soaring in outrage. "How can you demean the family that way? They'll have no respect for any of us if you go down there like a common nursemaid!"

"Mrs. Rankin, I have never been ashamed of working with my hands!" Kara flashed back, the old hurt out in the open. Octavia and Celestine, terrified at the anger between the two white women, backed off into a corner of the kitchen.

"I might have expected something like this!" Emilie Rankin was ashen, trembling. She turned her back on Kara and ran out of the kitchen. "Amory! Amory, come here, you hear me? Now you'll see if I was right or not! Amory!"

Kara hovered in the hallway, outside the library door. Emilie was throwing a full attack of hysterics. Amory shouted for Celestine, who was familiar with these sessions. In a few minutes, Emilie, crying frenziedly, was helped upstairs to her room. Jupe had been sent off to bring Dr. Scott.

"Don't be upset, Kara," Amory said gently, when she'd reported the scene in the kitchen. "While the family doesn't enjoy these nerve attacks of my wife's, I suspect they fill a need in her life. I don't want you to blame yourself in any way, do you understand?"

Only Amory and Kara appeared at the midday meal. Emilie had sent for Tim, right after Dr. Scott left. Celestine hurried up the stairs with the tray for Tim and his mother. Annabel had developed a headache, and Daphne was tending to her needs. Annabel was increasingly annoyed with Jasmine. Later in the afternoon, when Kara lay resting across her bed, too upset to read, Annabel came to her room.

"Kara, do you mind if I borrow Daphne tonight? I want her to put my hair up in curlers. I'm going into New Orleans with mama tomorrow, just for the day. Now that the heat's letting up, mama wants to go over to Mallard to see the Sèvres china they've been advertising. She thinks a . . . a change," Annabel chose her word delicately, "might be good for her."

"I'm sure it will," Kara said politely. "And use Daphne whenever you like." Annabel did that anyhow.

"I was thinking," Annabel said, and Kara sensed that whatever was about to be divulged had been thoroughly discussed with her mother-in-law. "Since I can't abide Jasmine, and you seem to like her so much, maybe we ought to switch maids. You never use Daphne to do your hair or sew for you, but you seem to enjoy having Jasmine do for you." Jasmine brought her bouquets from the woods and brewed her mint tea.

"I'm fond of Jasmine," Kara acknowledged, her mind racing. Of course she would prefer Jasmine! Daphne was so cold, so unbending. "I'll have to talk to Mr. Rankin first," she said.

"Mama will be pleased," Annabel pointed out, as though this would be a paramount consideration. "She likes to have Daphne do her hair and sew for her. We could share her easily enough."

"I'll talk to Mr. Rankin," Kara promised. "Right away." So she was supposed to do this to appease Emilie Rankin. But since she preferred Jasmine, she might just as well.

When Kara explained the new problem to Amory, he smiled grimly.

"They're cagey ones. But what about you? Would you prefer Jasmine?" He looked at her closely.

"Yes." Kara nodded earnestly.

"Then we'll let them get away with this." He chuckled, his eyes wise. "You see, Kara, they're after Annabel's getting papers to her own slave. I never did get around to transferring Jasmine's papers to Annabel, but she figures you'll give Daphne's to her in the trade. But don't worry, you'll have Jasmine's papers right away."

"It doesn't matter," Kara put in quickly.

"It does matter," Amory said gruffly. "The girl belongs to you. You'll have her papers."

Both Kara and Jasmine were delighted with the switch.

With Kara, Jasmine lost some of her shyness, spoke more freely in her musical accent, a blend of Sea Island, Georgia, and Louisiana, plus a sprinkling of Haitian French. Jasmine insisted on brushing Kara's hair every night, cared for her clothes with devotion, brought her coffee in bed each morning despite Kara's protests that she could have it downstairs with breakfast. Jasmine, like all the house slaves, had domestic chores apart from caring for Kara's needs, but she bore herself with a special pride because she was "Lil Missy's girl."

September waned. The cotton crop was coming in well.

Charles jubilantly prophesied they'd be harvesting right up to December. Emilie and Annabel had resumed their social afternoons of calling on neighbors, since the "summer spell" was past. They were pleased at Kara's reluctance to accompany them, and at her sudden withdrawal to her own room, when guests came calling. The ball had been an exhilarating adventure, but Kara still cringed from more intimate socializing with the plantation ladies.

"Kara's quite tired from the summer," Emilie would explain to her visitors. "She's not yet accustomed to our heat."

Tim talked eagerly about their going into New Orleans for a couple of days. Emilie registered eloquent disgust each time Tim mentioned this in front of the family, and Tim, for once, was trying to overcome her objections. It seemed as if they needed Mrs. Rankin's approval for everything they did!

Kara brightened at the light knock on the door.

"He be a fine day," Jasmine said with a brilliant smile as she moved her slender body into the room with fluid grace. "Nice fo' walk." Jasmine knew about Kara's morning strolls down to the quarters. She brought the cup of coffee to Kara.

"Oh, Jasmine, take that coffee away!" Kara recoiled from the rich fragrance that assailed her nostrils. She averted her head, her stomach churning. But not before she saw Jasmine's startled, hurt gaze. "Jasmine, I'm sorry," she apologized weakly. "I just don't feel right this morning."

Jasmine's eyes widened. She smiled broadly.

"Well, now ah ain't su'prised none, Li'l Missy," she crooned. Her eyes triumphant now. "How long yo' pas' yo' time?"

Kara's eyes widened.

"Jasmine! I'm not sure."

"Long 'nuf so yo' be *enceinte*," she said with pride, and giggled at Kara's questioning glance at the unfamiliar word.

"Carry baby," Jasmine translated. "Yo' think now. How long pas' yo' time?"

"I forgot how time was going by," Kara said, her mind racing. "It was must two, no, three weeks."

"Oh, dis be one fine baby," Jasmine smiled. "Fus' baby in dis house since Marse Tim be bo'n."

"That's why I've been so tired. And so sleepy all the time." She was *pregnant.* The words jumbled about in her mind. "Oh, Jasmine, yes. Yes!"

"Ah bring yo' mint tea with li'l piece co'n bread. Dat what my mama give her lady, back at Sea Island. Yo' don' move from dis bed, yo' heah? I bring mint tea and co'n bread. That settle yo' stomach fo' sho."

Kara leaned back against the pillows, relieved that the nausea was retreating. Not yet trusting herself to sit upright. *She was carrying a baby in her.* Tim's and hers. Tim would be happy.

Amory would be pleased. Kara remembered his words to Tim, "Give Kara a child, Tim. And your mother a grandchild. She'll let up on you. She'll have somebody new to spoil."

Emilie would be happy with the baby, and would leave Tim alone. Tim was, at last, going to be hers. Tim could be so full with love, he would adore his child. He would love her for making this possible. Everything would be different now. The baby would bring them together.

Jasmine came back with the mint tea and a square of Octavia's fluffy cornbread.

"Yo' need fill yo' belly with somethin' in the mawnin'," Jasmine said importantly. "No coffee, *tea.* Octavia lemme go fetch fresh mint from de garden."

Jasmine and Kara exchanged pleased glances. So Octavia knew, too. The slaves in the house always knew everything first.

"Soon yo' be needin' new clothes. I sew. Skinny one lik' yo' show right off. Oh, dat Marse Tim, him gonna be so happy!"

Jasmine fussed over Kara until she finished the corn bread to the last crumb and drained the fragrant mint tea.

"Yo' res' a while, ya' heah? No go runnin' off to de quarters no mo'."

"Oh, Jasmine, I'll be fine now," Kara laughed. "Of course, I'll go down to the quarters. As long as you keep bringing me mint tea every morning," she said teasingly, and was touched by the glow of pleasure her words brought to Jasmine's liquid amber eyes.

Jasmine left with the tray. Kara cautiously swung her feet to the side of the bed and sighed with relief because the nausea had definitely subsided. She was turning into a southern lady, behaving this way, when there was nothing wrong with her but what was natural. Mama all but had her little ones right in the fields!

Kara dressed impatiently, eager to see Tim. To tell him. Dressed, she inspected her reflection in the mirror. Her color was high with excitement, her eyes brilliantly blue. She smiled, happily, to herself.

She hurried down the carpeted corridor to Tim's room and knocked lightly on the door, then with more vigor. No answer.

She opened the door. Her mouth parted, eager to share her news. The bed was in disarray. Tim was gone from the room. Kara raced out into the corridor again, down the staircase.

The crisp, late-September morning was exhilarating. On a morning such as this Tim must surely be riding. She directed her steps toward the stables. Tim was not there.

She remembered, vaguely, the area in which he rode. To the east of the fields.

Kara walked swiftly, following the tracks of the horse, then spied—just ahead—the gleaming dark stallion Tim preferred to ride. He was tied to a tree.

She ran the last few steps.

"T—" she stopped, a hand on her mouth.

Jupe. Head thrown back, eyes shut strangely tight. His powerful black body glistening with sweat. His full mouth parted in a kind of silent anguish. And on his knees before Jupe, was Tim. The back of his head to Kara. His hands gripping Jupe's taut thighs.

And then she knew, and swayed with a sudden wave of sickness. She turned away awkwardly, ran, not knowing where she was going. But she had to get away from there.

"Kara! Kara, wait!" Urgency, desperation, lacing Tim's voice as he raced after her. "Kara."

He caught up with her, forced her physically to halt. His hands clutched painfully at her shoulders, and she winced. His breathing was labored.

"Kara, I must talk to you," he pleaded in an anguished whisper.

"Why?" she taunted, her eyes unable to meet his. "There's nothing to tell me."

"Kara, I thought it wouldn't be this way, once we were married. I—I prayed it would be all right. In New York it was."

"How did I let you down?" she cried out, sick with discovery, bewilderment. "What did I do wrong?"

"Not you, Kara." His face was tense with shame. "Me. It's always been that way. Mama found out and sent me up to New York to marry. She said if I married, she wouldn't tell Papa and Charles. Married, I'd be all right. She meant," he said bitterly, "that I would have a cover. But don't leave, Kara. Please don't leave! Somehow, I'll find a way to make it up to you," he promised, his eyes frenzied. "Anything you want, Kara, just tell me."

"I can't leave," Kara told him tonelessly. "And I won't talk, not to anyone. I am going to have your child, Tim. For his sake, I'll stay."

"Kara." Tim said, astonished. "Oh, Kara."

He made a move to touch her. She recoiled.

"Don't touch me, Tim," she warned intensely. "Don't ever touch me again."

"Kara, whatever you say," he said pleading. "Just stay with me. We'll raise the child together. Nobody need know, Kara, no one will ever know."

"I told you, Tim, I'll stay." She said it evenly, looking directly at him now. "My child is a Rankin. He belongs here. But everything must be right for him. He must never know. I want my child to grow up to be proud of his father. This I demand."

Chapter Twelve

Amory leaned back in his deep chair, gazing somberly into the blazing fire in the library fireplace. The damp chill from the rain that had been falling steadily all evening was penetratingly uncomfortable.

"Papa, can't you understand the possibility in switching over?" Charles said earnestly. "With every acre in cotton, we're constantly gambling. If we experiment with a few hundred acres in cane and the cotton crop goes bad, we've still got the money for the cane."

"Charles, I approve of your thinking," Amory conceded. "But with cane you need expensive equipment. Do you know what it costs to set up a sugarhouse?"

"I know. But I've been thinking this out for months." Charles leaned forward, his face taut. "We can grow cane, and as soon as it's cultivated in the spring, we can turn sheep to graze between the rows of shoots. Papa, I've studied this deeply. The sheep won't touch the cane; they'll just fatten up on the grass, without their costing us a cent for feed. We'll have a double crop on our hands!"

"Charles, we don't have the cash outlay this year for anything as expensive as a sugarhouse," Amory said carefully. He refrained from mentioning the money Charles had drawn to set up that girl on Ramparts Street. Not that that was much compared to the equipment the sugarhouse would require.

Charles hesitated. "What about Mama's money?"

Amory's face tightened. How many times did this come up to smack him in the face? Damn his father-in-law, for leaving everything outright to Emilie that way. The old plantation sold, the money tied up in securities now in Emilie's name. *Hers.* And she made sure he understood that.

"Charles, you know Mama's money is never touched," Amory reminded him cynically. Except when Emilie was out to make an impression. Emilie's money paid for Tim's expensive months in Paris. Emilie enjoyed bragging about how much that cost. Emilie paid for Tim's trip to New York, and that excursion of hers and Annabel's two years ago, when they brought back from New York those ridiculously expensive gowns to show off before the other plantation ladies. "That is," Amory amended drily, "Mama's money is never spent for business purposes." Hell, he didn't even know how Emilie distributed the money in her will. That was done privately.

"It's a shame," Charles said heavily. "The potential is so great."

"The potential of the South, Charles," Amory sighed, "is nil. If I were fifteen years younger, I'd sell out, head west. The South is in a terminal illness."

Celestine padded quietly into the doorway, hesitated cautiously.

"What is it, Celestine?" Amory asked, more sharply than he intended.

"Ole Missy say, come up, please, to huh room. Please, suh," Celestine said. "Her feelin' kinda pohly."

"Thank you, Celestine," Amory said, and sighed. If Emilie was "feelin' kinda pohly," she was upset about something in the house. "I'll go up directly."

"Yessuh."

Amory rose reluctantly to his feet.

"I might as well call it a night, too." Charles suppressed a yawn. "Let's go on upstairs."

The two men walked silently up the long marble staircase. Amory paused at his wife's door while Charles walked, shoulders hunched tightly, down the corridor to his own room. For a man of Charles's nature it was rough to lead the double life that circumstances had forced upon him. But damn it, Annabel had no right to walk around with that injured expression all the time because she suspected about that girl on Ramparts Street. She wasn't letting Charles in, was she? A man denied by his wife had a right to go elsewhere. Charles came back from the long drive into New Orleans with a relaxed expression, a kind of glow about him. It had been a long time since Charles looked that way. Bless the girl for that.

Amory knocked lightly at Emilie's door.

"Come in," she called out, her voice high-pitched, strident. Emilie was standing by the fireplace, lacing and unlacing her hands in that manner that told him she was agitated.

"Celestine said you wanted to see me, Emilie." He was in no mood for one of her attacks of nerves.

"Yes, Amory." Her eyes smoldered vindictively. "That Kara, Amory, she's after Tim to move away from Manoir!"

"How do you know?" he hedged.

"Tim came to me a little while ago. He said he'd like to have a house in New Orleans for the winter months. Don't tell me Tim dreamed that up, that was Kara's idea." She moved toward him, her hands working nervously. "Amory, I won't have Tim moving into New Orleans alone with that girl. You talk to him!"

"Emilie, a house in New Orleans is out of the question. I

can't afford it, you know that," he said, faintly bitter. "A townhouse, with the slaves he'd need to maintain, is out of the question."

Emilie pointedly ignored the financial angle.

"Tim's entirely too immature to be away from here," Emilie pursued righteously. "Amory, you talk to him, do you hear? It's that girl, of course, thinking she can lead him, and all of us, around by the nose."

"Emilie, my money is tied up in cotton," he said calmly. "Unless you give Tim the money, he's not stirring out of this house."

"Anyhow, you talk to him." But Emilie was mildly mollified.

"All right," he sighed. "I'll have a talk with Tim. In the morning."

When Amory left Emilie's room, his first impulse was to go to his own room and read in bed till he fell asleep. Instead he headed downstairs again. Curiosity was tugging at him about Charles's girl. Charles was reticent; he acknowledged the situation but did not elaborate. He was keeping a *placée* on Ramparts Street; he said nothing else. Yet Amory sensed that the relationship was becoming a deep one. Hell, why not? He had a cardboard marriage with Annabel.

In the library Amory settled himself in his special chair for one last drink of the evening. With a start of astonishment, a streak of pride, he was aware of desire stirring in him. Thinking about Charles and his quadroon. All these weeks, these months, he'd been watching that young Jasmine. Knowing that she was going to be his. Weaving fantasies about how it could be with her. Knowing nobody was getting there until he decided the time had arrived. Leave it to Octavia to make sure of that.

Amory rose to his feet, strode down the corridor, back toward the kitchen wing, where his voice wouldn't carry to the upstairs bedrooms.

"Octavia! Octavia!"

He waited, knowing she slept lightly.

"Yessuh. Coffee?" Octavia asked amiably.

"The girl," he said quietly. "Jasmine. Make her scrub down in a tub. Send her up to my room." His eyes not quite meeting hers.

"Me do." Octavia nodded gravely. "Her come soon. Me make sho'." A touch of sadness in her eyes.

"Octavia." He hesitated, ran the tip of his tongue pensively about his lower lip. "Tell her I'll have a nice present for her."

In his room Amory lit the fire, hovering there until a blaze crackled in the fireplace. The girl would know what was expected of her. She was old enough. Fifteen. There wasn't another female on the plantation her age who hadn't been broken in.

His thighs tightened in excitement. Make it good for a virgin, and she was yours for life. Unless the virgin was his wife, he taunted himself with the old bitterness. Women like Emilie and Annabel were half-women. There wasn't a black woman who wasn't superior in that way.

He walked to a window and gazed out at the relentlessly falling rain. There was a light knock on his door. So light he thought, at first, that he'd imagined it.

"Come in."

The door moved open slowly. Eyes downcast, Jasmine walked into the room. Beauty in her movements, in the fine bones of her face and body. Trembling.

"Are you cold, girl?" Amory asked gently. "Cold, Jasmine?" he repeated, aware of her shyness, her alarm.

"Nossuh," she whispered, eyes on the floor. Knowing why she was here.

"Come over here by the fire," he said, making a point of keeping his voice low, unrushed. "More comfortable here."

Obediently, she moved toward him. The glow of the fire emphasized the delicate sculpture of her face, her slimness. Taut nipples protruded beneath the cotton dress that was her sole garment. Amory wet his lips.

"Jasmine, I'm not going to hurt you," he said softly, "Now take off your dress."

Without an instant's hesitation, she reached for her skirt, swept the faded cotton over her slim length, over her head. Stood there in brown nakedness, hardly darker than Charles, Amory thought, after a summer in the fields. Amber eyes still averted. A sweep of dark lashes forming a semicircle high on her cheeks.

Outside the rain was pelting down, the wind raging. Shutters were being fastened for the night. Somewhere, a horse whinnied. But here, before the fire, with Jasmine a statue before him, Amory could hear nothing. He looked only at her. Gazing at the marble-smooth breasts, the narrow hips, the flat pelvis.

"You mustn't be afraid, Jasmine."

He watched her face while his hands moved gently about her. Her mouth parted slightly. Eyes still afraid to meet his. The warmth of the fire caressing her nakedness.

"Wait," he said, and strode across to the wide, high bed, to sweep off a blanket, the feather bolster.

Amory improvised a bed before the fire, gestured to Jasmine to lie down. With doelike grace she obediently lowered herself to the bolster, lay back. His throat tightened in anticipation as he dropped, awkward from the lack of exercise, to his knees beside her. His hands moved expertly over the tense torso while he whispered encouragement to her.

"It's going to be all right, Jasmine," he murmured. "You

don't think I'm going to hurt you, do you?"

"Nossuh," she lied, a pinkness showing beneath the brown of her face.

Outside the wind was whipping through the trees, lashing at a loose shutter somewhere about the house.

She cried out once. Then a soft moan escaped her mouth, a moan not of pain but awakening passion. And then he, too, felt the explosion out of life, the anguished ecstasy, more beautiful than life itself.

Jasmine stood hunched before the dying fire, pulling her dress over her body. Amory fumbled in the top drawer of the oak chest. He crossed to Jasmine with the length of cloth, silken and colorful in his hands.

"Make yourself a dress from this. You'll be the prettiest little thing at the church service Sunday morning."

Her eyes wide with childlike pleasure, Jasmine accepted the fabric.

"Thankee, suh!" Her eyes met his. "Me go now, suh?"

"Go, Jasmine," Amory said with a chuckle. "You're a good girl."

The storm had eased off into a light rain. He hesitated about throwing another log in the fire. But sleep was long in coming. Damn, why must he always wind up with this guilty feeling because he'd taken a slave? They expected it. He wasn't an animal, he treated the girl right.

This was the way of the South. All this talk up North, for years now, about abolishing slavery. Yes, freedom must come. Eventually. It was against nature to enslave human beings. Immoral. But how many of them were prepared to survive in freedom?

Amory awoke after a brief few hours, as was his habit.

Morning sunlight spilled into the room. He looked out the window. Branches broken by the force of the storm lay here and there about the grounds. Chrysanthemum bushes crouched low to the ground. But the fresh after-storm scent in the air was refreshing.

Kara wasn't at the breakfast table. Three mornings in a row she'd come down late. Celestine came in to serve Amory, chattering excitedly about the minor havoc wrought by the storm. Dramatically she relayed the message that three roofs had been swept off. The occupants of the cabins had spent the rest of the night in the infirmary.

"Mister Tim come down yet?" Amory asked when Celestine brought him a plate laden with grits, eggs, and curling strips of bacon.

"Me see he go to stables jes' now," Celestine said blithely. "Me catch fo' you'?"

"Catch," Amory ordered humorously. "Tell him to come have a cup of coffee with the old man."

Celestine padded off hurriedly, cutting through a side room to head off Tim. He couldn't blame Tim for liking the idea of a townhouse in New Orleans. Not much out here for the young folks. But he'd wager it was Tim's idea. Not Kara's.

Amory ate with gusto, listening to the sounds outside—Celestine's high, light voice, incongruous with her bulk, yelling to Tim with an air of importance.

"Marse Tim! Marse Tim! Yo' papa want yo', right away, suh!"

Tim strolled into sight, with Celestine not far behind, bringing another cup for him.

"Good morning, Papa."

"Tim, have coffee with me," Amory said with a leisurely smile, but his eyes rested intently on his second-born. "Your mother tells me you've got something in your head about setting up a house in New Orleans."

"Mama said no," Tim told him quickly.

"No trouble between Kara and you, is there?" Amory asked cautiously.

"No, of course not!" Tim's voice was unusually high.

"Kara and you can go down to the city regularly, now that the summer is over," Amory said, compromisingly. "I don't know why you suddenly want to spend most of the year down there."

"I—I thought it would be better for Kara," Tim said, watching his father. The young whelp knew he had a soft spot for Kara. "She's pregnant. Mama might not take too well to that."

Amory sat at the table, quietly glowing. A child. His grandson. After all these years of waiting.

"About time, Tim!" Amory voiced his enthusiasm noisily. A grandson to carry on at Manoir. A kind of immortality, in knowing the line went on. Poor Annabel. This would be a jolt for her. "When does Kara figure the child is due?"

"April," Tim said quietly.

"Tim, you know who ties up the liquid funds around here." Amory said bluntly. "Besides, more than ever your mother's going to be against your leaving. She's going to bust her stays when she hears about the baby." He cleared his throat uneasily. Her first reaction was sure to be shock. "When do you plan on telling her?"

"I thought maybe you would." Tim's eyes were troubled.

"Tim, your mother would never forgive either of us," Amory growled. "Finish your coffee and go on upstairs and tell your mother she's going to be a grandmother."

Emilie would be resentful at first. For years she'd hoped Annabel would provide an heir for Manoir. Annabel was manageable. Kara was more determined. And so quickly Kara was succeeding where Annabel had failed. But once Emilie accepted Kara's pregnancy, she'd wait impatiently for the baby's arrival. Another Tim. To be fussed over and spoiled and molded in her way.

But this was Kara's child. Kara wouldn't allow Emilie to take over. Kara wasn't Annabel. Emilie and Kara would be battling for control from the minute the baby arrived. Damn it, he wished he could give them that house in New Orleans!

Chapter Thirteen

Autumn in Louisiana would have been Kara's favorite season, except for Emilie Rankin's increasingly oppressive solicitude for her health. Emilie objected at every slight physical effort Kara made, harangued constantly that she rest, that she take a tonic, recounted endless old wives' tales about the road to a successful delivery. As Amory had anticipated, the expected child had become the focal point of Emilie's life.

Emilie and Annabel arrived home from trips to New Orleans with lengths of fine cotton, which Daphne was commissioned to transform into delicate baby clothes. Yet, despite all the fuss, Kara was agonizingly aware of the covert hostility in both her mother-in-law and sister-in-law. Her pregnancy was an affront to Annabel and secretly resented by Emilie. And Amory, sensing these undercurrents, went out of his way to show his affection for Kara.

Tim was grateful for her silence. Relieved, too, that no marital demands were made upon him. Weeks later, Kara would again find herself suddenly sick when she thought of Tim and Jupe out there in the fields. All that pretense of making love to her. When all he wanted was a child.

Kara determinedly continued her morning appearances at the quarters. She felt an almost desperate need to keep herself busy. Fortunately she was feeling exceptionally well, except for a morning squeamishness during the earlier weeks. The children looked forward to her appearance, and she enjoyed being with them, teaching them. Charles would walk over to the quarters each morning. He was friendly, concerned.

Poor Charles, Kara thought sympathetically. Just last week Emilie, prattling on long-windedly when Annabel was lying down upstairs with a headache, had told her of Annabel's contempt for men, how her father had gambled away the family plantation, just before her marriage to Charles, and had moved on with her mother to Texas. How Annabel and she felt that men were animals, that that was all they wanted.

Papa was so pleased about the baby. Mrs. O'Casey was making a christening dress, and no matter what Mrs. Rankin said, that was the dress the baby would wear. She hoped papa would like his Christmas present. Tim had bought six fine shirts in papa's size and personally sent them out in time to arrive in Ireland for Christmas. And for Mrs. O'Casey, Kara had shipped off a dainty brooch, which she knew the old lady would show off at Sunday Mass.

With the approach of Christmas the social life among the plantation ladies grew hectic. Kara, because of her "condition," was pointedly omitted from all the socializing. Actually she preferred the long hours spent each day with Amory, listening to him talk so eloquently about world history and local politics. Amory, too, wished that Tim would become involved in politics.

Every morning Tim rode. In the afternoons he painted. Two or three times a week, in the evenings, he took a carriage into New Orleans, to amuse himself at the gambling club he'd recently discovered. There was no more talk about their spending a couple of days in New Orleans, or driving down to the theater. In Louisiana *enceinte* ladies remained within the protective shadows of their homes.

Tim was pleased about the baby, which Kara found bitterly amusing. He was scrupulously attentive to her. The way he might have been attentive to a specially cherished sister. Not even Emilie, so attuned to Tim, was aware of the break in their marital relationship.

But at night Kara lay awake, staring at the ceiling. Remembering the brief period when her marriage had seemed real. Remembering how it was to be loved. Remembering her own startlingly eager response. It had all been a lie. But she would have her baby. The baby would make up for everything else, she vowed.

Kara lay reading on the bed, propped up against a nest of pillows. A hand resting on the swell of her belly, as though to embrace the child within. She stiffened, dropped the book beside her. Aware of the first flutter of movement within her. Waited with poignant eagerness for a repetition of that small flutter. Life. Her baby kicking! She lay back, her face alight with a fresh kind of joy. Waiting for a small foot or hand to assert itself again. Her first instinct to tell Tim.

Downstairs, she heard Dr. Scott's carriage pulling away from the entrance. He hadn't remained long. He was probably angry that Mrs. Rankin had called him out to the house because she had a mild cold. Mrs. Rankin was sure she was one step removed from pneumonia. She'd insisted Kara not remain in the same room with her. "You must think of the baby!" she'd exhorted virtuously. Emilie Rankin was never honest, even with herself; there was always the playacting.

Kara rose from the bed suddenly restless. Perhaps she ought to go downstairs to inquire about her mother-in-law's health. Not that it was serious, Kara thought humorously, but it was the polite thing to do. Passing Emilie's room, she could hear her upbraiding Celestine for not tucking under the covers to her liking. But those complaints never ruffled

Celestine; she'd lived with them too long.

"Emilie's fine," Amory was saying in the library. His voice edged with irritation. "Stop worrying, Annabel, Scott knows his business."

"But this is a treacherous time of the year, and she's so delicate," Annabel insisted. "I just think he might have stayed with her longer than that. In and out he went," she wound up indignantly.

"He's got sick people to see, Annabel," Amory said brusquely. "He's sending out medicine for her."

"What a pity Mama has to miss the opera tonight." Annabel sighed. "She was so looking forward to it."

"How's Mrs. Rankin?" Kara asked politely. She couldn't yet adapt herself to calling Emilie Rankin "Mama," as Annabel did.

"A cold," Amory shrugged. "She'll be all right." He squinted thoughtfully at Kara. "Ever been to the opera, Kara?"

"No." Kara brightened, reading his mind.

"Let's have Tim take you in tonight. We have the box," Amory said, pleased that Kara might enjoy this diversion.

"Papa, how can you suggest such a thing?" Annabel was visibly shocked.

"Honey, the way you ladies dress, nobody's going to know about the baby. Besides, plenty of *enceinte* ladies go to the theater and opera," he said smiling. "But I don't see why Kara has to sit with them off on the side when we have a box of our own."

"But all the riding," Annabel was tense, suddenly very nervous. And for a poignant moment, Kara saw her reliving the tragedy of her own miscarriages. "Why, anything could happen."

"I'm healthy as a horse, Annabel," Kara insisted gently.

"I'll be fine. Really I will."

"Mama's going to be terribly upset," Annabel warned, her voice still high.

"Emilie's not going to know about it until the four of you come back home," Amory growled. "Is that clear, Annabel?"

For a heated instant their eyes clashed. Then Annabel lowered her eyes.

"Yes, sir," she said quietly.

Dinner was scheduled early to allow for the drive into New Orleans. Charles seemed faintly anxious about Kara's making the trip. Several times through dinner, she glanced up to find his gaze resting on her. He was remembering Annabel's five miscarriages. But *she* wasn't going to lose this baby. Not with her Irish determination!

Jupe brought the carriage around before the entrance, and the two couples settled themselves for the long drive into New Orleans. The air was deliciously crisp—like autumn in Ireland, Kara thought with pleasure—you could hardly believe it was December.

"I'll probably sleep all the way in," Annabel said distantly, and immediately leaned her head back and closed her eyes. That relieved her of making conversation. Charles was on edge as though he would have preferred not to go to the opera tonight.

Kara drowsed for most of the trip, lulled by the movement of the carriage. Faintly aware of the animated political conversation between Tim and Charles. Charles was upset about the corruption in the local government. He talked about how the Democrats had brought down Chris Lillie from Tammany Hall up in New York, to teach them Tammany Hall tricks.

The carriage rumbled into the city. Kara, as ever fascinated by the sights and sounds of New Orleans. Jupe deposited them at the Théâtre D'Orleans. Tim solicitously helped Kara from the carriage, while Charles assisted Annabel. By the time they'd moved into the theater, it seemed that every seat was occupied. What a display of ladies' finery! What an air of anticipation!

"Everyone's determined to be here to enjoy the first note of the overture," Charles said. "Opera is taken very seriously in New Orleans, Kara."

"Oh, I wouldn't want to miss a note," Kara said, excited, her eyes meanwhile enjoying the spectacle of New Orleans society.

The socially elite sat in boxes, like theirs, on the first level. The tier above was occupied, mainly, by beautiful mulatto women, resplendent in jewels and brightly colored gowns, strikingly decolletage, which the white ladies would never dare to wear.

At the very top sat the blacks. Amory had explained to Kara that, among the New Orleans citizenry, was a group of free Negroes, some skilled slaves who'd managed to buy their freedom by unbelievable labor, or received their freedom because of some special services, or for bravery in war, or slaves freed by white fathers. Most of these free Negroes were carpenters, tailors, mechanics, small businessmen, who lived lives far different from the plantation slaves.

Charles leaned forward across Annabel to point out Mayor Crossman to Kara, and Tim joined in by naming other prominent New Orleansians in the audience. Tim was well into the convivial mood of the assemblage. He waved, here and there, to familiar faces; and Kara felt herself being scrutinized and discussed by those whom Tim greeted. They all knew, of course, about his Irish bride. Kara sat, cheeks flushed a becoming pink, with a ready smile for those who stared. Annabel sat composed and impersonal. She might have been alone in the theater.

Every now and then, Charles glanced compulsively toward the middle tier. Curious, Kara followed his gaze. A girl sat there staring with a small, fixed smile in their direction. Very young, exquisitely beautiful, with masses of honey-colored hair, a white satin dress forming a sheath over her body.

The girl was a mulatto; of that Kara was certain. Annabel had spoken with contempt about the mulatto women—the *placées* who dared to show themselves at the opera and theater, and who were grouped apart from the whites and the blacks. The girl lifted one slender hand in a private gesture of salute, and Kara, her face hot, averted her gaze. It was eavesdropping, to witness that tiny, poignant exchange between Charles and the ethereal beauty in the "colored" tier. This was why Charles was reluctant to attend the opera this evening! To sit here with Annabel, while that girl sat above.

The musicians took their places now. The conductor lifted a hand. Instantly, an expectant silence gripped the audience. They heard the strains of the overture. The curtain rose. Kara sat forward, entranced by the Donizetti music, thrilled and excited that *Lucia di Lammermoor* was based on a Sir Walter Scott novel.

The opera was performed exquisitely. The audience's response was dramatic, exciting. Bravos, hands clapping, canes pounding. Floral tributes tossed upon the stage. Almost reluctantly, the audience took its departure.

At Vincent's they joined the after-theater patrons, browsing about the glass cases of patés, brioches, éclairs, meringues, choosing this and that, discussing their selections, until Charles marshaled them to the counter where he paid for their elegant array of delicacies, to be taken back to

Manoir for the pre-bedtime coffee. Tim, still talking to people, smiling, shaking hands.

Jupe arrived to pick them up, and they settled themselves again in the carriage for the return trip. Again Kara dozed. To dream, oddly, of a honey-haired girl in white satin who, somehow, threatened her safety.

Kara was caught up in a last-minute rush to finish her Christmas presents for the children in the quarters. With Jasmine's help, she made rag dolls. Each doll with some small, special trim of significance to its future owner. Alone in Kara's room, they spent pleasant hours each day relaxing with this activity, while Emilie and Annabel visited neighboring plantations. In the evenings there were balls, which Tim decorously didn't attend out of deference to Kara's condition and to which Charles, unhappily, escorted Annabel.

Just five days before Christmas, Kara decided she must give each little girl a length of ribbon for her hair. She'd seen the wistful looks when she'd impulsively pulled a satin ribbon from her own hair to tie the pert pigtails of an eight-year-old.

"I know it's a long drive, Tim, but could we go into town today? I do so want to buy ribbons for the children, and this is so close to Christmas."

"Jupe could shop them for you, or Horatio," Tim pointed out. But his eyes said he wasn't averse to a trip into town. Tim was always eager to go to New Orleans.

"I'd like to choose them myself," Kara insisted. "Each one different."

"Mama'll be angry," Tim warned, uneasy. "When you're this far along." It was Mrs. Rankin who counted the weeks before the baby arrived, rather than Kara. "Why don't we have Jupe drive."

"*I'm* having this baby, Tim," Kara interrupted firmly, and

Tim flushed. "I can make the trip with no trouble at all. This baby is planning to stay," she said with an attempt at humor. "He knows when he's well off."

"Sure it's going to be a boy?" Unexpectedly, Tim grinned.

"I don't care which," Kara declared, "so long as it's strong and healthy."

It was painful to stand here this way with Tim, knowing they'd made this child together, and to know how he was. So many nights she lay awake, remembering the nights they'd lain together. Remembering the newly awakened passion which she'd discovered with such joy. But now she was full with child, and her husband would never come to her again.

Tim, candidly uneasy about his mother's reaction, accompanied Kara into New Orleans. The city was full of the Christmas spirit. The streets were thronged with carriages. drays, people on foot. Kara gave Tim directions. She knew exactly which shop would have the ribbons. Annabel had bought ribbons there for the baby's clothes.

"The shop is just another block down," Tim said, as Kara searched the store fronts. He was plainly nervous about her being jostled in this teeming traffic. "How do you feel?"

"I feel fine," Kara smiled. She was perfectly healthy, and having a baby was a most natural state.

As the carriage turned a corner, Kara sat up stiffly. Horatio, in that discarded gentleman's finery of which he was proud, was sitting atop a carriage. Amory was home. Mrs. Rankin and Annabel were visiting. Horatio must have brought Charles into town.

"Tim, could we stop here for a minute?" Kara asked. Tim hadn't noticed Horatio yet. He was busily engaged in watching a parade of slaves down the other side of the street. "I'd like to see something in a shop right here."

"Jupe, hold it here," Tim called out.

Tim helped Kara from the carriage. She sent a swift glance in Jupe's direction. He gave no indication that he'd spied Horatio, just ahead. Kara walked to a shop window attractively dressed with pewter and old glass. Charles wasn't inside. With a show of lively interest, she moved on to the next shop window. Inside the small jewelry shop she spied Charles, his back to her.

The girl was with him, the one Kara had seen at the opera. More beautiful close up this way. The features delicate. Dark shadows beneath heavily lashed eyes. A gaze of adoration on her face as she looked up at Charles. Charles held her hand tenderly, gazing into her eyes. He slipped a ring on her finger. It was almost like a marriage ceremony.

The girl placed her free hand at the top of her stomach, and suddenly, Kara knew. The dark shadows beneath the girl's eyes. The protective hand that caressed a yet-unformed child. Charles's *placée* was pregnant. And Charles was in love with the girl.

Kara swung about with awkward haste and crossed the banquette to where Tim waited for her. She smiled with an effort.

"Let's go on to the ribbon store."

Chapter Fourteen

Three days before Christmas Kara received a package from her father, addressed to Mr. and Mrs. Timothy Rankin. Kara opened it with tears of homesickness filling her eyes. Within the many protective wrappings lay a book of poems—*Sonnets from the Portuguese* by Elizabeth Barrett Browning. Chosen for Papa, no doubt, by Mr. Watterson.

Feeling a rich closeness to her father, Kara deposited the book on a table close to her bed. She'd read it in the restless nights when she lay alone and thought about the baby growing in her. Perhaps she might even use the book in her reading lessons with Jasmine. It was astonishing how quickly Jasmine was learning. So it was against the law to teach a slave to read, Kara thought defiantly; it was a ridiculous law.

There was a growing tension between Tim and Kara, even though she'd hoped this awkwardness between them would subside. Emilie, as usual, contributed to the situation with her constant coy remarks about the "new father." As Kara's belly increased in size, so Tim's discomfort mounted.

Now Kara was painfully aware of side glances between Jupe and Tim, of Tim's nocturnal disappearances, either about the plantation or down in New Orleans. She suspected Octavia knew. It was there in the dark, troubled eyes when they rested on Jupe or on Tim. It was there in Octavia's desperation-edged coaxing that Amory choose a wife for Jupe.

"Marse, him ought be makin' babies fo' yo'," Octavia chided repeatedly. "How come yo' don' find him a wife?"

"Let him find his own," Amory would insist with a chuckle.

This was one of Amory's small defiances against the system, like having built the one-room church in the quarters, which Emilie caustically referred to as "Amory's Folly," though it was Emilie herself who insisted that the slaves attend church regularly.

"Ole Miss bettuh not cetch us not goin' to church Sunday mawnin'," Celestine said emphatically one day when Kara was alone at breakfast. "Her have a fit!"

Celestine glowed with pleasure at the arrival of the holiday season, though the slaves had little reason to celebrate. There was a festive air about the whole plantation.

On Christmas Eve the family sat down to dinner early, because custom decreed that the "little niggers" from the quarters were to be brought up to the house to hang their stockings on the wide mantelpiece in the parlor. In addition, this year they would sing Christmas carols for the family. They had been rehearsing with Kara for weeks.

Mrs. Rankin appeared annoyed. Amory had been late coming to the dinner table. She was waiting now for Celestine and Jasmine to leave the room before she pounced on him.

"Amory," Emilie began with that quality of voice that inevitably set Kara's teeth on edge, "Mr. Dent tells me you're giving a whole week's holiday to a group of field hands."

Amory looked up warily, exchanged a swift glance with Charles.

"That's right, Emilie, we do it every year. Charles and I discussed it." It was Charles's decisions about the plantation that usually prevailed, but protocol called for his consulting with his father in instances such as this.

"But forty slaves, Amory!" Emilie's voice was rising stridently. "Do you realize what that's costing us?"

"My mathematics are quite good, Emilie," Amory assured her drily. "They turned out more work than I had call to expect from them, because they knew they'd get this vacation. I'm not selling them short."

"Oh, Amory, you are the most impractical man," Emilie said exasperatedly. "First it was this business with the Christmas stockings."

"Every plantation in the South allows that, Emilie," Amory shot back. "What does it cost us to buy some peppermint sticks and some hard candies?"

"Octavia's been secretly baking cookies for two days," Emilie informed him vindictively. Kara gazed quickly at her plate; she was responsible for this activity. "Do you know how much butter she's used? But I don't dare say anything because Octavia'll sulk for days, and the table will suffer for it. A fine thing"—she turned to Annabel for backing—"when you have to worry about upsetting a house slave."

"I hear there's some talk down in New Orleans about putting up a monument to Mr. Clay," Tim said anxiously, hoping to bring a new element into the conversation.

"I don't know why they had to hold those ceremonies down in New Orleans two weeks ago," Emilie said with a shrug. "Why, I read in the *Picayune* that it was the largest group of people ever seen at one time in New Orleans. And everybody knows that Daniel Webster comes from New Hampshire, where they have abolitionists hiding under every rock! Even if Mr. Clay and Mr. Calhoun were southern gentlemen."

"Emilie, the ceremonies were honoring the memories of three of our greatest men." Amory's voice was laced with annoyance. "How many times in history will we have three such giants in our government? We can't realize how much they've done to preserve the Union. And we've lost them all in the span of two years, at a time when we're so hungry for leadership!"

"I don't like the way the Congress is treating the Southern states," Emilie bridled. "And now with a Democrat going into the White House in March, no telling what's going to happen next."

"Mama, I didn't know you were interested in politics," Charles jibed gently.

"I'm just naturally against Democrats. Papa always said you couldn't trust a one of them, they were all against the banking interests. And the planters' best friends," Emilie wound up with a glint of satisfaction, "are the New York bankers."

"I sometimes wonder," Amory drawled.

"Mr. Pierce is a gentleman, though, mama," Annabel said quickly. "I'll just bet, even if he does come from New Hampshire, that he'll put some southerners into his cabinet."

Emilie sighed.

"It's such a pity that General Taylor had to die that way. For a while we had a Louisiana planter and a Whig in the White House, and we can be proud of that."

"General Taylor is probably the last President the Whigs will ever elect," Amory prophesied. "He rode in on his military victories."

"Amory, what a terrible thing to say!" Emilie stared at him in indignation. "Papa always said it was unladylike for women to become involved in politics, and of course, Papa's word was gospel to me, but I'm sure that women wouldn't make such a mess of politics as you men do."

"Oh, Mrs. Rankin, and Annabel," Kara included her sister-in-law in her ingratiating smile. Intent on diverting the conversation because Amory's face was growing taut with frustration, as was apt to happen if he discussed anything more serious than the weather with his wife. "My father sent a lovely book of poems by an English lady named Elizabeth Barrett Browning. Perhaps you'd like to read them?" This was Christmas Eve. Kara reinforced her determination to be friendly with the other two women.

"Thank you, I would," Annabel said politely while her mother-in-law ignored the offer.

"I bought a collection of poems in New Orleans last week, *Les Cenelles*." Tim seemed astonished that Kara and he might share this interest. "They're all in French, written by seventeen mulatto poets who lived at one time or another in New Orleans."

"Tim, do you speak French?" Kara asked with candid admiration, and then blushed. "Of course, you do," she said quickly. "You lived there." For one brief moment she'd forgotten the ugliness between them.

"Kara, would you like to speak French?" Amory asked, his eyes inspecting her keenly.

"I think it would be wonderful!" Kara's eyes shone wistfully.

"Emilie, there must be a French tutor somewhere among your plantation ladies. Arrange instruction for Kara," Amory ordered.

Emilie gazed at him with mouth agape in amazement, nodded stiffly, then apparently dismissed the whole matter from her mind. Mrs. Rankin was a penny-pincher when the penny was used on anyone other than herself.

"I ordered that new book by Mr. Audubon," Emilie announced with pride. "*Quadrupeds of America.* Mr. Audubon is a Louisianian," she added loftily.

Charles, who loved the land and the animals, asked questions about the book; but Emilie was obviously buying it solely because Mr. Audubon was a native of her state. She knew little of its contents. Later, Kara promised herself, she'd asked Amory what "quadrupeds" meant.

Celestine and Jasmine came in to serve the pecan pie and coffee. Kara remained silent, tired now by the exertions of the day. She had spent most of the morning in the quarters, rehearsing her choir, and the afternoon making amusing Christmas cards for the children.

"If we're all through," Amory said briskly, when seconds of Octavia's superb pecan pie had been turned down because its richness prohibited too heavy an indulgence, "why don't we go into the parlor? I'll tell Octavia to send to the quarters."

He relished the small ceremony with the children. Kara was glad she'd spent so much effort in preparing the musical surprise. Amory would enjoy it.

The family settled themselves about the parlor, Emilie rather disdainful because she "didn't hold with spoiling the slaves." Annabel appeared startled when Kara asked her if she would play the piano when the surprise choir sang their Christmas carols.

"Why, yes." But Annabel cast an uneasy glance at her mother-in-law. "I'll try to follow them."

Annabel and Emilie began to talk with a quiet conspiracy that excluded Kara, about the prolonged illness of a neighboring lady whom Kara suspected was a hypochondriac. Tim was slouched in a chair, staring somberly into the fire while he sipped at an after-dinner cordial. Kara listened to Amory and Charles. They were talking, again, about that Hungarian man. That Mr. Lajos Kossuth who'd received such an ovation at a mass meeting in Lafayette Square in New Orleans back in March. Mr. Kossuth had tried, very gallantly, to free his people, and had failed. It was strange to see folks flocking to honor a man like that, when right here all the black people were without their freedom.

The children from the quarters—shy, abashed, some giggling, all bright-eyed with the wonder of the occasion—trooped into the parlor. Their empty stockings were clutched in their hands. Amory immediately took charge, joshing with them, discovering a pocketful of sweets to distribute among them. Kara was proud of the swift glances they shot in her direction, the understanding that the sweets must not be devoured until after the singing.

Amid much conviviality, and with even Tim entering into it, the stockings were hung impressively across the mantelpiece. Kara rose to her feet, crossed to the little ones, to marshal them into a group at one side of the room while she explained about the entertainment. Amory was delighted. Mrs. Rankin stared as though this were a personal affront.

Annabel took her place at the piano, with an apologetic smile at Emilie. The high, young voices rose in poignant melody. Tim watched seriously, seemingly touched. Charles listened with a half smile. His eyes opaque.

The little ones sang three carols as planned, received their vociferous applause, mainly from the menfolks, with self-conscious titters, then were herded out by Octavia and Celestine. Both had eyes that shone suspiciously. Kara was sure the children's hands would be crossed with a cookie before they crawled into their beds for the night.

Jasmine and Celestine appeared with New Orleans coffee and a plate piled high with golden pralines. Annabel dutifully played Debussy at Emilie's request, while the others sat sipping their strong, hot, chicory-spiced coffee and nibbled Octavia's perfect pralines. Charles was restless. He rose to his feet, suppressing a wide yawn, and excused himself for the evening when Annabel left the piano. Charles was always the perfect gentleman to his wife.

Tim was not in the room. He had left with the children.

Despite her advancing pregnancy, Kara spent her mornings at the quarters. Prodded by Amory, Emilie came up with a French tutor for Kara shortly after New Year's. He was engaged at the consent of his employer, a neighboring plantation owner, to come over every Monday and Thursday afternoon. Jean Simone was a slender, fragile-looking young man with dark hair and intense eyes, and he was delighted with Kara's earnestness. His scrupulous courtesy found favor with Emilie, though she resented the money paid to him on Kara's behalf. Tim and Jean Simone seemed to get on very well, and many a time Tim would interrupt a lesson to talk to Jean.

Late in February, Emilie and Annabel decided to go into New Orleans for a day of shopping. Tim offered to accompany them. He wanted to choose a frame for Kara's portrait, on which he had been working, though Kara privately suspected he would never finish it. She hadn't posed for him in weeks. Not until Tim and the two women were leaving did Kara realize that Jean had promised to meet Emilie at Maison Blanche to help her choose materials for new draperies. Jupe, unfamiliarly sullen, drove the carriage. His eyes were accusing when they rested, fleetingly, on Tim.

Amory and Charles were to drive into town in the evening, to meet the ladies and Tim for dinner at Antoine's before going on to a concert with Ole Bull and a child prodigy named Adelina Patti. It was unthinkable that Kara should show herself in public in her seventh month of pregnancy.

Kara spent this morning, as usual, with the children in the quarters. Amory, to Kara's delight, made a point of joining her for lunch because he knew she would be alone. They had hardly sat down when Charles sauntered into the dining room.

"Celestine!" Amory roared. "Bring a plate for Mister Charles!" He grinned at his son. "To what do we owe this honor?"

"I figured Mama and Annabel might be upset if I fell asleep at the concert," Charles chuckled quietly. "I'll lay off for the afternoon. Dent has everything under control."

Charles looked relaxed, happy. Kara knew it was because of the child. She wondered if Annabel suspected about the girl. She must. Annabel had a new, harsh way of talking to Charles that was a wordless rebuke.

"Charles, Dent is really working out, isn't he?" Amory asked seriously.

Charles sighed. "Dent seems fine. I don't know why I keep getting this queer feeling that something isn't exactly right."

"You're not accustomed to an overseer with the manners of a dandy," Amory joshed. "He turns my stomach sometimes. Oh, excuse me, Kara," he apologized quickly.

"I feel the same way," she laughed. "He thoroughly disapproves of me, of course. Of anybody Irish." She'd overheard Dent talking about the Irish with Mrs. Rankin. To Mr. Dent they were noisy, brash, offensive.

"Kara, have you read Mrs. Stowe's book yet?" Amory asked, with a sly glance at Charles.

"You mean there's a copy around Manoir?" Charles clucked good-humoredly. "Mama's allowing that?"

"You know your mother couldn't bear not knowing what that woman wrote," Amory tossed back with amusement.

"Who is Mrs. Stowe?" Kara asked curiously. Somewhere she'd heard the name.

"Harriet Beecher Stowe," Charles said briskly, "is a

plain-faced, dowdy little woman of forty-one who wrote a book called *Uncle Tom's Cabin.* She never lived in the South; she made some short trips across the Ohio River, I understand, when she was a girl living in Cincinnati. She knows absolutely nothing about the South. She wrote on hearsay."

"You must admit, Charles," Amory drawled with satisfaction, "that nobody has done quite as much for the cause of abolition as your dowdy little Mrs. Stowe, who I understand is determinedly against woman's suffrage and free love."

"Mrs. Stowe was being totally unfair," Charles insisted. "I don't deny that it's a bad system. No southerner in his right mind can deny that. I'd be glad to be rid of it, if I knew what could take its place and function. But we don't treat our slaves unfairly. You know many of them are attached to us." But his eyes were unhappy.

"What is that I read in the *Picayune* about a canal to be dug across Florida?" Kara intervened, as always uncomfortable when slavery was under discussion. "Where is Florida?"

"It's a state far to the east, and south," Amory said. "But I doubt that we'll ever have a canal across Florida. It serves no important purpose. For myself I'd suggest a canal across the Isthmus of Panama, which would connect the Atlantic and Pacific, and certainly facilitate world shipping."

"You're always ahead of your time," Charles said with affection. "It'll come, I wager, though not this year."

"Next year there'll be action," Amory prophesied. "Wait and see."

Kara looked at Amory. He was so kind and so knowledgeable. Yet she couldn't help wondering how a man like Amory, who so hated slavery, would at the same time have Jasmine come to his room. But then this was the South, a land so full of contradictions.

While they were lingering over coffee in companionable

conversation, Celestine came in with a handful of envelopes.

"Horatio, him bring de mail," Celestine announced importantly, placing the letters beside Amory's coffee cup.

Amory shuffled through the envelopes with a smile.

"Ever since they started postal delivery in New Orleans in fifty-one, we have to have this invasion of our privacy," Amory grumbled good-humoredly. "Just because you can now send a letter three thousand miles away for three cents, everybody thinks he has to write. Oh—" Amory paused, turned to Kara. "Here's a letter for you."

"Thank you." Eagerly, Kara grasped the letter, with a small smile of apology for her impatience, ripped it open. Knowing it would be from her father.

But it wasn't from her father. The letter was from the schoolmaster. Her father had died easily, in no pain, in his sleep. A small box of his personal effects were being shipped to her. He had been buried in the country cemetery beside his wife. Mr. Watterson's letter was compassionate, gentle. Her father had been delighted about his coming grandchild. The schoolmaster hoped the child would assuage her loss.

Kara stared at the carefully written, consoling words in the brief letter, which she knew had been difficult to write. Rereading, trying to assimilate. Slowly tears came into her eyes. Her throat hurt. She pushed back her chair, the letter crumpled in one hand.

"Please excuse me—" Her voice a husky whisper.

Kara ran.

"There must be bad news," Amory's voice was anxious. "Charles, go to her."

Chapter Fifteen

A monotonous drizzle washed the night earth. Kara lay on her back across the bed, fully dressed, tears spent. Hearing the carriage drive up to the house, halt there. She heard Charles walking across the foyer to the door, because the house slaves were already asleep in the kitchen wing.

How sweet Charles had been this afternoon. Consoling her in her grief while she relived the anguished memory of those dreadful days when she and Papa had watched the others die. And now Papa, who survived the famine, was gone. She was alone, with the baby she carried within her.

Charles had sent his father alone into New Orleans, to remain at Manoir in case she needed him. There was such consideration, such tenderness in Charles. How could Annabel be but half a wife to him? No, no wife at all. His marriage was to that girl in New Orleans.

Kara stiffened as the foyer filled with the sound of festive voices. Mrs. Rankin's voice, high-pitched, bubbling over as she talked.

"Charles, it was a grand evening," she said with satisfaction. "Not just Ole Bull and his violin. There was this child, Adelina Patti, no more than ten. Oh, what a voice!"

"She was great, Charles," Amory said with conviction. "A dark-haired, black-eyed child with the voice of an angel. I can imagine what the *Picayune* will have to say about her!"

"Charles, why didn't you come down to New Orleans?" Annabel asked coldly. "Folks were asking about you."

"I thought I should stay here," Charles began cautiously. "Kara."

"What is all this nonsense about Kara?" Emilie interrupted vindictively. "You would think, the way Charles and Amory act, that this was the first child ever born! Charles, I was very upset when your father said you were remaining at home. At least you could accompany us to dinner and a concert when we ask."

"Emilie, wait," Amory interceded. "We didn't feel Kara should be left alone tonight."

"I have had it up to here with Kara!" Emilie's voice soared, shrill and loud. "If Tim felt his wife's condition required his presence at Manoir, he would have remained here."

"Tim didn't know," Charles explained quietly. "Kara received a letter from home after you left. Her father died."

"Tim, you'd better go up to her," Amory suggested quietly.

Kara waited. Her heart beating wildly. She didn't want Tim to come to her. He wasn't like Charles. He wouldn't understand.

"Kara's probably asleep by now," Tim said evasively. "I'll talk to her in the morning."

Quickly, Kara left the bed, crossed to the door, and softly closed it.

Kara found herself growing increasingly impatient these final weeks of her pregnancy. She still walked daily to the quarters, though now Jasmine determinedly trailed along behind her. Tiring easily, still engulfed in the grief of her father's death, she napped in the afternoons, except those when

Jean Simone arrived to tutor her in French. The lessons were short, but Jean remained to linger, lengthily, in the library with Tim. Despite Emilie's annoyance—"Really, Kara, it's indelicate to allow a young unmarried man to see you this far in pregnancy!"—she insisted on keeping up the lessons, though the relationship between Tim and Jean made her uneasy. And Amory, not realizing the import of this friendship, insisted that the tutor continue to come to Manoir.

The evenings offered small cases of comfort. Amory usually joined the ladies in the parlor after dinner, as did Charles at least three or four evenings a week, so that Kara found herself drawn into the stimulating crossfire of conversation between Amory and Charles, while Emilie and Annabel talked quietly across the room, along interests of their own. If Emilie and Annabel thought it odd that Tim seldom graced the parlor with his appearance, they refrained from giving any indication of this.

With the approach of Saint Patrick's Day, Kara regretfully acknowledged that she wouldn't attempt the drive into New Orleans for the big parade. Sitting in one position for any length of time was agonizing. An hour and a half each way in the carriage was unthinkable.

"What a shame to miss the parade," Kara said wistfully while she sat beside the glowing fire, across from Amory. Annabel was dutifully playing the piano, while her mother-in-law smiled and nodded to the rhythm of the music. "I've never seen a true Saint Patrick's Day parade."

"I'll take you in to see the next one myself," Amory promised. "With the little one," he added expansively.

"He'll like that," Kara said, bubbling.

"Oh, so it's a he already?" Amory chortled. "You're sure?"

"I'm sure," Kara nodded firmly.

"Next year, it'll be a beautiful day," Amory predicted.

"Tomorrow it's going to be typical Saint Patrick's Day weather in New Orleans. Teeming rain all day long. The city will be a murky gray lake. But that won't stop the Sons of Erin. They'll lay a line of boards right down the middle of the street, and there they'll march."

"Amory, did you say something about rain?" Emilie demanded querulously from across the room. Annabel had abandoned the piano, and Emilie's voice carried extremely loud and clear.

"It looks like rain," Amory said. "You still plan on going up to Biloxi?"

"Oh, yes indeed," Emilie said firmly. "Annabel's cousin is expecting us. We've planned this trip for weeks. We're leaving first thing in the morning. Horatio will drive us."

Earlier than normal, Kara excused herself and went up to her room. She was restless tonight, unable to concentrate on the novel that her father-in-law had given her. In bed, she found it difficult to discover a comfortable position for sleeping.

Long after Amory and the two women had gone to their own rooms, Kara lay awake in the darkness. She heard Tim enter the house and climb the stairs. Recognizing him by the nervous clearing of his throat.

Kara, at last, fell asleep. A heavy, troubled sleep that was punctured by the sounds of a departure in front of the house. It was morning, she realized with a start, despite the lack of sunlight. She'd overslept. Just as well, she thought with satisfaction. She wouldn't have to bother seeing Mrs. Rankin and Annabel off for their trip.

Kara shifted about in the bed, seeking a position that would give relief to her back. This baby was becoming a heavy one to lug about, she thought tenderly.

The door was opened cautiously. Jasmine smiled at finding her awake.

"Yo' sleep good," Jasmine asked, floating into the room with lissome grace, Kara's morning cup of mint tea in her hand. "Him good mawnin' to stay in bed. Yo' res', yo' heah? No go to de quatuhs. Rainin' already."

"Oh, what a shame." Kara awkwardly pulled her bulk into a position to accommodate tea drinking. Noticing the small Spanish comb, such as she had seen in shops in New Orleans, which Jasmine wore in her hair this morning.

"Ah bring up breakfas' presently," Jasmine went on, moving to the windows to pull back the drapes. She shook her head. "Jes' look at dat sky. Him gonna poah like mad, yo' see."

Kara allowed Jasmine to keep her in bed for a while, obediently ate the overly large breakfast that Octavia sent up. Mid-morning, she left the bed, dressed, spent a restless while brushing her hair. She went down the corridor and stopped at the stairs. Amory's and Tim's voices came from below.

"I plan on going in to New Orleans right after the midday meal," Amory was saying to Tim. "I told Doctor Scott I'd stop by today for my regular checkup."

"I'll go with you," Tim offered quickly. "I need to buy paint supplies. Why don't we meet for dinner at Antoine's?" Occasionally Tim made an effort to ingratiate himself with his father. "Just the two of us. I'm in a mood for pompano."

"That sounds promising," Amory agreed, and glanced up the stairs as Kara descended. "But do you think it's wise to spend the whole day away?"

Kara forced a smile.

"Good morning, gentlemen," she said pertly in what she'd once overheard Mrs. Rankin label her "bar-room cordiality." "Though the weather looks bad."

"Good morning, Kara," Amory said with a wide, welcoming smile, while Tim merely nodded.

"Papa, the baby isn't due for five weeks," Tim said tensely, his eyes averted from Kara's swollen belly. "Kara, you don't mind my going into New Orleans today?" Stiffly polite.

"No reason why you shouldn't go in," Kara said cheerfully.

By the time they sat down to eat, the rain had turned into a steady drizzle. The kind this part of Louisiana knew well. Tim, however, was insistent that they make the trip into the city. While Celestine served them, Charles arrived in the dining room.

"No day for the fields," Charles announced wryly, seating himself at the table. "That rain's going to keep up till nightfall, at least."

Charles and Amory talked about the cotton crop that would be put in next month. Tim was silent, apparently concentrating on Octavia's fluffy chicken pie. Kara barely touched her food.

"You go upstairs and rest, young lady," Amory ordered her affectionately, when she stood at the door seeing Tim and him off to the carriage. Charles had already disappeared into the library, to concentrate on some paperwork.

"I will," Kara promised. "Jasmine will hunt me out if I don't."

"Tell Octavia not to bother about dinner for us tonight," Amory said. "There'll just be Charles and you."

"I'll tell her." Kara waved good-bye. Suddenly elated. It would be nice having dinner with Charles, she thought, and felt the color rush to her cheeks.

Kara came awake slowly, to the lulling sound of a heavy rainfall outdoors. Dusk shrouding the house. She felt uncomfortable. Her eyes opened wide suddenly. There was a dampness in bed. Her water had broken. The birth was approaching.

"Missy?" Jasmine ventured close, her eyes anxious. Almost seeming to sense what Kara was about to say. "How yo' feel?"

"I think it's close," Kara whispered. "Will you, will you please change the bed for me?" Jasmine understood. Her eyes glowed, with a blend of anticipation and fear, while she nodded vigorously. "It won't happen for hours yet," Kara said. "Not with the first one."

"Ah tell Marse Charles right away," Jasmine said briskly, walking to the commode for fresh linens. "Soon's ah git you comfortable agin in dat bed."

"Jasmine, I haven't had a single pain yet."

"In dat bed," Jasmine ordered with mock sternness. "Soon's it ready."

"Doctor Scott will have plenty of time to get here," Kara said while she allowed Jasmine to change her into a fresh nightgown. She listened uneasily to the wind blowing outside. Jasmine changed the sheets, then prodded her into the bed.

"Lemme git dis fire movin'." Jasmine lifted a log, thrust it onto the fire, then hurried out of the room.

She wouldn't be afraid, Kara told herself. This was normal. Mama had no trouble at all. By morning, if she were lucky, she'd hold her baby in her arms. She laid a hand across her belly, waiting for the first contraction. Awed by the miracle of birth.

Minutes later Charles came striding up the stairs. He hadn't expected to be alone with her this way. But there was plenty of time for Dr. Scott to arrive.

He knocked lightly on the door.

"Come in," she called back, almost blithely.

Charles opened the door, walked inside, grinned.

"I hear you're in business," he said humorously, his eyes gentle.

"It seems so." She was grateful for Charles's air of casualness. "But it's going to be a long time yet. Did Jasmine tell you to send for Doctor Scott?"

"Jasmine told me," he confirmed, "and I did. Jupe's riding down to New Orleans now. He ought to be bringing Scott back in about three hours." His eyes were faintly apprehensive as they dwelt on Kara. He's gone through the awful experiences of Annabel's miscarriages, Kara thought sympathetically. All those disappointments. How sad, for both Charles and Annabel.

"Doctor Scott is going to be furious when he gets here," Kara said ruefully. "He'll probably be sitting around half the night." She felt faintly embarrassed at discussing the intimacies of birth with Charles.

"We'll get him out here before this storm breaks loose," he said thoughtfully, then, frowning, he crossed to a window, gazed at the howling blackness outside. "You'd think this was September and hurricane weather, instead of March." He studied the storm for a moment, then turned away from the window. "The baby's arriving rather early, isn't he?" He kept his voice even, so as not to upset Kara.

"Anytime in the ninth month the baby's ready," Kara reassured him, "and I—I wasn't sure of dates." Color brushed her face. "I'm very close to the ninth month, if not already in it."

"I'll be right downstairs in the library," Charles said quietly. "If you want anything, send down Jasmine."

Kara lay back against the pillows, too keyed up to read. Grateful for Jasmine's gentle presence.

Charles had seemed suddenly anxious to be away from her. She wondered when *his* child was due? Already he was experiencing paternal anxieties, seeing her on the brink of delivery. This, Kara thought wryly, was a kind of dress rehearsal for Charles.

Downstairs, Charles sat down to a solitary dinner. In the stillness of the house, Celestine's voice and Charles's carried upstairs to her partially opened door. Kara felt a sudden pain. Then another awhile later. The contractions were beginning. Twenty minutes apart so far. Startling her with their intensity. Perhaps Dr. Scott would not be sitting around so long as she feared!

"Jasmine, do you suppose I could have some tea?" Kara asked, more out of restlessness than a need for nourishment. It seemed so futile, to be lying here in bed, doing nothing to speed arrival.

"Nothin'," Jasmine said with astonishing firmness. "Ah talk to Mama Belle, her say nothin'."

Kara stared uneasily at Jasmine.

"How's the storm, Jasmine?" Kara listened to the wind roaring through the trees, heard shutters banging ominously against the side walls until Charles called out to someone downstairs to fasten them. "Is it bad?"

"Is bad," Jasmine conceded somberly. "Gittin' wurse. Ah hear dat magnolia neah de house crack off two branches."

"Do you suppose Jupe can make it back with Doctor Scott?"

Kara clenched her hands, a little afraid of the prospect of the baby's arriving without Dr. Scott's consoling presence. In these months, she had come to depend completely on his being here.

A sudden contraction, minutes earlier than she'd anticipated, starting a new time cycle, wracked her body, the hard knot in her belly bringing forth a line of sweat across her forehead.

"Dat one bad," Jasmine said sympathetically, reaching for her hand.

"Yes," Kara admitted, her voice shaky. "That one was

bad." She leaned back, exhausted from the effort of choking back a cry. Steeling herself for the next one. She glanced intently at the clock. "If the roads are passable, Doctor Scott ought to be here in another hour or so." She tried to sound matter-of-fact.

"Ah tell Celestine sen' one dem lazy boys git Mama Belle," Jasmine decided, her eyes opaque.

"Jasmine, not yet!"

"Dis rain bad, ah bring Mama Belle up while she kin git here," Jasmine said simply. Mama Belle was arthritic, in her seventies. A quarter-mile walk was an effort. "Yo' rest, Li'l Missy."

Jasmine went out into the corridor, leaned over the banister, called out shrilly: "Celestine! Celestine!"

"Jasmine, what is it?" Charles called back quickly, his voice coated with anxiety.

"Ah tink dem boys bes' bring Mama Belle up to duh house," Jasmine said, and further explanation was unnecessary. "Storm bad, bes' her be here."

"All right, Jasmine," Charles said. "I'll send for Mama Belle." Celestine was already beside him, asking questions in her high-pitched voice.

Charles shouted orders downstairs. He wanted a small cart taken down to the quarters to bring up Mama Belle immediately. Then he stalked up the staircase, to her room. Jasmine had the door semiclosed. Charles knocked.

"Come in," Kara said.

She forced a smile seeing Charles's worried face.

"Things may be happening a little faster than we thought," Kara said, with a lightness she didn't feel.

"Marse Charles, yo' stay," Jasmine said, bulwarked by the importance of the occasion. "Ah go fetch cloths."

"Jasmine's afraid Doctor Scott won't get through in this

storm," Kara said, striving to sound natural, though the hardening of her belly told her the next pain was imminent. They were coming much faster now.

She clenched her teeth, closed her eyes, caught up in the agony of the thrust within her. Never suspecting it would be this bad! All the times she'd watched, never knowing it would be like this.

"Kara!" Charles, his voice sick with anguish, sat down beside her, caught her hands in his, gripped them tightly.

"I'm sorry," she gasped, when the pain subsided. "You'd better go downstairs."

"No," Charles said, his face white beneath his perennial tan. "I'll stay with you. The baby won't come for a while yet." But he looked uneasy.

"Not for a while," she told him. "Will Mama Belle be able to make it up here in this weather?"

"She'll make it," Charles said quietly, "if I have to go down there and carry her up myself. I told the boys to take the cart," he added with a faint smile, "so there should be little difficulty. But why in hell did Tim have to go to New Orleans today?"

"To buy paints." Kara tried to seem amused. "Besides, what could Tim do?" Bitterness touched her. *She was glad Tim was in New Orleans.* Glad Emilie and Annabel were out of the house.

Jasmine returned with a pile of clean white cloths, prepared for the birth; but still, Charles remained beside Kara. His eyes reflected his uneasiness each time she battled with the pain. Kara lost track of time. All that mattered now was to cope with the avalanches of pain that were overtaking her with relentless regularity.

Jasmine moved in and out of the room, preparing for the ultimate moment. Her face was etched with concern when she walked in to set the small cradle beside the bed. Outside the storm was raging with near-hurricane force. Kara flinched as they heard a tree go down, close by. Dr. Scott would never make it in this. If he had even left New Orleans, which would have been foolhardy, he'd be forced to take refuge in a nearby plantation.

A pain bore her down, with searing force.

"Oh, the baby, no!" she cried out. "No!" They were coming so quickly, one on top of another.

"Jasmine, go see if Mama Belle is coming!" Charles said tensely, half rising to his feet.

"Is time yet, Marse Charles," Jasmine murmured, but her eyes were worried. "No baby born dis quick."

"Charles, I shouldn't be putting you through this," Kara whispered, while he stroked the spill of hair across the pillow.

"Next time will be easier," Charles consoled.

"No! No next time!" The words were wrenched from her.

"Kara, every woman says that at a time like this," Charles chided gently.

"No more children with Tim," she gasped, blunt with pain. "You're his brother. Don't you know? Tim wants nothing of a wife. He'd rather go to Jupe!"

Charles whitened. His eyes were shocked.

"Kara, you're sure?" His voice was strangled with disbelief.

"Charles, I saw him." She shut her eyes with distaste, "With Jupe." Her voice sank to a whisper. "Months ago."

Charles was silent, battling to accept what she had just told him. Remembering small incidents, the little signs he'd disregarded.

"That's why Mama sent him up to New York," Charles said quietly. "Hoping he'd marry."

"She ordered him to marry," Kara said intensely. "He

didn't dare come home without a wife."

"Tim never wanted to come home from Paris, but Mama insisted. She can be a very stubborn woman." Charles sighed. "Mama was responsible for bringing me back from Princeton at the end of my second year, though she tried to push this off on Papa. Most times I've been strong enough to fight back at Mama, but Tim never learned how, even as a child. I guess he turned that way in a kind of revenge." He gestured helplessly. "I didn't know, Kara. I swear, I didn't know."

"I was pregnant. There was nothing to do but live a lie. I think Tim was glad when I found out; there was no need to pretend anymore." Her knuckles were white as she clenched her hands into two small fists, "It was too late to go home."

"This is your home," Charles said tightly. "Your child is a Rankin. Perhaps the only Rankin to carry on the line." His eyes were dark. *His* child could never bear the Rankin name. "Kara, if you ever need help, come to me. I'll help. I promise."

Suddenly Kara shut her eyes tight, groped for Charles's hands. The wrenching within her washing out everything except this tidal wave of pain.

The door swung wide. Jasmine hovered beside the small, aged black woman, her spare hair a snow-white cap, her eyes squinting with fading vision. But her hands were magic. The stories about Mama Belle's prowess were many in the quarters.

"Marse, yo' go," Mama ordered, instantly taking charge. Placing a hand on Kara's belly and nodding sagely. "Dis heah chile—him in one big hurry."

Kara lay with eyes shut, conscious only of the need to rid her body of this child. Mama Belle's hands moving competently about her. Mama Belle urging her to bear down.

"Him big baby," Mama soothed. "Him try to come."

A big baby, and she was small through the hips, Kara realized groggily, lapsing into a minute of merciful semi-consciousness between each pain.

"Yo' help, Li'l Missy," Mama urged. "Yo' help. Beah down hard wit de nex' one, git this baby wheah him belong."

Kara cried out in her anguish. Her cries echoing through the house. And Charles grit his teeth each time he heard her.

"De haid!" Jasmine murmured with exhilaration. "Mama, him come!"

"Soon, Li'l Missy," Mama crooned. "Now yo' help, right now!" Kara, her hair damp with perspiration, concentrated on thrusting with the pain. "Oh, him broad shoulders," Mama clucked. "Jasmine, look. Come on, Li'l Missy, yo' push him out!"

With a gush of pain that enveloped her whole consciousness, Kara strove to expel the baby. She heard the first querulous whimper, collapsed into a semisleep of exhaustion.

"Her," Jasmine said with astonishment. "De baby a her!"

Kara awakened to the sound of the rain lashing against the house, but the wind had subsided. Close by, Jasmine crooned a Haitian lullaby. Kara forced her eyes wide, felt a rush of happiness as her eyes fell on the baby in Jasmine's arms.

"Let me see, Jasmine." Kara's voice still tired yet joyous. Her child was a girl rather than the boy she'd expected. "Is she all right?" A sudden rush of anxiety in her voice.

"Marse Charles, him say her puhfect," Jasmine said smugly, as she gently handed the baby to Kara. "Her one big girl."

Kara closely inspected the tiny bundle in the crook of her arm, red-faced, minute hands flailing the air even while she slept. Fingers and toes as they should be, Kara checked, remembering her mother's old superstition. *Her Daughter.*

The tiny mouth opened. The baby wailed.

"Her hongry," Jasmine said smiling, reaching for the baby.

"I'll feed her, Jasmine," Kara said, flooded with affection.

Jasmine's eyes widened with shock.

"Li'l Missy feed huself? No, me bring dat Aphrodite to de kitchen. Her got plenty milk. White lady don' feed her baby," Jasmine clucked, her eyes tender.

"This one does," Kara said firmly.

Jasmine appeared troubled.

"No milk maybe two, three days," she wheedled. "Yo' let Aphrodite give dis li'l lady her supper. Her hongry."

"All right," Kara conceded, allowing Jasmine to scoop up the baby. "But just for two or three days." No one could deprive her of the right to feed her own child. This baby was hers. Nobody would tell her what to do with her daughter.

Kara started at the knock on the door.

"Come in."

The door opened. Tim walked inside. His face was tense, self-conscious, faintly guilty.

"Papa and I had to wait for the storm to break. Doctor Scott came to us at Antoine's, but it was impossible to get through for hours. Doctor Scott's downstairs having himself a drink; he'll be right up." His arms moved compulsively to the bundle Jasmine cradled in her arm.

"We don't need Doctor Scott," Kara said. "Jasmine, let Mister Tim see his daughter."

Tim stared absorbedly, with an air of complete disbelief, at the wailing, red-faced bundle. He forced a smile.

"She's beautiful, Kara. Like you."

Beaming, Jasmine sauntered out of the room, down the corridor to the stairs. Tim hovered uneasily before Kara.

"Kara, I'll make it up to you," he promised huskily, and she realized how deeply moved he was by his daughter.

"Whatever you want, Kara, I'll do." And the ring of determination in his voice convinced her of his sincerity.

"Tim, go into politics," she pleaded urgently. With Tim in politics, they would have to move into New Orleans. Somehow, after tonight, it would be difficult to remain in the same house with Charles, knowing he belonged to someone else. "Tim, for the three of us, go into politics!"

Chapter Sixteen

Charles walked out of Fred Dent's modest house, after a shot of bourbon with the overseer. With a sense of relief. Damn, why did he continue to feel a peculiar distaste for the man? Dent was doing a fine job, the first overseer that satisfied him among the half dozen he'd tried out during the past six years. Maybe he'd built this up in his mind because of a subconscious reluctance to turn over the major operation of the plantation to a stranger. For all his hawking about the work he put in, it was the most important thing in his life. Until Odette came along.

He walked with a sensuous pleasure in his surroundings, the glorious signs of spring everywhere. Red and white oleanders blazing on all sides. Pink, white, and lavender crepe myrtles gently glowing. Cape jasmine, the waxen blossoms of the magnolia, red roses and snow-white lilies, yellowish pink mimosa, and the heavily sweet honeysuckle vines.

Approaching Manoir with his wide, compulsively fast strides, he heard Annabel at the piano, experimenting on the keyboard as she sought the proper notes for a children's song. He frowned slightly. Mama was being too coy, the way she insisted on a birthday cake for the baby tonight. Sheelagh was one month old.

Charles's face softened as he thought about the baby. Kara's milk-white skin and auburn hair, her expressive mouth. Tim's eyes, Tim's nose. Papa jokingly said the baby looked like him, Charles recalled with a flicker of humor, and everybody outside the family had always found a strong resemblance between Tim and him. Physical only, he told himself wryly, remembering Kara's startling confidence. Sometimes he was sure she was embarrassed about telling him, but the moment had demanded it. He felt an alarm rising within him when he remembered Kara's travail. Would it be that difficult for Odette? He could feel himself breaking out in a cold sweat.

God, what a difference that baby had brought into the house! Papa would sit by the hour, watching her. Mama fussed, with great ostentation, Charles thought drily, but for Mama this was a dramatic, new role, the fond grandmother. Somehow he distrusted the depth of her affection, and this distrust made him uncomfortable. It was as though his mother had been suddenly exposed to him in the cold, harsh light of truth, for the first time.

Annabel had softened strangely. It was astonishing to see, and Charles completely believed this, the rich affection that Annabel harbored for the baby, even in this short span of time. Of course, Annabel wasn't happy. How could she be, with no marriage between them? But she'd brought this about! Not just the bed business, nothing existed to hold them together anymore. They might be two strangers sharing a house. But damn it, he wished she wouldn't feel so subservient to Mama, as though she must always agree with everything Mama said.

Charles crossed the gallery and walked into the foyer. Climbing the stairs to his room, he heard Mama in Kara's room, talking in that nervous, high-pitched voice of hers. Before the baby came, she had never set foot in Kara's room.

"Kara, I'm older than you and I've raised two children," Mama was declaiming in her injured manner. "This weather is treacherous. Sheelagh should have another blanket on her."

"I don't think so," Kara said politely, yet Charles sensed a tenseness in her. "She's such a warm baby."

And Mama would keep on arguing, and then tear out of the room with rage in her eyes, Charles guessed as he strode down the hall to his own room. These minor crises between Kara and Mama—Kara was polite but determined to stick to her ground—were gnawing away at everybody's nerves. He'd had his own run-ins with Mama through the years, but never with the frequency that Kara was encountering.

In his room Charles washed up, changed for dinner. He planned to ride down to New Orleans tonight, to be with Odette. How beautiful she was, pregnant, her belly so far out with the baby. The last time he'd been anxious, fearful they'd harm the baby, but Odette had calmly told him it would be all right with them, almost to the last.

How he wished he could tell Papa about this other child! With luck, a son. Papa knew about Odette; he had to know about the money arrangements. He never asked questions. But it would be wrong to talk about the child here, under the same roof with Annabel.

Annabel had changed so much after that first year of their marriage. After the first miscarriage. Before, she had at least been warm, affectionate, though never really responding in bed. But after the miscarriage, she'd become so passive. Enduring. Damn, it had been rotten that way. They wore out their marriage in the first year.

Annabel's parents had been so puritanical, so heavy on the religious side. Once, only once, had she said something that it was a punishment because she had been wicked. She had been lustful. She had wanted to lie with her husband, when the sole purpose of coupling was to produce children. Well,

Charles told himself drily, she had successfully killed off those "lustful" feelings, she had become a stick of wood, a receptacle for his steadily diminishing passion. When she'd turned him away, completely, after the last miscarriage, he had not been unduly disturbed.

It was possible she was suspicious about his trips into New Orleans. All right, it would be abnormal if she were not suspicious. But damn it, he couldn't spend the rest of his life like a man in priesthood. He was only twenty-eight.

By the time Charles came downstairs, his mother was in the library with Annabel and his father, complaining again about her imagined palpitations, the emphasis being that Kara was responsible. She talked on in her querulous, faintly strident voice, with Annabel attentive, and his father obviously more concerned about reading his newspaper. Upstairs, the baby cried lustily.

"Chess tonight?" His father gazed up to ask with interest.

"I'm going down to New Orleans," Charles explained guiltily and was instantly conscious of Annabel's lowered eyes and his mother's sharp glance of annoyance. Damn, did the whole family have to sit in judgment?

"I'll play with Kara." Amory said, smiling smugly. "Another six months and she'll be beating the hide off me."

"Why is the baby crying?" Emilie demanded impatiently. "I do think Kara is terribly headstrong in handling that child. Nobody can tell her anything. Tim ought to talk to her. After all, Tim is the father," Emilie smiled vindictively. But Mama knew about Tim, Charles thought unhappily. She'd known a long time.

Celestine pattered into the room to announce dinner. Emilie ordered her to run upstairs and inform Kara.

"And tell Miss Kara to give the baby some sugar water,"

Emilie called imperiously after Celestine. "Poor little thing, she's probably hungry."

They moved from the library into the dining room. Kara appeared just as Daphne was bringing in the ox-joint soup. Jasmine had been assigned to full-time nursemaid duty, with Daphne shifted to help with the serving.

"I'm sorry to be late," Kara apologized, faintly breathless. "I didn't want to come down until the baby was settled."

"Did Celestine tell you about the sugar water?" Emilie demanded. Kara stiffened.

"Where's Tim?" Charles broke in stiffly, and saw Kara relax a bit. These encounters between Emilie and Kara were reaching a discomforting stage. "Did anyone call him for dinner?"

"Tim went down to New Orleans," Emilie said, as though Kara would hardly be aware of this. Tim had been going to New Orleans for the races all winter long, Charles recalled. Usually, he had Jupe drive him in. Sometimes he took along that effete French tutor, Simone. "For the races," his mother confirmed. "He'll probably stay in town for the evening, at his club," Emilie smiled tightly. It was a coup in her mind, for someone not a resident of New Orleans itself to be elected to membership in Tim's club. She was prone to lay such social victory to her own family connections and money.

"Tim brought home an interesting book on flood control," Kara contributed, glad to have the conversation diverted to innocuous channels. "It's by a Mr. Charles Ellet, Jr., and it talks about the need for reservoirs to help in flood control. He claims the twelve hundred miles of levees just isn't enough."

"More than that, I'm concerned about our doing something to clear the swamps between the city and Lake Pontchartrain," Amory said briskly. "All that evil-smelling slush, the stagnant water, with that cypress grown so dense the pollen yellows the rain. Every spring I'm uneasy about an epidemic, the way the drainage can find no runoff. And what affects New Orleans affects us," Amory added firmly.

"Amory, you've been howling every spring for the last twenty years about yellow-fever epidemics," Emilie reproached, her face grimacing. "They're not going to let anything like that happen again."

"Are you forgetting 1833?" Amory taunted. "And several subsequent summers? We were lucky out here at Manoir, it didn't touch us. But remember the thousands of people who died? So fast they couldn't be buried!"

"Amory, you're not to talk that way at the dinner table!" Emilie snapped indignantly.

"If Tim is serious about becoming involved in politics, in running for assistant alderman next election, he ought to concentrate on the need to clean up the swamps. I was talking with Lumsden over at the *Picayune*, he tells me they're going to get behind it. Tim would do well to coast along with that."

Charles listened attentively. What was this business about Tim running as assistant alderman? Odd, considering Tim's attitude toward politics in general. Or was Tim seeking a cover for his spending so much time in New Orleans? Involuntarily, Charles's eyes swung to Kara. Her color was high, her eyes bright. She was listening closely while Amory and Emilie Rankin discussed Tim's potential as an alderman. Kara was pleased, Charles realized with astonishment.

While Daphne slid plates of baked red snapper with brown oyster sauce before them, Emilie pointedly moved away from the discussion of Tim's future. Still a bit ambivalent about this, Charles surmised.

"Amory, you're always talking to those newspapermen," Emilie prodded. "Whatever happened to that business about removing Bible reading from the schools? Which is," she said emphatically, "the most awful thing that could happen, in these days when folks are just so bad."

"The protests have died down," Amory reported drily. "Not that they were taken seriously. But the Bible is safe in the New Orleans public school system. More important is how they're using that million dollars John McDonogh willed to the school system three years ago."

"I don't hold for all that public education," Emilie said disdainfully. "Not every mind is equipped for learning. Sooner folks realize that, the better. I don't hold with all this education for young ladies; I don't think it's genteel."

Charles frowned. That was a stab at Kara, who sopped up learning like a hungry hound dog over a bowl of gravy-rich grits.

"Kara, I do declare your waistline is as small as ever," Annabel said in a burst of warmth, as though embarrassed by Emilie's snide insinuation. Charles was aware of a reluctant urge on Annabel's part to befriend Kara. But his mother wasn't likely to allow that.

"My waistline snapped right back," Emilie picked up smugly, "right after both Charles and Tim. It was never over seventeen inches until my nerves began to go, and Doctor Scott put me on so much medication. Oh, I was always getting compliments on my waist and my feet."

Charles lapsed into an introspective silence, broken by occasional comments to his father. Kara, eyes flooded with tenderness, listened at regular intervals for sounds of the baby. His mother and Annabel were engaged in their usual inane prattle. God, he wished dinner were over! That he was down in New Orleans in that small perfect room with Odette. Odette figured the baby would come sometime in July. Right now, it seemed as though July would never arrive.

* * * * *

April, with its balmy days and cool evenings, moved into May. The imminence of the hot weather was prodding city people into preparing for the summer exodus from New Orleans. Those who could afford this luxury. The thermometer moved uncomfortably high as the days rolled by, but the rains were slow in arriving. In the city even the cobblestone streets were thick with dust, with carriages and wagons digging ruts between the stones. Odette rarely left the small white house on Ramparts Street.

Tim, to Charles's astonishment, had leaped into the fight for better sanitary conditions in New Orleans. He seemed to be enjoying the attention he was receiving. God knows, he made a handsome, eloquent figure, Charles conceded. And people were always drawn to Tim. Perhaps that ingratiating charm would be of some practical value, after all. As Papa had been saying for years, New Orleans was just one step away from disaster, considering its lack of proper sanitation facilities. It would be interesting to watch Tim's progress in this fight.

Driving into New Orleans late in the month, Charles was considering renting a small house for Odette by the lake, for the summer. He was uneasy, the way a couple of doctors were talking about the fever. Of course, all those rumors about a sailor being brought into Charity Hospital with the fever had been vigorously denied. The city council reproached the local "alarmists," though the group with whom Tim worked announced plans for coping with yellow fever. This was nothing more than a smart political move, people were saying scathingly.

Every New Orleanian firmly believed that the fever attacked only those who were not yet acclimated. Still it was foolhardy not to take precautions. He would persuade Odette to leave her beloved New Orleans for the hot months. There was no financial problem involved.

When the carriage approached the outskirts of the city, they were deluged by rain. The dust-thick roads seeming to drink with a year-long thirst at first. The rain was falling far heavier than usual, seeming as though it would pour down from the black skies for the rest of the night. The savage onslaught washing piles of garbage to the banquettes. Water beginning, already, to fill up the gulleys and gutters.

The swamps would be a mess, Charles thought uneasily. With the city lying lower than the levees, with its lack of underground drainage, New Orleans would be facing a sea of stagnant water within forty-eight hours. The rotten little mosquitos were everywhere already, and they would breed without bounds with the water standing everywhere, growing its stinking green scum. Conditions like this brought the fever; more and more doctors were becoming convinced of this.

At the small white house Odette received him with her usual warmth.

"You look tired," he said anxiously, gazing at the small, exquisite face. Blue eyes darkly circled. Her shoulders seeming to droop from the effort of carrying the extra weight of the child. "You must rest, Odette."

"I am, my love," she said quickly. "Please, do not worry for me." Her smile was dazzling. "I will give you a magnificent son." She knew how much he wanted a son.

They ate one of their perfect suppers, and then the girl was dismissed, with orders at Charles's stern injunction, to return by midnight.

"I don't want you to be alone," he said firmly. "And tonight I won't stay over." He smiled gently at the consternation in her eyes. "I don't trust myself to stay over," he explained with infinite tenderness. "From this point on, we must consider the child."

Odette thought for a moment, then smiled with deep happiness.

"Charles, you are so good to me," she whispered softly. "And always so right. But I will make you happy," she promised, "without disturbing the child. There are ways," she added shyly, and when their eyes met, Charles felt desire already rising in him. These girls were reared by mothers wise in the ways of the world. Odette would know how to bring him to the ultimate point of satisfaction, even with her belly so swollen with pregnancy that he dared not enter.

They lay together across the wide, soft bed, with the candlelight casting delicate shadows across her lovely face, and even her misshapen body was beautiful to him. How fortunate he was, to have found Odette, after the fallow years.

Tomorrow, he must ask around about a small house near the lake. Tim seemed so certain that the cases of fever were being hidden, that this summer showed signs of being a bad one. He must get Odette away.

"Charles, this is good for you?" she inquired anxiously.

"Yes," he said, his voice deepening. "Yes!"

Charles was jubilant when he found a vacant cottage right away, even this late in the season. He brought over a group of slaves to fix the interior. By the end of the week, he told himself with satisfaction, he would be able to bring Odette out here. Away from the stagnant waters that permeated New Orleans. Mosquitos here, yes, but not like in the city. The nights would be cool. They would sit on the gallery and watch the moon over the water. Dr. Scott, too, agreed it would be better for Odette. When her time came, Dr. Scott would drive out to the lake.

The slaves had started painting the house this morning, Charles thought happily, as he sat down to dinner with the family. Celestine appeared to tell him nervously that there was a man at the back who said he must speak to him immediately.

Charles excused himself and strode from the room, catching up with the scurrying Celestine, who seemed to fear that Emile Rankin's obvious annoyance at this intrusion might be vented on her.

"Celestine, who is it?" Charles demanded anxiously.

"Dat boy who come from Doctuh Scott's," Celestine said, her eyes fearful. The house slaves knew Dr. Scott's boy, from the frequent trips when he brought out "nerve medicine" for Emilie. "Him won't wait till yo' finish eatin'."

"That's all right, Celestine." Dr. Scott. Odette didn't expect the baby for another six or seven weeks!

Charles dashed ahead, out to where the earnest-faced young black boy waited for him.

"Doctuh Scott say bes' yo' come into New Awleans," he said gravely. "He say tell yo' de baby, him comin'." He took a deep breath. "Me no bring de carriage," he apologized. "Doctuh Scott, him say faster on de horse."

"I'll saddle up and go right into town. You go into the kitchen and tell Octavia I said to give you something to eat. All right, boy?"

"Yessuh!" He flashed a brilliant smile.

Charles rode the fastest stallion in the stables into the city, anxiety tugging at him every inch of the road. It was natural for Dr. Scott to send for him; he'd insisted he wanted to be with Odette when she delivered. Yet something of the urgency in Scott's boy transmitted itself to him.

Charles's heart was pounding as he approached the house on Ramparts Street. Through the lighted windows he saw the handsome wall hangings, the polished candlesticks of which Odette was so fond, the girandoles. The bedroom windows were discreetly masked.

Charles tied up the stallion, crossed to the door, and entered without bothering to knock. Odette's maid was hurrying into the bedroom with a water-soaked towel. She nodded nervously to Charles and moved to the bedroom door, opened it, walked inside.

"Charles!" Dr. Scott's voice called to him. "You may come in if you like."

His throat tight, Charles strode into the bedroom. Odette lay back against a mound of pillows. The face over-high with color, the honey hair dark with perspiration across the high forehead.

"Charles," Odette whispered. "Oh, Charles, I hoped you'd come." He rushed to sit beside her. Sick within because he saw the pain in her eyes and remembered the time with Kara. And now it was Odette's time.

"Will it be soon?" with Odette's hands in his, he turned to Dr. Scott. "How much longer?" The glint of concern in Scott's eyes alarmed him.

"Soon, we hope," Scott said, just as Odette suddenly writhed in anguish, and the mulatto darted forward to touch her face with the wet cloth. "She's so small. The baby's quite large, even though he's a few weeks early."

Odette suddenly screamed aloud, thrashing about the bed. Charles moved swiftly to restrain her.

"It's been this way for hours," Scott said heavily. "Perhaps you'd better wait outside." He leaned over Odette, placed a hand over her belly as she braced herself for the next pain.

"No!" Charles thundered. "This is my child, my—" He stopped himself from saying "my wife," but Dr. Scott understood. "I'll stay with her till the baby is here."

Himself drenched in perspiration, Charles pulled off his jacket, sat at the edge of the bed while Odette battled the pains. At Dr. Scott's orders, he held her down lest she fall off the bed. Sickened with helplessness, he saw the bruises on her arms. Dr. Scott was visibly upset, the maid terrified.

"The baby's coming the wrong way," Dr. Scott announced, his face pale. "If I can turn him, it would be easier for her." Frowning with determination, he tried to manipulate.

"No!" A fierce cry escaped Odette. "Nothing to hurt him, you hear? Let him come the way he wishes!"

"It's useless trying to turn him," Scott admitted, striving despite Odette's exhortations.

"Doctor Scott, can't you do something for her?" Charles trembled as Odette screamed again and again, and the slender body thrust about the bed in anguish.

"It's coming," Dr. Scott said tersely. "A foot, Charles—" One tiny foot lay, toes curled upward, in Dr. Scott's hand.

Another scream wrenched itself from Odette, to be followed by the second foot. Charles was terrified by her paleness.

"Doctor Scott," Charles said hotly, "do something for her!"

"Charles, it is in God's hands," Scott said tiredly, intent on taking the baby. "Let me do what I can for the child."

"Odette." He leaned anxiously over her because suddenly she seemed without will, without pain.

And then a cataclysmic convulsion of her body, and a thin, small wail echoed through the room.

"Your son, Charles," Scott said exhaustedly.

But Charles hardly heard him. His eyes were fastened to Odette's colorless face.

"Doctor Scott!" he cried out in alarm. "Dr. Scott—"

"I'm sorry, Charles," Scott said quietly. "She's gone."

Chapter Seventeen

Kara awakened to the pleasurable scent of the outdoor flowers, their perfume enhanced by the downpour of the night. Outside the grass was still wet, even though the sun had been up for hours. Kara slept later than usual these days. She was nursing the baby, in spite of Emilie's undisguised horror.

Kara shifted slightly, to rest on her side; she opened her eyes, gazed upon the sleeping Sheelagh, in her netting-swathed cradle beside the bed. How beautiful she was!

It was astonishing how devoted Tim was to Sheelagh. It was a small miracle, to him, that he'd shared in her creation. But he still continued to live that other, secret life of his. She knew. Mrs. Rankin knew. It was discomforting for her, sometimes, to study with Jean Simone and know he was so enamored of Tim.

"I thought I heard the baby," Annabel said with an unsure smile, when Jasmine opened the door. "Is she awake?"

"She's stirring," Kara whispered. "Come on in, Annabel." She was glad that Annabel had opened up this way.

Jasmine waited till Kara drained her teacup, then took the tray and left the room. At a nod from Kara, Annabel removed the mosquito netting, scooped up Sheelagh, who'd begun to cry lustily, and brought her to Kara. This was becoming almost a morning ritual with Annabel.

"Oh, my, she's a hungry one this morning," Annabel murmured, carefully cradling the small head.

"She won't be in a few minutes," Kara laughed. "But what an appetite!" Mrs. Rankin still complained that there was something coarse about a white lady suckling her child, when there were a half-dozen women slaves with plenty of milk.

Kara guided the eager, small mouth to her full, blue-veined breast, winced as that mouth tightened on the nursing-tender nipple. In moments like this, she could forget the lie she lived. Moments like this made up for the emptiness of the nights. The emptiness of a life without a husband.

"Kara, how does it feel?" Annabel's eyes were fastened wistfully on the baby. Her voice painfully self-conscious. "To nurse a child—"

"The world stands still," Kara said simply. "I feel fully a woman." And then added quickly, realizing Annabel would never nurse a baby. "She tugs this way, and I have this odd feeling down here." She touched her belly briefly, eager to make Annabel understand. "Like a tiny contraction. Not painful. Just a tiny drawing in, that reminds me each time of the miracle of birth."

She'd believed, that night, that she would never forget the pain. But a woman forgets. Not that she would ever have another child, Kara thought with a sense of loss, which made Sheelagh all the more dear. Tim would never come to her that way again. Color tinged her cheeks because it wasn't Tim she wanted anymore. The man she wanted was Annabel's husband. And that, too, could never be.

Kara and Annabel sat together in companionable silence, broken only by Sheelagh's small grunts as she nuzzled. Half an hour later, with the baby in Jasmine's care and Annabel having coffee with Emilie, Kara made her way out of the house and headed for the quarters. She stopped to admire the exceptionally lush velvet-red roses, of which Horatio was so proud. Looked up and saw Charles riding toward the stables. She lifted a hand to wave. The hand froze. Her throat tightened. Charles had not even seen her. When they'd been no more than a dozen feet apart. He seemed so distraught, in a hurry to go somewhere.

For the rest of the morning, while she made a game with the children of mopping up the leaky, wet cabins, she remembered the way Charles had looked. She'd seen faces like that during the famine. With death on every side, and nothing one could do to halt it.

Kara left the quarters, the children trailing behind her gleefully to the very edge. Tim had gone to New Orleans for a meeting with that committee of his. Excitement welled up in her as she considered Tim's activities. He was truly involved in this cleanup campaign down in the city. He had a gift for making himself believe completely in a cause, and talked with an enthusiasm that aroused others. But she also knew his growing involvement in local politics was part of the tacit agreement between them. "Anything you want, Kara, just tell me."

If Tim were elected assistant alderman, they'd have to move to New Orleans. Already, Mrs. Rankin was beginning to be impressed with the possibilities. No pushing for the house though. The right moment would come, and Mrs. Rankin would make the offer herself. It must come from *her,* must appear her own idea. Mr. and Mrs. Timothy Rankin, in their winter home in New Orleans! And yet, Kara felt a startling consternation. Not to see Charles every day. She would miss him, she knew that. But perhaps it might be better being away from him.

Kara walked into the house, up the long, curving stairway to her own room. Jasmine smiled from the pile of laundry she was folding. Sheelagh was awake, just beginning to utter small complaints.

"All right, you greedy little girl," Kara chided affectionately as she lifted the baby from the cradle, and laughed at the already groping mouth.

She seated herself by the window, hoping for a breath of fresh air, brought the baby to her breast. Holding Sheelagh close, knowing her own richness. When the baby had drunk to her satisfaction, Jasmine took charge of her again. Kara hurried downstairs, hearing sounds in the dining room. Mrs. Rankin was always annoyed when Kara was late for a meal, even though it was Sheelagh she was feeding. Mrs. Rankin could never completely forget that her granddaughter was half poor-Irish. Sometimes, Kara suspected, her mother-in-law resented the attention Sheelagh attracted among the family. As though this lessened her own position in the house.

As she walked with her quick, small steps down the corridor to the dining room, Kara heard Charles's and Amory's voices in the library. The door wide because of the oppressive midday heat.

"Charles, you can't take care of these details," Amory was saying with an urgency that slowed Kara's steps. "I will have them arranged."

"No, Papa," Charles said, his voice oddly empty. "I'll drive down to Florville Foy this afternoon. I must choose the tomb myself."

Kara stopped.

"I'll go with you to the cemetery," Amory offered gently.

"No, Papa. Just her mother and I. If you went, Mama would be terribly upset."

"Charles, she doesn't have to know," Amory said impatiently.

"Somehow, she'd find out. No, Papa."

The girl had died, and Charles didn't wish her memory sullied by a battle with his mother.

"The child, Charles?" Amory sounded suddenly exhausted.

"He's fine. Six weeks early but big. He—he's the image of you, Papa."

Tears blinding her, Kara retraced her steps. Unable to walk into the dining room and face her mother-in-law. That girl had died, giving Charles his son. The son that must forever be publicly denied, because that was the way these things were done in Louisiana. The son that was the image of his handsome grandfather. But the blood strain was tainted. His mother was a quadroon.

Kara watched Charles with silent anguish. Knowing his pain. Wishing, wistfully, that she might say the words that would ease his grief. He spent long hours in the fields as usual, glad now, for that outlet. Nightly, he rode into New Orleans. To be with his son.

Occasionally, Annabel looked upon Charles with concern, without realizing the cause of his unhappiness. Believing, perhaps, that he was fretful about not being able to carry out his ideas about moving into cane, as Amory and he constantly discussed. Mrs. Rankin didn't believe in investing her money in Manoir, though Amory agreed with Charles that this could be advantageous. She made it abundantly clear that her own money remained in securities and real estate. Her mother-in-law enjoyed withholding money from Amory and Charles, Kara realized with distaste. Emilie Rankin enjoyed power.

June rolled along. Hot, wet, mosquito-ridden. Sheelagh was fretful from the heat, but thriving. Jasmine watched her constantly, to keep away the mosquitos, washing her down with cool cloths when the sun baked the house. Hardly a day passed without a heavy rainstorm. The weeds sprang up in wild abandon, despite the efforts of Horatio and his crew to cut them down. And everywhere, Kara thought with impatience, the pesky mosquitos. But that was part of the Louisiana summer. Only a little worse this year.

Night after night Kara lay awake, her insomnia only partially caused by the physical discomfort of the summer. Restless, she would leave her bed to sit by the window, hopeful of a breeze. Hearing the sounds in the night. Jasmine slipping quietly into Amory's room. Tim after some secret rendezvous. Jupe? Or someone else. Once she had spied him meeting Jean Simone.

She had been relieved when Mrs. Rankin insisted that the French tutoring cease for the summer. It upset her to be aware of the relationship developing between Tim and the tutor. The cautious hot looks, the whispers. She tried not to think about Tim with Jean, as he had been with Jupe.

Most nights, Charles would ride home in the wee hours of the morning. It became a ritual for Kara to wait there by the window until Charles was in the house.

Tim was spending much of his time in New Orleans, with his mother complaining that the weather was too uncomfortable for him to be traveling back and forth with such frequency. By the end of June, it seemed as though the summer had existed for many months already. His mother seemed hardly aware that Charles made even more frequent trips into New Orleans. But then, Charles was not her "darling Tim." Emilie Rankin had lost control over her older son long ago. But she would never let go of Tim.

"Amory, I wish you'd talk to Tim," Emilie said exasperatedly when they sat down to dinner one evening. Tim was not yet home. Ignoring Kara's presence—as though he didn't have a wife. "It's absurd for him to be wearing himself out in this heat!"

"Emilie, this is a matter between Tim and Kara," Amory reminded her, his voice edged with sharpness. "If Kara feels he's overdoing it, I'm sure she'll talk to him."

For an ugly instant Emilie's eyes clashed with Kara's. She knows we have no marriage, Kara thought, and she's glad! *She knows it's a sham marriage.* Kara felt suddenly giddy. Felt herself mercilessly exposed. Vulnerable. But Emilie couldn't say this aloud, to anyone. Not even to Amory. It was an ignominious secret they must share in silence. But Emilie Rankin felt a sick kind of triumph because her son did not go to his wife's bed.

Celestine and Daphne, faces glistening with perspiration, their thin calico dresses clinging to their bodies, moved in and out of the dining room with platters of food. Emilie always ordered these heavy hot meals. Strange, Kara suddenly realized, how she'd begun to think of her mother-in-law as Emilie instead of Mrs. Rankin since Sheelagh was born. As though the baby strengthened her position in this house.

"Charles, you're not eating," Annabel protested quietly, frowning at him. "I know it's hot, but you have to eat."

Annabel played these little games with herself. As though to pretend that her marriage still existed. Three women in this house, and not one with a man who truly belonged to her.

"There's Tim now," Emilie said with a small, pleased smile, then jingled the table bell. Daphne quickly appeared. "Daphne, bring in another pitcher of iced tea, please, with plenty of ice. Quickly now. Mister Tim will be thirsty from his trip."

Tim walked into the dining room with a smile of apology, took his place between his mother and Kara. He looked exhausted, uneasy.

"Tim, I won't have you wearing yourself out this way," Emilie shot a fleeting, furious glance at Kara, as though blaming her for being at the root of his activity in New Orleans. "No more running around this way until the weather settles a bit."

"I don't think any of us should be going down into New Orleans for a while," Tim stated somberly, and Charles stiffened to attention.

"Why not, Tim?" Amory asked carefully, his eyes questioning.

Tim took a deep breath.

"The yellow fever," he said unhappily. "They're trying to keep it quiet—it's terrible for business—but there's definite evidence of the fever. Along Lynch's Row, in the uptown Irish district, the French section. Isolated cases all around town." Tim stared at the tablecloth, aware of the stricken faces about him. "We're in for an epidemic, I'd swear to that."

Alarm whitened Emilie's face. "Tim, don't talk that way. You know the fever is fatal! But it won't affect us out here." Her breathing was heavy. "Amory, we'll close off the plantation to everybody, you hear? Charles, nobody comes in from the outside! From this minute till this awful thing is over!" Hysteria edged her voice.

"I've been afraid of this for years," Amory said gravely. "The way they've neglected the sanitary conditions down in the city. Every time Doctor Scott opens his mouth to utter a warning, they call him a calamity howler!"

"We'll all stay right here at Manoir, and nothing's going to happen all the way up here," Annabel said, with a warning glance about the table. "Mama, would you like me to send Daphne upstairs for your nerve medicine?"

"I think you should, Annabel," Emilie conceded, fanning herself frenziedly. "My heart's just pounding like crazy. Now I don't want to hear another word in this house about the fever. And we let it be known we won't be socializing for the summer. You never know who could be bringing in the fever!" Her eyes were overbright, her hands trembling.

After dinner Emilie retired to her room, with Annabel in solicitous attendance. Kara, unnerved by the imminence of an epidemic, joined Amory and Tim in the library. Charles quietly disappeared. The Tim who spoke to them tonight was one she'd never known.

Talking with a terrifying eloquence about what he'd discovered in the city.

"All you have to do is walk into New Orleans, look around you, and you know it's spoiling for pestilence. Water in puddles everywhere, ugly green with stagnation, perfect breeding places for the damned mosquitos. The city's slops thrown in there daily to make it worse, garbage, dead cats, dead dogs, everything foul!"

"Your committee's been fighting for weeks," Kara said earnestly. "Has nothing been accomplished?"

"Nothing," Tim said flatly. "We've made a lot of noise. We've had petitions signed. We're politicking, they claim," he pointed out bitterly.

"But they must realize you're right," Kara pointed out. "What with this happening." For the first time since that day she tried so hard to wash from her memory, Tim's eyes met hers directly. "You'll be the only candidate for alderman who foresaw the epidemic."

"Kara's right," Amory said drily. "You'll stand a much better chance for nomination and election."

Kara's face was hot as her mind swept to the fall election. This was the right road for Tim and her, and particularly for Sheelagh. Whatever Tim and she could build up together, it was for Sheelagh. The only child they would ever have.

Kara heard the ominous sound of thunder outside. Lightning flashed across the sky. More rain, to fill more puddles, provide more breeding grounds for mosquitos. Epidemics always came when the mosquitos were particularly bad, Amory had said.

As was customary in the summer, the thunderstorm subsided within the hour. By the time Kara had given Sheelagh her late-evening feeding, the oppressive heat, mitigated during the rain, had returned full strength. Not a breath of air stirred among the trees.

Kara sat by the window, fanning herself tiredly. Pushing away the mosquitos who insisted on invading the bedroom, their noisy clamor persistent, annoying. From time to time Kara glanced at the cradle, where Sheelagh slept unmolested beneath her netting. Everybody kept saying the mosquitos were not dangerous except Amory and a few physicians like Dr. Scott.

Kara sighed, trying to thrust aside a stirring alarm. Tim was so sure the politicians, the business people, the newspapermen, were hiding the truth about the presence of the fever in New Orleans. The death rate, Tim said, and Kara remembered the statistics he quoted, was rising alarmingly. That could only mean the fever.

Others in the house were also restless tonight. Kara could hear the nervous coughing of her mother-in-law down the hall. Amory had not yet come up to bed. As on most wretchedly hot nights, he remained down in the library, reading and drinking. Only a little while ago, she'd heard Octavia bringing ice to him.

Kara leaned forward intently as she heard a carriage coming up the roadway. Every sound magnified in the stillness of the night. Horatio pulled up before the house. A pause. The horses clomped back towards the stables. The downstairs door opened. Then a door opened upstairs.

"Amory, is that you?" Emilie called out petulantly.

"It's me, Mama." Charles, his voice strained. "I've just come back from New Orleans."

"Charles, how can you go down there?" His mother's voice soared perilously. She was in the hall now. "You were at the table when Tim told us! There's an epidemic!" Kara heard Emilie's heelless slippers padding to the head of the stairs. "Charles—" Shock, disbelief, ricocheted in her voice. "Charles, what are you holding?"

"My son," Charles said, his voice desperate. "I couldn't leave him in New Orleans. I had to bring him home."

An animal-like scream issued from Emilie. Kara rushed instinctively to the door, paused here, her hand frozen to the knob as she listened.

"Amory! Amory!" Emilie screamed hysterically. "You come here! I won't have my home desecrated this way! Amory, make him take his black bastard out of my house!"

"Mama, he's your grandchild! Your blood!" Charles' voice was hoarse with anguish.

"No! No!" Emilie screamed over and over again, while Kara clung to the door, sick within. "You take that black thing away!"

Annabel rushed from her room, crying out to her mother-in-law in alarm.

"Mama! Mama, what is it?" Annabel was trying to soothe her, with no inkling of the cause of Emilie's distress. "Mama, please."

Amory bolted up the stairs. Kara reached for her wrapper, pulled it snugly about her. She heard the stinging slap of Amory's hand across Emilie's face as he sought to break her hysteria. Emilie collapsed into uncontrollable crying. Amory and Annabel would be busy with her for hours now. Kara was well versed in her mother-in-law's lesser "attacks." She could easily envision the scope of this one. Emilie would cling to her bed for days.

Kara, with a sudden decision, pulled her door wide. Emilie was being half carried into her own room. Amory's face was chalk white, but not out of concern for his wife. She ran down the corridor, almost tripping in her hurry. Charles stood there, desolate, still, the tiny, wailing baby in his arms.

"Charles," she called out urgently as he turned away, head down, shoulders tense with defeat. "Charles, wait."

Charles lifted his eyes to meet hers. How exhausted he seemed!

"Kara, I had to bring him home. The nurse refused to stay in New Orleans; she left tonight for her people up the river. They're running, Kara, they're all running from the fever."

"Bring him into the library," Kara said softly. Pushing down her first instinct to take the baby from him. "Come along, Charles," she coaxed, but womanlike, leaning forward to inspect the tiny bundle. Remarkably like his grandfather, even at this age. One day he'd be startlingly handsome, with fair hair and skin no darker than Charles's.

"The wet-nurse didn't show up tonight," Charles explained, his eyes haunted. "He must be hungry." They went down the stairs, Charles still holding the baby.

"I'll bring Daphne from the kitchen wing," Kara said gently. "She's still nursing. Her child doesn't need the milk. Your son does."

Kara prodded Charles into a chair in the library, gently touched a tiny, flailing hand. Poor baby, so indignant. So hungry! Hunger, for Kara, held a special urgency. She hurried to the kitchen wing, the sounds of Emilie's wild sobbing relentlessly following her. She found Daphne asleep on a comforter in a pantry.

"Daphne . . ." She leaned forward, touching the woman's

shoulder. "Daphne." Daphne moved with a start, a sudden fear. Her eyes opened. "Daphne, I need you," Kara said quickly. "Please come with me."

"De li'l one?" Daphne asked uneasily, rising to her feet. Despite Daphne's coolness toward her, Daphne loved little Sheelagh. Her own baby was cared for in the quarters, brought to her for nursing. Actually, Daphne's child was old enough to be weaned. "Her sick?"

"No, Sheelagh's fine," Kara reassured her quickly, already moving back toward the main part of the house. She hesitated. "Mister Charles has brought a baby home," she said simply. "He's hungry. We want you to nurse him until Mister Charles can make other arrangements." Daphne would understand because slaves had to understand. With her devotion to Annabel, Daphne would loathe the baby, Kara thought unhappily. But the baby must be fed tonight. Charles was in no condition to go running down to the quarters in search of a wet-nurse.

Daphne followed Kara into the library. Kara nodded to her to sit in a chair far from the window, where the mosquitos were less likely to bother her. Obediently, she sat, waited. Kara crossed to Charles, gently took the baby from him. Daphne pulled a breast, rich with milk, from the neck of her calico dress, brought the baby to the nipple. Instantly, the thin wail quieted. The noisy sucking, the faint grunts of satisfaction echoed through the room.

"Po' li'l fella, him so hongry," Daphne crooned. "Yo' eat all yo' want, yo' heah?" She was oblivious of their presence now.

"I can't keep him here in the house," Charles said tightly. "I can't take him back to New Orleans to that pestilence. I gave up the lake cottage."

"Let me keep him with me tonight," Kara said. "If he

cries, your mother will think it's Sheelagh. In the morning, take him down to the quarters, to Mama Belle." Suddenly, she wanted so much to keep Charles's son in her bed tonight, to cradle him in her arms. "You can build a cabin close by, Charles; in one day, you can have a crew put up the frame of the cabin," she rushed on, seeing the idea take root in his mind. "I'll bring down netting. You must close off all the windows, the door, to keep away the mosquitos. He'll be all right there, Charles."

"I didn't think, when I brought him home, what it would mean to Mama," Charles said heavily. "I didn't think about Annabel." His eyes darkened with pain. "I thought only about Christopher."

"That's the way it must be," Kara said passionately. "You think first, always, of your child!"

"I'll keep him in the cabin, the way you say, Kara." Charles nodded determinedly, his voice a whisper though they knew Daphne heard nothing. "I work hard with Dent, train him in every angle of managing the plantation." Kara's eyes widened in prescient alarm. "And if Dent seems capable of running Manoir by the end of three months, I'll take Christopher and move on. To Texas or California."

Chapter Eighteen

A ribbon of early morning sunlight filtered in through the drapes. Kara awoke with a start, a sense of hurtling through space, remembering last night's happenings. She turned on her side, an arm moving out to encircle Christopher. But he wasn't there!

She sat up, alarmed, while her eyes searched the room. There he was, cradled in Daphne's arms while he noisily nursed. Daphne seated in the Boston rocker which Amory had ordered for Kara when Sheelagh was a few days old.

"Him de hongriest li'l fella ah ever did see," Daphne said with satisfaction. "Ah figuh it time he eat."

The two women exchanged contented smiles, then Kara leaned over to inspect her small daughter. Sheelagh would sleep at least another hour, she thought with the familiar rush of tenderness at this first morning sight of the little one.

It must be hardly five o'clock, Kara guessed from the position of the sun in the sky. At least there was some relief from the heat this early. She rose from the bed, dressing with compulsive haste while Christopher grunted his pleasure. She could hear Annabel talking soothingly to Emilie down the hall. Poor Annabel, she must have spent all night at Emilie's bedside.

The baby relinquished the nipple, lay back, smiling. Daphne turned inquiringly to Kara.

"Put him on the bed," Kara said gently. "I'll take him down to Mister Charles presently." Only for an instant did Daphne reveal her disapproval of Charles. Daphne, of course, was devoted to Annabel. Daphne, like Annabel, was a cold woman, with little use for the act of creating a child.

Daphne left the room, to go downstairs to begin her daily routine in the kitchen. Not for hours would she be taking up Annabel's breakfast. Kara reached for Christopher, held him close, her face brushing the velvet softness of his cheek. Wishing this were her child, Charles's and hers.

With the baby asleep in her arms, Kara went down the wide marble staircase, trying to brush away the ugliness of Emilie Rankin's screaming and ranting last night. She stopped at the library. Charles was there, stretched out on the sofa, still asleep.

She stood before him, her heart pounding. The depth of her feeling for Charles frightening her. He mustn't leave Manoir. She couldn't bear it if he went to Texas or California, as he'd talked about. Never to see him again.

"Charles." She leaned forward, touching him with one hand. "Charles—" How exhausted he looked, even in sleep.

He moved beneath her gentle prodding; frowned. Coming awake with reluctance.

"Hmmm?" He opened his eyes tiredly, struggled to focus on Kara.

"I'll have Octavia bring us coffee," she said quietly. "The baby has had his first feeding."

Charles was suddenly fully awake.

"Kara," he said with startling intensity. "Kara, how would I have survived last night without you?" He sat up. "I'd better go on down to the quarters." His eyes settled with tenderness on his son.

"After coffee," Kara stipulated, placing Christopher in his

arms. "No one will wake for hours." Not entirely truthful, but Charles understood. His mother and his wife were awake, but neither was apt to descend to the lower floor this morning. Emilie would cling to her bed for days, and Annabel would play the faithful companion.

In the early morning stillness Kara went to the kitchen to ask Octavia to bring coffee. While Charles and she were drinking, with Christopher lying within protective arm's reach of his father on the sofa, Amory walked into the room. Yawning widely, eyes bloodshot and somber.

"When I was able to get downstairs again last night, you were asleep in here," Amory said self-consciously to Charles, with questions in his eyes. "We—we had our hands full with your mother for a while. I sent Horatio in for Doctor Scott, but he couldn't be located." Amory sighed heavily. "Tim's right, yellow fever's moving in fast. The death figures, Horatio reported, are staggering."

"We can't go into New Orleans until the epidemic's over," Charles said uneasily. "It's too dangerous."

Amory leaned forward toward Christopher, a glow of pleasure in his eyes.

"Here, let me take that little fellow," Amory said expansively. "Can't a grandfather have a look?"

Charles explained about the plans to keep Christopher in a cabin at the edge of the quarters until it was safe to move him back to the city.

"One of the field hands gave birth two days ago and the child died. She'll have milk for Christopher," Charles said. "I'll take Artemis out of the fields and put her in charge of the baby."

Together, Charles and Amory left with Christopher, a bond between the two men that brought tears to Kara's eyes. But Amory wouldn't have the strength to fight his wife and bring his grandson into the house. Tradition was too strong in this house of the South. And there was Annabel to consider.

Feeling strangely alone, Kara returned to her room, pausing there by the small cradle with an intense wish that Sheelagh would awake, would be hungry. She was conscious of a compulsion to be sitting there in the Boston rocker, with Sheelagh at her breast. To feel, this instant, the tugging at a nipple, the not unpleasant, mild contractions deep in her belly as the baby took its sustenance. The overpowering, joyous feeling of being fully a woman.

Three days later, while Kara was in the quarters supervising the children in the community vegetable garden they'd just begun, Charles appeared and beckoned her to join him. Some of his urgency communicated itself to her. Anxiously, but with a smile and a quick word of approval to the children, Kara walked up to Charles.

"Kara, you mustn't come to the quarters anymore," he said earnestly. "We have two cases of yellow fever in the infirmary."

Kara gasped as she searched his grave face.

"Maybe it's something else, something not serious."

"Mama Belle is positive," Charles told her. "She's been through enough of these sieges to know. It starts off simply enough. These two complained in the fields yesterday about headaches, slight chill. The driver thought they were malingering. It happens sometimes," he conceded, without meeting Kara's eyes. "But today, both men collapsed in the fields. I won't come up to the house again until it's over. Have Horatio bring down a bundle of clothes for me; leave them at the edge of the quarters. You mustn't come down here." He hesitated. "I'll keep Christopher in isolation in the cabin, with Artemis."

"Charles, I'm not afraid," Kara said. "Let me help."

"No, Kara, you stay away from the quarters," he insisted.

"But Charles, I could be useful."

"You have Sheelagh to think about," he told her brusquely. "Keep an eye on Christopher for me." His voice lost its edge. "See what you can do about getting netting for us down here. Mama Belle wants to close up every opening in the cabins, to keep out the mosquitos. We'll need a hell of a lot."

"We'll find it," Kara promised.

"Don't let Papa come down here," Charles urged. "Not with that heart condition. He'd never survive the fever. Tell him to order the netting, and all the quinine he can lay hands on, from Baton Rouge and Biloxi." He sighed tiredly. "Mama and Annabel will have to know. We must close the plantation to outsiders, sit this out, and pray."

Kara hurried back to the house with her mind in turmoil. Her memory too fresh with the agonies of the famine in Ireland to contemplate the imminent epidemic with calm. But she mustn't panic, she told herself sternly. There would be enough to cope with when Emilie was told. In the back of her mind was the uneasy realization that no doctors would be coming out to Manoir, with New Orleans in such a calamitous state.

In the ensuing days neighbors, disregarding the warning from Manoir, came calling when they learned the fever was isolated in the quarters, though both Emilie and Annabel lived in terror of an outbreak within the house itself. Neighbors reported on the panic that was riding herd over New Orleansians. Anyone who could leave the city was running. This was made more difficult because towns up the river and along the coast were clamping on embargoes. Armed guards were being put up to keep out refugees from New Orleans.

Every trapped resident blamed something else for the fever. It came from the rotting wood, from "specks in the air," it was the "pestilential effluvia" created by digging all those canals around the city.

Everybody espoused another cure, though the survivors among the stricken were few. Quinine, opium, lime water, sulphur. The superstitious put onions in their shoes. Bloodletting was painfully practiced. One doctor prescribed oyster juice. Everything was tried with an unbalanced rush of hope, and discarded for something new when the results were nil.

Frantic city officers tried a variety of efforts to rout the fever. The banquettes were ordered spread with layers of lime. Cannons were set up at street corners, their roaring booms calculated to clear the air of "effluvia." Barrels of tar were lugged into the streets and fired.

In the quarters at Manoir, Mama Belle, tottering about on arthritic limbs, was everywhere, ordering scrupulous, daily cleaning of the cabins, feeding quinine to slaves who were more afraid of the medication than the fever. Mama Belle was faithful to the "Creole treatment" for the fever utilizing hot mustard baths, hot aromatic teas, and castor oil. She refused to allow bloodletting and exhausting emetics and purgatives, as was popular among the whites. Charles knew the mortality rate under her ministrations would be lower than in New Orleans. Still, despite all her efforts, seven slaves died in the infirmary within ten days. Charles, sick with frustration, ordered their bodies, their clothes, and the pallets on which they had lain burned.

The main house remained, thus far, unscathed. Daily, Kara came down to the edge of the quarters to speak with Charles, fifty feet between them. It was Kara who ordered meals for Charles, and she took them down herself to his sternly honored borderline. Emilie and Annabel moved about the house in an aura of fear, speaking in low, subdued tones.

Kara, deprived of her hours with the children at the quarters, spent them instead with Christopher, who was thriving. Artemis, delighted with her new status as a "house slave," was devoted to Charles's son. Kara suspected, though Amory avoided any such confrontation, that Christopher's grandfather was a frequent visitor.

At the end of the second week Kara noted Sheelagh's lack of hunger and was immediately uneasy. Jasmine was exhorted to remain by her cradle every moment that Kara was not there. When Kara returned, after having left food for Charles, she found Jasmine washing Sheelagh's tiny, angry face with a wet cloth. Her throat tightened with alarm.

"Jasmine, what is it?" Her voice sounded unnatural.

"Her hot," Jasmine whispered, eyes wide with fear. "Not high fever, Li'l Missy," Jasmine said quickly. Kara turned white. "Li'l bit, dat's all."

Kara rushed to the cradle, leaned forward to touch the small forehead. Fever. Oh yes, she was running a fever! Though fast asleep, Sheelagh murmured fretfully, moved about restlessly.

"Stay with her, Jasmine," Kara ordered. "Keep washing her down."

Kara darted about the house, searching for Tim. Angry at not finding him. Amory had left this morning for Baton Rouge, in hopes of buying a fresh supply of quinine. Upstairs, in Emilie's room, Emilie and Annabel talked in their subdued, uneasy tones. Then, as she was about to return to her room, Tim strode in through the front door.

"Tim, where have you been?" she demanded impatiently.

"Walking," he said cheerfully. "This house depresses me." Tim loathed being quarantined, missed the excitement of New Orleans.

"Tim, you must go down to New Orleans." Her voice rose. "The baby, she's running a fever!"

"Kara, are you sure?" Tim looked stricken.

"I'm sure. You must go down to New Orleans and find Doctor Scott!" Dr. Scott would know what to do. With a need to cling to something, Kara told herself that Dr. Scott was their one hope of saving the baby.

"Kara, I'll never be able to find him. No doctor is in his home; they're working, night and day, in the hospitals!" But he was ashen. "How could I find him in that madness?"

"Tim, this is your child!" Kara trembled, knowing the course of the fever. "Find him!"

"Kara, have you lost your mind?" Emilie's voice intruded furiously. She hovered at the head of the stairs. "I won't allow Tim to set foot in that pestilence-ridden city!"

"This is our child!" Kara blazed. "You have no right to tell Tim what to do!"

"*He* is my child! He won't go down there!" With surprising strength, and without hysteria, Emilie's voice echoed through the house. "I won't allow him to be exposed to that! You don't care," she went on with scathing contempt. "But he's my son and I love him. He's not leaving Manoir!"

"Kara, I won't be able to find Scott. If there was a chance, I'd go. You know that, Kara." Desperation laced Tim's voice as his eyes sought hers, pleaded for reason, Kara knew he was right. The city was in chaos. Dr. Scott, if found, couldn't spend the time to come out here to treat one patient when thousands required his attention in New Orleans. Tears in her eyes, she swerved away from Tim, ran.

Running to the quarters, she at last was forced from physical exhaustion to slow down her steps. Not stopping, this time, at Charles's imposed barrier. She found him outside the infirmary, directing the putting up of fresh mosquito netting.

"Kara!" He frowned in reproval. "I told you not to come down here!"

"Charles, I had to," she gasped. "Sheelagh. She's running a fever, she's fretful. I wanted Tim to go for Doctor Scott, he won't."

"Kara, he can't." His agitation was instantly apparent, though he strived for calm as he held her comfortingly by the shoulders. "Wait, I'll get Mama Belle. We'll send her up to the house."

In Kara's bedroom, while Kara and Jasmine fearfully watched, Mama Belle leaned over Sheelagh. Tim hovered in the door, pale and shaken, clenching and unclenching a fist.

"Dis heah chile ain't got no yella fevuh," Mama Belle diagnosed with reassuring serenity. "Her got dem teet' tryin' to come t'rough. Ain't no mo' dan dat," she wound up complacently. "Me fix somet'in' put on dem gums, her feel bettuh. Dat fevah, him go way quick, yo' see."

Kara never left the cradle, though Tim kept asking her to let him take shifts. And then, by the end of the third day, Sheelagh cried with the familiar hunger warning. Crying and laughing simultaneously with relief, Kara scooped up the baby, pulled her into her arms, took her to a breast painful with its fullness. As long as Sheelagh was all right, the world was beautiful.

Down in New Orleans, the epidemic continued relentlessly. Amory, back from Baton Rouge, stormed about the house, haranguing about the devastation that could have been avoided if the city had taken precautions. Emilie, terrified, refused to allow Amory to discuss the epidemic in front of her.

More than ever, Emilie was effusive in her avowal of devotion to Sheelagh, making it obvious that she was at the same time rejecting Charles's son. Christopher was never mentioned in the house, except between Amory and Kara. Amory took great pride in his first grandson who, he reiterated jubilantly, had the good sense to resemble him. But there was a new bitterness in Annabel, of which Kara was increasingly aware. Annabel was drawing more within herself, though ever solicitous of Emilie. Sometimes Annabel sat staring into space, off in a world of her own, wanting no part of theirs. Tim was restless, impatient at being confined to Manoir, riding much, striding alone about the grounds.

Every evening, Amory talked at great length with Kara and Tim, who sat with him in the library. The three were held together by a common determination not to be overwhelmed by the horror of what was happening in New Orleans, and the knowledge that the sickness could still strike at them, though the epidemic in the quarters seemed over.

Amory, pleased with his captive audience, expounded at great length, with much canniness, on the intricacies of local and state politics, which Kara found fascinating. He spoke with enthusiasm about such news of the world as came to them in their present circumstance.

"I tell you, if Commodore Perry can bring off this treaty with Japan," Amory said with satisfaction, "it'll be the beginning of a whole new era for the world. One country can't live alone that way."

"I don't understand what's happening," Kara admitted with her characteristic candor. "Why did Commodore Perry go to Japan?"

"We assume he's there now," Amory chuckled. "Judging from when he left President Fillmore sent him with a letter to the head of government, the shogun, proposing mutual trade between Japan and the United States. Of course we won't know anything for a while," Amory surmised. "The Japanese won't jump in right away, they'll give it thought. Perhaps we'll know something by next spring." He squinted narrowly at Tim. "What about you, Tim? When the spring elections roll around, are we going to have an alderman in the family?"

"I have to get the nomination first, Papa," Tim reminded him diffidently, and shot a passing glance at Kara. "Once the epidemic is over, we can start talking to people." But his eyes were brooding. For Tim, politicking was an acting role. He had to prime himself for the performance.

By mid-September, the tide seemed to be turning in New Orleans. The death rate took a heartening dive. The weather changed dramatically. The rains stopped. The sun beat down with less intensity. Pleasing breezes swept in from the lake, and the mosquitos disappeared.

Cautiously families began to return to the city. Slowly the stores began to reopen. Then suddenly the city surged into normalcy. People were talking about the theater season and the opera. The restaurants were again thronged with customers.

Charles went into New Orleans and found a small house he could rent, where he could set up Christopher with Artemis. And fresh alarm welled up in Kara because she remembered his determination, before the disastrous summer, to prepare Fred Dent to take over as overseer, in complete charge of Manoir.

Charles was not completely sold on Fred Dent, Kara reminded herself. Despite his admission, within the family, that Dent appeared to be doing a satisfactory job. Up till now, no overseer had remained at Manoir longer than seven months. Charles said that the turnover at all the plantations was shockingly heavy. Emilie, of course, doted on Dent because he poured on such absurd flattery. Even Annabel seemed to like the man. But Kara, like Charles, harbored an unfocused distrust.

★★★★★

Again Tim was traveling regularly into New Orleans. To Kara's astonishment, she and Tim were beginning to be invited to social events in the city. To small dinners, to the masked balls, the opera, and the theater. Tim invariably accepting because this was part of the political buildup.

It became a determined game with them to play, in public, the handsome, devoted young Rankins. Emilie was alternately proud and outraged at their emergence as one of the most popular young couples in wealthy New Orleanian circles. Kara was aware of Emilie's jealousy, her constant reminders about her own beauty as a girl. Cannily, Kara allowed Tim to argue with his mother about the extravagant dresses that he chose for her at the smartest modistes on Chartres Street. His taste was impeccable; Kara was learning much from him. She smiled apologetically and shrugged when Emilie laced into her, with increasingly less finesse, about wardrobe expenditures. To Tim these were campaign costs.

For election time, in the spring, Tim had planned an energetic race for one of the assistant alderman slots. He was hinting already to Emilie about the necessity of having a house in New Orleans, if he were to run for city office, a house large enough for extensive entertaining.

Kara relished the fullness of her days and nights. The mornings at the quarters, two afternoons weekly studying French, now that the epidemic was past, with Jean Simone. And now, the evenings in New Orleans, playing this exciting new role. Always, much time with tiny Sheelagh, though Kara knew Jasmine was as attentive as herself. Yet with all this, Kara felt herself existing on a precipice of disaster.

Emilie constantly carped about Kara's gowns, her hair, her effervescent manner, the way she insisted on bringing up the baby.

"Kara, I hope you have the good sense not to let it be known you're nursing the baby. Folks would be shocked," she said over and over again until Kara wanted to scream.

Emilie seemed to bait Tim's annoyance, as though she enjoyed being the martyred mother, now deserted by her favorite son. Because she saw this new interest as a failure in herself. She was losing her son. Kara was nervous; they'd counted on Emilie's pride in a son active in politics to put across the house in New Orleans.

Emilie often invited Fred Dent into the house socially. For dinner, for a casual evening of conversation. The poor man had no family, Emilie would murmur smugly. When he was doing such a fine job, the least they could offer was a little hospitality. Kara watched with apprehension. Dent was moving into a position never enjoyed by any other overseer.

Kara was concerned about the long evening conferences in the library between Charles, Amory, and Fred Dent. Part of this was due to Charles's plans to give the usual holiday time off to the good producers among the field slaves. Also, he was testing a new system, approved by Amory, of allowing a few favored slaves the right to raise what could amount to a bale of cotton for themselves, on their own time. Charles felt this had worked out well and wished to continue it, on a wider basis, with the spring planting. Fred Dent, like Emilie, was strongly averse to such liberality.

On December 22, two months after the epidemic was legally declared over, New Orleans would celebrate Thanksgiving. Kara and Tim were invited to a large celebration dinner at the townhouse of influential friends of the Rankins, who were becoming aware of Tim's political aspirations. Emilie was indignant that she and Amory were not included in the invitation.

"Emilie, we're the older generation," Amory twitted her,

while she bridled at what she considered an insult. "Rene can only invite so many, and he wants to help the boy." He winked at Kara. "Though how the hell they're going to reciprocate all this hospitality they've been enjoying lately, I don't know. New Orleansians don't take well to traveling this far out of the city for their socializing in the winter months."

Emilie looked at Amory, startled, yet aware of the validity of his statement. Kara lowered her eyes. A house in New Orleans, she visualized with towering excitement. Close by Charles's charming small house where from time to time she visited little Christopher. And felt pangs at Artemis's maturing attractiveness, at Artemis who seemed to flower in her new position.

"Perhaps we could give a dinner at the Saint Charles," Emilie suggested reluctantly.

"Damned expensive," Amory complained. "And that's just one time. If the boy's going to make his mark in politics, he's going to have to entertain heavily."

"I don't want to hear anymore about it tonight," Emilie said peremptorily, yet Kara knew the seed had been planted. She knew, also, that the price of that house would be Emilie's constant presence at any parties Tim and she would give. Emilie's high-handed interferences. But she could endure this, she told herself, if it put Tim into an assistant alderman's seat.

Driving into New Orleans with Tim for the Thanksgiving Eve dinner, Kara talked about Sheelagh. The conversation between Tim and her settled, invariably, around Sheelagh or politics. Always, an invisible wall, discomforting but insurmountable, was between them.

Kara was tense. She knew that the outspoken Creole family who was entertaining them, like most of their guests, was adamantly against the naturalized Americans in New Orleans, particularly the Irish and German. They knew only that Kara had lived in New York. It upset her that Tim made a point of glossing over her Irish background. Her knowledge of French, slight as it was, was treated with rousing admiration. And New Orleans, Tim said with candid satisfaction, always approved of beautiful women.

Twenty guests sat down to dinner in the elegant dining salon, with the menu one which would have been acceptable even at the fabulous Saint Charles Hotel. Vermicelli, gumbo filé, leg of mutton with caper sauce, a loin of veal, oyster patties, beef a la mode, calves feet *à la Padcaline,* rice, beans, pickled cucumbers. Bread pudding with brandy sauce, gooseberry pie, Creole bonbons, and Genoese perlies were served afterward, along with dishes of filberts, pecans, almonds. Kara particularly enjoyed the French café au lait that wound up the meal.

Their host, an expansive, elegantly groomed, corpulent man in his fifties, still with an eye for the ladies, cornered Kara later in the evening. Kara had been paying flattering attention to a Creole dowager who, Tim had whispered earlier, carried much weight with her politically powerful husband. Their host was gallant, charming, yet beneath his apparently casual probing, she guessed he was testing her potential as the wife of a prospective assistant alderman. Knowing, naturally, that a Rankin in politics would inevitably aspire to higher office.

Kara turned cold inside, although she continued to talk vivaciously to her host. She had seen Tim quietly leave the lush parlor. In the company of a rather handsome, foppish older man. She forced herself to smile brilliantly, though her pulse raced, while her companion spoke with eloquence about the growingly corrupt political scene.

"Mr. Rankin, my father-in-law, is most upset about conditions," Kara said earnestly. "This is one of the reasons Tim has grown so interested in the assistant alderman's seat." She looked at him, awaiting his reaction. There was none. "He feels that we're disgracing the state with the kind of politics we're practicing."

"We need young blood," her host acknowledged grudgingly. Yet Kara knew, from what Amory had taught her, that a few influential Creole families resented the growing prominence of Americans in the political arena.

"Tell me about Paris," Kara coaxed ingratiatingly. "Your wife tells me you were there only last year. I think Paris must be the most fascinating city in the world."

Panic brushed her when the hostess announced that supper was about to be served. Until she saw Tim slip unobtrusively into the room again. A few minutes later, the other man appeared, smiling faintly, meeting Tim's eyes for one loaded instant.

While they sat down to a supper of cold roast turkey, Tim whispered to Kara with sardonic amusement.

"I gather I just sewed up the Creole vote. Monsieur Aumont was most enthusiastic about my running."

Kara told herself she should be bursting with happiness. Tim was on his way. The house in New Orleans would surely come through now. When they returned from the Thanksgiving Eve celebration, late as it was Tim went directly into the library to talk to his father. Kara lay awake until she heard Tim, coming up to his own room, an hour later. She guessed that Tim would discuss her own success with their host. He would hardly mention his private conference with Monsieur Aumont, she thought with a freshly acquired cynicism. Thus, it seemed, were political alliances formed.

Christmas Eve passed fairly uneventfully. Except that while Kara's young choir sang their carols in the parlor, Sheelagh took her first steps. Emilie was indignant that Kara didn't immediately put a stop to such nonsense.

"She's much too young," Emilie protested, while Amory marshaled the giggling young choir into the library to receive treats he had stashed there for tonight. "Her legs will be bowed for sure!"

Emilie was further outraged when Tim proudly took one of Sheelagh's tiny hands firmly in his and urged her to further adventure. Earlier than usual she retired to her room, with Annabel solicitously at her side. Belatedly, Kara realized that Emilie's anger could hold up the house in New Orleans. Well, she would learn to be diplomatic, if it was necessary. It did not come naturally, to bow down before her mother-in-law.

Monday morning, with work scheduled as usual in the fields after the holiday hiatus, Kara resumed her routine of going down to the quarters. After the epidemic, Charles had conferred with Amory, and it had been decided to build another group of cabins so that each family might have a cabin of their own. Hardly luxurious, Kara conceded wryly, but to the field hands this was heaven-sent. Charles kept insisting the system couldn't be reshaped in a year, while Amory was increasingly pessimistic about the future of the South.

There was much talk about secession. Both by the southern slave owners and the northern radical abolitionists. Of the white population in the slave states—a total of roughly six and a quarter million—only two hundred and fifty-two thousand families owned any slaves. And of that only one-third owned ten slaves or more. So that this whole ugly institution was being supported for a small group of rich southern planters, at the expense, possibly, of the well-being of the rest of the people!

Amory had talked about how that Mr. Edward Everett, who had been governor of the state of Massachusetts and president of Harvard College, was calling for secession from the South, though he suggested it be done "like reasonable men." But to divide the country would be unthinkable. And for what? So that those rich southern planters could continue living immorally on the lives of slaves! And Kara felt sick because the Rankins were one of those rich southern-plantation families.

"Li'l Missy! Li'l Missy!" The young black children, yet too young to go to the fields, greeted her with their usual glee. "Heah come Li'l Missy!"

In the deliciously crisp morning air, warmed by the sun, the children played with Kara. Later they solemnly settled down to the numbers game Kara had devised, to teach them to add and subtract. When she was finally ready to go, they tried amid joyous laughter to persuade her to remain longer, as usual.

"Tomorrow," Kara promised. "Now go to Mama Belle for your milk," she ordered with mock sternness. *"Vite."*

Kara fondly watched them scamper away to the cabin where Mama Belle dispensed milk each morning. An innovation arranged by Kara. In three or four years the older ones would be out in the fields. Would she ever grow accustomed to the fact that her very existence depended upon the labor of these people? Yet Charles insisted they would be completely lost alone, without a "marster" to guide their lives.

Kara walked down the dusty dirt road between the two rows of cabins, heading back for the house. Amory had gone into New Orleans with Tim this morning. Tim had told her, secretly, that his father and he were going to check on New Orleans real estate, to be ready when Emilie made up her mind to invest. The house, of course, would be Emilie's in title.

Emilie had been visibly impressed by Monsieur Aumont's offered support. She now mentally saw herself as the mother of a rising young politician. Amory prophesied optimistically that it was a question of time before Emilie broke down. At the same time, Kara sensed, Amory was annoyed that it was necessary to appeal to Emilie. The money should be in both their names, but Emilie's father hadn't wished that. Nor had Emilie.

On impulse, Kara turned off for a detour through the fields. She was restless, her impatience to be out of Emilie Rankin's house already at the painful point. Emilie was constantly at her throat over Sheelagh, she could do nothing right. She complained about the money Tim spent on her wardrobe, and even Amory was a little annoyed at that.

In New Orleans she would be able to see little Christopher, whom she adored, almost every day. Tim and she could have Charles over for dinner at least once a week. That was natural enough, when he made the long, tiresome trip into town practically every day, to see his son. They'd have an extra bedroom for whenever Charles wished to sleep over, she decided.

Kara started at the sound of a faint cry of protest. Thrown out of her introspection, she frowned, her eyes scanning the wooded area to her right.

"Aaah!" A louder outcry this time. An anguish that seemed to escape despite an effort at control. "Aaah!"

Her heart pounding, Kara strode between the towering pecans. Her face turned hot as she heard the sharp smack of leather against flesh. She felt sick inside. And furious. No one flogged a slave at Manoir! Both Charles and Amory took pride in that.

She stumbled in her haste, caught herself against a tree trunk, froze at the unexpected sight close by. Annabel, hands clenched, peered out from behind the protective girth of an old tree. Unaware of Kara's presence. Her eyes fastened on something out of Kara's vision. Her thin, disapproving mouth faintly parted now. A vein in her throat distended. A convulsive shudder ran through Annabel's body, and a low moan escaped her. A moan of passion.

"Aaah!" The slave's anguish rose to an animal-like shriek. "No mo'! Please God, no mo'!" But again, leather cut into flesh, and Kara fought down a wave of nausea.

She spun around, retreated from the sounds of that sickening symphony. Charles! She must tell Charles! But the painful outcries of the victim halted her. She circled around a cluster of pecans, toward the clearing, instinctively searching for a way that would spare Annabel the humiliation of discovery.

Fred Dent stood before a slave with hands tied together above him, lashed to a low bough of a tree. Adam, Kara recognized with a shock, a field hand whom Charles brought into the house now and then for odd jobs and whom Charles had talked about training for carpentry. Dent, a look of savage satisfaction on his face, lifted the leather whip again while the tall, brawny Adam, his back laid painfully open, red and ugly, his face glistening with the perspiration of his agony, gritted his teeth in anticipation of another lash.

"Stop that!" Kara called out sharply. "We don't flog slaves at Manoir! Stop it!"

Dent's face flushed with fury as he faced Kara.

"This don't concern womenfolk, Miss Kara," he said coldly. "This is a man's business. This black nigger was malingering, trying to get out of doing an honest day's work. It's my job to hand out discipline where it's needed. You go on up to the house."

"It's not your job to flog anyone, Mr. Dent!" Kara's head was high, her eyes flashing. "You are not to flog the slaves!"

Her face hot, tears stinging her eyes, she turned and marched toward the fields. Aware that Annabel had fled the area. Why had Annabel stood there, watching that way? Looking like that?

All at once, it dawned on her. Annabel, who denied her husband a place in her bed, found that kind of pleasure when Fred Dent flogged a big black buck.

Chapter Nineteen

Kara looked for Charles in the near fields. He was not there. Then she remembered he had mentioned some project in the far fields, a considerable hike for her to undertake. Yet she churned to report Dent's monstrous behavior. She paused, forcing her mind to focus on how she was going to tell him. Guiltily, she recognized a covert exhilaration in her because she had accidentally come upon a means of ousting Dent from Manoir.

Perhaps it would be better to wait. Find out a little more first. Talk to the slaves in the infirmary. Ask questions. *Yes, she would find out everything possible about Fred Dent's treatment of the slaves.*

With her objective set, Kara walked back to the quarters. The youngsters were crowded together in Mama Belle's cabin, still having their morning milk. She went into the infirmary. In the first floor room to the left, she spied one of the female field hands who was laid up with a swollen leg.

"Good morning, Rachel." Kara tried to sound casual. "How's the leg?"

"Him swell up awful bad," Rachel said stoically. "Mama Belle, her say me cain't wuk in de fields maybe two, t'ree mo days." Her dark eyes watchful, as though expecting some rebuke.

"You do what Mama Belle says, you hear?" Kara said good-humoredly. "The doctor will be out Friday to hear the complaints at the infirmary. If the leg isn't well by then, the doctor will give you medicine." Kara hesitated, seeking to frame the words as casually as possible. "Rachel, I'd like to ask you something. Does Mr. Dent use the whip often?" Her face felt hot, but her eyes were steady on Rachel.

"Oh, Li'l Missy." Unexpectedly, Rachel chuckled. "Ever' Monday morning, him line up de young niggers fo' whuppin'. Him say, niggers no good less'n dey git a li'l taste of de whip. Dem got too easy time on Sunday."

"For no reason at all he flogs the hands?" Kara stared sick with shock.

"On Sunday, dey go tuh chu'ch, and Monday mawnin' de young, spry ones, dey git a few hits acrost de back."

Both Kara and Rachel started at the sounds of new arrivals in the infirmary. Two slaves brought in Adam, mercifully unconscious now, and deposited him on a pallet. Kara shivered at the sight of his laid-wide back, the raw redness of torn flesh.

"Go bring Mama Belle," Kara ordered, steeling herself. "Tell her to bring salve, and clothes." And later, she would tell Charles about his fine Mr. Dent, whom Emilie invited into her parlor.

It was almost an hour later when Kara caught up with Charles. He had returned from the fields on one of the stallions, to eat the lunch Octavia sent down from the house for him.

"Kara." Charles smiled his welcome. "You're down here late today."

"I was waiting for you." She returned his smile, though her eyes were grave. "It—it's about Fred Dent." She hesitated, suddenly self-conscious, felt the telltale color stain her cheeks.

"What about Dent?" Charles asked quietly.

As calmly as she could, Kara reported the flogging, recognizing the fury the news unleashed in him. She added what Rachel had told her about the Monday-morning routine. Charles's face hardened. He clenched a fist as he swore under his breath, then apologized to Kara for his rough language.

"Something about that man bothered me from the beginning. Kara, he'll be off our property by nightfall. I promise you that. We don't allow anybody to flog a black at Manoir. That's unconscionable!"

Horatio came striding toward them, basket in hand.

"Octavia send yo' chicken, Marse Charles," he said expansively. "Nobody cook chicken like dat Octavia."

"Kara, have lunch with me," Charles asked persuasively, while Horatio pulled up a table and a bench. "Octavia always sends down enough for a whole field crew. Come on, sit down," he prodded. "Don't worry, I'm getting rid of Dent," he reassured her. "You know I will." But his eyes were troubled. Because now it would be impossible for him to move on, to Texas or California, with Chris.

It was like an unexpected picnic, Kara thought, relishing this private time with Charles. The conversation was sternly impersonal, though Charles's eyes rested upon her, intermittently, with a warmness that set her heart thumping.

"Kara, do you realize what the government has done by adding forty-five thousand square miles to its territory, with this new purchase?" Charles said earnestly. "For ten million dollars we've brought ourselves a practicable railroad route all the way to the Pacific Coast." But she didn't enjoy the wistful glint in Charles's eyes as he contemplated the Far West. "Of course," he acknowledged, "this is just a provisional treaty, it'll take some doing before it's ratified," Charles's eyes grew opaque, shutting her out. He was thinking, she guessed unhappily, that he might have been part of the growing West, if she hadn't found out about Fred Dent.

"Perhaps all the excitement over the new land will settle business conditions," Kara suggested. "Your father's concerned about that."

"He's jumping the gun," Charles said. "Talking about a financial crisis before the year actually begins. Of course Papa has a special sense about such things," Charles conceded. "He's even worrying about bank failures. That's all we need now, with the country as divided as it is."

Kara diverted the conversation to Tim's efforts at working for improved sanitary conditions in New Orleans. They talked until Charles announced it was high time he returned to the fields. Kara rose to her feet, fearful that she had betrayed herself with her eagerness to be with him.

"I must get back to the house. I haven't seen Sheelagh all morning." Her face softened as she visualized her tiny sprite of a daughter, her hair and eyes, her mouth, Tim's eyes and nose. "How's Chris?" Over the holidays it had been difficult for her to get into New Orleans, where her first stop was inevitably Charles's house.

"Chris is great," Charles said tenderly. But sadness lurked behind his eyes because his child could not be reared at Manoir.

Not until after dinner, when the family was gathered in the library, did Charles announce he had discharged Fred Dent. Emilie was visibly upset.

"Charles, I'm sure if Mr. Dent flogged a slave, he had a good reason," Emilie insisted imperiously. "Did you talk to him?"

"I talked to him," Charles said carefully.

Kara was conscious, as the words flew about the room,

that there was a silent conspiracy among the men to refrain from telling Emilie that it was *she* who had discovered Fred Dent's sadistic habits. Annabel, tensely silent, kept her eyes on the floor. In high-handed agitation, Emilie decided to forsake the library, inviting Annabel to join her in her room. A few moments later, Charles left. Kara knew he was going into New Orleans to spend the night with Chris.

"Tim—" Amory leaned back expansively in his chair and something in his voice snapped Kara to attention. "Your mother feels it might be wise for Kara and you to have that house in New Orleans. After all, if you're announcing for the assistant alderman's seat at the meeting on Thursday, you'll need a local address."

"I've been using Charles's house," Tim said with a faint smile, but Kara was aware of his excitement. "I doubt that anybody's going to question me on that score." His smile was sardonic. Every Louisianian knew the corruption in New Orleans politics. "But why hasn't Mama told me?" He rose from his chair, crossed to the fireplace.

"Your mother will announce it when she's good and ready," Amory said drily. "But it must be soon. Kara, you don't know about this," he cautioned. "Until Emilie makes her dramatic announcement. But she had me arrange for a transfer of funds from her New York bank to our New Orleans bank. You'll have the house."

Tim announced his candidacy. With the manipulations of Louis Aumont, Tim won a place on the Whig slate. On his own, he picked up support from the new Independent party, which had been organized by a group of merchants two years earlier, and which chose "nonpartisan" candidates who might be favorable to business interests. Both Amory and Charles were Democrats, but Monsieur Aumont, like

Emilie's deceased father, was devoted to the Whigs, much favored by the larger planters because of their sympathy for banking interests.

The same evening on which the *Daily Picayune* carried the news of Tim's candidacy, Emilie interrupted the sober dinner conversation about the crisis in the Crimea, to report she was buying a townhouse in New Orleans, which "Tim and Kara are welcome to use for the winter." Emilie, it was clear, was to have the final say about furnishings and would be a frequent visitor.

Tim's elation, eloquently and lavishly expressed, elicited smug, contented smiles from his mother.

"Tim, you know I always want what's best for you," Emilie purred. Her fleeting glance in Kara's direction was rich with vindictive triumph. Why, Kara wondered bitterly, when Emilie knew there was no marriage between Tim and her? Why was it so important to Emilie to be sure she rated first in her younger son's affections? "Papa always insisted it wasn't genteel for ladies to concern themselves with politics, of course." This was an oft-repeated slap at Kara, who was candidly fascinated by the machinations of politics. "But when it's my son, my baby, who's running for office, I can extend this much help." She reached across the table to pat Tim's hand.

"Thank you, Mama." Tim was playing the devoted son to perfection.

"Tim, if we're going to be doing a lot of entertaining in New Orleans, I must buy new gowns," Emilie said enthusiastically. "I do want you to go shopping with me. I put such faith in your taste. And bring along Jean Simone," she added girlishly. Emilie suffered Jean Simone's presence two afternoons a week as Kara's French instructor, but she greeted him warmly in the evenings as Tim's friend.

Each night the Rankin dinner table ricocheted with discussions about the speedily purchased townhouse, which Amory "just happened to hear about at the propitious moment," Kara gritting her teeth to stop raising objections now and then to the furnishings which Tim and his mother were choosing for the house. As though she didn't exist, Kara thought, frustrated. Rarely did Tim challenge his mother's choices, which leaned toward the ostentatious. Amory was active in planning Tim's campaign, enjoying it, though he shrewdly retreated in deference to any express decision made by Louis Aumont, whom he considered an ace politician.

"*You* should have been in politics!" Kara said earnestly over a luncheon she shared with Amory. Her eyes were glowing with affection. "What a governor of Louisiana you would have made!"

"I'll leave that for my younger son," Amory jibed, and briefly his eyes met Kara's, and a fresh ambition was born in both. Kara's heart beating fast as she saw this possibility looming in the years ahead. Why not, with Amory to guide Tim? With men like Louis Aumont behind him, and the Rankin money? Sheelagh growing to young ladyhood in the governor's mansion.

"The state's loss," Kara said softly, "that you have never become involved in government."

"I talk much," Amory said whimsically. "I don't have the drive to do." His eyes squinted in deep concentration. "Once, it might have been possible for me. But everyone takes a step somewhere along the road that recharts his entire life. When I stepped into the management of Manoir, I was in an irreversible pattern."

Under Amory's tutelage, Kara was sopping up the intricacies of local politics. A conservative bloc of merchants was fighting to maintain control of New Orleans, fearful of the rise of political machines based on immigrants and laborers, who invariably voted Democratic. Now the city was rife with "reform," "independent," and "citizens" movements.

In February the American party, the Know-Nothings, was founded and was vociferous in its denunciations of immigrants. The *Semi-Weekly Creole* declaimed that both Irish and Germans failed "to comprehend the genius of our republican institutions, and regard with disfavor the restraints of law and the operations of long established usages." The *Daily Creole* wrote: "Immigration is the fountain of abolitionism, Europe is pervaded by a hatred of Negro slavery." The *American Exponent* claimed that the "foreign influence is alarmingly increasing and endangering the permanence and purity of our republican institutions."

Even the *Picayune*, usually neutral, came out in support of the "principle of the new party that Americans should rule America."

Kara kept a stiff smile on her face though she churned inwardly at the shocking denunciation of immigrants. It was the Irish who labored for years, under unbelievably trying conditions, to build the New Basin Canal. Irishmen worked the cotton presses, drove the cabs and drays. The Sicilians, the Italians, the Germans all performed essential services for their adopted city! The Sicilians were active in the dredging of shellfish. Italians handled the vegetables and oysters. Germans were metal workers, shoemakers, brewers. Where was the city's loyalty? The American party continued to draw new followers, catering to old-line Whigs, Creole Democrats, everyone of American birth.

Tim enjoyed his new role, thrust himself wholeheartedly into campaigning. The New Orleans house was furnished and staffed; Kara and Tim launched a rigorous entertainment schedule, with Emilie and Amory in constant attendance. Kara suspected that Amory's capitulation to Emilie's insistence that they be involved socially was for two reasons. He relished the chance to spend much time with both Sheelagh and Chris, and to avail himself of the services of Jasmine, who had accompanied Kara to New Orleans. Kara knew of the nocturnal visits Jasmine made to Amory's temporary quarters in the townhouse.

New Orleans, always rising to hot feelings on national issues, was in an uproar when the American steamship *Black Warrior*, on a routine voyage from New York to Mobile, was stopped at Havana on February 28 and seized by the Spanish authorities. Amory conceded that the Spanish probably suspected that the ship carried arms for revolutionaries, which he, like many other Louisianians, was sure it didn't. Secretary of War Jefferson Davis loudly demanded that action be taken against Spain.

"Thank God, Marcy is a cool-headed man," Amory declared during a heated after-dinner discussion. "A secretary of state with Davis's temperament would have us at war tomorrow. This is not a time for hawks."

"But Monsieur Soule, our ambassador to Spain, can surely handle this," Emilie protested, frowning at the injection of this serious note. She protested, regularly, about the way Amory and Charles brought the problems of the world to the dinner table. "He's a fine gentleman." Monsieur Soule, a Louisianian, stood high in Emilie's special graces.

"We'll see," Amory said shortly, exchanging a skeptical glance with Charles. "With all that trouble in the Crimea, let's hope we don't get ourselves involved in a war with Spain."

"That would be senseless," Charles gestured his impatience. "But all wars are senseless." Amory had lost an older brother in the War of 1812. All these years later, he still harbored a bitterness against war, which he shared with Charles.

"Amory, does this trouble affect Tim's campaign in any way?" Emilie asked, a glint of unease in her eyes.

"No, it won't upset the applecart," Amory said firmly.

"Amory, he is going to win, isn't he?" The prospect of failure upset her.

"We hope so, Mama," Tim said warily, before his father could answer. His mother had no patience with failure.

"He's going to win," Kara said determinedly, eyes flashing, "I know he will!"

Tim's political career was becoming the focal point of Kara's waking hours, except for the time she spent with her daughter. Tim's success in politics was for Sheelagh; Tim would become a father upon whom Sheelagh could gaze with pride some day. It was unnecessary for her to know her father's failing as a husband.

As election day drew closer, the campaign fighting became rough. Not unusual for New Orleans, Amory pointed out with bitter humor.

"I remember the year the New Orleans Democrats hired a Tammany Hall man to come down from New York, to indoctrinate them in the intricacies of rigging the election."

Election day loomed gray and chill. A heavy fog surrounded the city. Kara fretted because, as a woman, she was denied the ballot. Up in New York women were fighting against this denial. At a convention last year in New York City, women had come from as far west as Cleveland and Chicago to unite for women's rights.

Quite early in the morning, Amory stopped by the house.

"Kara, under no circumstances are you to leave the house," he said seriously, "It's bad this year. I saw a mob hunting down Irish, Italians, and Germans and beating them into unconsciousness. Then they dragged them over the cobblestones by their feet." He shook his head in distaste. "To keep them away from the polls."

"What about the police?" Kara demanded.

"They look the other way," Amory said grimly. "Either because they support them, or they are scared to get involved."

"But that's so wrong!" Kara burst out.

"That's politics in New Orleans," Amory reminded her. Neither would acknowledge vocally that these were the people voting for Tim.

Amory remained to have coffee with Kara, then hurried off to Tim's campaign headquarters. Kara roamed restlessly about the house, feeling herself caged in, a prisoner. To Kara's relief, Emilie had chosen to remain at Manoir election day.

"The excitement will be just too much for my nerves," Emilie decided. "I don't want to know a thing about it till it's all over." She cringed at the prospect of having to face defeat.

Kara spent the morning playing with Sheelagh in the nursery. In the afternoon, despite Amory's warning, Kara had Jupe drive her over to Charles's house for a brief visit with Chris. Kara felt oddly self-conscious at Charles's house, as though Artemis might suspect the jealousy that rode herd over her each time she was in the presence of Christopher's nurse.

Kara returned to her house for a solitary dinner, served by Jasmine, in the ornately furnished dining salon, with its wrought-iron chandelier holding fifty lighted candles. A dinner for which she had little taste. The street crowds were becoming raucous. Even here, Kara could hear them. There were growing complaints about the police, about how they were paid off to look the other way. Driving home in the carriage, she'd heard disconcerting news about troubles at the polls. She was nervous for the Rankin menfolk, who were at Tim's campaign headquarters.

"Li'l Missy don' eat," Jasmine scolded when she saw Kara's barely touched plate. "Aphrodite make dis special," she coaxed, pushing the plate of pecan pie before Kara. "Her know yo' lak."

Kara forced a smile. "I'll eat every crumb." She felt so useless, staying here in the house on a day as important to their lives as this one.

Kara was in the small rear parlor sipping her coffee when she heard the staccato of the knocker on the front door. Instantly, she was on her feet.

"I'll go to the door," she called out to Jasmine, who was already running down the hall. "It's probably Mister Tim."

Breathlessly, she rushed to the formal entrance, to pull the door open. Charles stood there, smiling quietly down at her. How tired he looked! All this traveling back and forth between Manoir and New Orleans. She fought down an impulse to reach out and touch him.

"Papa and Tim are staying over at the office until the bitter end," he said indulgently. "We can't know for sure yet, but it looks as though Tim will make it. I couldn't resist stopping by to tell you."

"Oh, Charles!" Kara glowed with pleasure. "Come in and have coffee with me. Jasmine!" she called, without waiting for confirmation. "Jasmine, bring coffee for Mister Charles."

They sat in the small, high-ceilinged back parlor, on chairs drawn close to the marble fireplace, and Charles reported on the progress of the election.

"You know Papa," Charles chuckled. "He won't accept a victory until every last vote is in and counted, but he concedes he's highly optimistic."

Along with coffee, Jasmine brought a tray of cold meats and bread, which Charles and Kara shared with candid enjoyment while Charles filled her in on small vignettes of the day.

"We should all have a celebration supper," Kara said on impulse. Warmed by Charles's nearness. Aware, again, of that questioning look in his eyes as they rested on her. Knowing about Tim. Her face stained with color. Right now, this minute, she wished Charles would take her in his arms. "Charles, let's have a celebration supper," she repeated, stammering slightly because she knew he looked upon her with desire that matched her own.

"That would be premature, a victory party," Charles chided gently, pulling his eyes away from hers in that electric instant where each silently acknowledged the feeling in the other. Each knowing she had dismissed Jasmine for the night. If he reached out, if he touched her, she could deny him nothing! But Charles rose to his feet. "It's been a long day."

"Thank you for stopping by," Kara said softly. Exhilaration surging through because she knew that Charles wanted her. A meager consolation to which she would cling when she lay alone, later, in the ornately canopied bed upstairs, which had never known a male presence.

Amory, Charles told Kara, would be driving directly to Manoir once the victory was certain. Kara went with Charles to the door, stood alone in the foyer with a towering sense of loss when he was gone. At loose ends, she returned to the rear parlor to sit alone before the fireplace. Sitting in the chair still warm from Charles's body. She leaned forward to poke at the red coals in the grate, caught up in the tumultuous emotions that enveloped her.

She was in love with Charles. She couldn't deny it any longer. She rose from her chair, roamed aimlessly about the room. Straightening a picture that didn't need to be straightened, moving a vase, smoothing the damask of a chair. What would have happened if she hadn't met Tim? How much she had loved Tim, there in the beginning! She closed her eyes, remembering the nights in his arms aboard the *Crescent Queen.* The miracle of discovery, and then to learn it was all a lie. Because of Emilie, Kara thought with churning frustration. Emilie drove Tim into it with her constant fussing over him, her overpowering demands. Tim was not as strong as Charles; his mother smothered him, refused to allow him to be a man. Poor Tim.

Kara left the parlor and went upstairs to her own room. She never waited up for Tim. They saw each other at meals, when Tim was home. Mainly, they saw each other when they entertained, or were entertained. But tonight she would wait up for Tim.

Impatiently Kara changed into her night clothes. The filmy, delicate chiffon that Tim had brought for her at Stewart's in New York, which she had worn aboard the ship down the Mississippi, and never since. Over the chiffon, the white satin wrapper. On her feet the heelless matching slippers. When Tim came home, she would be waiting for him.

A night chill swept over the house. Kara went into Sheelagh's room, where Jasmine lay sleeping on a cot, to make sure her daughter was properly covered. She leaned forward, with a rush of love, to press her mouth against the small, velvet face. God, she wanted another child! A son!

Downstairs in the rear parlor again, Kara poked at the coals, enjoying the rush of uneven heat. Outside, a drunken group loitered along the street, singing a ribald parody of a song currently popular. Kara flinched as she heard the words, damning the immigrants who dared to call New Orleans home. One day, not too distant, it would be the immigrant vote that would control Louisiana politics.

Kara heard the rumble of a carriage out front, heard the carriage draw to a stop. Someone opened the heavy double doors to the carriageway. That would be Jupe. She hurried to the foyer to wait for Tim.

Moments later the side door opened. Tim hovered in the entrance. Tall, slight, handsome, smiling. His face unfamiliarly flushed. He'd been drinking.

"Tim?" Her eyes searched his for reassurance.

"You've won, Madam Alderman," he bowed mockingly. "Kara, you look beautiful." Instinctively, Kara made a move toward him. Tim made a barely perceptible retreat. His eyes were sardonic, amused. "What a pity it's going to be wasted."

Sick with humiliation, Kara lowered her eyes. She had offered herself to her husband, in that split-second of hope that there could be something for them, and she had been rejected.

"Marse Tim!" Jupe called sharply, and lunged to catch him before he fell. "Me git him to bed, Li'l Missy," Jupe said. "Him be all right." Then, unexpectedly, Jupe grinned. "Dis one fine night, Madam Alderman."

Chapter Twenty

Jasmine opened the heavy oak door and came in with Kara's morning tea.

"Him bad day, Li'l Missy, how come yo' not stay in bed?" she scolded.

Kara laughed and slid beneath the covers, so that Jasmine could position the tray across her lap.

"Jasmine, please bring Sheelagh in," she said, her eyes shining. "Do you realize this is her first birthday?"

"Drink yo' tea fus'," Jasmine insisted. "Me bring huh soon 'nuf. Her wit' huh gran'ma, gittin' spoiled somet'in awful." Jasmine shook her hand in disapproval. Emilie Rankin was not one of Jasmine's favorite people.

Annabel and Emilie had stayed over last night while the men returned to Manoir because Charles was reluctant to leave the plantation solely in the care of the new overseer. They'd be back in time for the dinner. A formal dinner party to celebrate Sheelagh's birthday. Formal, at Emilie's insistence.

Kara leaned back against the mound of pillows while she sipped at her mint tea. Tim would breakfast in his room and then disappear from the house until it was time to dress for dinner. He was working hard with the committee to improve sanitary conditions in New Orleans. Soon summer would be here again, casting shadows of last summer's epidemic. Kara sighed. In a few weeks they must return to Manoir for the hot spell.

She had so hungered for this house of her own. But it wasn't her house. Emilie spent almost as much time here as at Manoir. Emilie's high-handed way with the slaves upset Kara, caused a certain amount of sullenness among them because their loyalties were to Kara. Emilie still relished the new social life to which she was exposed, yet increasingly there were the complaints, the hurt feelings over imagined slights.

So often Emilie brought Annabel with her to the New Orleans house, making Kara feel the intruder. Mornings, Emilie and Annabel spent in Emilie's room. In the afternoons they went for a drive along Shell Road if the weather was pleasant, or shopping about New Orleans. A fainthearted invitation to join them, in the beginning; now no pretense of welcoming her company.

Kara's introspection was broken by the exuberant arrival of her daughter. They shared an ecstatic morning reunion, and Jasmine whisked Sheelagh off for play while Kara dressed. She was glad she had canceled out today's French lesson. Jean was gnawing at her nerves, the way he secretively watched the door for Tim's return to the house at the close of her lesson. Knowing that Tim deliberately timed his return to coincide. Nobody suspected Tim, not with his devoted wife and daughter always part of his conversation. Oh, Tim was bright enough!

Kara moved about the house, taking care of small details for the party. The flowers arrived. She arranged them, though she suspected her mother-in-law would have acerbic comments about the results. She made sure Aphrodite polished the silver, which Emilie had brought down from Manoir. Giggling under Octavia's good-humored prodding, she sampled the superb bonbons which were being prepared for dessert. The birthday cake rested on a table in pink and white magnificence.

Mid-afternoon, with Emilie and Annabel both taking "beauty naps" in preparation for the dinner party, Kara impulsively decided to go and see Christopher. Knowing there would be little daytime frivolity during Mardi Gras, she walked the dozen blocks to Charles's house. She felt happy walking briskly through the New Orleans streets, brushing shoulders with the working people.

At Charles's pleasant but unpretentious house, she knocked and waited for admittance. Carmelita, one of the Manoir field hands raised to status of house slave, ushered her in with an eagerness that was at the same time laced with apprehension.

"How is Chris?" Kara inquired. "I haven't seen him in a couple of days."

"Him still sleep," Carmelita gestured affectionately, but her eyes were uneasy as they traveled upstairs. "Any minute him wake. Yo' sit, Lil Missy, have coffee. Me bring him down."

"Don't wake him," Kara said, walking to the front parlor. "I'll wait a while to see if he wakes up."

Carmelita called out excitedly to someone in the rear of the house to prepare coffee for Kara, and hurried up the stairs to Christopher's bedroom. In a few moments she returned, effusively apologetic. Christopher was still fast asleep.

"I'll just sit here and have coffee," Kara said. "Don't bother about me, Carmelita, go on about your work." She smiled reassuringly.

In a couple of minutes Carmelita returned with a cup of pungent hot coffee, whose aroma seemed to permeate the lower floor. Assured of Kara's comfort, Carmelita hurried off again. Kara leaned back in the small, damask-covered chair, enjoying the delicious hot brew. Relaxing, away from her own house, where Emilie's stamp was so indelibly imprinted. She looked around, envisioning herself mistress here. Sheelagh and Chris, growing up together. Charles and she everything to each other.

Suddenly Kara was restless. She wouldn't wait for Chris, after all. She rose to her feet, gently put down her coffee cup, crossed quickly to the double door that led to the foyer. Involuntarily, hearing voices, Kara glanced upward.

Artemis emerged from Charles's bedroom and walked down the hall to check on Christopher. Standing in the doorway of his room stood Charles. Jacketless. Buttoning his shirt front.

Color flooded Kara's face. Hastily, she retreated into the parlor, her heart pounding. While Christopher napped, Charles had taken Artemis. He had come back to New Orleans earlier to lie with Artemis.

Trembling, Kara sat down again. She had suspected this, she tried to rationalize. Charles was a man; he needed a woman. Annabel refused him. Throughout the South, men with rejecting wives turned to slaves. But she was jealous. She was jealous of a slave!

Kara waited, striving for poise, until Christopher was brought down to her. The word of her presence must have been passed along to Charles. He remained upstairs. She played briefly with Christopher, who was an affectionate, playful baby, and then she turned him over to Artemis, who hovered nearby in case she was needed. Kara making a point of avoiding Artemis's eyes. Fearful of giving herself away.

"He's a darling wee one," Kara crooned, giving Christopher a final hug. "I don't see him for two days, I miss him."

Kara returned to her own house, sought out Sheelagh as

though for reassurance. But she was a woman, she thought with sick frustration. Not only a mother. A woman, young and in love.

The house resounded with festivity as the guests arrived for dinner. Chandeliers aglow with hundreds of candles. Flowers everywhere. Jasmine had been instructed to keep Sheelagh upstairs until it was time for the birthday cake to be brought to the table. Emilie was smug with the triumph of Tim's election, Amory quietly pleased. Tim himself had arrived home late and did not appear until the guests were ready to go to dinner.

Octavia had prepared a magnificent array of dishes, with Aphrodite and Jupe quietly serving. The table conversation was strongly political, under Amory's guidance. Emilie tried futilely to divert the talk into what she considered less masculine channels, and sat with a pursed mouth and a vindictive glint in her fading eyes. Tim was ingratiating, handsome, deferential to the ladies. Kara knew that more than one woman who graced the table was envious of her position as Tim's wife.

With much fanfare, to Kara's distaste, Sheelagh was brought down to the dinner table and propped into a chair beside her grandmother. The guests politely respectful before Emilie's maudlin extravagances.

"Oh, not so much cake for Sheelagh," Kara protested when Emilie ordered a huge wedge to be placed before the bubbling young guest of honor.

"Kara, how can you?" Emilie clucked in reproach. "It's her first birthday. My beautiful darling."

Kara barely touched her own plate. What was the matter with Emilie, stuffing Sheelagh that way? Cake, ice cream, and now bonbons! Kara turned appealingly to Tim. Ever so slightly, he shook his head.

They mustn't incur his mother's anger. Already Tim and his father were talking about a seat in the state legislature two years hence. That would prove expensive, with the kind of politics being waged in Louisiana these days.

"Oh, she's just so much like me at her age!" Emilie said. "I had that same delicacy, that same grace. Papa couldn't resist spending a fortune on my clothes."

Suddenly, alarm tugged at Kara as she gazed at her daughter. She rose to her feet, moved quickly to Sheelagh.

"Excuse me," Kara said shakily, and scooped Sheelagh into her arms.

"Oh, Kara, what is the matter with you? Always fussing." Emilie frowned in annoyance.

A minute later, in the privacy of the foyer, Sheelagh was violently sick all over the front of her pink lace dress.

There were people in the nation, including Amory Rankin, who feared, in this year of a lagging economy, that the country was heading toward another depression. One that would be worse than the depression of '47. Amory spoke, with increasing gloom, about the division arising in the country.

In late May, just as Kara and Tim were preparing to move back to Manoir for the summer, Congress passed the Kansas-Nebraska Act, which provided that two new territories, Kansas and Nebraska, were to be formed from the Indian land that lay west of the bend of the Missouri River and north of 37 degrees latitude. Included in the bill was a provision that allowed the people in the new territories to make their own decisions about slavery.

"Of course, Douglas put in that rider," Amory jeered with dry amusement, while he gathered with his sons and Kara in the library at Manoir for one of their "small cabinet meetings."

"Stephen Douglas is one of the sharpest minds in the nation, and one of these days you'll be seeing him make a try for the Presidency. He can't win without the South, and he knows it's damned unlikely that slavery is going to exist within a single mile of that territory. Still, it's going to create a hell of a storm in the North."

"Papa, you're beginning to sound like an abolitionist," Tim drawled with amusement. "You want to ruin me in New Orleans?"

"I'd like to see Charles and you out of the South," Amory said bluntly. Involuntarily, Kara glanced at Charles. His face wore a polite, tense mask. "I don't like what I smell in the air. I don't want to see my sons fighting for something I don't believe in!"

"Papa, don't talk about war." Charles was pale now, his voice unhappy. His father was apt to jibe about his hatred of killing. Charles refused even to "possum hunt." "War is immoral, it's uncivilized."

"I'm convinced," Amory said with bitter humor, "that we are living in an uncivilized era. Never in the history of this country have we been so desperately in need of a leader. For years we've turned our backs on our giants in the Senate and elected nonentities to the Presidency. How, with men like Clay and Webster and Calhoun available, could we have elected Zachary Taylor?"

"Papa, you're talking about a southern gentleman, a slaveholder," Tim chided. Kara glanced sharply at him. He had been drinking heavily since dinner. This was a new, disturbing habit.

"No man could have been more unfit for the Presidency than General Taylor!" Amory exploded. "He knew less than a field hand about national or international affairs. He was unread, prejudiced."

"But he had the vote-winning appeal of a victorious general," Charles said. "People don't vote with their minds, it's the emotions that rule. Fillmore, of course, walked in when Taylor died suddenly that way, but how can we account for Pierce's election?"

Amory chuckled. "Charles, that was a bastard of a choice! Begging your pardon, Kara," he apologized wryly. "Damn the conventions for nominating two men like those two that year. Neither of them had an outspoken opinion on anything controversial. General Scott is a pompous, egotistical boor, to boot. We voted for the lesser of two evils." Amory sighed heavily. "And now the three giants are all dead. Who is there to lead us, at a time when we're so desperately in need of leadership?"

"What about Stephen Douglas?" Kara inquired.

"He's going to lose support in the North," Amory prophesied, "with his supporting this new act. I hear that Mr. Greeley wrote in his newspaper, the *Tribune*, that the Kansas-Nebraska Act would create more abolitionists in three months than that man Garrison and the other abolitionists could make in fifty years."

"I was impressed a few years ago, it was in early 1848, I think." Charles squinted thoughtfully. "This congressman from Illinois, Abraham Lincoln. Of course, there's been little heard from him since, but he spoke eloquently against the war. He said that Illinois officers fell while leading brave Illinoisans to 'robbery and dishonor, in aid of a war of rapine and murder.' He said," Charles paused, trying to recall the exact words. "He said that six thousand men were sent to Mexico to record their infamy and shame in the blood of poor, innocent, unoffending people, whose only crime is weakness."

"We have problems of our own right at home," Amory

said grimly. "Tim, what progress is your committee making with the sanitation conditions?" He didn't have to remind Tim they were approaching another summer. Possibly another epidemic.

Tim frowned.

"Much rhetoric is flying around," Tim admitted. "We've denounced New Orleans as one of the dirtiest and sickliest cities in the nation. We've heard our 'Acropolis of the South' unpatriotically referred to as the 'Necropolis of the South.' But damn it, we're accomplishing little! Nobody wants to listen. With fifteen thousand dead last summer, and a repetition possible this summer, we talk to deaf ears."

"So far there's been no outbreak," Amory said cautiously. "I was talking to Doctor Scott just the other day."

Tim rose impatiently to his feet.

"So far, but that's by the grace of God! Not by any efforts the city itself is making."

Kara leaned back, listening intently to the flow of talk about her, in her hands a book which would be her bedtime reading. Reading selected for her by Amory, and discussed with him as she finished each segment. Against her stern determination to concentrate on what was being said, Kara's mind returned to her uneasy belief that Amory guessed how Charles and she felt toward each other. Guessed and was gravely concerned.

Yesterday afternoon Charles had come in from the downpour. The others were all out of the house. Celestine had brought them coffee and returned to the kitchen wing. They might have been completely alone in the house, and Charles had looked at her, knowing that. For a poignant, painful moment she thought Charles would reach out, draw her into his arms. But Charles's control had faltered only a instant. Whatever he wished, she would have done. She had no will of her own where Charles was concerned.

"It's late," Amory announced abruptly, puncturing her introspection. "Let's call it a night."

Tim elected to remain downstairs, and Kara caught the faint glint of disapproval in Amory's eyes as they rested on his younger son, already pouring himself a refill. Upstairs in her room, Kara settled herself in bed for her night reading. Her private college, Amory had dubbed these night sessions.

The night was sticky, afflicted with a noisy mosquito symphony. Under her protective netting, Kara tried to concentrate on the open book across her lap. Perspiration beaded her forehead. Her nightdress clung to her body. After a few minutes, with a gesture of impatience, she freed herself from the netting, crossed to the windows to open them wider. More mosquitos, perhaps, she conceded, loathing the ugly, persistent buzzing, but considerably more air.

Kara traveled from one long, narrow window to the next, relishing the slight breeze that moved into the room. The heavy scent of the honeysuckle vines below and the piquant sweetness from the rose bushes were pleasing. She lingered at the last window, her eyes straying about the grounds as she fanned away the mosquitos with one hand.

Tim was striding toward a carriage, perhaps seventy-five feet down the road. The man in the carriage leaned forward to lend Tim a hand up to the seat. The spill of moonlight rested on a familiar profile. Jean Simone.

Quickly, with a tightening in her throat, Kara retreated from the window. This nocturnal meeting was deeply disturbing. Somehow she must stop this relationship. Tim was being reckless. If Louis Aumont found out, he would be furious; he would withdraw all his support!

Kara stood in the shadows, trying to think logically. First, she must stop the French lessons. The summer heat was sufficient excuse. Give Jean less reason to be about Manoir. Louis Aumont, with his position, was above reproach. There were politicians about town who resented Tim, entering politics at twenty-six. A wife and child might not be sufficient cover, if Tim were discovered.

New Orleans would forgive a gentleman any affair of the heart that revolved about a woman. An affair with another man would annihilate any career.

Chapter Twenty-one

Kara moved through the summer feeling as if she were caught in a vacuum. Simultaneously welcoming and dreading the constant contact with Charles. Occasionally gripped in the exquisite agony of being alone with him over tall glasses of iced lemonade while other members of the household were sequestered in their rooms. Glorying in the awareness of his feelings for her, even while tormented by the futility that faced them.

It was impossible to travel to New Orleans. Again there were alarming outbreaks of yellow fever all around the city proper. Nothing to match last summer's shattering epidemic, but still, people were dying of the fever daily. Doctors warned that the death toll could rise as high as twenty-five hundred before the hot spell departed.

Every afternoon, religiously, Charles rode to the small lakeshore cottage he had rented for Chris and the household slaves. Quite often, Kara and Amory would drive over to see Chris, sometimes taking Sheelagh with them. Kara nurtured a compulsion to bring the two little ones together. It delighted her to hear Sheelagh demand imperiously, "Cis, Cis! Go see Cis!"; even while she was brushed with alarm lest Emilie hear and throw one of her "attacks." Emilie and Annabel still kept a wall between Charles's son and themselves. For them the baby didn't exist.

In September Kara and Tim prepared for the move back

to New Orleans. The yellow fever had disappeared when the summer rains departed. After the heat, the near-isolation, at Manoir, Kara yearned for the social life that had begun before the summer. Charles, too, was shifting Chris and his entourage back to his New Orleans house.

Kara undertook a heavy schedule of small, political dinners, with Emilie playing the dowager queen, always in attendance. Kara was relieved that Tim appeared to be losing interest in Jean, who, nevertheless, hovered about even without the protective cover of tutoring Kara. Jean was alternately hurt, wistful, reproachful; but Tim was wrapped up in his commitments for the September state elections. Louis Aumont was running for the legislature.

During the September 1854 elections, sections of New Orleans were turned into battlegrounds between Irish and Know-Nothing gangs. Election groups prowled the streets of New Orleans, beating and stabbing immigrants. Hoodlums were hired to spread terror about the city, while the outmanned police force looked on helplessly, some said, paid to look the other way. With mounting horror, Kara observed the increasingly overt occupation. Amory suggested that Tim try for an investigating committee before the situation moved beyond control.

Tim tried to evolve a solution to the problem of the street battles. He was quietly told to keep his peace. The important task was to put Louis Aumont into the legislature.

Louis Aumont, in this election, repeated the activities of Judah Benjamin, who, some years before, pulled off a coup that put him into office. Aumont's aides, just prior to election, handed out cash to hundreds of Louisianians so that they might buy licenses for carriages or cabs. As a property owner, a man was entitled to vote. The new licensees had no prospects of ever owning even a wheel of a carriage, but the license entitled them to cast a vote for Louis Aumont, who happily paid for each such act in cash.

Louis Aumont was elected to the state legislature. Amory, displeased by Aumont's tactics, which were rumored about the state and indignantly denied, nonetheless predicted that Tim would run for the legislature two years hence. It was time to try for office on the state level. With Aumont in office, Tim's chances were improving.

Charles was bluntly critical of Tim's fellow travelers. Amory cynically pointed out that this was the method of operation at this level, by all parties. Results were what counted. Aumont was better for the state than his competition. When Aumont would go to Baton Rouge for the legislative sessions, Tim would accompany him as top aide.

Meanwhile, Amory and Charles talked heatedly, night after night, with Kara an absorbed listener, about critical federal problems. Stephen Douglas, so anxious to unite the Democratic party, to hold the Union intact, was being bitterly attacked in the North. The black-haired Douglas, a spectacular figure with his huge head above the stocky body, argued eloquently before the Senate or a public audience. Was booed out of a meeting in Chicago. His life was threatened.

In October, while Tim was out of the city with Louis Aumont, Jean came to Emilie with a proposal to start a French Club among the American ladies in the outlying areas. Flattered, Emilie undertook the formation of the club, with Manoir to be the scene of these cultural meetings. Kara overheard her say to Annabel that she was afraid "that young man" was developing a romantic feeling for her.

Kara pointedly did not join the French club. She pleaded a heavy entertainment schedule, plus the fact that she actually was not eligible as a resident of the city. At that time, Kara was intrigued by the young congressman about whom Charles had talked earlier, who had a run-in with Mr. Douglas in Springfield. Amory was following his activities with keen delight.

Mr. Lincoln delivered a speech at Springfield, which he repeated in Peoria ten days later, and which was then published. Amory declared this speech, which he read with deep appreciation to Kara, to be one of the great speeches of their lifetimes. A new leader was arising. A leader, Amory conceded with candid trepidation, for whom the South would profess little affection.

"Lincoln isn't speaking for himself," Amory said with conviction. "This is no politician's speech, not even a speech on behalf of his own state. The man speaks for a great principle. He didn't chastise the South for holding slaves—he admits our constitutional right to own slaves but—he comes right out and expresses his hatred for this institution." Amory leaned back, savoring the words he was about to quote, " 'because of the monstrous injustice of slavery itself, because it deprives our republican example of its just influence in the world, causes the real friends of freedom to doubt our sincerity and especially because it forces so many really good men amongst ourselves into an open war with the very fundamental principle of civil liberty.' "

"How would we approach this gradual emancipation that I understand Mr. Lincoln preaches?" Charles asked quietly.

"Then you believe emancipation will come!" Kara pounced, her eyes lighting. Usually Charles did a hasty retreat when Amory and she probed in this area.

"Kara, I believe in the freedom of man," Charles confessed. "But we've wrought a monster here in the South, and I don't know how we'll stumble out of it. Short of war," he added somberly. "And war is the last thing I wish to see."

"I appreciate the way Mr. Lincoln closed that Springfield speech," Amory said with quiet respect. "The way he urges every lover of liberty, North and South, to join in considering slavery not as a 'sacred right,' but as a *national problem,* that we must 'join together in the great and good work' so that not only shall we save the Union but that we shall have done so in such a fashion that succeeding generations, the world over, will bless us."

"I'd like to believe that Chris will grow up in a world that will see no wars. But I'm afraid." Charles stared into space. "And if it comes, it'll be fought on southern ground."

Kara shivered. She had seen too much of death. The years of the famine would never completely leave her. If war came to the South, she would take her child and run! But people wouldn't let war happen here. They knew the cost. Somehow, a way out must be found.

Kara was pleased that Tim was so deeply committed to his alderman's duties, along with the frequent consultations with Louis Aumont. The trips to Baton Rouge at regular intervals with Aumont. There was little occasion, she told herself optimistically, for Tim to be with Jean.

Jean, a young Frenchman with all the graces and great charm, was invited to some social events that Kara and Tim attended. Kara made a deliberate effort to keep Tim at her side on such occasions, triumphant in the indulgent asides she overheard about her "devotion to that handsome young husband."

Kara sensed, with satisfaction, that Tim was beginning to be bored with Jean, who appeared sullen and unhappy in Tim's presence. She wished Emilie would break off her absurd friendship with the French tutor, who was so ridiculously pampered by the ladies in Emilie's elite clique.

Without the diversion of her mornings at the quarters, Kara spent much of her time after breakfast, when Sheelagh was happily at play, reading the out-of-town newspapers Amory had ordered mailed to her. She was fascinated by the drama of daily living in New York, Philadelphia, the District of Columbia, Boston.

Kara stored up information gleaned from the newspapers to repeat to Tim at dinner, aware that Amory expected this of her. Tim had no patience for acquiring news of the country, although it was important to his career. It became a ritual each evening at the dinner table for Kara to brief Tim on daily events about the nation. About the world. To drill him on facts her bright mind deemed important for him to know. She achieved a wry satisfaction in Tim's tacit respect for her ability.

After dinner, Tim disappeared into those all-men meetings, thick with cigar smoke and the scent of bourbon. When there was some important measure under consideration, Kara would remain downstairs until Tim returned to tell her what was happening. She suspected he refrained from reporting some of the dirty politics practiced. This was of no consequence. Amory took pride in keeping her knowledge broad. This was part of her education.

The nights remained Kara's special torment. She read in bed until sleep came from sheer exhaustion. Emilie and Annabel continued to move in and out of the townhouse at regular intervals, though with less frequency than last winter, to Kara's relief.

At Christmas, Kara, Tim, and Sheelagh went to Manoir for a few days. Kara bearing gifts for the children in the quarters, who greeted her with much excitement. Christmas Eve brought tears to her eyes because Daphne, who had always appeared so cold and disapproving of Kara, had secretly been training the children in Christmas carols, and now marshaled them into the house to sing for the family after the stocking-hanging ceremony.

"How sweet they are," Kara whispered to Charles, with tears filling her eyes while Daphne calmly hurried the children out of the house again. Amory, in rare high spirits, tagged along, stuffing pockets with candies.

"All children are sweet," Charles said, and she knew he was thinking about Chris, already tucked into bed now, back in New Orleans.

Christmas day was quiet, uneventful. The day after, Emilie decided to go calling on the Bradfords, and wanted to take Sheelagh along to show her off. But Sheelagh was determinedly against this.

"No." Sheelagh shook her head stubbornly and turned to her mother. "Go see Cis! See Cis!" She tugged urgently at Kara's skirt, while Kara tried to conceal her confusion.

"Who is this Cis?" Emilie demanded, annoyed.

"A—a child she plays with beck in New Orleans," Kara stammered, inadvertently glancing at Annabel, who stared intently at her. For a painful moment, Kara's eyes met Annabel's. Annabel whitened. She knew, Kara thought unhappily, she knew about Charles's son being in New Orleans. "Sheelagh misses seeing him."

"I'm her grandmother," Emilie bridled, and turned on her granddaughter with rage in her eyes. "Why is it more important to see this little boy than to be with your grandmother?"

"See Cis!" Sheelagh repeated. A determined Botticelli cherub.

"Kara, why don't you talk to her?" Emilie's voice rose perilously. "I'm her grandmother! I come before some child she happens to play with sometimes."

"Sheelagh didn't mean it that way," Kara said uneasily.

"She's not even two; she doesn't know how to express herself sometimes."

"She's old enough to know who she prefers," Emilie shot back coldly. "Sheelagh prefers some stranger to her grandmother. It's all in the upbringing. Annabel, we'll go without her."

Kara knew that Emilie would be affronted for days because she felt that Sheelagh had slighted her. She wished, tiredly, that her small family was back in New Orleans.

The Rankin clan was in the dining room next evening, at dessert and coffee, when the current overseer appeared at the front door and asked to see Charles.

"What's happened?" Emilie asked fretfully, when Horatio was done whispering in Charles's ear. "Couldn't it wait until after dinner?" Emilie had never truly forgiven Charles for having discharged Fred Dent. This was obviously some word from Dent's replacement. No carriage had drawn up outside.

"I'll let you know after I talk with Mr. Roberts, Mama," Charles said with an ironic smile.

Emilie picked up her tale of complaint over some imagined slight administered by the Bradfords, but Kara noted how Amory's eyes moved compulsively to the corridor. In a few minutes, they heard the heavy front door open and close again, and then Charles's muted footsteps returning to the dining room.

"What was it, Charles?" Emilie frowned in annoyance at the intrusion.

"Mr. Roberts reported that the headman just made the night check. A slave is missing. Adam." Charles was grave, wary.

"Then how can you sit there over sweet-potato pie?" Emilie bristled with indignation. "Are you letting an investment of ours just walk off the plantation? Charles, I never will be able to understand you!"

"Mr. Roberts is quite capable of handling a search party," Charles said, his voice edged with sharpness. "If it's possible, he'll catch Adam and bring him back."

"You don't care!" Anger glazed Emilie's eyes. "You hope he gets away!"

"I can't forget that flogging he took," Charles said heavily. "That never should have happened." He took a deep breath, turned to his father for support. "If Adam is caught, we'll put him up for sale."

"If he's caught he ought to be flogged until he's half dead!" Emilie blazed. "I wonder sometimes that we still have Manoir, with all this ridiculous kindness toward the slaves. They don't understand that kind of treatment. They have no sensibilities."

Kara's eyes moved compulsively to Annabel. Annabel's hand trembled as she lifted a forkful of pie to her mouth. Her eyes opaque.

Kara tried to concentrate on her coffee, while Emilie droned on about Charles's and Amory's "unbusinesslike attitude toward the slaves," as she quoted her beloved "Papa." Outside, in the distance, they could hear the dogs barking noisily in the night.

Neither Charles nor Amory had much taste for after-dinner conversation tonight. Tim, complaining of having overindulged at the dinner table, retreated to his own room after a few minutes in the library. Annabel, at Emilie's nightly command, sat at the piano and dutifully played Chopin. Earlier than usual Emilie suggested they call it a night.

Kara's first thought, when she awoke to the crisp, cool morning, was about the runaway slave. She hoped, with a startling intensity, that he would escape. Charles, too, wished that. Charles never forgave himself for that flogging; it would be a kind of poetic justice for Adam to escape. That was one of the traits in Charles which Kara deeply loved, his deep sense of justice.

After breakfast Kara decided to go down to the quarters to spend some time with the children, in her old pattern. Yesterday she had taken them a mass of photographs collected from magazines, and now was wondering if she had, perhaps, been thoughtless in exposing them to a world they could never enjoy. Charles and Amory, she knew, were both off in the north fields right now. She'd heard them talking together en route to the stables.

In the quarters Kara romped with the youngsters for well over an hour, all the while wondering about Adam, yet inhibited about inquiring. Last night she'd lain in bed listening for sounds that would tell her of the success or failure of the hunting party. There had been no indications.

"All right, that's all today," she said finally to the children, picking up a toddler for an affectionate hug. "I must go see Mama Belle at the infirmary."

"Mama Belle, her sick," an older one said seriously. "Her got de misery."

Anxiously, Kara left the children to walk rapidly toward the infirmary. Just within the entrance she froze. Annabel, her back to the door, stood beside the pallet on which Mama Belle lay.

"I brought you some soup, Mama Belle," Annabel said solicitously while the old woman flashed a toothless grin of appreciation. "I heard you were sick."

"Me be fine in a li'l bit," Mama Belle said, reaching for the soup that her "white folks" had brought down for her. "Don't worry yo' li'l head 'bout Mama Belle."

But Annabel's gaze had left Mama Belle, to rivet to the other room of the infirmary. There, Adam lay prone on the floor, one trouser leg slit high about the thigh to allow for the splint on his leg. His face taut with sudden anger, his eyes staring into space.

Wordlessly Kara spun about, unnoticed, and left the room.

In the beginning of the new year, with an eye to a seat in the legislature, Tim petitioned the state body to establish a Board of Health, which was already under discussion because of the heavy tolls of yellow fever in the summers of '53 and '54. The campaign, a stiff one, was vigorously supported by the *Daily Picayune.* However, there were those, like the mother of the prospective legislator, who expressed dissenting opinions.

"Amory, I think it's just terrible," Emilie complained. "To advertise to the whole world about all the folks who died of the fever these last two summers. Can you imagine what that's going to do to business?"

"It's tampering with Providence," Annabel declared unhappily. "If God didn't want those folks to die, He wouldn't have sent the fever."

Nevertheless, the state legislature passed a law establishing a Board of Health, and Tim adroitly managed to acquire some additional luster as a politician from this passage, though his role was minute. Now, at the advice of his "small cabinet," Tim began to talk about the necessity for laying rail lines which would connect New Orleans with such cities as Mobile and Saint Louis and eventually with all the major cities of the country. New Orleans was the economic leader of the South. Let her live up to her potential.

The spring aldermanic elections were relatively peaceful,

for New Orleans, for which Kara was grateful. The continued belligerency toward immigrants unnerved her. For a time she battled with her father-in-law to advise Tim to take a stand against such idiocy; but Amory, while sympathetic, bluntly pointed out that politics allowed no room for sentiment. Once elected to the legislature, Tim would be in a position to fight such bigotry. But first Tim must win that seat. It wasn't going to be easy. They must brace themselves for the election in the fall of '56.

With the approach of summer, Kara and Tim made the usual trek to Manoir. Charles shifted Chris and the New Orleans household staff to a lakeshore cottage. Politics would be at a standstill during the hot, rainy season, and Tim was outspokenly elated. Kara, too, was glad for this respite, even while she knew that, within a week, she would grow restless in the lazy, isolated existence at Manoir.

The Rankin clan settled down to its usual summer routine. Kara watched Tim nervously when Jean appeared to lead Emilie's French club discussions. Tim had seen little of Jean during the spring. Tim was polite, faintly aloof to the tutor. Kara hopefully decided the affair was over.

By midsummer Kara was already anxious to return to New Orleans. She spent her mornings in the quarters, as always when she was at Manoir. And as always, shocked when the older children were shifted into the fields at twelve, though Charles explained that they were considered only "one-quarter hands."

"Damn it, Kara," he exploded one morning in the quarters, when Kara expressed her unhappiness because a particularly bright twelve-year-old, whom she was teaching to read, had been sent out to chop cotton. "What's the point of coddling them past twelve? I can't send them to school, it's against the law." He blatantly ignored Kara's private efforts in this direction. "They'll get into trouble just hanging around the quarters when they get big."

"Why can't they be trained for jobs?" Kara persisted. "The bright ones. And don't give me that story about the blacks not being capable of learning!" Kara shot back, her eyes alight. "Your father told me that right in New Orleans we have a black architect, five jewelers, four doctors, eleven music teachers, and fifty-two merchants."

And Kara remembered an article Amory had given her to read, which quoted Frederick Douglass. The words etched in her memory, filling her with a personal guilt. "Every hour sees the black man elbowed out of employment by some newly arrived immigrant whose hunger and whose color are thought to give him a better title to the place." Many of these newcomers were Irish. It was the Irish who were pushing the free blacks out of the heavy laboring and menial jobs. How wrong for the Irish, who suffered such discrimination themselves, to push around the "Nagurs," battling them in the railyards and coal mines and around the docks. Even the Irish women were replacing the free blacks as cooks and maids and washerwomen. In New York, in all the key cities. She remembered her own first days in New York. Remembered what Pat, Meg's brother-in-law, had said about free Negroes in New York. "Hate 'em. Comin' in, messin' up things for honest white folks. They be ruinin' jobs for the likes of us. We're gonna have to organize agin 'em, wait and see!"

"Kara." Charles's serious voice brought her back to the present. "I wanted to train Adam to be a skilled carpenter. I hired him out for this purpose. He tried to run away again. I had to bring him back to Manoir." He sighed. "I'm afraid I'm going to be pushed to sell him. Once a black as bright as Adam tastes the whip, he's no good anymore."

"Charles, do you blame him?" Kara burst out.

"No," Charles said bluntly. "But I must cope with the situation. I can't have these constant efforts at escape. You know what's bound to happen; others would join with him. I'll ask around at the neighboring plantations, find a good place for him. I won't sell to just anybody."

Charles left to return to the fields. Kara went back to the house. In the afternoon everybody napped. Kara roamed restlessly about the lower floor, glad when a thunderstorm broke through the torpid summer heat to provide minor relief. She stood at a window, terrified by the claps of thunder, the flashes of lightning, yet drawn to watch the display.

Something in the fury of the storm echoed her inner emotions. To be so close to Charles, close enough to touch, and to be forced to play this polite game. When she knew he loved her the way she loved him!

Kara smiled faintly, reliving the unwary moments when their eyes met, when hands accidentally brushed. He wanted her, the way a man wants his wife. With tenderness, with passion.

Exhausted by the summer heat, Kara fell asleep earlier than usual. The book she had planned to read lay unopened on the table close at hand. But after the first, drug-heavy sleep, she threshed about restlessly beneath the mosquito netting, stirred into wakefulness.

It was hot! Both Emilie and Annabel had announced they were taking the "hot-weather pills" which Dr. Scott had prescribed to assure them a good night's sleep. Kara refrained from such medication. She pushed aside the netting, suddenly thirsty. The ice in the pitcher had long since melted and was now a tepid three inches of water. She must go downstairs for something to drink. She pulled a wrapper about her slender form, heard a sudden clamor outside, unnaturally shrill in the night stillness.

"Yo' keep away from him, yo' heah? Keep yo' dirty hands off dat boy!" Jupe's voice came from below.

"Jupe, stop it!" Tim yelled, his voice strident. "Stop it before you kill him!"

Kara ran to the window. Jean Simone was sprawled on the ground, Jupe straddling him, pounding his face with blows.

Kara raced from her room, down the corridor, and knocked urgently on Amory's door. Her heart pounding because she could still hear Tim's voice, barely in control as he pleaded with Jupe to stop. Thank God, Emilie and Annabel had taken those pills; they would sleep through a hurricane.

The door opened. Amory, struggling into his robe, stood there, bleary-eyed but anxious.

"Kara, what the devil's going on?"

"Jupe," she gasped. "He's beating up Jean Simone. Tim can't stop him!"

"Go wake Charles," Amory said, instantly alert. "I'll go out there. Tell Charles to hurry," Amory urged, already striding toward the stairs.

But Charles had already been disturbed by the fracas downstairs.

"Kara, what's going on?"

"Jupe. He's beating up Jean. Charles, he could kill him!"

Kara followed Charles down the stairs, almost tripping once on the hem of her wrapper. Charles reached out a hand to steady her. Their eyes met for a charged moment, both of them aware of what must have happened out there beside the house. Jean and Tim at a rendezvous, with Jupe an uninvited third.

Outside, Amory struggled ineffectually to remove Jupe from the bloodied Frenchman beneath him. Tim, white and stricken, stood helplessly watching, frozen into immobility.

"Jupe!" Charles leaned forward to clutch at the massive black shoulders while Amory shouted, "Jupe, stop this! Stop this!"

Charles and Amory pulled Jupe away from the semiconscious man on the ground. Tim, his face taut, reached for a handkerchief, dropped to his knees to sop up the blood that poured from a gash.

"Jupe, I told him to go away," Tim was saying tiredly, as though he had repeated this a dozen times. "Didn't you know? I told him to go away."

Kara turned away from the anguish in Amory's eyes as he listened to Tim. Amory knew.

"We'd better get Jean inside," Kara said quietly. "Horatio will have to ride into New Orleans for Doctor Scott."

"He's not going to die, is he?" Tim asked, his voice shaking.

"I doubt it," Amory said drily. "Jupe, you'll have to help us. Come on, man."

Jupe was trembling, his eyes glassy. He was suddenly terrified at his actions. Wordlessly, Jupe bent to scoop up the prone figure on the ground, needing help from neither Amory nor Charles.

"Take him into the small bedroom toward the back," Amory instructed, glancing apprehensively at the upper windows. No sign that either Emilie or Annabel had awakened.

Inside, Amory shouted for Octavia and Horatio. They quickly appeared. Octavia frightened when she spied Jean's battered body, the scratches on Jupe's face. She was shipped off for hot water, clean clothes. Horatio was ordered to take the carriage into New Orleans, to bring back Dr. Scott. Daphne and Celestine, cowering in alarm, appeared in a doorway. Amory waved them back.

"Li'l Missy?" Jasmine called in a small voice, halfway down the stairs. "Li'l Missy, yo' be awright?"

"It's nothing, Jasmine," Kara said. "Go back to Sheelagh."

Amory, with Octavia's help, worked over Jean, who was regaining consciousness.

"That black!" Jean gasped shakily. "He is going to hang for this! I will see to that!"

Tim was ashen, his eyes fastened on Jupe. Kara feared his knees would buckle.

"Tim," she whispered quietly. "Come with me. Tim."

Kara tugged at his sleeve, and he allowed her to guide him from the small, sparsely furnished bedroom to the library. Seated in a chair by the window, Tim stared into space as though drugged. Kara brought him a glass of bourbon, pressed it into his hands. He gulped it down.

"Kara." He gazed up at her, his eyes brilliant with emotion, his voice astonishingly strong. "Kara, you find some way to get Jupe out of this, or I'm walking out on the whole deal. *You* be the alderman, Kara. *You* run for the legislature."

"Tim! Tim, don't talk that way."

"You get Jupe out of this, Kara," Tim warned. "Get him out or the whole show is over."

Chapter Twenty-two

Kara stared at Tim in disbelief.

"Tim, you don't know what you're saying!" But her eyes fastened on Tim; she knew he meant it. But how could she save Jupe from legal punishment? Help him escape? How? She knew about the much-hated underground railroad; it was discussed in scathing language by many of their neighbors, with deep respect by Amory and herself. How was she to contact these people? The immediacy was terrifying. "Tim, how can I help Jupe escape? I know nothing about these things." Her face ashen, her voice a hoarse whisper.

"I'm not talking about escape." All at once, Tim was secure, calm. "You want me to play the politician. It's important to you and Papa." His smile was caustic. "You're bright, Kara, Papa's always talking about that. You figure out how to get Jupe off the hook."

Trembling, Kara tried to assimilate what Tim was asking her to do. And Tim meant it. Jupe was his Rock of Gibraltar in this world. Tim would go out and play the charming, ingratiating young politician who won fresh friends and votes daily; but he intended to have Jupe always there in the background.

"Stay here, Tim," Kara said, her mind scrambling for a way out. "Let me talk to Jean."

"All right." His eyes were a mixture of desperation and hope.

Kara returned to the small downstairs bedroom. Octavia had been dismissed. Amory and Charles were trying to calm Jean, whose pain was aggravated by his indignation.

"How is he?" Kara asked softly.

"He'll survive," Amory reassured her. "Some cracked ribs, I suspect. Doctor Scott will have to patch up that cut on his head, I've done what I could. The bruises will fade away." Amory was haggard. How awful that he had to find out about Tim this way!

"That black bastard will hang!" Jean was insisting, his eyes ablaze with vengeance. "Attacking me that way! And as for Tim," he accused, "he did nothing to stop him!"

"Tim tried," Kara intervened, softly, and hesitated, gearing herself for what must be done. "Please, may I speak with Jean alone?" Kara's eyes pleaded with Amory and Charles. They looked at her in utter disbelief. "Please," she said urgently. "It's important."

"Where's Tim?" Jean asked guardedly, when they were alone.

"He's shaken up," Kara said, and winced seeing the smug acknowledgment on Jean's face. "I made him stay in the library till he gets hold of himself again. Jean," she took a deep breath, "Tim doesn't want you to take action against Jupe." She looked at him directly, her fists clenched.

"What do you mean?" Jean tried to raise himself, outraged. He gasped in pain, gingerly lowered himself into a prone position again. "Of course, I shall prosecute."

"No," Kara said with gentle firmness, her face belying her inner turmoil. "No, Jean, *you will not.* Nor will you see Tim again. You will forget tonight ever happened."

"You have lost your mind, madame!" His eyes blazed furiously.

"You will stay away from Tim. You will do nothing to incriminate Jupe," she repeated slowly. "Because if you do, I will go to all those ladies whom you instruct at fancy fees, and in the deepest confidence I will tell them that I sent Jupe to horsewhip you because you made improper advances to my husband. You lead a comfortable life among the plantation ladies. You don't want to lose that."

"You wouldn't dare!" Jean flushed an ugly red. "That would involve Tim."

"*You* made improper advances, Tim rejected them. But a wife with my Irish temper wouldn't be satisfied with apologies," she improvised, realizing she was gaining ground. "Oh, they'll believe that I sent Jupe to rough you up. They've never really accepted me as a southern lady. They'll enjoy such a juicy tidbit of gossip."

Kara's eyes held his, unflinching before the accusation in his. She smiled faintly with a confidence she didn't really feel. Knowing she walked a tightrope.

"Only if you guarantee that Jupe will be sent away from Manoir," Jean stipulated sullenly. "I have to know he will never be here again. And you must swear not to tell Madame Emilie and Madame Annabel," he continued with petulant defiance.

"No one will know," Kara promised. "Just us, who were here tonight. The slaves won't talk, they'll be afraid to. Jupe will be sent away. Tonight."

Kara joined the three men in the library. Jean could be left alone until Dr. Scott arrived. Tim was slumped in his chair, his eyes on the floor, a bourbon refill in his hand. He was drinking too much, Kara thought detachedly, but not so much that outsiders would notice.

Amory stood at the window, staring out into the night. His distress revealed itself in the tautness of his shoulders, in the hand at his side that unconsciously clenched and unclenched.

Like Charles, when he was disturbed, Kara thought.

"Well?" Charles forced a smile, his eyes inquiring.

"Jean won't press charges," she said quietly. Tim's head shot up. "But we mustn't mention tonight to the ladies. I promised this. Jean will continue as before with his French tutoring. And I promised that Jupe would be sent away from Manoir." Her eyes clung to Charles. She felt the threatening weight of Tim's gaze. "Charles," her voice dropped to a whisper, "would you take Jupe into your house?"

Gently, Charles nodded, his face serious.

"I'll send you Zeke in his place." Charles turned to Tim. "Is that a fair exchange?"

Tim averted his eyes. "Fair enough."

"I'll go out and tell Octavia," Kara said softly. "She's terribly upset."

Again it was a relief to Kara to return to New Orleans. She sensed that Tim, too, was glad to leave Manoir behind. These final weeks of the summer had been strained. Tim was unhappy that his father and his brother knew about his shadowed relationships.

Kara told herself she was glad that Amory knew. No need, now, to keep up some of the small pretenses before him. She felt a fresh closeness to Amory. At the same time, she was conscious of a festering concern in him because of what he sensed between Charles and her.

In September Kara and Tim resumed the frenzied rounds of entertainment. Tim was active in the election campaigns, though he had little taste for the corruption that was rampant. But he was earning favors that he would call in, during next fall's election, when he himself would be running for the legislature.

The fall elections were declaimed a state disgrace, fraught

with wholesale violence and bloodshed. The legislature refused to seat four American party candidates who had been elected, on the grounds that they had won by fraudulent means. The legislature passed a rash of stricter voter-registration laws, designed to eliminate floaters. The state body made the city of New Orleans responsible for whatever damages were wrought by roving mobs during election campaigns. Amory, as usual, was cynical about the efficacy of these laws.

In the winter, under Amory's tutelage, Tim began to campaign quietly for a seat in the legislature. Kara suspected that Tim was seeing Jupe, but this was an area where she knew she must not intrude. And as part of the agreement, she knew that Tim was determined to win the election, for her. Amory repeatedly warned that this would be a far tougher goal to attain than the aldermanic seat Tim now held. Kara refused to consider defeat. Tim's political success was for her a substitute for marriage. All of her being was tied up in the moves that brought Tim nearer the legislature, nearer the governership.

Emilie and Annabel came less frequently to the New Orleans house. The glamour had paled. It was Amory who was apt to arrive for dinner and stay the night, to indulge in earnest, searching, after-dinner talks about Tim's political format. Sometimes, Amory and Tim would go to the Aumont house, not to reappear until far into the night. Sometimes, Charles would join them for dinner.

Kara kept prodding Tim to urge an enlargement of the public-school system in New Orleans, with Amory backing her up.

"I know it's a fine public-school system that we have," Kara conceded. "And one of the few in the South. But there's room for improvement." A zealous glow showed in her eyes.

"Tim, that will buy you votes among the Irish and the Italians and the Germans, no matter what their party affiliations."

"She's right, Tim," Amory agreed.

"Someday," Kara said softly, "blacks will attend these schools, too, side by side with whites."

"Not in our lifetime," Amory grunted. "Nor in Sheelagh's lifetime." He leaned forward to pick up a small volume which lay on a table nearby. "Did you read Cervantes, Kara?"

"Yes." Kara's face glowed. "What a beautiful book."

"Pity that there's no room in our civilization for a knight on a white charger, a Don Quixote."

Amory cautioned her not to pressure Tim. Some of her enthusiasm diminished. She was impatient to see things happen for the good! As a legislator, Tim would hold substantially more power. He had such eloquence, he could sway people. He could be a power in improving conditions in this state.

"The nearest thing we've ever had to that in this country," Charles contributed quietly, "was Thomas Jefferson. What a shame he isn't alive today."

"I remember Jefferson with the greatest of respect and admiration," Amory said, "but in times like this there is no place for Jeffersonian democracy. The federal government must play a strong role in national life. Only the federal government can hold the nation together. But we've embarked on an age of mediocrity in leadership. Pierce wants a second term, but I doubt the Democrats will give it to him. There's a lot to be said for the Republican party."

"Papa," Charles reproached. "No matter how you try to dress them up, they're still a bunch of abolitionists."

"And are we different at heart?" Amory challenged strongly. "We own slaves, but do we believe this is right? There's much that's wrong in this country. We founded our nation on the principle that 'all men are created equal.' Then we interpreted that to mean 'all men are created equal, *except* Negroes.' Now we have the Know-Nothings, who declaim that 'all men are created equal, *except* Negroes and foreigners and Catholics.' Where the hell is it going to end? When will *we* be excluded?"

Amory was increasingly pessimistic about Tim's chance at a seat in the legislature. Kara suspected that this was based on his knowledge that she would be painfully disappointed if Tim should lose. Amory warned bluntly that they must play politics to the hilt, that they must cross party lines for votes.

Kara launched on a private campaign for the Irish vote, which was considerable in New Orleans. With Amory as her escort, with her socially elite American-Creole circle completely unaware of these activities, Kara went to the waterfront to fight for the Irish votes. She walked along the banquettes of the Irish Channel, where Irish women sat on the steps, and their men rocked close by and passed the beer. Kara attended Irish wakes and swapped stories about the old country. With tears in her eyes she talked about her family in Ireland. And listened to their tales of woe.

Amory gloated over the votes he was sure Kara would bring over to their side in the election next fall. And Kara remembered Emilie's words about the Irish: "They drive the drays and trade on a flair for low politics."

Kara campaigned not only for Tim, but also for those involved in the local spring elections because, as Amory stated with sardonic humor, "one hand washes the other." She was also intensely concerned about the presidential elections. Like Amory and Charles, she was worried about the tensions in the country.

Early summer was a time of crises. On May 21, proslavery men invaded the town of Lawrence, Kansas, where efforts were being made to maintain Kansas as a free state. Eight hundred men—under Sam Jones, the proslavery sheriff of Douglas County, and J. B. Donaldson, the U.S. marshal—stalked into the town, broke the presses of the *Herald of Freedom* and the *Kansas Free State*, confiscated weapons, destroyed a local hotel, and burned the house of Dr. Robinson, who had been illegally named governor by the Free-Soil voters. A member of the "posse" was killed and two injured, presumably through carelessness in destroying the hotel. None of the local citizenry were harmed, yet northern newspapers and abolition orators cried out vociferously against the "Sack of Lawrence."

On May 24, John Brown, with his four sons and two other men, viciously massacred five proslavery men on Pottawatomie Creek. A warrant was issued for Brown, but he escaped from the territory into Nebraska.

Also in May, the tensions over slavery erupted within the august walls of the United States Senate. The tall, commanding Senator Charles Sumner of Massachusetts—a fanatic antislavery leader—delivered a speech which lasted two days, May 19 and 20. The speech was pompous, redundant, exaggerated, charged with malicious emotions. On the next day Senator Sumner was caned in the Senate chamber by a furious young representative from South Carolina, Preston Brooks, a nephew of one of the men the senator had maligned. While Brooks was forcibly restrained, there were those in the Senate chamber who openly approved.

Early in June the Democrats met in Cincinnati to nominate a candidate for the Presidency. Pierce wanted a second term. He was rejected, and James Buchanan was nominated. Amory was disgusted.

"Hell, the man's a manipulator," Amory complained. "Look at his record. I admit he has a certain charm," Amory conceded grimly, "but every move is calculated. And try to get him to face any controversial issue! He dodges every time."

"It'll be the South that will put him in," Charles sighed. "Wait and see."

Surprisingly, Emilie avidly followed the Democratic convention news.

"Oh, Mr. Buchanan is such a handsome man," she gushed repeatedly. "What a shame he's chosen to remain a bachelor."

The Know-Nothings nominated Millard Fillmore; and the Whigs, their party disintegrating, followed suit and nominated Fillmore too. On June 17, the new Republican party, growing in strength, met in Philadelphia and chose Frémont as their candidate.

Amory and Charles, following the convention closely, though they would hardly vote for a Republican, considered Frémont a disastrous choice. However, they were intrigued with the emergence of Abraham Lincoln, briefly, as a possible candidate for vice-president. Although Lincoln received 112 delegate votes, William Dayton of New Jersey was nominated.

Amory had developed into an avid admirer of Lincoln, particularly since his speech at the state convention in Bloomington, when Lincoln had so eloquently warned the members of that convention that unless the violence in Kansas was halted, "Blood will flow, brother's hand will be raised against brother."

At Manoir in the summer of 1856, the entire family, including Emilie and Annabel, were involved in the mechanics of furthering Tim's campaign. The ladies gathered regularly in the library to address envelopes which carried appeals for Tim's election. Emilie was loosening her personal purse strings, so enamored was she of her possible position as "mother of the legislator." Without question she turned over huge sums to Amory, who applied them to areas where the money would buy votes.

Tim, under Amory's coaching, followed the lead set by the *Daily Picayune*, and called for the development of manufacturing in the South, so that the South might benefit from the tariff. Tim made a handsome, appealing figure on the podium as he discussed a newly announced process of destructive distillation which could produce oil from rosin, which oil could take the place of whale oil. The price of whale oil had risen scandalously, from nineteen cents a gallon in 1840 to ninety-five cents a gallon in 1856. The pine forests of the South offered fresh wealth.

Tim pleaded for clean government at a time when he knew, as did every politician in the state, that voters went to the polls using names taken from tombstones. That gangs hung out near the polls each election day, prepared to gouge the eyes of the opposition who tried to vote.

On election day in New Orleans, many a man checked his pistols, sharpened his knives, and stood ready to kill. On election day the citizenry could be certain of constant physical violence. A man intending to vote could never be sure that he would not have his head bashed in with brass knuckles by supporters of men he opposed.

Under such conditions Tim ran for election to the legislature in September 1856. Election day was humid and uncomfortable. A few mosquitos, supposedly gone for the year, returned to buzz queruously about, as though this were still midsummer. Kara, fretting anew over her own inability to vote, paced about the New Orleans house.

Amory voted in his parish and immediately afterward was driven into New Orleans to be with Kara. Emilie and Annabel decided to remain at Manoir.

"Don't tell me a thing about the election until it's all over," Emilie had warned imperiously. "The state of my nerves just won't tolerate that kind of anxiety."

Tim had left immediately after breakfast, with Jupe and Horatio as his protectors, to meet with Louis Aumont.

"Kara, sit down," Amory said. They were both in the library, waiting hopefully for some word about the progress of the election.

"He has a good chance, hasn't he?" Kara's eyes pleaded for reassurance as she obediently sat down beside her father-in-law. Amory poured coffee for them.

"Kara, you know as much as I do," Amory said honestly. "We've done everything we could." He sighed. "There's much about elections in this state that turns me sick. Aumont plays as dirty as the next man, but what other way is there to run for election? Bad government is formal government in New Orleans," Amory said grimly. "Let's hope Tim wins, so that he can be instrumental in a cleanup."

Jasmine brought Sheelagh downstairs, ready to take her to Charles's house so that she could play with her beloved "Cis."

"Jasmine, not today," Kara protested nervously. "Not with the wildness in the streets. I'm sorry, darling," she said, kissing Sheelagh's forehead. "You'll go visit with Chris tomorrow."

"Want to see today!" Sheelagh's eyes blazed with indignation. "Now!"

"Come on, young lady, none of that," Amory scolded with mock sternness, and scooped her off her feet. Sheelagh gurgled with delight.

After a few minutes of horseplay, Amory relinquished Sheelagh to Jasmine again, and the pair left the library. Kara turned somberly to him.

"What happens if Tim loses?" Her eyes were apprehensive. "Do we try again in two years?"

"Let's not think beyond tonight," Amory suggested warily. "We have a powerful machine moving for Tim. Let's be optimistic."

"All along you've warned me Tim might lose," Kara chided affectionately. "And now you want me to be optimistic?"

"Get out the chess set and let's play."

"Now?" Kara gazed at him in disbelief. "How can we play chess on election day?"

"Kara, this is one election," he emphasized gently. "There'll be more coming up. Now you learn to ride with the tide, young lady, or you won't have the stomach to go through these times."

"When will we know?" she asked as she walked to the commode to get the carved-ivory chess set that Amory had given her for her last birthday.

"The figures will start coming in early tomorrow. By tomorrow night, we should have the results."

"I can't wait till tomorrow," Kara burst out.

"You can," Amory reassured her with a chuckle, "Now sit down and let's see if I can trounce you, young lady."

Amory fell asleep in his chair in the library, after eating heavily of Aphrodite's skilled cooking. Kara sat across from him, trying to read, her mind distracted by the roving, noisy crowds in the streets. It was a fairly calm election, as New Orleans elections went, Kara thought with a flicker of dry amusement.

She wished Tim would come home, to give them some idea of the voting turnout. He ought to come home, to his father and to her. He was closeted somewhere with those men who made up Louis Aumont's political machine.

Eventually the streets quieted. Only an occasional raucous outburst shattered with night quiet. Jasmine tiptoed into the library.

"Bring in some coffee, please, Jasmine," Kara asked, her nerves taut with the waiting. "We might as well go on to bed. We won't learn anything tonight."

Tim wouldn't bother to come home. More and more he wasn't bothering to come home at night.

Kara awakened Amory when Jasmine returned with a pot of steaming hot café au lait. Sheepishly, Amory pulled himself erect in his chair and grinned at her.

"I'm a fine comfort on election eve," he apologized.

"We might as well go to sleep," Kara said, her eyes averted. "I doubt that Tim will come home tonight."

"Kara," Amory said, his voice anguished, suddenly appearing ten years older. "Where did I go wrong with Tim? Where did I fail him?"

Though exhausted from the tensions of the day, Kara lay sleepless until the orange-and-pink streaks of dawn brushed the sky. Only then did she succumb to slumber, to dream, to toss about in the hot September morning. Quite suddenly she came awake, opened her eyes.

Daylight. Tim standing by the bed. Unshaven, dark shadows beneath his eyes, his hair uncombed.

"Tim." She sat up anxiously. Afraid.

"I came to report, Kara." His smile was bitter. "While the figures won't be complete for another five or six hours, it seems safe to say that I've been elected to the state legislature."

"Oh, Tim!" She sat upright, her eyes shining.

"You've won again," he drawled. "Please tell Papa."

Tim spun away from her, strode across the room to the

door. And Kara watched, a tightness in her throat, a sickening awareness of what she had read in Tim's eyes. Contempt for his wife. *Tim hated her.*

Chapter Twenty-three

Kara would have enjoyed accompanying Tim to Baton Rouge for the coming session of the legislature, but Tim had made it clear, right after election, that he meant to attend these sessions alone. Kara warily brought up the subject again, the morning before he was to leave.

"This is politics, Kara," Tim said with a new edge of superiority in his voice. "Not a place for women."

"Your father would like to go and see you in the legislature," Kara said stubbornly. Amory had been hinting blatantly for such an invitation. "Why were you so sharp when he brought it up last week?"

"Because in Baton Rouge, Kara, I operate on my own," Tim said coldly. "I can't tuck Papa in my pocket and let him tell me how to vote on measures that come up. Papa and you must learn that when I go into those chambers, *I* am the legislator."

"Of course, Tim." Kara struggled to sound natural. More and more she was encountering these outbursts of hostility. "But you must realize how much it means to your father."

"I gave him what he wanted," Tim shot back. "And you, I gave you what you wanted. Now leave me alone."

Wordlessly, tears stinging her eyes, Kara rose to her feet and ran from the room. She remained upstairs until Tim left the house. Late in the afternoon, Emilie and Annabel came in from Manoir to shop on Chartres Street. With the men, the three of them were to go to the Saint Charles Theater that evening.

Tim would appear in time for dinner, Kara surmised with her freshly born cynicism. Tim catered to Mama because, of late, he was constantly wishing for some new extravagance that Amory would bluntly turn down. He was enamored now of the trotting races, constantly plotting to ask his mother for an extremely expensive team. By being elected, Tim considered himself due such rewards.

It was Charles who appeared late, holding up dinner for twenty minutes, much to his mother's annoyance. Aphrodite's dinner, as always, was superb; but Emilie found fault in an effusively polite vein that was new to Emilie's manner, and very disconcerting for Kara.

"I tell you these things for you own good, Kara," Emilie gushed. "If you don't take a firm hand with Aphrodite now, you're sure to have problems later. I've been through this."

"I hear Bishop Polk is still working to raise funds for his University of the South," Charles said to his father, with an effort to derail his mother's petty tirade. His mother was especially fond of Bishop Polk.

"Yes," Amory said with a show of enthusiasm. "I sent him a check last week. Modest, I'm afraid." He smiled apologetically. "But you know the expenses at Manoir this year."

Emilie smiled vindictively. "Amory, I think Charles and you were out of your minds, going out and buying all those beds for the quarters. They could have gone on sleeping on the old ones!"

"No, Mama," Charles said firmly. "They could not."

Emilie stared at him, mildly rebuffed, then swung her attention to her husband.

"Amory, is there any truth in that rumor about an uprising

over at the Bradleys?" Emilie frowned in distaste. "We heard some talk."

Amory was suddenly sober.

"They've had some mild trouble. Bradley had to sell a troublesome black." Amory gestured for quiet because Jasmine was approaching the dining room with the next course. "But there's nothing to be concerned about, Emilie," he continued.

"The Bradleys are lovely folks," Annabel contributed with conviction. "I can't imagine anybody wanting to start trouble for them. It's all those agitators up North, saying such terrible things about us."

"Bradley has a way of pulling in the reins," Charles said with honesty. "I'm not actually surprised that he gets some bad reaction."

Emilie stiffened in impatience. "Charles, you're impossible. Oh, Amory, Annabel and I met Madame Aumont at Olympe's this afternoon. She's so enthusiastic about railroad stocks. You know, she has a sixth sense about these things; her husband always listens to her advice," Emilie said archly. "She says he's buying heavily."

"I have no money for railroad stocks," Amory said with ironic humor.

"I was thinking of my money," Emilie smiled with importance.

"Not in railroad stocks," Amory growled with unexpected firmness. "I don't trust all this expansion in the railroads. There's been far too much speculation. I don't consider rail stocks a safe investment in today's market."

Tim made much of his mother, was impersonally polite to Annabel and Kara. He wasn't actually with them, Kara thought uneasily, distrusting this outside world of his. But he'd be all right in Baton Rouge. He'd spend much of his time with Monsieur Aumont, who was highly respected in legislative circles.

In the coming months Kara found herself seeing less and less of Tim and was increasingly concerned about how he handled himself in Baton Rouge. Amory quietly checked, he reported to Kara that Tim was performing well, ingratiating himself in quarters that counted politically. He was listening to his mentor, the canny Louis Aumont.

Every time Tim went off to Baton Rouge, Amory insisted that Kara and Sheelagh stay at Manoir. Kara dreaded and at the same time looked forward to these intervals on the plantation. She enjoyed the leisurely days, the quiet evenings, even though Emilie was an abrasive companion at regular intervals.

It was exquisitely painful to be alone with Charles in the quarters. Alone if she discounted the presence of the children, the ill in the infirmary, Mama Belle. But at the quarters, away from the family, she could look at Charles without the constant fear of being discovered.

And she loved his son as if he were her own. Chris was a delightful Botticelli angel. In New Orleans she spent time daily teaching the children to count, to add, to recognize the letters of the alphabet. Sometimes, noting the resemblance between the two cousins, which was poignantly beautiful.

As always, Kara herself was learning. Amory, the master chess player, regularly dissected the intricacies of politics for her, on every level. Yet sometimes in the evenings, at Manoir or at Kara's and Tim's New Orleans house, Amory, Charles, and she would become absorbed in some impassioned discussion, and suddenly she would become aware of the troubled look in Amory's eyes as they moved from her to Charles, and back to her again. Seeing nothing for Charles and her. Seeing his own helplessness.

Kara, like Amory and Charles, was disturbed by the increasingly angry talk about a dissolution of the Union. Only two days after Buchanan took office, and Louisiana was instrumental in voting him in, the Supreme Court handed down the decision that said Congress had no power to legislate slavery either in or out of the territories, and therefore the Missouri Compromise was unconstitutional. This was a terrible blow to the antislavery cause, and actually did much to divide the North and South even further. In the North the Fugitive Slave Act became almost impossible to enforce.

Buchanan was having his problems in the Utah Territory where the Mormons, under the dictatorship of Brigham Young, acted as though they were independent of the United States. The Mormons' habit of living in a state of polygamy, which Young dubbed "the seed of the church," aroused bitter opposition in the rest of the country. More disruptive was the determination of the Mormons to resist the rule of the United States government.

Late in the summer, business conditions were causing grave concern. In August the Ohio Life Insurance and Trust Company in Cincinnati suddenly failed. It had put too much capital into rail stocks. In early September other banks and business houses failed. At dinner at Manoir, Amory spoke unhappily about the panic that was arising.

"It's overexpansion," Amory declaimed, while Emilie and Annabel continued a private conversation about a ball being given by the Bradleys. Emilie was mildly affronted by a new friendship Annabel had developed with one of the Bradley girls. "All that gold coming into the financial markets. People spending money as though it grew on trees. All the speculation. I tell you, we're going into a panic that will be as rough as the one in thirty-seven."

"We've got twenty-one thousand miles of railroad built,"

Charles said, shaking his head. "But how much of that is operating?"

"Can't something be done?" Kara asked. "Can't the government step in?"

"We'll be the last to feel it, here in the South," Charles surmised. "We're fortunate; we have plenty of European markets for our cotton."

"Business conditions will have sharp political repercussions," Amory conceded. "Particularly on the national level."

"Oh, Amory," Emilie said impatiently, breaking off her conversation with Annabel. "Must you always bring business to the dinner table? That was one thing Papa never permitted."

Early in 1858 the groundwork was laid for Tim's campaign for a second term in the legislature. Again Emilie sold securities to finance the race. Kara, now a veteran campaigner among the Irish, went regularly along the Irish Channel until late May. Then she went with Sheelagh, as usual, to Manoir for the summer. Yellow fever was still taking heavy tolls during the hot, wet months. New Orleans was to be avoided.

In 1858 it was announced that the cost of laying tracks for New Orleans' proposed streetcars would cost seven thousand dollars a mile, a prohibitive figure. That same year saw the laying of the trans-atlantic cable that linked the United States with Europe. Queen Victoria sent a ninety-word message to President Buchanan, which flashed across the ocean in sixty-seven minutes. The cable went dead immediately after. It was conceded that it would be a number of years before regular service could be established.

At Manoir, Emilie continued to be aggrieved at the friendship that had developed between Annabel and Betsy Bradley. This summer Emilie and Sheelagh were having a succession of nasty encounters. Late in August there was a particularly bitter battle between Sheelagh and her grandmother.

"Sheelagh, you are to stay in your bedroom all afternoon," Emilie had decreed. "In this heat it's absurd not to take a full afternoon nap."

"Don't want a nap," Sheelagh grumbled, gearing herself for battle. As soon as her grandmother retired to her room, Sheelagh knew she would be spirited off to spend the afternoon with Chris, at the cottage by the lake. She knew, also, that she must not mention this to her grandmother.

"Sheelagh, don't be impudent." Emilie frowned impatiently. "You'll go to your room and nap. Kara, where's that girl of yours?" Emilie harbored an intense dislike for Jasmine.

"No nap," Sheelagh shrieked. "You're not my mama!"

"Sheelagh!" Emilie's voice was shrill with anger. "How dare you talk to me that way!"

Emilie lashed into a tirade against her five-year-old granddaughter that made Kara tremble. It was impossible to quiet her, once she had started. In a few moments Emilie called hysterically for Dr. Scott.

"Grandma just loves herself," Sheelagh announced, tears spilling over when Emilie was upstairs in the care of Celestine and Annabel, and Horatio in route for Dr. Scott. "Why can't we go home, Mama? I don't like this house."

"I'm sorry, darling." Kara gathered Sheelagh into her arms. "We'll go back as soon as this heat is over."

Recovered from her "attack of nerves," Emilie went off to spend a few days with Madame Aumont at her lakefront house. Annabel pointedly remained behind. Emilie considered it improper for Kara to remain the only white woman at Manoir.

Each afternoon, promptly after lunch, Annabel rode off to

spend two hours with Betsy Bradley. At the same time Kara usually went off with Sheelagh and Jasmine to visit Chris. But today, Kara was particularly exhausted from her morning down in the quarters. The heat had been unbearable.

"Jasmine, I'll stay here and nap," she decided. "You take Sheelagh over to see Chris."

"Yes'm," Jasmine said placidly. "Come on, baby," she held Sheelagh's hand affectionately. "We go git dat no' count Horatio take us over der."

Horatio, too, was in the conspiracy to keep Chris's presence a scant half-hour's drive from Manoir a secret. There was little the slaves didn't know. Jasmine had told Kara that Artemis had developed a strong romantic interest in Jupe, who was polite but wary.

A few minutes later Annabel came down the stairs.

"Are you going out in all this heat?" Kara asked Annabel.

"I promised Betsy I would be over," Annabel explained with that glint of faint disapproval in her eyes which was ever-present when she looked at Kara. "I must send for Horatio."

"I'm sorry," Kara apologized. "I just sent Sheelagh and Jasmine out for a ride along the lake with Horatio. Sheelagh's so restless in the summer."

Annabel stared in sharp annoyance.

"I wish you'd told me earlier, Kara. Zeke is out too. With Tim in the city. But there must be someone in the stables who can take me over."

"Do you think you should go to the Bradleys today?" Kara asked with concern. "After the disturbance last night?"

Annabel uttered a low sound of impatience.

"So some slaves escaped last night." She arched her eyebrows. "Whatever does that mean to the Bradleys? They'll run some ads in the newspapers and the slaves will be brought back." But the Fugitive Slave Act was hardly being enforced these days. Not with the way feelings were rising up North.

"I just don't think it's advisable." Kara said, though she found it futile to argue with Annabel.

"I appreciate your concern," Annabel said with cold politeness, "but it's entirely unwarranted."

Annabel swept past Kara toward the rear of the house. "Celestine! Celestine! I need a carriage."

Annabel leaned back in the carriage, fastidiously touching her damp forehead with one of the hand-rolled handkerchiefs that Betsy Bradley had made for her. Oh, she'd be glad when the summer was over! She'd be glad when Kara took herself and her daughter back to New Orleans.

She hated the way Charles looked at Kara sometimes. In that ugly, hungry way. At times she was sure there was something between them. Kara was always making up to Charles in that sweet way of hers. And everybody knew Kara's background. Tim was probably suspicious about the two of them, but he didn't seem to do anything about it.

Annabel frowned as the carriage rumbled along in the semitropical heat of late August, and her mind dwelt on her husband. Charles probably had a woman in Ramparts Street again. As for the child, Mama was magnificent, the way she wouldn't let that black baby in the house!

If Mama hadn't been the way she was, she might have taken in the baby herself. But Mama would have just about died. She looked out the window, a little regretful, wistful. She could have had a child that way, without Charles coming near her. Sometimes, she wished she could bring herself to let Charles come to her bed. But not after what she had gone through. Never again.

Betsy understood about men. She swore she'd never

marry. It was so nice to have Betsy for a friend. Betsy was so affectionate. It was like they were two young girls again. She wished she could stay over some night, and just talk to Betsy. But Emilie liked to have her at home for breakfast. And when Emilie was away, like now, she couldn't leave Kara alone in the house with Charles.

The carriage turned off into the pecan-lined road that led to the Bradley house. Annabel smiled in anticipation. The carriage pulled up to a stop before the portico. Ebenezer hopped down to help Annabel from the carriage, then returned to the seat to take the carriage off to the stables until Annabel sent for him.

Annabel walked up the stairs, crossed to the front door. How quiet the house was on a hot afternoon like this. Everybody would be napping, of course. Except Betsy. Betsy would be waiting for her.

Annabel rapped sharply on the door, waited for someone to respond. Oh, these lazy slaves! All of them dreaming out in the kitchen probably, eating the Bradleys out of house and home. Betsy said it was shocking how butter and molasses kept disappearing from the kitchen.

She pushed the door open and walked into the elegant foyer. It was equally hot inside. Annabel lifted a handkerchief to her forehead as she walked toward the rear parlor, which was the one room sure to get a breeze on a day like this.

"Betsy," she called, hearing a slight rustle. She walked into the parlor. Her smiled faded. She froze as she spied Adam by the window, stuffing a silver vase into a knapsack.

"Adam, *what are you doing?*"

Adam straightened up, his eyes staring boldly at her. "What yo' do heah today, Young Missy? How come yo' heah?"

"That is none of your business!" She felt a dryness in her

throat. A feeling inside that brought a flush of color to her cheeks. Adam, tall, blackly handsome, stood near-naked before her. His bare chest, bare thighs, glistening with sweat. His teeth startlingly white when he unexpectedly smiled at her.

"Hey, Adam!" a voice yelled from down the hall. "Come on, man, let's get outta heah!"

"Yo' wait a lil bit!" Adam called back, and in a few strides he crossed to the door and slammed it shut.

"Where are the Bradleys?" Annabel demanded, her heart pounding.

"Dey run away," Adam gloated. "We come back aftah las' night, and us take what us want. Dey run!" he repeated, licking his lower lip with his tongue. "Maybe half hour ago. Dem ugly white folks." He moved slowly toward her. "Yo' purty, Young Missy. Lotsa times ah look at yo', and ah think, ain't her one purty piece!"

"Get away from me!" Annabel screamed. "Get away!"

But his strong black hands pulled her against him. One hand ripped at her dress, tearing the bodice to the waist. She opened her mouth to scream, but his mouth covered hers.

She beat him with her hands as he gripped the small, white-veined breasts, and his thighs moved hotly against her. Annabel stopped struggling.

She felt the sofa beneath her, felt her clothing being disarrayed. His hand touching her, invading her. She sobbed wildly, a blend of terror and passion. She shivered at the hard, hot touch of his maleness.

"No, no!" she sobbed, even while her body responded.

"Ah gib yo' somet'in' yo' want, Young Missy," Adam boasted. "Yo' don' fool me none. Ah see yo' lookin' at me. Lookin' down deah!" Triumph in his voice as she moaned, and moved beneath him.

She cried out in her passion, her nails ripping into the bare black shoulders above her until blood showed.

"Adam! Adam, you ain't got no time to fool wit' dat white gal! Come on!" Another burly black hovered, grinning, in the doorway.

Adam pulled away. A broad grin on his face.

"Yeah," Adam said complacently. "Yo' hot as a pistol. Sho' wish ah could stay awhile."

Adam lifted the knapsack to one shoulder, stalked out of the room. Annabel, her face hot, eyes overbright, hair spilled about her shoulders, struggled into a sitting position. Trembling, her breathing painful.

Fighting a wave of nausea, Annabel tried to pull her dress together. In a daze, she stared at the spill of her breasts, which had known the touch of black hands. She had been violated by a black man! *And she had wanted him to do that.* She was a bad woman. Like one of those whores in the saloons down in New Orleans.

She staggered to her feet, her mind in turmoil. She couldn't go back to Manoir. A black man had used her. Everybody at all the plantations would whisper about it.

"Oh God!" she cried, her hands covering her face. "Why did you let this happen to me? Why?"

Chapter Twenty-four

Kara tossed about on the bed, beneath the protective mosquito netting, seeking sleep in the discomfort of the afternoon heat. After ten minutes of threshing about, she realized the effort was futile. Despite her tiredness she was too alert, mentally, for sleep.

Restless in her room, she went downstairs to the library to search for a book that Amory had mentioned last night. The front door slammed shut, and the heavy thud of impatient footsteps crossed the foyer.

Impulsively, Kara moved out to the hall. It was Charles.

"Did the heat get you down?" Kara inquired sympathetically as he approached. "I'll ask Octavia to make you a pitcher of lemonade."

"Not now," Charles said with an unfamiliar brusqueness, and Kara stared at him in shock. "I'm sorry, Kara, there's trouble over at the Bradleys." He swung in at the entrance to the gun room, and Kara followed him. "Half a dozen slaves escaped last night. They've come back, apparently to try to instigate an uprising. The Bradleys managed to get away," he reassured her quickly. "The menfolk are at the Conways organizing a posse." Reluctantly he brought down a shotgun from the wall, stared at it with distaste.

"Charles, it'll be dangerous over there! Not you, not with a gun." Her voice betraying her terror.

"I have no choice, Kara," Charles said gravely, rummaging in a drawer for ammunition. "But I won't use this," he promised, pointing to the gun. "It's for scare tactics." He forced a smile. "I recoil from shooting a 'possum."

"Charles." Kara gasped. "The Bradleys, you said! Annabel went over there!"

"When?" Charles was ashen.

"About an hour ago. Perhaps an hour and a half. Charles, we didn't know."

"She probably left with the Bradleys," Charles said, but there was fear in his eyes. "Kara, don't say anything to Papa about what's happening. I don't want him involved."

"You're going to the Conways?"

"We're meeting at the edge of the Bradley place. It'll be faster that way." He loaded the shotgun.

"Charles did—did anybody say that Annabel was with the Bradleys?"

"A rider drove over to inform me of the uprising. He didn't hang around to discuss it. He's arousing half the county."

Charles hurried off to the stables. Kara went to a side window, saw him charging off on one of Amory's prize stallions. She glanced up at the sky, suddenly dark and ominous.

Kara paced fretfully about the room. Worried about Charles. Blaming herself for not stopping Annabel.

Mr. Bradley kept too tight a rein on his slaves; feelings must be ugly over there. She couldn't stay here, just waiting. Defiantly, she hurried from the house, out to the stables. Rumors must have circulated about the uprising. She saw the terror in the eyes of the stable hand as he brushed a horse.

"I'm taking the carriage," she said. "Bring it out for me, please."

"But Li'l Missy." His eyes were wide with alarm.

"Do what I say," she ordered impatiently.

Through the hot summer afternoon, with a sudden downpour drenching her as she clung to the reins, Kara urged the horses to greater speed. Finally, she saw the entrance to the Bradley plantation.

A dozen horses were tied up before the multicolumned, gleaming white mansion. But everything was so still. A tightness in her throat, Kara jumped down from the carriage and hurried to the house.

She recognized some of the men, stern-faced, talking in low voices, who hovered in the foyer.

"Miss Kara, what are you doing here?" Jack Conway asked uneasily. "This is no place for a lady."

"Is it over? Is everybody all right?" Her eyes roamed down the long, narrow hallway, seeking Charles.

"A couple of slaves got themselves killed," Conway reported. "The others are up for floggings, down in the quarters."

"Where's Charles?" she asked, her throat suddenly dry. "Where is he?"

"He'll be out here directly," Conway said evasively, but Kara was already racing down the corridor, to the room from which a cluster of somber-faced men were emerging. She pushed past them.

Annabel lay on the floor, her head in a pool of blood, her face lifeless. The gun still clutched in her hand.

Kara would have fallen if Charles hadn't leaped forward to catch her.

Annabel was buried in a tomb in the small family cemetery a hundred yards west of the house. Throughout the service, Charles stood white-faced and attentive. Remembering the first, good years, the early years of their marriage when Annabel was his wife. Emilie sobbed throughout. She would miss Annabel desperately.

After the service, when the neighbors had expressed their condolences and left, the family gathered in the library. Tim excused himself, mumbling about an appointment with Louis Aumont in New Orleans. There was a meeting about a piece of legislation that would be coming up in the fall.

"Tim, today?" Emilie protested. "Can't it wait?"

"How does it help if I sit around Manoir?" Tim said defiantly.

"I don't like all this traveling back and forth between New Orleans and Manoir," Emilie reprimanded. "There've been a lot of deaths from the fever, although they try to hide it. Doctor Scott says we shouldn't take chances."

"I'll be all right, Mama," Tim said, and crossed to kiss her. "I'll stay in town tonight, be back by dinner tomorrow." Pointedly ignoring Kara.

Daphne, her eyes red from crying, brought in tall glasses of iced tea, with a pitcher for refills, and, sniffling, left them again.

"Oh, I don't know how Annabel could have done this to us," Emilie sighed. "I was always so good to her. How could she leave me this way? She knew how much I depended upon her company."

"My God, Emilie, nobody did anything to you," Amory thundered. "It was done to Annabel!"

"Don't you raise your voice to me!" Emilie's own voice rose with the familiar shrillness that the others recognized as a danger signal. "How dare you, Amory Rankin! After all I've been through these last three days!"

"Calm down, Emilie," Amory said wearily. "Celestine!" he called. "Celestine, go upstairs and fetch Miss Emilie's medicine."

Amory deliberately diverted the talk into that impersonal

channels. Paul Morphy was doing so well in Europe on that chess tour of his, everybody was sure he would return to New Orleans with the title of the world's greatest chess player. Another Vigilance Committee was being talked about, to police the elections next month.

"Will Tim win another term, Papa?" Charles asked quietly, knowing this would capture his mother's interest. "What do you think?"

Emilie's head shot up. "Of course, Tim will be reelected," she said coldly. "That's his seat for as long as he wants it." Her faint smile was smug. "I bought that seat for my son."

Kara sighed. Tim was in the legislature, would probably be returned there. Yet all the years ahead seemed so painfully empty. But there was Sheelagh. Sheelagh made up for everything. Bless her! But there were the nights Kara lay alone, and desired her brother-in-law. Charles was free now. But then he would probably take himself a wife when the year of mourning was over.

As Emilie had predicted, Tim won with a comfortable margin. But the election was scarcely past before Amory started talking, with Kara and Charles, about Tim's running for governor in '59. After a family dinner at the townhouse, early in November, when Tim had left on his nocturnal haunts, Amory, Charles, and Kara sat down to an earnest discussion. For the first time Kara was uneasy.

"At Tim's age?" she protested, her eyes swinging to Charles for support. "Wouldn't it be wiser to wait until the sixty-four elections? Or even sixty-eight?"

"In 1860 Tim will be thirty-one," Amory said briskly. "If he doesn't make it then, it's a four-year wait, and I don't like what's happening in the country. Besides," Amory resumed with enthusiasm. "I believe it's Tim's youth, his personality, that'll help us put him in. These are trying times, people are upset. We'll be able to sell Tim."

"It'll be rough, Papa," Charles was doubtful. "This is a hell of a lot bigger than a seat in the legislature."

"Charles, in Louisiana anything is possible, if you know the right people, spend enough money. Your mother doesn't care what it'll cost to put Tim into the governor's mansion."

"I want it, too," Kara said passionately. "I want Sheelagh to grow up, knowing she once lived in the governor's mansion. I want her to have respect for her father. The governor!" Her eyes clashed with Charles's, saying what she could not bring herself to put into words. Never, *never,* must Sheelagh suspect the truth about her father.

"The Democrats are fairly sure to push Wickliffe," Charles said seriously. "He's a fine man, has a good record as a state senator."

"Tim won't run on the Democratic ticket," Amory said with triumph. "He'll play it as an independent. We will plot our strategy well, keep Louis Aumont on our side and we have a fighting chance. That's all I ask, Charles." His eyes softened as they dwelt on his older son. "I know you have no stomach for our brand of politics, and Charles, I respect you for that. But this is politics in our country, and we have to operate within the framework. I'll do anything, short of murder, to put Tim into the governor's mansion."

Not until after Christmas, when Kara, Tim, and Sheelagh were at Manoir for the holidays, did Amory broach the possibility of the governorship to Tim. They were at the dinner table, with Celestine having just served Octavia's magnificent rum cake and coffee, when Amory, smiling with satisfaction, announced to Tim that his mother had agreed to finance his race for the governorship.

"We don't make any public announcements until late in

March," Amory said cagily, "but word will circulate in the proper circles."

Tim gasped in disbelief. "Papa, you're out of your mind." His face flushed with color. "Louis will be furious."

"Louis was furious for about twenty minutes," Amory conceded. "I convinced him you were what we needed in the governor's mansion. The voters are tired of old men in office; look at the way Buchanan's foundering. They want new, young blood. Louis knows you'll take care of him, Tim, once you're elected."

"No." Tim's eyes flashed stubbornly. "I won't run, Papa. I'm way out of my depth. Even in the legislature, I'm out of my depth."

"Tim, you're doing a fine job," Kara said exchanging worried glances with Charles. Herself defiant because she knew Charles agreed with Tim.

"I am tired of being a puppet." Tim spoke with a cold, furious calm. "I am tired of speaking Papa's thoughts, Charles's thoughts, Kara's thoughts. I'm tired of always being somebody else. I will not run for governor."

"Oh, Tim," Emilie chided, tears filling her eyes. "How can you do this? We're all thinking of you."

"I'm sorry, Mama." Tim pushed his chair back, rose from the table, strode out of the room.

"Tim doesn't mean it," Emilie declared, reluctant to relinquish the dream of seeing herself in the governor's mansion. The Queen Mother. "Amory, talk to him."

"Let me," Kara said quickly, her eyes pleading with her father-in-law.

"All right, Kara." Amory sighed tiredly. "Talk to Tim."

Kara found Tim in the library, pouring himself a drink.

"Your mother's upset," Kara said quietly.

"Mama is always upset." Tim's smile was sardonic. "In a

few minutes she'll be screeching hysterically. Celestine and Daphne will come running. Horatio will ride off to bring Doctor Scott back. *But I am not running for governor.*" He slammed a fist on the teakwood table before him. "I have had it, Kara, with this rotten politicking!"

"Is sitting forever in the legislature better than moving up to the governorship?" Kara challenged. "Tim, you have never in your life done anything for your father. He's such a brilliant man, he's never had a chance to prove himself. Tim, he has one of the finest intellects in this state; let him share this with you!"

"My, you're a solicitous daughter-in-law," Tim jeered. His eyes contemptuous as he swigged down his bourbon.

"Not just for your father," Kara said evenly. Color stained her cheeks. "For Sheelagh, too. Give her this much to hold onto through the years, give her pride in your being her father. Take Sheelagh with you to the governor's mansion."

Tim stared at her for a few seconds, then he poured himself another, potent drink.

"All right, Kara, I'll run for governor. That's not saying I'll win. But it's the last thing you'll ever ask of me. Is that clear? *The last thing.*"

Chapter Twenty-five

At the New Orleans house, late night conferences were held regularly on behalf of Tim's campaign. Tim occasionally sat in on these conferences, which included Amory, Louis Aumont, political bigwigs whom the two men were wooing, and Kara.

Kara had won the respect of her father-in-law and Aumont by quietly stated observations.

"You're young, Kara, but the head is old," Amory expressed with satisfaction.

Kara, now, was an acknowledged member of the group.

"This is a hell of a lot rougher than putting the boy in the legislature," Aumont said seriously, at the conclusion of a meeting. "But what a prize, at his age!" Aumont's eyes glowed.

"Louis, we can do it!" Amory rose from his chair and paced the room. "The proper strategy. Every road solidly covered."

"Money," Louis drawled. "What we cannot do by twisting a few arms, we will buy. Never in the politics of Louisiana has a situation been so right for manipulating."

Tim would be good for the state, that was the important consideration. He'd have some debts to pay, yes, but he wouldn't allow wholesale corruption. He would listen to Amory and Louis Aumont, and the state would be healthier.

Charles was outspokenly against it. He insisted it was morally wrong to run Tim. Wickliffe was the man for the governorship. Wickliffe was opposed to secession, as Tim was, so long as the South could remain in the Union with honor. Without the intervention of corrupt politics, the Democratic party would vote him in with no difficulty.

Kara sat back in the small, brocade-covered chair in her front parlor, and listened while Amory and Louis planned a public announcement of Tim's role in next Thursday's *Daily Picayune*. Everybody of political importance on their side had already been briefed. The race would be rough, but Kara was optimistic. It was so important to her that Tim win.

"Announce it on Saint Patrick's Day," Kara suggested. "The Irish are great for omens. Announce it on Saint Patrick's Day and it'll be a good-luck sign. Tim and I can give a party after the parade." She glowed with enthusiasm. "We carried the Irish vote in the last election!"

"Set it up with the *Picayune* for announcement on Saint Patrick's Day," Amory said jubilantly to Louis. "By God, the Irish will relish having one of their own for First Lady of the state."

Kara concentrated completely on Tim's campaign. It was essential to keep her mind involved in some demanding channel, so she would forget about Charles's widower status. She realized, with misgivings, that he was the prey of every unmarried woman in their ever-widening social circle. Charles, of course, refrained from socializing; he was determined to observe the year of mourning for Annabel. But at his father's insistence he was frequently present at political dinners and gatherings, where Kara unhappily observed the feminine eyes that were cast on him. She was aware, too, of the open glances Charles sent in her direction, and knew the intensity of his feelings for her, which for a moment would lift her to rapture, and a moment later would shoot her down into the depths of frustration.

Emilie, missing Annabel, became a vexing problem to

Amory in her determination to meddle in political planning. She was more overtly vain, fussing over her hair, her gowns. Bringing dressmakers out to Manoir, shopping extravagantly at Chartres Street. Amory protested in outrage when, early in April, Emilie commissioned Olympe to design her a gown to wear at Tim's Inaugural Ball.

In the South, as early as the spring of '59, Jefferson Davis of Mississippi was being spoken about as a presidential candidate for the Democratic party in the 1860 elections. Northern Democrats were certain Stephen Douglas was the man to bring the country together. It was popularly conceded that Buchanan could not win reelection.

Abolitionists were denouncing the southern slaveowners with the exaggeration that had brought Calhoun to say that abolitionism "originated in that blind, fanatical zeal which made one man believe that he was responsible for the sins of others; and which, two centuries ago, tied the victim that it could not convert to the stake."

Sex was being dragged into the picture, with Wendell Phillips characterizing the South as "one great brothel where a half-million women are flogged to prostitution."

The South, in outrage, responded by denouncing the treatment of free laborers in the North, where thousands of white children labored fourteen hours a day in mills and shops, at an age when slave children were free to play, or, at most, were "one-quarter hands" in the fields. The South quoted statistics which showed the factory system in the North enslaved white workers by tying them economically to endless, exhausting labor.

To the northerners the whole South was wrong, not merely that small segment that owned slaves. They had no patience with the problems of the southerners, whose whole economy was slave labor. There were those in the South who could see no way out of financial devastation if slavery were abolished. Division became an ever-increasing threat.

In June Kara would normally have gone to Manoir for the summer. This year she was delaying because of her involvement in the campaign. Also, Dr. Scott was highly optimistic that the improvements in New Orleans sanitary conditions would rid the city of the fever this summer. So far not one case had been reported. Kara checked on the kitchen. There was a dinner this evening, and she made a point of remaining close to the preparations on such occasions.

"Everything smells so good, Aphrodite," she sniffed appreciatively, knowing Aphrodite would beam and work doubly hard to make the dinner a success. "I'll starve till dinnertime."

"Yo' sit yo'se'f down in de din' room," Aphrodite said affectionately, "and ah tell dat lazy Zeke to bring yo' in a plate."

Kara looked sharply at her. Zeke usually drove Tim about New Orleans.

"Is Mister Tim home?" Rare, for Tim to be home in the daytime.

"Him in de dinin' room raht dis minute, havin' hisself some coffee."

"I'll be there, Aphrodite," Kara said, and hurried out of the kitchen.

Tim sat at one end of the dining table, hunched over his coffee. He looked as if he hadn't slept all night, Kara observed quickly. He hadn't shaved this morning. His eyes, when they met hers, were dark with unease.

"Is something wrong, Tim?" She sat down beside him, alarm churning in her.

"That campaign we've been working on," Tim drawled. "We're in trouble."

"How?"

"Louis," Tim said huskily. "He suffered a heart attack last night. I stayed at the house. He died at four this morning."

"Oh, Tim!" Shock rocked her. Late yesterday afternoon Louis sat in the front parlor, drinking with Amory. He'd looked tired; he always did, it seemed lately. "Tim, I can't believe it."

"You'd better," Tim warned grimly. "Because where do we go to replace Louis? Who's got his kind of power to throw on my side? Who can we buy, Kara?" His eyes were mocking.

"It's dreadful about Louis," Kara was striving to be matter-of-fact. "But he wasn't a young man, it isn't a tragedy."

"It could be a tragedy for you," Tim shot back, his eyes oddly triumphant. "And for Papa. And for the unholy party."

"Tim, we're not giving up." Kara's eyes blazed with resolution. "Not after we've come this far. After the funeral we'll sit down and work out a solution."

"Let's talk about that right now," Amory's voice intruded. Kara and Tim swung around, startled. He stood in the doorway, his face drawn, visibly shaken by the announcement of Louis's death. "I heard this morning," Amory said slowly. "Over at the Saint Charles. I came right over; I've been upstairs with Sheelagh."

"Louis swung a powerful block of votes," Kara said quietly. "What happens to that now?"

"There's going to be a mad scramble for control." Amory sat down at the table, squinting in thought. "We've got to act to channel that control behind someone we can handle."

"Who has Louis's kind of power?" Tim taunted. "He's handled that block of votes for thirty years! They've never been really behind me, it was Louis who brought them in."

Between them, they threw out names at random, with

Amory discarding one after another. Anxiety etched their faces as they arrived at no decision.

"What about Monsieur Renoir?" Kara asked on impulse.

"That old man?" Tim smirked. "He's been inactive for years."

"Renoir is a highly respected figure in Creole circles." Amory nodded, a glint in his eyes. "In some ways more so than Louis was."

"But he hasn't been a power in politics for fifteen years," Tim protested. "The man must be seventy."

"If we can talk Renoir into coming back into activity, we'll be in a much healthier position," Amory pointed out. "Without that block, we're on thin ice."

"Who can talk to him?" Kara's eyes swung from her father-in-law to Tim. "Who was close to Louis that would have influence with Renoir?"

"I have an idea," Tim said quietly, a faint smile playing about his mouth. "His wife."

"Cecile Renoir?" Kara stared at Tim. Disconcerted.

Cecile was Renoir's second wife, half her husband's age. A flamboyant, darkly attractive woman given to many flirtations. It was said that Renoir, at his age, merely looked the other way. Otherwise he would be fighting duels three times a month.

Amory, too, was startled at this suggestion.

"It's said that Madame Renoir has considerable influence with him," Amory conceded, but he frowned with distaste.

"I think we could manage to direct that influence," Tim said softly. "I met Cecile Renoir at the gambling tables several nights ago. She seemed highly sympathetic."

Suddenly, the air was charged with tension.

"You're going to try to get through to Renoir by way of his wife?" Amory growled.

Tim's eyes were coldly in command when they met his father's. "Do you know a better way, Papa?"

Kara lowered her eyes, her face flooded with color. Amory recoiled, shocked, angry, disturbed. For the first time, he questioned his judgment in pushing Tim toward the governorship.

Tim, who found it distasteful to fulfill his marital obligations, was, for the sake of his political career, prepared to bed the unfaithful wife of a highly respected Creole gentleman who could, most likely, insure that election for him.

Dr. Scott's prophecy about the paucity of yellow fever cases this summer proved accurate. By late August of '59 only 92 cases had been reported, compared to 4,855 in '58. The efforts of the Board of Health were lauded as New Orleans and the surrounding area breathed relief at this respite from summer death. Tim was eloquently crusading for a new water system for the city, the urgency of which had been highlighted by the million-dollar fire back in April.

Kara was disturbed by Tim's liaison with Cecile Renoir. They had discussed this dispassionately. It was an expedient. Still, Kara was aware that Tim deliberately flaunted the affair before her.

She was exceedingly uncomfortable in social situations where Cecile, smug in what she obviously considered a conquest, was openly patronizing to her. Charles was all indignation about Tim's relations with Cecile. Coming downstairs from her room late one night at Manoir, Kara overheard Charles and his father in the library. Their voices carried distinctly in the stillness of the night. Kara paused at the foot of the stairs, the telltale pink staining her cheeks as she realized she was the subject of their discussion.

"Papa, what the devil is Tim up to?" Charles demanded angrily. "Hasn't he enough to do with campaigning to stay out of Cecile Renoir's bed?"

"Leave the boy alone," Amory said evasively.

"He's a man," Charles said impatiently. "Thirty years old! And what about Kara? I've seen the way that Renoir slut talks to her. How dare she!"

"Charles, Cecile Renoir takes a new man to her bed every month," Amory said bluntly. "We need Georges's support. Cecile is assuring that."

"So Tim is stooping to electioneering in bed," Charles said, his voice laced with contempt. "Papa, is that what you want for him?"

"I want the governorship for Tim," Amory said, so quietly Kara had to strain to hear. "I want every man, woman, and child in Louisiana to look up at Tim and say, with respect in their voices, 'There goes Governor Rankin'."

In late August New Orleansians were predicting that the fantastic new French Opera House being built by James Gallier, Jr., the thirty-two-year-old son of the man who had built the Saint Charles Hotel, the Pontalba Buildings, and the City Hall would, indeed, be delivered for the winter opera season. Tim's campaigners made much of Gallier's youth, heralding this as an era of new, young blood. Men were working day and night, in shifts, in order to deliver the "lyric temple of the South" by the end of November. Rossini's *William Tell* was chosen for the opening night.

And in Cecile Renoir's opulent, ostentatious, white-and-gold bedroom, Tim stood, this evening as on many other evenings, briskly clothing himself, while the langorous Cecile stretched out against the satin sheets, her dark hair cascading about her shoulders, her firm, full breasts provocatively displayed.

"Tim, I do not understand your running off this way," she

pouted, her dark eyes flashing another invitation. God, didn't this woman ever get enough, Tim asked himself impatiently? "Tim, I thought you loved me."

"Georges will be coming home soon," Tim said tersely. "We don't need that kind of situation on our hands."

"Georges is snoring in a chair at his club," Cecile said contemptuously. "Tim." She sat up, her breasts spilling over the extremely low-cut wrapper. Tim, gritted his teeth, compelled himself to stare avidly at the lush view she provided.

"Cecile, don't tempt me," he reproached, while his stomach churned with distaste. "We can't afford gossip at this point in the campaign. Nor do I want to be challenged to a duel by Georges." He forced an amused smile. He couldn't wait to remove himself from this room. Her perfume, her woman scents, nauseated him.

"Georges won't challenge you to a duel," she drawled. "At his age? It would be suicide. Tim, when you are governor," Cecile announced with satisfaction, "I shall rent a little house in Baton Rouge."

Tim smiled, as though enjoying this prospect; he moved to the bed to kiss her with calculated roughness.

"Good night, Cecile," he murmured with a wistful sigh of reluctance, seemingly at leaving her, then strode from the room.

Outside, in the late-evening humidity, Tim took a deep breath of air. Thank God, he was out of there. He would go over to the Saint Charles and have himself a drink. Did she mean that, about taking a house in Baton Rouge? He'd have to find some way of stopping *that.*

Zeke pulled up closer to the entrance, and Tim climbed into the carriage. Anticipation rose pleasurably in him. All kinds of people congregated at the Saint Charles tavern.

"Go on home, Zeke," Tim ordered, stepping down from

the carriage. "I won't need you anymore this evening."

The carriage rumbled off over the cobblestones. Tim approached the entrance to the tavern. At the door he hesitated, whirled about after a moment, and left the Saint Charles.

He strode left, purposefully, whistling softly to himself. Within five minutes' walk was the small tavern where Tim retired when he wished not to be recognized. Tonight, after the repugnant session with Cecile, he yearned for the anonymity, the comfort that he might find in a place frequented by the less fashionable of New Orleans.

In the modest, dimly lit tavern with its array of wrought-iron chandeliers and wood-paneled walls, Tim seated himself at a small table at the rear, which, nonetheless, afforded a clear view of the entrance. He was on his third drink, already restless, when his eyes fastened on a pair of new arrivals.

The smaller, slighter of the pair, unusually handsome, fair-haired, features almost girlishly fine, frowned at the heavily populated tables, the crowded bar. He turned to whisper to his companion, a muscular, broad-shouldered, dark-haired, arrogant youth. What magnetism, Tim thought, admiring the taller boy. That one would have the barmaids chasing him like mad. Amusement welled in him. The barmaids would never know that he would have only contempt for the likes of them.

On impulse Tim raised a hand, beckoned to them when he captured their attention, indicating the available seats at his table. There was a brief consultation between them, then they swaggered toward him. About eighteen, Tim guessed, and faintly belligerent in their youth. Good thing they didn't know who he was. It would be a pleasant night's diversion.

"Sit here," Tim said, faintly aloof, politely impersonal,

though his eyes betrayed his interest. "Damnably busy tonight."

"We don't mind if we do." The dark-haired youth, his eyes boldly bright, lowered himself into a chair, nodding to his companion to follow suit. "So long as the beer comes along."

A waiter sauntered over, his eyes veiled. Polite because Tim, who came in on the average of once or twice a week, was easy with the dollar, and what did it matter to him if a gentleman took his kicks in peculiar ways.

"Beers," Tim ordered, quickly pulling forth his wallet to indicate this was on him. He was inwardly amused at the respect the sheaf of bills obviously elicited from the pair.

"I'm Jamie, he's Cliff," the blond youth said, after a meaningful glance at his friend.

"I'm Tim," Tim introduced himself casually. They had no idea he was the gubernatorial candidate, the one the betting money now said was sure to win.

Tim adroitly led the conversation into areas where the other two felt comfortable. They argued heatedly about the merits of teams seen at the races last season, talked about the mushrooming interest in baseball.

"Folks are crazy," Cliff complained contemptuously. "Them that says you can play baseball with ten men on a side! Even the newspapers say it's wrong!"

"I hate baseball," Jamie said petulantly. "It's the dumbest game I ever saw."

"Look," Tim suggested casually, with a deliberately admiring smile for Jamie, who was showing signs of being annoyed at the attention Cliff was paying to Tim. "I'm going next door to check into the hotel for the night. Why don't you two come up and share a bottle with me?" No need to play games with these two; they knew exactly what he was.

Jamie and Cliff accepted with alacrity. The three left the tavern, with a bottle of choice bourbon, and went to the run-down hotel next door. Jamie and Cliff waited self-consciously by the door while Tim checked in, paying in advance, and ordered glasses sent up. The clerk was obsequiously polite. The cut of Tim's clothes advertised his affluence.

Tim beckoned to the pair. Together they climbed the dimly lit stairs to the shoddy room Tim had rented for the night. It was small, low-ceilinged; the furniture consisting of a double bed, a washstand, and two straight chairs. When Tim lit the jet, the walls, paint-hungry, plaster peeling, came ashamedly into view. Jamie and Cliff settled themselves in chairs while Tim crossed to open the room's one window.

"Here come the mosquitos." Jamie's voice was shrill. "I just hate 'em."

"We'll have a drink in a minute and forget all about 'em, Jamie," Cliff said, winking good-humoredly at Tim. His eyes bold, sizing up Tim. Flattered to find himself in this situation.

The knock at the door sounded unusually loud, but Tim knew that was because he'd been listening impatiently for the sound of hotel help arriving with glasses. He wanted the hot warmth of another shot of bourbon nestling in his belly. He wanted to reach out and touch the masculine warmth of Cliff.

"You wanted these." A frowsy hotel maid walked inside, set the glasses on the washstand. Her eyes wise as they traveled from Tim to the younger pair. But she was effusive in her thanks when Tim dropped a silver dollar into her palm.

The room was sticky with the late-August heat, and the successive rounds of bourbon did little to ease this. The three sat in their shirtsleeves, drinking, talking, sizing up one another. Jamie turned white with rage when Cliff dropped an arm about Tim's shoulders.

"Take your hands off him!" Jamie shrieked, and lifted the nearly empty bourbon bottle.

"Jamie, what's the matter with you?" Cliff's voice was deceptively gentle. He stood beside Tim, his feet set far apart, a brash smile on his face. "Talking like that about a fine gentleman like Tim here. The way he's spent his money on us."

Too late, Tim interpreted the byplay between the other two. Watched, immobile with fear, when Jamie, with an oath, smashed the bourbon bottle across the back of his chair and lunged forward. Toward Tim. A large, rough hand closed in on his mouth lest he cry out. His eyes galvanized to the jagged neck of the broken bottle.

"Jamie," Cliff reproached with silken softness, "we oughtn'ta be doin' this."

Chapter Twenty-six

Kara sat at the breakfast table with Amory and thought how exhausted he appeared from the efforts of the campaign. Charles had been reproachful on a number of occasions these last weeks about the strain on his father. But the governorship was practically within Tim's hands, she remembered with exultation. In less than ten days they would be able to sit back and relax. The election would be over.

"Kara, you're just poking at your breakfast," Amory scoffed. "We can't have a peaked First Lady on election day!"

"I'm not really hungry," Kara said with a small smile. "It's all this heat."

But Amory knew better. He knew how she was being eaten away by the love she harbored for Charles. Always afraid some pretty young thing would come along, and Charles would take himself a wife. *Which was what he should do.* For Chris's sake and his own.

Amory frowned, listening attentively to something in the distance.

"Company at this hour of the morning?"

Out before the portico, a horse was being pulled to a stop. Celestine scurried to the front door, murmuring in reproach.

"Folks dat come callin' afore breakfast ain't got der haids screwed on right."

And then, moments later, Celestine stood in the entrance

to the dining room, stammering to Amory.

"Him be from de po-leece." She was frightened, uneasy. "Wanna see yo' raht away."

"What is it?" Kara asked quickly, feeling the blood drain from her face.

"Probably something about the campaign," Amory said with forced calm as he pushed back his chair. "Some of the boys may have gone too far in their enthusiasm." He smiled wryly. "I'll be right back, Kara."

Kara sat stiffly at the table, battling a compulsion to run behind her father-in-law, to listen to what the police officer had to say. But she remained at the table because, clearly, this was what Amory expected of her. She reached for her coffee cup and lifted it to her mouth, sipping the steaming contents without tasting.

Amory walked slowly back into the dining room. His face was ashen, his eyes distraught. Kara waited mutely.

"I must go immediately into New Orleans," Amory said, an unreal quality in his voice. "The police refuse to tell me what's wrong, only that it has to do with Tim."

"I'll go with you," Kara said instantly.

"No!" Amory shook his head.

"Whatever trouble Tim is in, I belong there," Kara insisted. "He's my husband." Before the citizens of Louisiana he was her husband. "I'll send Celestine to the stables to order the carriage."

They sat in near-silence during the hour-and-a-half ride to New Orleans. They drove into the late-morning bustle of Canal Street, turned up two squares to Saint Charles. They weren't headed for the police station, Kara suddenly realized. She turned questioningly to Amory as the carriage drew to a halt before a seedy hotel, a little more than a block from the grandiose Saint Charles.

"Kara, please sit here in the carriage," Amory said, his eyes avoiding hers. "Horatio will wait here until I come out of the hotel."

Kara sat, lacing and unlacing her fingers in agitation while Amory crossed to the unpretentious entrance. She waited, watching the morning hordes move along the banquettes without seeing, until suddenly she could not sit in the carriage another second.

"Horatio, wait," she said quickly, leaving the carriage.

The lobby was empty except for a rotund elderly man at the desk, who glanced up in astonishment as she approached him.

"The gentleman who just came in. Mr. Rankin," she said unevenly. "Where is he, please?"

"Upstairs. The third room down the hall." The man stared sharply at her. "But miss, I don't think you ought to go up there."

Kara, skirts lifted about her ankles, was already racing up the stairs. She heard voices emerging from an open door. The third door. The words were unintelligible, yet something in the quality of those voices was unnerving to her. Two men stood at attention at the door.

Kara slowed down. Her throat tight. Heart thumping. She forced a smile.

"I'm with Mr. Rankin," she began, and stopped dead at the consternation that crossed their faces. And then she heard Amory's voice, low but distinct.

"Yes, sir. That is the body of my younger son."

Kara's blood turned to ice. Her nails dug into the palms of her hands as she fought to retain control. She shut her eyes tightly, for a second, to shut out the horror on the floor. That was Tim on the floor. Tim dead. Sheelagh's father dead. Thank God, the body was covered. But for a long, long time she would find it difficult to sleep, remembering that dark-red stain on the threadbare rug, beside the covered body.

"Mr. Rankin," the policeman in charge spoke gently. Amory was not yet aware of Kara's presence, and the policeman appeared uncertain about telling him. "Have you any idea, sir, why he was murdered? The clerk remembers he arrived last evening." The policeman hesitated. "He came up here with two boys. About eighteen. We haven't been able to locate them yet!"

Amory's head shot upward. Tension in his shoulders as he lifted them defiantly, anguish in his voice.

"I'm sorry. I can tell you nothing."

Tim is dead, in a room he'd occupied with boys. The implication glaringly plain. People would talk. Nasty talk. Kara balled one hand into a painful fist, gearing herself for what must be done. She moved forward, reaching for Amory's hand as she spoke.

"I can tell you why he was here," Kara said with quiet dignity. "My husband was deeply worried about the young folks of our state. The wild ones in their teens. He was secretly working on a report about this problem. Regularly, he went out into the street and talked to them. Sometimes he would invite two or three of them to a room somewhere, so they could sit down and talk, openly and honestly. Two of these boys killed the man who, more than anybody else in this state, was trying to better conditions for them."

Chapter Twenty-seven

They stood in the dreary morning drizzle before the brick tomb, stuccoed and whitewashed, with a miniature ironwork gallery and narrow banquette, which was to be the final resting place for Tim's body. They listened to the minister eulogize Tim as son, father, husband, brother, and public servant. Just the three of them—Amory, Charles, and Kara. Emilie had been under sedation for three days. Sheelagh had been sent off to Charles's summer cottage to spend the day with her young cousin.

Fifty feet to the west stood a weeping cluster of slaves who had known Tim all his brief life. Octavia, sobbing as though this were her own child being laid to rest, a red-eyed Celestine, Mama Belle, Horatio, a haunted Jupe, allowed at Manoir for today's sadness. Moss hanging mournfully from the lush green trees and a cloying sweetness emanating from the profusion of late-summer flowers in bloom.

Amory had been insistent on privacy. No friends here at the family cemetery. Later today, in New Orleans, there would be a public memorial service. From time to time, as the Reverend Mr. Walters droned on endlessly, Charles glanced anxiously at his father. How exhausted both men appeared, Kara thought, herself white-faced and dazed from the efforts of these last three days. The three of them determined not to give way to grief, to retain their outward composure before the shock of the entire state. The people, from every level of government straight up to the governor himself, had filed in and out of Manoir to pay their respects to Tim's bereaved family. Nobody knew the truth. Thank God, she had brought that off successfully!

It had been worst for Amory than for any of them. Emilie, at least, was under sedation.

The minister was winding up his eulogy. Amory stood ramrod stiff, his eyes straight ahead, focused on the casket.

Daphne, obviously distraught, served coffee to the minister and the family in the front parlor. Even now they could hear Octavia's distant sobbing.

"Missy," Daphne whispered urgently to Kara. "Ole Missy, her downstairs. In de lib'ary."

"Is she alone?" Kara was suddenly uneasy. "Who's with her, Daphne?"

"Celestine be with her now," Daphne explained. "Me stay till her come."

"Daphne, bring Reverend Walters a bag of Octavia's pralines to take home to his wife," Amory said.

Obediently, Daphne went off to the kitchen. The Reverend Mr. Walters talked about the heartening drop in yellow-fever fatalities this summer. Everyone praised the efforts of the Board of Health in bringing this about. Kara remembered Tim's early enthusiasm at playing the role of the handsome young politician, which had gradually given way to a restless cynicism. She'd insisted he go on with the role. She had pushed him too hard. Because of that he lay in a tomb which, every morning, she would see when she went to her bedroom window. Her fault that Tim was dead. Tim, who hadn't wanted to be governor at all.

The minister rose to his feet, preparing to take his leave. Kara forced a faint smile as she, too, rose.

"Mrs. Rankin, you must be brave." The Reverend Mr.

Walters said with deep sincerity. "Please try not to ask questions. For a precious while he was yours."

"Yes." She nodded gently.

"I'll walk with you to the door, Reverend," Amory said graciously. He was relieved that the minister was leaving.

"You'll stay here at Manoir," Charles said quietly to Kara. "I'll arrange for Celestine and Daphne to go into New Orleans to pack for Sheelagh and you."

"Yes, Charles," Kara whispered, her eyes tender as they rested on him. How like Charles, to understand she could never set foot in that house of ghosts again. Too much that was ugly had transpired between Tim and her in that house. "Thank you."

"If there's anything special you'd like them to bring back from the house, let me know. Before we—we close the house."

"I won't want anything," Kara said quickly. "Except Sheelagh's toys." Painfully remembering the nights when Tim would arrive at the house with a new toy, to compensate for a broken promise to be home before Sheelagh went to sleep. "She'll want them." Then, quite suddenly, guiltily, she remembered. "Charles, I forgot to tell you. Daphne said your mother is downstairs. In the library. Celestine is with her."

"We'd better go to her," Charles said soberly.

Together Kara and Charles walked out into the hallway. Amory had closed the front door and was moving toward them. His face was drawn with grief.

"Papa," Charles said gently, "Mama is downstairs, in the library. The sedative must have worn off."

"Celestine is with her," Kara added, seeing the apprehension in Amory's eyes. She recalled, with a shudder, Emilie's wild hysteria when Amory had told her, finally, that Tim was dead.

"How will she bear this?" Amory sighed heavily. "How will she live?"

The three of them moved toward the library. The door was open wide. They could hear the gay, delicate tinkle of a music box, playing "Frère Jacques." Emilie, in a flower-sprigged wrapper, her hair down about her shoulders, sat on the sofa, surrounded by a collection of stuffed animals, toy soldiers, a much-battered drum. Tim's toys, once shown to Kara by Celestine in their storage place in the attic. Tim's toys, which his mother would not permit to be given even to his daughter.

"Amory," Emilie demanded petulantly. "Where have you been so long? And when is Tim coming back from play? Octavia says he hardly touched his breakfast. I know he must be hungry."

"Tim will be home soon," Amory put his hand on her shoulder with infinite gentleness. "Why don't you go upstairs and rest? I'll have Octavia bring him up to you."

"All right, Amory, but if he isn't home soon, you send for him. And if Papa drops by, be sure and tell me."

"Celestine!" Amory called out. "Celestine, take Miss Emilie up to her room."

"I'll take this with me," Emilie said with childish pleasure, clutching the small music box. "It's exactly like one Papa gave me when *I* was five."

Life held a strangely theatrical quality at Manoir. They all played a desperate game for Emilie's benefit. Emilie moved in her shadowed world where Tim was always a slightly naughty boy. Amory accepted this with a docility that startled Kara.

"It must be this way, Kara," he explained. "This is the only way Emilie can survive."

It was Charles who suggested that Tim's room, adjoining

Emilie's, be converted into a sitting room for her. With Daphne and Celestine taking turns at attendance, Emilie would live out her life in these two rooms, occasionally being taken for a walk outdoors but always eager to return to her rooms, where Tim's toys were spread about as though left there, minutes ago, by a child.

With Emilie settled into this pattern, Kara spoke of bringing Chris to Manoir. It seemed absurd for Charles and Sheelagh, who adored her cousin, to be constantly traveling into New Orleans.

"Yes," Amory approved vigorously. "Yes, we must bring Chris home."

Charles was pleased to have his son at Manoir. It delighted him to see Chris and Sheelagh, too young to be touched by the tragedies that had descended on Manoir within a period of a year, playing happily about the elegant old house. And he found satisfaction, too, in the pleasure Chris's presence brought to his father. Yet it was a period, for Charles and Amory, and for Kara, of painful adjustments.

"Kara, I don't think we could have survived without the children," Charles confided somberly. It was Christmas Eve, and Sheelagh and Chris, in party clothes, sat happily on the floor and listened to the children from the quarters raise their melodic young voices in a medley of Christmas carols, now an annual feature of the holiday season at Manoir. Sheelagh's and Chris's stockings hung with those of the small slaves on the expansive mantelpiece above the wide fireplace.

"Thank God for the children," Kara agreed softly.

"Mama, they sound so pretty." Sheelagh bubbled when the children were done and Amory was stuffing their hands with candies. "Mama, I love Christmas!" Sheelagh ran to hug her mother.

"Mama, I can sing, too!" Chris said ebulliently, and then

stood up, quite still, to sing, in his high-pitched voice. "Silent night, holy night."

Chris had called her "Mama." Color rode high in Kara's cheeks. How she wished, in truth, she was Chris's mother. Charles, too, had heard. He was turning away self-consciously. But for a poignant, shattering moment their eyes had met. Too many tragedies had befallen Manoir. More than ever, she thought with anguish, were Charles and she separated. The gap too wide to be ever crossed.

Kara was relieved when the holiday season, observed for the sake of the children, was past. She had taken over the running of the household. Jupe and Artemis had been absorbed into the household staff when Charles closed up his New Orleans house. For Octavia's sake, Jupe was permitted to remain at Manoir; this had been Amory's decision. Octavia was hopeful that Jupe and Artemis would be married. She had confided to Kara that Jupe was working up courage to ask Amory's permission. This he must do himself, Octavia sternly decreed.

But the days and nights were long for Kara. Always the feeling of existing on the edge of a precipice. So much unspoken between Charles and her. So much that could never be said. The shadows of Annabel and Tim forever between them. Sometimes she felt the weight of Amory's gaze, and wondered what thoughts ricocheted in his mind.

On the surface they appeared to be reconciled to the emptiness of their lives. In the evenings the two men and Kara sat in the library and heatedly discussed the difficulties that plagued the nation. Concentrating on the impersonal in preference to the personal. Yet pointedly ignoring local and state politics.

In February 1860 Abraham Lincoln made a speech at

Cooper Union in New York City, under the sponsorship of the Young Men's Central Republican Union. In a heavy snowstorm, fifteen hundred people turned out to hear Mr. Lincoln. He was escorted to the platform, on which sat the eminent Horace Greeley, David Dudley Field, and William Cullen Bryant. Mr. Greeley, in his welcoming speech, said this was the largest gathering "of the intellect and culture of our city" since the days of Webster and Clay.

Lincoln, in his broadcloth suit bought for the occasion, rose to make his speech, and history was made. Lincoln argued, with a fervor that held his audience to rapt attention, devastating Douglas's much-discussed views on popular sovereignty, insisting that the framers of the Constitution "certainly understood that no proper division of local from federal authority forbade the federal government to control slavery."

He appealed to the southerners to accept the Republican party, not revolutionary, nor radical, in fact conservative. The party had nothing to do with John Brown's nefarious raid at Harper's Ferry; it was against all acts of violence. He turned to the Republicans, urging them to help maintain peace by placating the South. But he wound up his speech with a proclamation that brought the crowd to its feet:

"Let us have faith that right makes right, and in that faith, let us, to the end, dare to do our duty as we understand it."

The speech was published in full by four New York newspapers and by others across the nation; it was issued in a special pamphlet by the *Chicago Tribune.* And at Manoir, Amory read the speech and passed it on to Charles and Kara.

"That man will be the next President of the Union," Amory guessed, his eyes deeply troubled. "And there will be a war to preserve the Union. The man will fight for his convictions, and he's already said, 'A house divided against itself cannot stand. I believe this government cannot endure, permanently half slave and half free.' War, Charles," he warned his pacifist son. "With Lincoln in the White House we will have war."

"Lincoln is a strong man," Charles said evasively. "He'll find a way out of this mess."

"There is no way, short of war." Amory sighed with frustration. "Since the beginning of this decade, we've watched it coming. Before the end of this year, you'll see southern states making a move to secede." His eyes dwelt first on Charles, then on Kara. "Kara, I know you've meant to sit out your year of mourning. I know Charles is waiting for that time to elapse." Startled, color rising to her cheeks, Kara swung involuntarily toward Charles. His eyes were on her, saying what he had never put into words. "Don't wait," Amory urged. "Marry now, take Sheelagh and Chris and go, far from here."

"Papa." Charles looked from his father to Kara, saw the hope springing up within her.

"Charles, this new state that's just come into the Union. Oregon. You've talked about it with such enthusiasm. Take Kara and the children and start a new life there. You can't live with the yesterdays. I'll arrange for funds to provide you with a fresh start." He smiled faintly. "Why must you wait until I'm dead to receive part of what will be yours?"

"Papa, this is my home," Charles said earnestly. "How can I run away when trouble looms?"

"Because a war would destroy you!" Amory suddenly blazed. "Like me, you have no stomach for slavery. You've seen no way out for the South, but you know it's morally wrong. You want no part of killing, and you'll be forced to kill. I want you away from here, Charles," Amory said forcefully. "The four of you. There will be bloodshed here in the South; I don't want you part of it. *Go, while there's time.*"

"Papa, what about you?" Charles asked unhappily.

"I must stay here with your mother," Amory said resignedly. "This isn't the end," he insisted. "There'll be much ugliness, but afterward we'll live again. I can endure whatever happens, if I know the four of you are in Oregon, far from death and destruction."

Three weeks later, Charles and Kara, with the children, started on the long journey to the Far West. Amory showed signs, still, of his grief; but satisfaction also showed in his eyes because he had brought off this marriage. He stood on the portico in the early-spring sunlight to see them off.

As the carriage rumbled away from Manoir, Kara heard, from an upstairs bedroom, the faint tinkle of a music box, playing "Frère Jacques."